The ASSASSINS *of* ISIS

The ASSASSINS *of* ISIS

*A Story of Ambition, Politics and Murder
Set in Ancient Egypt*

P. C. DOHERTY

ST. MARTIN'S MINOTAUR
NEW YORK

www.minotaurbooks.com

ISBN-13: 978-0-312-35960-7
ISBN-10: 0-312-35960-8

First published in Great Britain by Headline Book Publishing,
a division of Hodder Headline

First St. Martin's Minotaur Edition: November 2006

10 9 8 7 6 5 4 3 2 1

In honour of two great men,
Billy and Kenny Yip,
beloved husband and son
of Susan Yip of Woodford Green

List of Characters

THE HOUSE OF PHARAOH

Hatusu: Pharaoh-Queen of the XVIII dynasty

Senenmut: lover of Hatusu: Grand Vizier or First Minister, a former stonemason and architect

Valu: the 'Eyes and Ears' of Pharaoh: royal prosecutor

Omendap: Commander-in-Chief of Egypt's armies

THE HALL OF TWO TRUTHS

Amerotke: Chief Judge of Egypt

Prenhoe: Amerotke's kinsman, a scribe in the Hall of Two Truths

Asural: Captain of the Temple Guard of the Temple of Ma'at in which the Hall of Two Truths stands

Shufoy: a dwarf, Amerotke's manservant and confidant

Norfret: Amerotke's wife

Ahmase and
Curfay: Amerotke's sons

THE TEMPLE OF ISIS

Impuki: High Priest and Principal Physician

Lady Thena: Impuki's wife

Paser: Impuki's deputy

Mafdet: Captain of the Temple Guard

THE HOUSE OF GENERAL SUTEN
Suten: retired senior general
Lupherna: Suten's wife
Menna: Chief Scribe
Heby: Suten's valet

OTHER CHARACTERS
Nadif: officer in the Medjay, desert police
The Shardanna: a former member of the Sebaus
Djed: a member of the Sebaus
Hefau and Apep: snake men
Sithia: a courtesan, member of the Sebaus
Nethba: a Theban noble woman
Sese: father of Nethba, former royal archi-
                      tect
Rahimere: disgraced former Grand Vizier of Egypt

HISTORICAL NOTE

The first dynasty of ancient Egypt was established about 3100 BC. Between that date and the rise of the New Kingdom (1550 BC) Egypt went through a number of radical transformations which witnessed the building of the pyramids, the creation of cities along the Nile, the union of Upper and Lower Egypt and the development of the Egyptians' religion around Ra, the Sun God, and the cult of Osiris and Isis. Egypt had to resist foreign invasion, particularly by the Hyksos, Asiatic raiders, who cruelly devastated the kingdom.

By 1479 BC, Egypt, pacified and united under Pharaoh Tuthmosis II, was on the verge of a new and glorious ascendancy. The Pharaohs had moved their capital to Thebes; burial in the pyramids was replaced by the development of the Necropolis on the west bank of the Nile as well as the exploitation of the Valley of the Kings as a royal mausoleum.

I have, to clarify matters, used Greek names for cities, etc., e.g. Thebes and Memphis, rather than their archaic Egyptian names. The place name Sakkara has been used to describe the entire pyramid complex around Memphis and Giza. I have also employed the shorter version for the Pharaoh Queen: i.e. Hatusu rather than Hatshepsut. Tuthmosis II died in 1479 BC and, after a period of confusion,

Hatusu held power for the next twenty-two years. During this period Egypt became an imperial power and the richest state in the world.

Egyptian religion was also being developed, principally the cult of Osiris, killed by his brother, Seth, but resurrected by his loving wife, Isis, who gave birth to their son, Horus. These rites must be placed against the background of the Egyptians' worship of the Sun God and their desire to create a unity in their religious practices. The Egyptians had a deep sense of awe for all living things: animals and plants, streams and rivers were all regarded as holy, while Pharaoh, their ruler, was worshipped as the incarnation of the divine will.

By 1479 BC the Egyptian civilisation expressed its richness in religion, ritual, architecture, dress, education and the pursuit of the good life. Soldiers, priests and scribes dominated this civilisation, and their sophistication is expressed in the terms they used to describe both themselves and their culture. For example, Pharaoh was 'the Golden Hawk'; the treasury was 'the House of Silver'; a time of war was 'the Season of the Hyaena'; a royal palace was 'the House of a Million Years'. Despite the country's breathtaking, dazzling civilisation, however, Egyptian politics, both at home and abroad, could be violent and bloody. The royal throne was always the centre of intrigue, jealousy and bitter rivalry. It was on to this political platform, in 1479 BC, that the young Hatusu emerged.

By 1478 BC Hatusu had confounded her critics and opponents, both at home and abroad. She had won a great victory in the north against the Mitanni and purged the royal circle of any opposition led by the Grand Vizier Rahimere. A remarkable young woman, Hatusu was supported by her wily and cunning lover, Senenmut, also her First Minister. Hatusu was determined that all sections of Egyptian society accept her as Pharaoh Queen of Egypt.

Egyptian society was bound up with life after death. The

ancient Egyptians did not have the modern fear of what lay beyond death. They saw it as an adventure, as a journey into a land more wonderful, a paradise under the rule of the Lord Osiris. They talked of 'going into the Far West', and it was the duty of every Egyptian to prepare himself for this next stage of his existence. The journey, however, would have its perils. The dead would have to travel through the Underworld and into the Hall of Judgement, where their souls would be weighed in the Scales of Truth. The ancient Egyptians saw the heart as the symbol of the soul. Only those with a clean heart would be allowed into the Eternal Fields of the Blessed. The journey, therefore, posed its own dangers, but these could be overcome or circumvented if certain rituals were followed. The body had to be embalmed, purified and buried according to the Osirian Rite.

Beyond the grave the dead would need goods, servants, food and drink, and these were buried with them. The Necropolis on the west bank of the Nile offered a wide range of funereal goods, and the ancient Egyptians travelled there, on what we would term their holidays, to inspect the coffins, caskets and other paraphernalia. The priests of the various temples also did a roaring trade; their prayers were essential both before and after death to ensure everything went well. There was no exception to this rule; it was all-encompassing, from the lowliest peasant to the Keeper of the Great House, Pharaoh himself. Indeed, part of the succession rite was that a Pharaoh had to supervise the funeral of his predecessor and then ensure that the royal tombs and sepulchres were carefully preserved and protected.

The discovery of Tutankhamun's tomb in the 1920s illustrates what treasure houses these royal sepulchres truly were. They literally contained a king's ransom in precious goods, from alabaster jars to beds, couches and chariots. The temptation to steal is as ancient as the world itself, and it is only logical that the exact location of these tombs was regarded as a state secret. Royal architects went to great lengths to conceal entrances, and even placed traps to catch the unwary. Nevertheless, the lure of such riches was irresistible. We know from contemporary sources that one night's raid could make the lucky thief a millionaire. Of course, getting into a tomb, stealing the goods and transporting them away carried its own hideous risks. If a thief was caught he could expect little mercy and would face an excruciating death, impaled alive, either on the cliffs above Thebes or at the entrances to the royal valleys. Nevertheless, there were always those cunning and greedy enough to try their luck. The Pharaohs saw such pillaging as a direct attack upon themselves and their own greatness and strength. The Valley of the Kings and the other royal sepulchres are now a great tourist attraction, but in the reign of Hatusu they were also the scene of a deadly game of cat and mouse . . .

EGYPT *c.1478 BC*

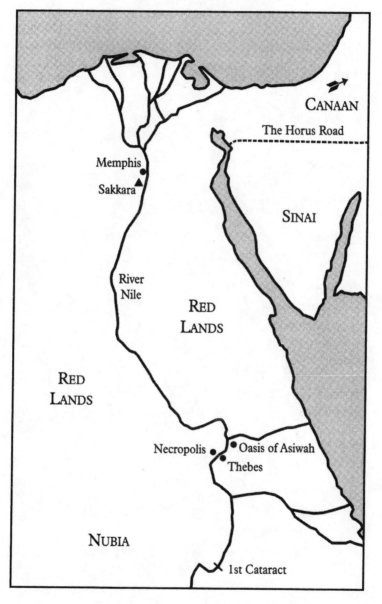

KERH: ancient Egyptian, 'darkness'

PROLOGUE

The violaters of the Houses of a Million Years could not believe their luck. They had swept into the Valley of the Nobles, a deep gully to the right of the soaring peak of Meretseger, the Silent One, which overlooked the Necropolis on the west bank of the Nile, opposite the temple complex of Karnak. The tomb guards had posed little problem, nothing which a silent knife thrust or the tight cord of a garrotte string couldn't resolve. Their leader had given them precise details regarding the princely tomb they were to ransack. Once inside the valley, garbed in black from head to toe, they had swept like ants along the branching trackways. None of them knew or recognised any of his companions. They were united by one stark purpose: the pillaging of a tomb, the rifling of treasures of the ages from a House of Eternity whose owner had long gone across the Far Horizon into the Eternal West.

Now they were finished, sweeping up the moon-washed valley. They had enough light to see their way, a long line of fast-moving figures laden down with booty, so excited they were oblivious to the roars, grunts and growls of the night prowlers, the lions, the hyaenas and jackals which lurked on that broad wasteland between the City of the Dead and the scorching desert which stretched like an eternity. They'd thought their night's task was finished when their leader paused, holding up his dagger. Abruptly he left the narrow track, plunging down the shale and sand, sending dust flying as he moved between two jutting crags on to an unseen ledge and a carefully masked cleft which concealed the door to another tomb. The leader gestured for the rest to follow, calling them down by imitating the 'yip, yip' of a night fox. The violaters, who took the name of the demon Sebaus, would never have dreamed of searching for such a place.

The group gathered in the small porchway and quickly dug away at the plaster-covered entrance. Once inside, the pot of fire was brought, pitch torches, taken from a sack, quickly lit and pushed into crevices along the wall. The Sebaus had long lost their fear of the Kingdom of the Dead. They glanced around, realising that the tomb consisted of four roughly hewn chambers, a main one with three storerooms leading off. The tomb had been hastily prepared. No paintings on the wall, no dried-out baskets of flowers, whilst the plaster coating hadn't been properly finished or smoothed down. Nevertheless the burial chamber and adjoining storerooms were full of costly artefacts: precious game boards, ivory shabtis, mother-of-pearl boxes, chairs and stools of the finest wood inlaid with precious metals, boxes of precious oils, caskets of brilliant jewels, trinkets, bracelets and floral collarettes. In the far corner a collection of costly weapons lay heaped: knives and swords in jewelled scabbards, a magnificent bow of honour. Next to this was an exquisitely carved wooden casket containing the canopic jars, but the real prize was the red quartzite sarcophagus with the wadjet, the Eye of Horus, painted on each corner. The Sebaus' leader, a former scribe, crouched down and read the hieroglyphs.

'Rahimere,' his muffled voice grated, 'former Grand Vizier of Egypt. Well, let's see what this lordly one holds.'

Using crowbars and mallets they prised the lid loose, letting it fall to the ground with a crash, ignoring the great crack which appeared along the side. They climbed up on to the side, staring down at the luxuriously painted coffin casket within. Tools were hastily brought, the lid wrenched off and the casket inside brought out and thrown unceremoniously to the ground. The Sebaus leader wrenched off the beautiful face mask, ordering one of his men to break it up while the rest began to plunder the mummy, unwinding the bandages, fingers probing and searching for the sacred jewels and amulets.

The leader returned to the sarcophagus. He swung himself up, lowered himself gently down and searched around. His hand grasped a costly leather case. He picked this up, opened it and took out a book wrapped in the finest linen. He had been expressly ordered to look for this and leave the case deliberately on the floor. He climbed out and gazed round the burial chamber. His companions, faces and heads masked and hooded, were now seizing whatever they could carry. Baskets were emptied, chests and coffers kicked over, sacks and pouches hurriedly filled. The leader of the Sebaus wiped the sweat from his brow and smiled contentedly. He knew none of his companions; he had simply been given his orders, precise directions, where to go and what to do, and had memorised every detail. He rejoiced in the great honour shown to him. Just before midnight he had gone out to the Dried Oasis to the north of the valley and met the Khetra, their silent, secretive master. The Khetra had stood hidden in the shadows, as he had done when the Sebaus leader had last met him, on that desolate island of Khnum to the north of Thebes. As usual, he had relayed his orders through another, so softly the leader couldn't decide whether the Khetra was man or woman. He could detect nothing but moving shadows and that pervasive smell of jasmine. Was the Khetra a woman? In the past the Sebaus leader would have found this disturbing, yet didn't Egypt have its own Pharaoh Queen? Wasn't the Khetra a deep fountain of knowledge about the Valley of the Kings and all its treasures? What did it matter! He or she was making all of them rich beyond their wildest dreams.

The Sebaus leader, cradling the book wrapped in linen, wondered where the Khetra could have acquired his knowledge about a hidden tomb like this. How could he have possibly known? Yet the orders had been quite precise, to follow the trackway above the two crags, reach the middle point and plunge down to the waiting ledge. The leader watched one of his gang empty a pure alabaster oil jar which had been filled with pearls. The wealth of this tomb spoke for itself. He recalled what he knew of Rahimere. Hadn't he once been the Grand Vizier who'd opposed Pharaoh Hatusu and been given no choice but to drink poisoned wine? His family had been disgraced and must have chosen this lonely, hidden spot to protect Rahimere in the afterlife. There were scores of such tombs; some were discovered by accident, but others would remain as they were, a hidden horde of treasures.

The Sebaus leader, cradling the linen parcel, walked over to the wall and unwrapped it. The book itself was composed of papyrus sheets sewn together with a strong twine; the writing was that of a learned scribe. The Sebaus leader, who had knowledge of such writing, began to read carefully, and as he did so, his heart skipped a beat. He hastily closed the book and rewrapped it in its linen sheet. The pitch torches were burning down and, going to the entrance of this man-made cave, the leader peered out. He glimpsed the stars low against the blackness of the heavens. His orders had been quite precise: to ransack this tomb and return to the Dried Oasis, where the Khetra would be waiting.

'Enough!' He turned to his companions. 'Take what you have.' He held up a hand, his wrist bracelet glistening in the light. 'Remember, nothing must be withheld, nothing taken. Theft by one of us is a danger to all.'

The gang nodded in understanding. The Khetra was ruthless; any theft meant instant death.

They left the tomb, slippering and slithering up the shale. A number of objects were dropped, but the leader, distracted by what he had read in the book, ordered them to be left. Speed was the order of the night; although it was still dark, they had to reach the oasis before dawn. They left the lonely valley, climbing over the limestone gullies, sinister shapes, the only sound their grunts and groans as they carried their heavy burdens. To their left glowed the lights of the Necropolis, and across the river was the shadowy mass of Thebes.

The Sebaus leader urged his men on, although he remained distracted. He was frightened, for deeper fears had now been stirred. The robbing of the royal tombs had already caused scandal in the city. The Medjay police and the chariot squadrons were being deployed, and troops would soon be dispatched. The situation was growing more fraught by the day. The leader climbed a rocky outcrop, skirting the tall posts driven into the ground bearing impaled corpses, now only tattered remains after the vultures and desert prowlers had taken their share. The lights of the city had disappeared. They were now on the borders of the Red Lands, yet they moved carefully, wary of foot patrols or chariot squadrons camped in some ravine. On the night air throbbed the heart-chilling roars of the night creatures.

The rest of the gang were climbing the rocky escarpment now, fanning out and peering down at the Dried Oasis below. The fire bowl was brought; a light flared, which was answered from the oasis, its bent, twisted trees black against the starlit sky. The Sebaus moved down the rocky outcrop and across to the oasis, where they squatted in a semi-circle, as they had been ordered to, around the crumbling wall of the old well. On the far side of this lurked other Sebaus who had not taken part in the raid, and somewhere in the trees beyond them was the Khetra. Orders were issued, the plunder collected, men were beckoned forward to be rigorously searched, the choice being indiscriminate.

Once the Khetra was satisfied, rewards were distributed, the profits from previous raids, now converted into gold, silver and precious stones. Some of the robbers were selected to take the new plunder to certain places in Thebes. No home or person was named, only this pleasure house or that beer shop, or some other anonymous location. All they had to do was leave the treasure; it would be collected, and sometime in the future the price would be paid.

At last the Sebaus dispersed and the oasis fell silent. The leader of the tomb robbers had been given strict instructions to remain. He did so, still cradling the book wrapped in its linen shawl.

'Come!' a voice whispered through the darkness.

The Sebaus leader moved around the well.

'Kneel.'

The tomb robber did so. He was aware of dark shadows coming towards him; the smell of jasmine was very strong.

'You have what I told you to find?'

'Yes, master.'

A pair of hands abruptly plucked the book away.

'Did you read it?'

'No, master.'

'You lie. You opened it when you should have been watching those who were with you.'

'Master, I—'

The Sebaus leader heard a faint sound, followed by the twang of a horn bow. The arrow took him deep in the chest, loosed so close it flung him back to lie coughing and kicking in the sand. The last words he heard, as he choked on his own blood, was the order for his corpse to be taken and buried deep in the desert.

Three days later a sweat-soaked runner raced up the Avenue of Sphinxes towards the soaring pylons of the Divine House, the Palace of Hatusu, Pharaoh Queen of

Egypt. The runner, the swiftest in the imperial corps, was covered in dirt. He had to wash and purify himself before being allowed into the entrance porch, where he was anointed and perfumed in preparation for being taken into the Kingfisher Chamber – a beautiful room with light-green-painted walls. The kingfisher bird was everywhere, its vivid plumage accurately depicted in a number of scenes, perched above ever-blue water or plunging life-like into some reed-ringed pool.

Inside the door the messenger knelt. The man squatting on cushions on the dais at the far end of the room ordered the gauze linen curtains to be pulled aside to reveal a strong man, his balding head glistening with oil. He had a soldier's face, with hard eyes and harsh mouth, and he was dressed in a simple white tunic, although costly rings glittered on his fingers. The messenger, beckoned forward, nosed the ground before the dais, then, grasping the step before him, gasped out his message to Lord Senenmut, Grand Vizier of Egypt, First Minister and, some claimed, lover of the Pharaoh Queen.

Senenmut threw down the map he was studying, hiding his alarm as he listened intently to the message. Once the runner had been rewarded and dismissed, he rose to his feet and strode through open acacia doors on to the balcony where Hatusu lay on a silver couch under a perfume-soaked awning. She was laughing and chattering with her maids, but broke off as Senenmut came across, catching his glance, and dismissed the maids.

'My lord?'

'They have found the tomb. Rahimere's. It has been robbed and the coffin opened.'

The lovely faience goblet slipped from Hatusu's fingers as she stared in horror.

'It can't have been,' she whispered.

'The tomb was robbed,' Senenmut confirmed. 'A leather case was found which must have contained the book. There's

9

no mistake. Rahimere died and took his secrets with him; now they're in the hands of some tomb robber.'

'So the Temple of Isis was right, the information they gave us.'

Hatusu crunched the broken glass under her sandal.

'Enough is enough!' she whispered. 'Ask Lord Amerotke to be here by dusk. I'll instruct him to root out these robbers. Somewhere in this city is a merchant or official who's helped them; he can be easily broken . . .'

AARAT: ancient Egyptian snake goddess

CHAPTER 1

Nadif, a standard-bearer in the Medjay, the desert police who controlled the approaches to the city of Thebes, loved to walk along the bank of the Nile as the sun began to set, changing the colours of both the city and the desert. He would stand by the bank, his left hand holding his staff of office, the other grasping the lead of his chained baboon; he'd half close his eyes and breathe in the delicious smells of the river, the fragrance of the wild flowers mingling with the stench of the rich mud and the odour of fish. He would listen to the various sounds: the calls of fishermen out on the river, the cries of swooping birds and the distant bull-like roars of the hippopotami. Tonight was no different. Whilst Baka, his trained baboon, peeled a piece of rotten fruit, Nadif stared across the Nile at the great City of the Dead, the Necropolis, where he was building his own tomb, preparing for that day when he would journey into the Eternal West.

'You can't see it from here.' Nadif always talked to Baka; in fact, the policeman found the baboon more intelligent than some of his men. 'But it's there, high in the cliffs, nothing special mind you, but I'm proud of it. There's a small temple outside, well, I call it a temple, and three chambers within. I wanted four, but the cost of these stonemasons . . .' Nadif shook his head, he couldn't believe the way prices had climbed. He had remarked on the same when, the previous day, a holiday, he had taken his wife and children across to the City of the Dead to buy some funeral caskets.

The policeman squinted up at the sky. His tour of duty would end when the sun finally sank. He would return to the police barracks just within the city gates, share a jug of beer with his companions and make his way home. His wife had promised a special meal: slivers of goose cooked over an open grill and flavoured with sesame, followed by fruit in cream. Afterwards they would share a cup of Charou wine and, once again, admire the replica caskets they had bought the day before. Nadif believed that was the best way: you could order what you wanted, buy miniature replicas and bring them home to show your friends and neighbours. He was quite insistent that his casket must prove to his descendants, when they visited his tomb to check all was well, that he had been a high-ranking officer in the Medjay.

'Aye, and before that,' Nadif jerked back the chain, 'I was a spearman in the Swallows.'

He closed his eyes. For six years he had served as an infantryman, an auxiliary to one of the bravest generals in the Egyptian army, Chief Scribe Suten. Suten had commanded one of the new imperial chariot squadrons, new because the chariot they used was lighter, more mobile, yet tough enough to withstand the rigours of the Red Lands, those yawning deserts which stretched out on both sides of the great river.

'Come on, Baka.' Nadif turned and walked along the footpath. Now and again he would pause to study the papyrus groves, those lush islands of green along the banks of the Nile. If there was danger, that was where it would lurk; it was not unknown for a hippopotamus to come lumbering out or, worse still, one of those great river monsters, the crocodiles, who sometimes decided to go hunting inland. Nadif himself had come across the remains of a tinker who had made the mistake of sleeping on this very path, he had been seized by one of the demons of the river and pulled back into the deep mud which fringed the edge of the pool.

'All we found was a head,' he murmured. 'Or at least the top of it.'

However, Nadif's reason for the patrol was not crocodiles or hippopotami, but to protect the great mansions of the wealthy which stood in their own grounds behind high walls some distance from the Nile. The policeman was always full of wonderment at such places. 'Palaces in their own right,' was how he described them to his wife. They had great oaken gates, soaring plaster walls and, beyond them, delicious cool gardens with orchards, lawns and pools of purity fed by canals from the Nile. Nadif knew all the gatekeepers and porters. Now and again he would stop to share the local gossip as well as a pot of ale or a plate of sugared almonds or figs. Each of these mansions was owned by one of the great lords of Pharaoh Hatusu's court: Lord Amerotke, Supreme Judge in the Hall of Two Truths at the Temple of Ma'at in Thebes; General Suten, Nadif's old commander-in-chief; and Lord Senenmut, Grand Vizier or First Minister of the young queen, and, some whispered behind their giggles, Pharaoh's lover, a former stonemason, an architect, now busy building Egypt's greatness in another way.

Nadif strode on. He didn't envy these people, but he did enjoy peeping into their lives. He had been given this part of the riverbank to patrol because General Suten never forgot those who served with him. Nadif was responsible for the area between the North Gate of the city and the Great Mooring Place. He patrolled four times a day whilst his companions filled the gaps. There was very little trouble usually, now and again the odd suspicious character, but Nadif had worked out a clever system. He and his companions carried a conch horn, which they used to raise the alarm. The servants of these great mansions would

15

then gather at the gates to provide any help or support the Medjay needed.

Nadif paused; soon it would be time to go back. He stared up at the sky, where the evening star had appeared.

'We will walk on a little further.'

Baka grunted and scratched himself, then paused to look at something he had found on the edge of the path. This turned out to be nothing more than the white skin of a piece of fruit, which the baboon immediately ate. Nadif began to sing softly under his breath. Baka responded with grunts of pleasure. The animal liked to hear his master sing that old refrain, a marching song about how young maidens often sighed at the approach of the Swallows and hid their sloe eyes behind beautiful fingers to disguise their desire for these warriors of Egypt. Nadif knew the words by heart: he had sung them on the parade grounds of Thebes and along the dusty desert roads; he'd chanted them as they camped around fires in lonely oases or on the war barges as they coursed down towards the Third Cataract to bring the Kushites to battle.

As Nadif recalled the days of glory, he was so absorbed that, at first, he thought the yelling and screaming were part of his memories of the Kushites bursting into the camp and trying to burn their boats. However, Baka was dancing frantically at the end of his chain and Nadif shook himself from his reverie. The hideous screaming was coming from one of the mansions behind their high walls, their gateways masked by clumps of date and palm trees. Nadif hurried across. The screaming was now louder, broken by the sound of a wailing horn and the clash of a cymbal, the usual sign for the alarm being raised. Already the gateways were opening, and porters and servants came tumbling out, curious as to what was happening.

Nadif broke into a run, going as fast as his damaged leg would allow. Baka was jumping furiously on the end of his chain. The evening had changed. The sun was going down and darkness swirled like a cloak to cover the world. The power of Seth, the red-haired god, would make itself felt. A buzzard screeched overhead, as if it too was hurrying to what might be a slaughter, whilst the smell from the river was one of rottenness rather than sweetness. Nadif noticed that the gateway to General Suten's house was open, and servants holding torches were hurrying out, one blowing hard at a horn. They were looking for him. Nadif took his own conch horn, put it to his mouth and blew. The servants turned and came hurrying towards him.

'What is the matter? What is the matter?'

Nadif paused to catch his breath, aware of the sweat running down his face. Baka lunged on his chain and the servants, wary of the creature's sharp teeth, hung back.

'You must come!' An old man gestured with his hand. 'Officer Nadif, you must come now, it is the master!'

'General Suten?'

'You must come!' the old man gasped. Nadif could still hear that heart-wrenching screaming, as well as shouts and cries from the garden beyond.

'General Suten,' Nadif repeated. Heart in his mouth, he recalled the general's face, his sharp eyes, the sunken cheeks, that nose curved like the hook of a falcon. The old retainer, however, was already ushering the other servants back, shouting at Nadif over his shoulder to follow. The standard-bearer strode through the main gate. At any other time he would have paused to admire the beauty of the garden, the tall sycamore trees, the vine trellises, the lawns and flowerbeds, the coloured pavilions and small ornamental lakes. Now, however, grasping Baka's chain, he hurried along the basalt-paved pathway leading up to the front of the house with its spacious steps, elegant col-onnades and porticoed walkways. He was aware of people hurrying around. Inside the house servants were already tearing their garments in signs of mourning. One young girl had clawed her cheeks and thrown dust on her hair.

A dog raced up, ready to bite Baka, but the baboon lunged in attack, paws in the air, and the dog slunk back.

They crossed the small hall of audience with its central fire, past the raised eating area with its beautifully coloured couches and divans and through kitchens smelling sweetly of the recently cooked savoury meats. General Suten's household, his wife Lupherna, Chief Scribe Menna and his body servant Heby, along with other principal retainers, were clustered at the foot of the steps leading up to the roof terrace.

'What is the matter?' Nadif shouted, beating his stick on the floor.

Lupherna, the general's young wife, came towards him like a sleepwalker. She was dressed as if for a banquet, a beautiful thick oiled wig bound to her head by a silver fillet, her dark sloe eyes ringed with green kohl. The nails on her hands had been painted an emerald green whilst her lips were carmined, yet her eyes were rounded in fear and she played constantly with the necklace about her throat.

'Officer Nadif.' She put her hand out; the Medjay grasped her fingers, they were ice cold.

'My lady, what is the matter?'

She gestured at the stairs.

Nadif brushed by her. Heby and Menna seemed in shock. Heby tried to stop him, but Nadif pushed him aside. The steps were built into the side of the house just beyond the kitchen door. Nadif climbed them slowly, Baka whimpering at his side. He reached the top and stared across the roof terrace, an elegant place with its wooden balustrade running around the edge. He noticed the long couch under its drapes of linen, the beautifully polished acacia-wood tables and chairs. In every corner stood flowerpots. The air smelt sweetly of the exquisite perfume of the blue lotus. Oil lamps had been lit and placed in coloured glasses, and for a while Nadif could see nothing wrong. In the shadows and flickering light from the lamps he glimpsed a writing table, another table bearing a wine jug and goblets. Then, near the couch, he saw the body, tangled in linen sheets. From where he stood, Nadif could make out General Suten, his scrawny arms, the marching boots he always insisted on wearing rather than the sandals or slippers of a scribe.

'Be careful!' someone shouted.

'Be careful of what?' Nadif snapped back.

'The snakes.'

Nadif paused, one foot on the top step. Now he knew why Baka had whimpered. He grasped the baboon's chain more securely and, recalling his desert training, remained as still as a statue, eyes peering through the gloom. At first he could see nothing, but then one of the linen sheets on the floor moved. Nadif controlled his panic as the horned viper, long and grey, came slithering sideways towards one of the warming dishes placed on the ground. As he watched, he realised that the entire floor of the roof terrace seemed to be covered by these highly dangerous snakes. What he had first thought were shadows now began to move, many of the vipers curling out from beneath the bed.

Nadif had seen enough. He clattered down the stairs even as he recalled the story about General Suten and snakes, how the old soldier hated them. When he reached the foot of the steps, he tied Baka to a ring in the wall.

'Who's been up there?' he asked.

'I have.' Lupherna had overcome her shock and was crying quietly, the tears coursing down her face, smudging it with paint. 'I heard his screams.' She put her painted nails to her mouth. 'I was going to join him as I usually did. I heard those hideous screams! I came to the steps. Heby was on guard here. I climbed up . . . well, we both did. My husband was on the edge of the bed, arms and legs flailing like a man trapped in a pool, unable to move. He had a snake here,' she pointed to her shoulder, 'and there was another on his leg. He was staring at me, Officer Nadif, and he was screaming.'

19

'Is this true?' Nadif turned to the plump-faced scribe.

'I was in the master's writing office,' Menna the scribe replied. 'I was working by the light of an oil lamp detailing how many jars we had taken from the oil press—'

'Yes, yes,' Nadif interrupted.

'Then I heard the screams. Is General Suten dead?'

'I don't know.'

Nadif now turned to Heby, a tall, handsome, middle-aged man. He could tell from Heby's face and the way he carried himself, that he was a former soldier.

'You are General Suten's body servant?'

'Aye, in peace and war. I have served him for twenty years.'

Nadif stared at the man's hard face, the cheeks slightly pitted, the nose broken and twisted. Heby's right ear was clipped at the top, whilst the wig he wore only half concealed the ugly scar which ran from the ear down to his neck.

'A Libyan.' Heby had followed Nadif's gaze; he touched the scar. 'Out in the western deserts he cut my ear, but I took his penis along with four others and burnt them as an offering to the god.'

'I'm sure you did.' Nadif stepped back. 'But shouldn't we do something about your master?'

'The snakes,' Heby replied. 'If we go on that roof we too will journey into the West. I don't think my master would want that.'

Nadif tried to hide his unease. He had met many people who had experienced the sudden death of a friend or relation, and their reactions were often surprising. Some became hysterical, others wept, a few became icy quiet; but these three were acting as if they were half asleep or drugged.

Nadif became aware of the clamour in the rest of the house. The hall of audience was filling with servants and the curious from other houses along the Nile. He immediately instructed all those not belonging to General Suten's retinue to leave. He dispatched a runner into the city to inform his superiors what had happened, and tried to impose some order. He ordered a fire to be lit in the hall of audience and organised the servants, telling them to put on heavy boots and gauntlets, anything they could find to protect their feet, legs and arms. From a servant he borrowed some leather leg guards and an apron for his front, wrapping his hands and arms in rolls of coarse linen, then, armed with poles and garden implements, he and Heby led the servants on to the roof terrace. Some were terrified and refused to go, but Lupherna, who now asserted herself as head of the house, promised all those who helped a lavish reward, and Nadif soon had enough volunteers to help him clear the roof.

It was a grisly, gruesome business. The horned vipers had emerged from their hiding places, attracted by the heat and food. Most of them were sluggish. A few were killed but the servants were superstitious and regarded the snakes as a visitation from a god, so Nadif compromised, and where possible the horned vipers were placed in a leather bag and taken away. Eventually they reached the general's corpse. Nadif ordered it to be taken below, and it was laid on a divan in the hall of audience. Lady Lupherna knelt beside it. She took off her wig, placing her jewellery beside it, then rent her beautiful robe and, taking dust from the fireplace, sprinkled it over her head and body, staining her face, chest and shoulders. She knelt keening, rocking backwards and forwards, as Nadif laid out the corpse and stripped it of its robe.

The general had been an old man, well past his sixtieth summer, and his body had been lean and hard. Nadif counted that he must have been bitten a dozen times, each bite mark a dark bluish red, the skin around it deeply discoloured. The general's face had also become swollen, the hollow cheeks puffing out, the lips full, with white froth dribbling out of one corner. Nadif found the

half-open eyes eerie, as if the general was about to look up
at him and snap out an order. He had glimpsed Suten from
afar in the uniform of a staff officer, his armour glittering,
the gold collars of valour and the silver bees of courage
shimmering in the sunlight. Now he looked like a pathetic
old man caught in a dreadful death.

A local physician was summoned from a nearby house.
He turned the corpse over.

'At least fifteen times,' he intoned. 'I'm not an expert; my
specialities are the mouth and anus.'

At any other time Nadif would have laughed at this
pompous physician.

'You don't have to be an expert,' he snapped, 'to count
how many times a man has been bitten.'

'I'm merely stating,' the physician retorted. 'It's rather
strange that General Suten didn't try to escape. He appears
to have allowed himself to sit there and be bitten.'

Nadif narrowed his eyes. 'What are you saying?'

'What do you think I am saying?' the physician replied.
'Here is a man who, according to you, lay down on his bed
and was bitten by a snake. What would you do, officer, if
you were bitten by a snake?'

'Run away.'

'But this man didn't. He sat there and allowed himself to
be bitten another fourteen times.'

'How soon would the poison work?'

'A few heartbeats,' the physician replied. 'Perhaps he was
in shock. That's what a rat does when it is bitten. It stays
still and allows itself to be bitten again. I've seen it happen.'

'General Suten wasn't a rat!'

Nadif gestured at the physician to join him, and led him
to the steps to the roof terrace.

'I'm not going up there.'

'Don't be stupid,' Nadif retorted. 'You will be well paid.
Anyway, the snakes are gone. From what I gather, they are
rather careful about who they bite!'

The physician's head came up aggressively.

'I'm only joking,' Nadif whispered. 'Follow me.'

When they reached the roof terrace, Nadif was pleased he had acted so quickly. Heby was now clearing up his dead master's papers and was instructing a servant to take the remains of the food and wine down to the kitchen.

'Leave those there,' Nadif ordered. Heby went to object, then shrugged. The servant left the tray on the table. Nadif ordered some oil lamps to be brought. He and the physician scrupulously examined the remains of the fish, bread and fruit, as well as the rich Canaanite wine in both jug and goblet. The physician didn't know what he was looking for. Nadif took the goblet of wine and poured the dregs on to a napkin, then felt the stain with the tips of his fingers.

'There, there,' he whispered.

'There, there, what?' the physician snapped.

Nadif handed him the napkin. 'Feel that.'

The physician did as he was told. 'Grains,' he said. 'Yes, as if some powder has been mixed with the wine.'

Nadif snatched up the goblet. He detected similar grains around the rim.

'It could be the wine,' the physician remarked. 'If it is drawn from the bottom of a cask, there is some silt.'

'I don't think so,' Nadif murmured. 'Smell the cup, physician.'

The self-proclaimed guardian of the anus did so. 'Oh, I know what that is.' He sniffed again. 'Any doctor would. I've mixed it myself. I served in the army as well, you know. There are certain wounds you can't heal.'

'What is it?'

'Poppy seed. I would wager my wife's honour on it. The general mixed poppy seed with his wine to make him sleep.'

'You mean he was poisoned?'

'No, I didn't say that. Poppy seed, used sparingly, will take away your cares and soothe you into a deep slumber. It will clear any pain you have of heart or body.'

23

Nadif turned round abruptly. Heby was looking at them strangely. Nadif waved him over.

'Where is it?' Nadif asked.

'Where is what?' Heby retorted.

'The poppy seed. Your master mixed poppy seed with his wine; he must have had a phial or pouch.'

'He never took poppy seed.'

Menna and Lupherna had also come up on to the roof terrace and joined the officer and the physician. 'General Suten never took poppy seed with his wine; there is no pouch up here,' the Chief Scribe declared.

'Are you sure?' Nadif asked.

'There is no poppy seed powder up here,' Menna repeated.

'Then if General Suten didn't mix the poppy seed with his wine, who did?' Nadif asked. He stared around. 'Let's search.'

Nadif went over to the bed. As he pushed aside the drapes, a leather pouch fell out. He exclaimed in pleasure. The pouch was small and tied at the neck, and it bore the insignia of the Temple of Isis. He undid the cord and handed it to the physician.

'Yes, it's crushed poppy seed,' the fellow replied. 'Lady Lupherna, you did not know your husband was taking this?'

She shook her head.

'He must have mixed it secretly,' Heby murmured. 'I knew he had visited the House of Life at the Temple of Isis, but . . .'

'Did he mix it with his wine tonight, I wonder?' Nadif asked.

'I have a better question for you,' Menna hissed. 'Here we have General Suten, bravest of the brave, a man who hated snakes, who had this roof terrace searched this evening to make sure there were none, and who is suddenly found bitten at least fifteen times whilst his roof terrace is swarming with those vermin.'

All of Nadif's doubts and confusions disappeared. He realised why Menna, Heby and the Lady Lupherna had been acting so strangely when he'd first arrived.

'This was no accident,' he whispered. 'I remember the stories about General Suten's fear of snakes. He was murdered, wasn't he?'

The physician wiped his hands on his robe. 'Murdered!' he exclaimed. 'Is this the work of the red-haired god Seth? General Suten was a hero of Egypt. May Osiris have mercy on us all. If he was murdered, someone will burn for it.'

The Temple of Isis was a sprawling compound of storehouses, mansions, living quarters, gardens, orchards and pastures. It surrounded the temple proper, dedicated to the Mother Goddess who worked so hard to bring Osiris to life after he had been slain by his vindictive brother Seth. The Temple of Isis proclaimed itself an oasis of calm, a place of healing, with its Houses of Life and Learning, dedicated to the study of medicine and the care and strengthening of Pharoah's subjects. Near the House of Life, the academy where the young men studied to be physicians, stood the House of Twilight, a place where those in mortal fear of their lives, attacked by some malignant disease, could receive specialist help and attention. They called it the House of Twilight because those who lived there hovered on the border between life and death, ready to make the journey into the Eternal West to rejoice in the everlasting fields of the green-skinned Osiris. Near the House of Twilight were the mansions and living quarters of the chief physicians and their helpers, men and women of great learning who gathered all the knowledge available on disease and its cure. Nevertheless, the priests of the Temple of Isis believed a dark shadow lay across their temple.

No one was more concerned about this than High Priest Impuki, physician, priest and politician, who, during his ten years of high office, had made the Temple of Isis even more famous. Now he sat in his small writing office next to the embalming rooms underneath the temple. It was a gloomy place even during daylight hours, as only a window high in the wall provided sunlight, but now, as darkness fell, the oil lamps and candles had to be lit. Impuki sat fanning himself and, as he often had during that evening, moaning bitterly about the heat. He prayed quietly that the hot season would soon pass, the Dog Star would appear and the Great Inundation would begin, when the rushing waters of the Nile would replenish themselves and refertilise the land. Until then the heat would be intense, the only relief being the cool of the evening and the fragrant breezes from the Nile.

However, at this late hour, Impuki was not so concerned about the heat as about the failure of the man opposite, Mafdet, Captain of the Temple Guard, to discover the whereabouts of four young hesets, temple girls, who had disappeared. Impuki glowered at the fellow. When this crisis was over, he promised himself, he would tell Mafdet to exercise more and eat less. He noted the soldier's bulging belly, the fat glistening thighs, and the jowls appearing on either side of this veteran's face. Impuki did not like Mafdet. Impuki was a physician, a great healer. He prided himself on the fact that he could recognise a killer when he met one. In fact he secretly categorised people with the names of animals, birds and reptiles. The temple girls were beautiful moorhens; the priests were geese. The physicians? Well, some of them reminded Impuki of mastiffs or monkeys. But Mafdet? Impuki thought of him as a scorpion.

Mafdet was a dangerous man, a former soldier who had fought with the redoubtable General Suten out in the Red Lands, and had been given this post as Captain of the Temple Guard because of his friends in high places. He now sprawled insolently in a low-backed chair, his linen robe slightly stained. He had taken off his ornamental leather breastplate and war kilt, whilst his sword belt had been unhooked and slung on the floor beside him, and he sat, legs apart, tapping one sandalled foot against the tiled floor, as if impatient and resentful at being summoned here. Instead of staring at the High Priest, or adopting a more reverential pose, Mafdet enjoyed ignoring him. He stared up at the heavy-beamed roof or glanced across at the writing desk piled high with papyri and writing implements as well as the cups and phials Impuki used in the study of medicine.

'I'm sorry to call you here, Captain.'

'With all due respect, my lord, I don't think you are.' Mafdet turned his head and stared directly at the priest.

'I beg your pardon?' Impuki leaned his elbows on the table, joining his hands to conceal the anger in his face.

'You don't like me, my lord,' Mafdet said. His accent was harsh, lacking the soft culture of Thebes. He liked to emphasise that he came from the north, from the town of Henes, in the Delta, where life was not as comfortable and easy as it was in Thebes. 'My lord,' he repeated, wiping the sweat from his face with one hand and drying it on his robe, 'you don't like me, and now you hold me responsible.'

'And why don't I like you?' Impuki asked, intrigued at the captain's insistence on having this conversation.

'You don't like me, my lord, because I am a soldier, I come from the north, my manners are rough and I like my food and drink. I have as much experience of life as you do. I have served Pharaoh and her father most loyally. I have held positions of authority. I was an officer in the retinue of Lord Rahimere, once Grand Vizier of Egypt.' Mafdet could have bitten his tongue. Rahimere had died in disgrace, and it was best not to mention him. 'I was recommended to this post by the Commander-in-Chief General Omendap,' he added hastily. 'I am a good captain of the guard; nothing disturbs the peace in the Temple of Isis.'

'I don't like you,' Impuki lost his temper, allowing his

tongue to run away with him, 'because . . .' He paused, fighting for breath. 'I think you like killing, Mafdet.'

The soldier snorted, shook his head and glared at the High Priest from under his eyebrows.

'And that's another thing I don't like about you,' Impuki added. 'The way you stare at me. As for keeping the peace in the temple . . .'

Mafdet picked up his war belt and eased the sword in and out of its scabbard, a threatening gesture not lost on Impuki.

'I don't like you, Mafdet,' the High Priest decided to return to his confrontation, 'because I think you like killing. You are a bully, you swagger around, you drink and eat like a pig!'

'Do I do my job?' the soldier asked. 'Where have I failed? Is there any disturbance, do trespassers scale the walls? Are temple treasures stolen? Are the pilgrims and worshippers not carefully marshalled and controlled?'

'The hesets.' Impuki spat the words out. 'Four of our temple girls have disappeared, dancers and singers, consecrated by their parents to dance in the Holy of Holies and give praise to the Mother Goddess, virgins who have taken a vow never to leave the safety of these precincts. In the space of a few months four of these girls have disappeared without trace.'

'If a young woman has an itch—'

Impuki banged the desk with his fist. 'These are sacred girls, dedicated to the Goddess, not temple prostitutes! No one has seen them leave, they have not returned to their parents' houses. According to the High Priestess,' Impuki snorted in derision, 'they were happy enough.'

'So how is that my fault?' Mafdet sneered. 'How can I be held responsible for their disappearance? If you decide to scale the walls, my lord, and run away, what can I do to stop you?'

'Well, the walls could be patrolled.'

'They already are, by your priests and my guards.'

Impuki picked up the fan and wafted it in front of his narrow face. He could feel the anger seethe within him. The muscles at the back of his neck were tense, whilst his mouth was as dry as if he had been facing a desert wind. He closed his eyes and tried to control his breathing, and when he looked again, Mafdet was sitting, legs crossed, arms hanging down by his sides, staring up at the ceiling, humming quietly.

'I'll have you dismissed,' Impuki declared. 'I'll make an appeal to the court. I have the Divine One's ear. You'll be discharged to join the other lazy veterans in the beer shops of the Necropolis or the slums of Thebes.'

'If you do that, my lord,' Mafdet straightened the chair, 'I, too, will ask for an audience before the Divine One, or my patron General Suten, or perhaps Lord Senenmut, Pharaoh's Chief Minister. I will tell him about the secret doings of this temple.'

'The secret doings?'

'Well, my lord.' Mafdet sighed and patted his stomach, smacking his lips as if eager for a drink. He looked longingly at a jug standing near the doorway. 'It is remarkable how many men and women come to this temple and die in the House of Twilight.'

Impuki stopped wafting his fan. 'What are you implying? Our patients are old and very ill; they come here to die and we make their last days as comfortable as possible.'

'They still die,' Mafdet answered cheekily, 'and before they do, they write out their wills and leave most generous legacies to the temple.'

'We don't need their money and you know that,' Impuki answered. 'They wish to repay us for our care and skill. You will find this common practice in other temples; the income we receive from such legacies is a drop in the pool.'

'And there are other matters,' Mafdet continued.

'What matters?' Impuki could now feel the sweat soaking his body. The buzzing of the flies over a dish of sweetened dates seemed to grow, an irritating sound which set Impuki's teeth on edge; for the first time since this confrontation had begun, he felt a prick of fear in his gut. How much did Mafdet know? What was he hinting at?

'If you have anything to say, now is the time.' Impuki drew a deep breath. 'If not, I think it is about time to dispatch you to your duties. I want you to search the temple gardens, the groves, the undergrowth, the orchards, all those lonely places.'

'And what am I looking for, my lord? Do you think the temple girls are hiding there, giggling behind their fingers, eager to play hide and seek?'

'We have many visitors to this temple,' Impuki retorted. 'The sick in body and mind come here. They visit our schools of life, they make offerings in our chapels and seek the advice of our priests and physicians.' He took a deep breath. 'It is possible that we have admitted a sinner, a man who likes to prey on young women—'

'Nonsense,' Mafdet interrupted. 'One thing I know about our temple girls is that they have powerful voices. If any man touched them, their screams would be heard all over Thebes.'

'How do you know that, Captain? Have you tried to touch one yourself?'

'I have heard rumours.'

'The young women of this temple are dedicated to the Mother Goddess; they are not the playthings of a drunken soldier.'

'To echo your words, my lord, if you have any allegation to make, do so. I am friendly with these girls. I tease them. If I wished to hire one to satisfy my own pleasure, then I would do so honourably.'

'I'm giving you an order, Captain. Instead of sitting in your guard house tonight, search the temple grounds.

It is months since the first heset disappeared; she may even have been a victim of a quarrel amongst the girls themselves. I fear you must search for a corpse.'

'At night?' Mafdet objected.

'You can carry a torch,' Impuki retorted. 'And it is something best done under the cloak of darkness so that we don't raise suspicion. Let us forget our quarrels. The parents of these girls are now petitioning the court. The Divine One herself has taken a great interest in their fate. As I said, I want you to search the orchards and groves, those lonely parts of the temple grounds. Look to see whether the ground has been disturbed, make a careful note of where you go. Tomorrow morning report on which areas you have covered.' Impuki waved his hand. 'Now you may go.'

Mafdet belched noisily. He slowly picked up his leather breastplate, kilt and war belt, gathering them into a bundle, scraped the chair back as noisily as possible and stamped out of the chamber. He climbed the steps into the temple grounds and stared up at the night sky. The heat had now gone, the breeze was cool and ripe with the smells of the temple gardens. In the distance he could hear the faint sound of the chapel choirs rehearsing for the morning sacrifice, and from the bull pens came the lowing of the cattle being prepared for the sacrifice once the sun returned. Servants hurried by, busy on their various tasks. The Temple of Isis rarely slept. There was bread to be baked, meat to be cooked, wine jars to be brought up from the cellar, temple forecourts to be cleaned and sprinkled, animals to be tended to, the countless tasks of a busy temple. Above all, there was the care of the sick, both those in the House of Twilight and those who would be allowed to sleep in the forecourts, the poor and crippled, who had spent money and time reaching the temple in the hope of a cure for their illness.

A group of young temple girls came by dressed in their billowing white robes and heavy black wigs. They chatted amongst themselves, shaking sistras or clattering tambourines. One or two glanced flirtatiously at Mafdet before wafting by in a cloud of perfume. The Captain of the Guard watched them go, then slowly made his way through a grove of trees to his own small, square-built house which adjoined the temple barracks. He unlatched the door and went in, revelling in the smell of cooking oil which mingled with a small pot of cassia he had placed in the centre of the table. Mafdet liked things clean; he always insisted that the tables, benches and furniture, every pot and jug, be scrupulously scrubbed by his orderlies. Jars of perfume were to be left out to sweeten the air; as Mafdet always remarked, he'd had his fill of smelly latrines and pits. Now he was Captain of the Temple Guard he would have the same luxuries as those plump priests.

Mafdet went to the rear of the house, into the stone-floored bathroom and latrine. Using a thick cloth, he picked up a small pot of fire placed there and brought it back into the centre of the room. He placed it on the table, took off the lid and blew carefully. The flame, a wick floating in a small pool of oil, flared vigorously. Mafdet used this to light other lamps before returning to the bathroom, where he washed his hands and face in a bowl of herb-strewn water and wiped himself clean with a napkin. During the day he had a servant to tend him, but at night he liked to be by himself. He had business to do, plans to make, money to count. He thought of High Priest Impuki and smiled, baring his teeth like a dog. 'My lord Impuki this, my lord Impuki that!' he hissed. 'Well, my lord Impuki,' he filled a beer jug and sipped appreciatively, enjoying the harsh tang of the brew, 'perhaps I know more than you think.' He recalled the High Priest's angry face and his instruction to search the grounds. Mafdet sat down on a stool and laughed softly to himself. He would do nothing of the sort. If the temple gardens were to be searched it would be during the day. He had no intention of jumping to the High Priest's every whim and wish.

Mafdet finished his beer. He felt tired and sleepy. He recalled what Impuki had said about the temple girls, and smiled quietly to himself. As he thought of a certain heset's golden body squirming beneath him, his eyes grew heavy and he promised himself a short sleep before resuming his drinking. He put the beer cup down and went and lay on the long couch which served as his bed. For a while he drifted in and out of sleep. Memories came and went: of the chaos caused by Rahimere's fall, followed by service out in the Red Lands; of sleeping with one eye open, ever ready for those Libyan marauders to come slipping out of the darkness. Ah well, that was all over; now a life of comfort beckoned. Mafdet fell asleep.

He was slapped awake brutally, startled by a cup of cold water thrown into his face. He lurched forward, only to discover that his hands were bound above his head whilst his legs were held fast by cords which bit into his ankles. He tried to speak, but the linen cloth stuffed into his mouth made him gag and fight for breath. Mafdet turned his head. Was this some sort of nightmare? Yet he was in his own house; the oil lamp still glowed. He glimpsed a movement, and a shadow detached itself from the darkness and came towards him. Mafdet gazed in terror as the head came into view, the face hidden behind a jackal mask. The intruder was cloaked in black, and the sinister features of that mask, the glittering eyes, cruel snout and sprouting ears, reminded Mafdet of the city executioner. He shook his head, trying to understand who this terrifying figure could be, and why it was here.

'Mafdet.' The voice was low and throaty. The Captain of the Guard couldn't decide if it was female or male. 'Mafdet, you have sinned against the Goddess.'

Mafdet shook his head and strained with all his might against the cords around his wrists and ankles, but they were tightly bound and the cords held. He struggled, trying to lift his body, but it was impossible.

'Do you remember, Mafdet?' The voice came like an echo in a dream. 'Do you know what happens to those who commit sacrilege against the Goddess?' Mafdet could only stare at this monstrosity from the Underworld. 'You have to be punished, Mafdet.'

The Captain of the Temple Guard felt his tunic being raised. He tried to scream as his loincloth was wrenched away, and his body convulsed in agony as the knife, pressed against his genitals, thrust deep.

BEHEN: ancient Egyptian, 'murderous'

CHAPTER 2

The Hall of Two Truths in the Temple of Ma'at at the heart
of the Waset – Thebes, the City of the Sceptre – lay silent.
So expectant was the crowd gathered at the back and along
the sides of the hall that they forgot to stare round. They did
not admire its painted pillars and columns of dark green and
light blue with gold lotus leaves carved around the base and
silver acanthi at the top. Nor were the spectators distracted
by the marble floor, polished and shiny so it seemed as if you
were walking on water: so clear it acted like a mirror and
caught the reflections of the silver flowers, butterflies and
birds carved on the ceiling. The Hall of Two Truths was truly
a chamber of beauty as well as justice. Its wall paintings
depicted Ma'at, the Goddess of Truth, in many poses and
roles: as the beautiful young woman, the divine princess,
kneeling before her father Ra; as the judge, standing in
the Hall of Judgement with the jackal-faced Anubis and
the green-skinned Osiris as the Divine Ones assembled to
weigh a soul and determine its final fate. In other paintings
she was portrayed as a warrior princess fending off the
destroyers, the creatures of the Underworld, who exulted in
such names as Devourer of Faeces, Gobbler of Flesh, Supper
of Blood, Grinder of Bones. Next to these she appeared in
more peaceful roles holding the scales of justice or stretching
out the feather of truth.

37

All these paintings and carvings reminded everyone assembled in the hall that this was a court of justice, a place of judgement, where men and women faced the all-consuming power of Pharaoh and suffered the consequence of her displeasure. Here, sentence of death was passed, the dreadful decree which dispatched criminals to a suffocating death in the desert or to be hung in chains from the Wall of Death outside the city.

Now, in the first weeks of the Inundation, in the third year of Pharaoh Hatusu's reign, sentence of death was to be proclaimed. The onlookers in the court either gasped or held their breath, for the trial recently ended manifested how the Pharaoh Queen, scarcely a woman of mature years, had tightened her grip on the collar of Egypt. When Pharaoh's power was strong, the princely tombs in the Valley of the Kings and the Valley of the Queens were left untouched. If Pharaoh weakened, the powers of darkness always made their presence felt, either in attacks on the temples or in the raiding of tombs across the swollen waters of the Nile in the City of the Dead. Such raids had recently taken place, and all manner of men and women had been involved. Priests of the mortuary temples, priestesses of the serpent goddess Meretseger, whose shrine overlooked the Necropolis, merchants and soldiers, high-ranking ministers and officials: no fewer than two dozen people in all had been arrested. Hatusu, her face mottled with fury, had met her councillors of the Royal Circle and demanded such raids be brought to an end. Now the man responsible for Pharaoh's justice, Chief Justice Amerotke, was about to pass judgement. He had been left in no doubt that he was to show all of Egypt how Hatusu had tightened her grip on the Kingdom of the Two Lands.

Hatusu herself had come down to the court early that morning to lecture Amerotke in his chamber behind the shrine. The Chief Justice thought Pharaoh had never looked so beautiful: her flawless skin drawn tight, eyes sparkling with life, the blood running fast and free. She was so angry she could not stay still, but walked up and down, linen robes swishing, her multicoloured sash swinging backwards and forwards to the clatter of bracelets and necklaces: these reflected the light from the torches and lamps so it seemed the Pharaoh Queen shimmered in an aura of fire. She had even pressed the pearl-encrusted fan used to keep her cheeks cool against Amerotke's neck.

'You are sure they are guilty, my lord?' she demanded.

'Of course, Divine One.'

Amerotke kept his eyes on the Uraeus, the spitting cobra, which lunged from the centre of the circlet around Hatusu's head. In many ways, he thought, the Pharaoh Queen in her present mood was more dangerous than any snake.

'I want those criminals dead.' Hatusu took away the fan, snapped it open and began to use it vigorously. She turned, and stared down at her Chief Minister, Senenmut, his thick-set face impassive as he squatted on a footstool and watched his divine mistress engage in not such a divine tantrum.

'You must not, my lady, be seen to interfere,' Senenmut declared. 'The tombs were invaded, the criminals caught; justice will be done.'

'I want them all to see justice is done. I want people as far north as the market towns of the Delta who stare out over the Great Green to know that I am Pharaoh. I want people who live beyond the Fourth Cataract to tremble at the sound of my name.'

'They already do.'

Amerotke leaned against the wall and crossed his arms. Hatusu was not angry with him, she was just indulging her well-known temper. In truth he realised this cunning Pharaoh Queen was delighted at what he had achieved.

'They will see you as mighty of form,' he continued, 'strong of heart, beloved daughter of Pharaoh, Lord of the Two Lands, she whom Nekhbet the Vulture Goddess has covered with her feathered wings, she whom Horus protects as he burns millions.'

Hatusu now hid her face behind the fan.

'She to whom,' Amerotke continued his teasing, 'the priests of Amun, Isis and Osiris offer incense to the clash of cymbals and the braying of trumpets. She who wears the double crown and the feathered headdress, whose words leap down from her mouth.'

Hatusu's rage subsided. She stood for a while listening to Amerotke imitate an imperial herald, then began to laugh, shoulders shaking, fingers going to cover her mouth. She had thrown the fan at Senenmut and hitched more closely around her shoulders the beautiful jewel-encrusted Nenes, the coat of glory, worn only by Pharaoh. Now she clapped her hands in appreciation.

'If you ever wish to become a herald, Amerotke, I can arrange that, but in the meantime . . .' She drew so close Amerotke could smell the beautiful Kiphye perfume, the juice of the resplendent blue lotus. Up close Hatusu's eyes reminded him of a leopard's, almost amber-coloured, whilst he knew those beautiful lips, parted so prettily, could curl in a snarl. She lifted her hands, sheathed in their blood-red gloves, and gently touched Amerotke's face. 'Three years, Amerotke, I have been Pharaoh, and you are right. I am the beloved of the gods. I am the smiter of the vile Asiatics, the crusher of the rebellious Kushites, and before me the People of the Nine Bows tremble. My ships cross the Great Green, my war barges patrol the Nile, my chariot squadrons go deeper and deeper into the Red Lands. My soldiers build wells, fortify oases, map roads; they set up inscriptions and monuments to my glory. My troops patrol the Horus path across Sinai, I demand the princes of Canaan flood my court with tribute, wines, wool and precious timber. But what is the use of that,' she pressed her fingers against his cheek, 'if I can't even protect the sepulchres of my kin, my father, brother, mother and husband? You know

what they did, Amerotke, those miscreants? They looted
the tombs, desecrated the mummies. They stripped them
of jewels, gold and silver, selling them like trinkets in the
marketplace. What do you think, my lord Amerotke, the
princes of Canaan will say when a merchant approaches
them and offers to sell jewels which once protected my
dead father's eyes? What does that say about the power of
Hatusu?'

'My Lord Amerotke is not to be blamed.' Senenmut spoke
up. 'He is the one who hunted these villains down and
brought them to justice.'

'Ah yes. Justice!' Hatusu stepped away. 'Make sure my
justice is done, make sure it is published and shown that it
has been done.' She snapped her fingers at Senenmut and
swept out of the chamber.

That had been three hours ago, just before dawn. Now
Amerotke sat enthroned on the dark-red-quilted Chair of
Judgement, its acacia wood inlaid with silver and gold, the
back of the chair rising above him from which a tasselled
awning stretched out above his head. Both the arms and the
feet of the throne were carved to represent a lunging lion
with the face of Sekhmet, the destroyer goddess. Amerotke
stared across at the group of men and women manacled
and chained, guarded by Asural, the burly Captain of the
Temple Guard, dressed in full ceremonial armour, sword
in one hand, club in the other. Around Asural stood the
temple police, whilst Amerotke knew that in the courtyard
outside, the death carts had been assembled. On a cushion
at Amerotke's feet knelt Lord Valu, the Eyes and Ears
of Pharaoh, the royal prosecutor, keeper of the Crocodile
Diadem. Amerotke knew the ritual. Valu would ask for
justice, for sentence of death to be passed on all those he'd
presented to the Goddess.

'This is my decree.' Amerokte grasped the flail and the
rod, the symbols of justice; he crossed his arms, imitating
Pharaoh when she issued a decree. 'The crimes you have

committed are a blasphemy which stinks as high as heaven, offensive to both man and god. You entered the Holy of Holies, the Houses of a Million Years. You opened the coffers and caskets of the great ones, and plundered their treasures, sealed there for all eternity. You disturbed the dead.'

Amerotke paused as the onlookers gasped and sighed, for that was the real crime: not the theft, but the disturbance of the dead. What happened to their corpses in this life would influence their Kas in the next.

'You used corpses as torches, setting alight the mummies and embalmed remains of divine children.' Amerotke stared at these criminals, men and women now almost indistinguishable, the dirt and muck of the prison dungeons staining their bruised flesh and torn clothes. 'Very well.' He picked up a scroll and handed it to Valu. 'Here are the names of the prisoners. Ten of the men shall be impaled alive at the entrance to the Valley of the Kings; the women will be buried alive beside them. The rest can hang in chains from the Wall of Death.'

'And the treasure they stole?' Valu asked.

'Everything these criminals robbed,' Amerotke continued, 'is to be sealed and brought here to the Temple of Ma'at, and placed in the embalming rooms below. The goods will be purified and inspected by Lord Senenmut before being returned to their proper place.'

Some of the prisoners were starting to shout and weep. Asural and his guards began to walk amongst them, thrusting cloths in their mouths to gag them.

'This is Pharaoh's justice,' Amerotke continued, 'and as it is written, so let it be done.'

Lord Valu smiled, his fat face creasing in pleasure. He scrambled to his feet, bowed to the judge who had made his job so easy, and backed away before turning, snapping his fingers and shouting at Asural to escort the prisoners out to the waiting death carts.

Amerotke put the flail and rod down on the small table

before him which carried the Books of Judgement. The court began to empty. He took off the heavy symbols of office, the beautiful cornelian pectoral, the bracelets and rings, as well as the chain of justice around his neck. He felt exhausted. He had trapped these criminals, he had proved, or at least Lord Valu had, that each had been guilty of a heinous crime. He could well understand Lord Valu's pleasure, for most of the work had been done for him when the evidence was handed over to his House of Scribes.

'My lord?' Amerotke looked up. Asural had returned, helmet under his arm. 'Shall I replace the bar?'

Amerotke nodded. The Captain of the Temple Guard, helped by one of his men, lifted the bar of sweet-smelling cedar wood and placed it across its three trestles. This separated the place of judgement from the rest of the court; it was only removed when the judge was about to give sentence.

'Is my lord ready for the next case?'

Amerotke got to his feet and walked over to the speaker, a fresh-faced young scribe who squatted with the rest, a writing tray across his lap. He crouched down and smiled at his kinsman, Prenhoe.

'Are you so eager for justice, Prenhoe? Are you not tired after writing so long?' He tapped the pots on the writing tray which contained red and black ink. 'Don't they have to be refilled? Aren't your fingers tired and your mouth dry? Or have you forgotten all other appetites except your hunger for justice?'

The other scribes now began to join in the teasing.

'We have to wait,' Amerotke continued, 'at least until Lord Valu and Asural return.' He got to his feet. 'Prenhoe, take some refreshment.' He pointed towards the Chair of Judgement and the table before it with his insignia of office. 'But make sure you guard what is there. Oh, by the way, where is Shufoy?' Amerotke stared round. Usually his manservant was never far away. 'The ever-dancing dwarf', as Asural

43

called him, would come hastening up to his master once any case was finished to discuss its finer points. Amerotke couldn't remember seeing him during the trial.

'You sent him on an errand, don't you remember, my lord?'

'Yes, it was a message,' Amerotke agreed, 'but not a journey! I hope he is all right.'

The Chief Justice strode towards the door, straining his ears; he could easily distinguish Shufoy's voice amongst the rest. Amerotke always worried about the dwarf who had become his companion and manservant. Shufoy was one of the 'Rhinoceri'; his nose had been removed for a crime he hadn't committed and he'd been banished to live with the other Rhinoceri in their dusty, dirty village many miles from Thebes. He had appealed against his punishment. Amerotke had investigated the case and found a hideous miscarriage of justice had taken place. As recompense, he had taken Shufoy into his household, and the little man had repaid him with undying loyalty and friendship. Despite his appearance, Shufoy had a keen mind and nimble wits, and was a constant companion to Amerotke and his family. He was forever plotting schemes to make himself wealthy. He had trained as a physician, sold medicines, proclaimed himself to be an astrologer and even offered to tell fortunes. Of course, all the schemes had failed, but not without provoking a great deal of laughter from Amerotke and the rest. Shufoy was a pleasant antidote to the pomposity and burdensome protocol of the court.

Now Amerotke wanted to discuss certain matters with Shufoy, and at the same time he was fearful for the little man's safety. Shufoy always accompanied his master through the streets of Thebes, and Amerotke had seen various merchants study the dwarf carefully. They viewed him as a grotesque. It was not unknown for the likes of Shufoy to be captured, bagged, bundled aboard a barge and taken either up or down river to be sold to some travelling troupe of itinerant players to serve as a mascot or fairground attraction.

'Don't worry,' Prenhoe called out. 'I'm sure Shufoy will be safe.'

Amerotke turned and stared back at the place of judgement. He went over and picked up the pectoral, the chain of office, the precious rings and bracelets, placed them in a coffer on the table and locked it securely. Still anxious about Shufoy, he sat down on a cushion, stretching his legs and arms, ignoring the curious looks of the scribes, who wanted to get away. They were hungry and eager to visit one of the temple cookshops.

'I wish to see the judge!' The woman's high-pitched voice echoed from the portico. 'I wish to see Chief Justice Amerotke. Let go of me! I am Lady Nethba.'

Amerotke groaned and put his face in his hands.

'You should see her.' Prenhoe hurried over and crouched before the judge. 'I didn't tell you this, master, but last night, I had a dream. You were walking by the river bank. Shufoy and I were riding on the back of a crocodile, which plunged into the water. I thought I was going to drown when I saw the ibis bird above me. I opened my eyes—'

'Were you still asleep?' Amerotke asked crossly.

'Yes, I was.'

'So how could you open your eyes? Never mind.' Amerotke patted Prenhoe's knee. 'Bring the lady in.'

The young scribe hurried away and returned with the lady Nethba. Amerotke had glimpsed her on other occasions but had never spoken to her. A tall, harsh-faced woman with the imperious features of an eagle, glittering eyes, sharp nose and a jutting mouth, her cheeks slightly furrowed, she had rather strange hands, her fingers so long and thin they reminded Amerotke of a spider's legs. She was dressed in a light blue cloak, the hood pulled across her head because she wore no wig, and her only concession to fashion was some face paint on her cheeks and black kohl under her eyes; this had been done hastily and was beginning to run. She extended a hand as Amerotke went to meet her. The judge grasped this and brushed her fingers against his lips, a gesture of respect for this daughter of one of Egypt's greatest architects.

'My lord Amerotke, I am so pleased you will see me.'

'Not here.'

Amerotke smiled. Calling for Prenhoe to bring him a jug of sweet ale, cups and apple bread, the judge took the lady Nethba into the small whitewashed room which served as his writing office and private shrine, a comfortable chamber with a desk, stools, chair and a bench along the far wall. He tried to keep it as clear as possible, a place where he could sit and think. He courteously showed Lady Nethba to a stool and pulled across another so that he could sit opposite. They exchanged pleasantries while a temple usher served the ale and bread. Amerotke was pleased to eat and drink; his throat was dry, whilst he hadn't broken his fast, having been summoned from his house long before dawn by Pharaoh's messenger.

'My lady.' Amerotke put his cup on the floor and leaned over to clasp one of her hands 'It is good to see you. You wish to speak with me?'

'It is my right,' Lady Nethba replied. 'As a daughter of an Imperial Fan Bearer, I have the right to appeal to Pharaoh's principal judge. My father was given that title and privilege for his work in the Valley of the Kings. Oh, my lord, I am so pleased that you caught the villains responsible for those robberies.' She would have carried on, but Amerotke squeezed her hand.

'My lady, time is short. How is your father the lord Sese?'

'He is dead.'

'I beg your pardon?'

Lady Nethba's lower lip trembled. 'He travelled into the Far West a few days ago. He had complained of pains in his belly. I had taken him to the Temple of Isis. My lord, he was in good health.'

'Your father had passed his sixtieth year.'

'He was still vigorous,' Lady Nethba retorted, 'and all he had were gripes in the belly. They wouldn't let me see him. They took him into the House of Twilight to examine his stomach. He was there four days. I received a message that my father was dying. I was preparing to go there when another messenger arrived: Father was dead. By the time I reached the temple, all I had to collect was my father's corpse. Oh, and a letter he had signed and sealed leaving a generous bequest of gold and silver to the Temple of Isis.'

'And?' Amerotke asked.

'I don't believe it, my lord. I believe my father was murdered, killed by those priests and physicians. In his fevered state he was encouraged to sign away part of our wealth.'

'But the Temple of Isis is famous for its skill and its riches. My lady, surely you misunderstand them? Your father—'

'My father is now being embalmed. I have appealed to the Divine One.'

At any other time Amerotke would have closed his eyes and groaned, but he wished to remain tactful and diplomatic.

'I have asked the Divine One for his death to be investigated. I have asked for you, my Lord Judge, to study the circumstances and tell me what happened. I know the Divine One will not refuse me.' Lady Nethba's face broke into a smile. She thrust her ale cup into Amerotke's hand. 'I'm pleased justice will be done.'

'Where is your father's corpse?'

'At the Temple of Isis; it lies in the Wabet, the Place of Purification, awaiting the embalmers. I have asked my own physician to be present when this takes place.' Lady Nethba sniffed and blinked quickly. Despite her apparent arrogance and harshness, Amerotke could appreciate this noblewoman's love for her father and her deep anguish at his unexpected death.

'I promise you,' the judge held up his hand, 'I will do what I can.'

When Lady Nethba had left, Amerotke sighed and loosened the sash round his robe. He felt damp with sweat and realised how agitated he had become. He tried not to think of what was happening to the prisoners. Only two would survive, young women who had been sentenced earlier to life imprisonment at one of the prison oases far out in the eastern desert. He and Lord Valu were to question these later.

Amerotke had brought those involved in the tomb robberies to judgement, but he remained uneasy. He believed there was more to the matter than he had discovered, such as those shadowy figures known as the Sebaus, who were responsible for the actual robberies and were therefore more deeply involved than those who had merely received and sold the plunder. He had warned the Divine One about his suspicions but Hatusu had only half listened; she was more concerned with what goods had been recovered. Amerotke had spared the two women, former courtesans, in order to explore his doubts further, but the rest would experience hideous execution. Yet what choice did he have? All those involved in the robberies had committed treason, blasphemy, sacrilege and, above all, murder. They had been responsible for the deaths of at least eight mortuary guards, whose corpses had been found in rocky culverts near the Royal Valleys.

A knock at the door startled him. Asural, still dressed like the war god Montu, leather helmet under his arm, marched into the chamber.

'The criminals, my lord, have gone, handed over to the executioners. Lord Valu has granted your request: each prisoner will be given a cup of drugged wine before sentence is carried out.'

The captain of the guard paused, alarmed by Amerotke's pale, drawn face. Usually the judge was strong and vibrant; now he crouched on his stool like a man full of sorrow.

'My Lord . . .'

'I am well, Asural. You know what it's like: nobody deserves death, not really.'

'They did.' Asural pointed to the tray on the floor. 'I'll send a temple usher in for that. You need food, tender lamb grilled over charcoal, with a goblet of cool charou. You should eat and rest. The court will not reconvene during the midday heat; perhaps you should go for a walk, then sleep?'

Amerotke, embarrassed by such care, thanked him hurriedly. Asural left, and the judge crossed to a tall reed basket in the corner. He undid the seals, lifted the lid and took out the copper container which held the court's scroll for the next case.

'Poor General Suten,' he murmured. 'Bitten to death by snakes.' He removed the copper top and shook out the scroll, then unrolled it and read the few paltry facts he had gleaned. The door opened behind him.

'Shufoy, where have you been?'

There was no reply, and Amerotke turned swiftly. Shufoy was never so silent! His heart leapt as the two assassins, garbed in black from head to toe, separated, crouched and edged towards him, daggers out. The Chief Justice backed against the wall, grasping the copper container. The assassins, one of whom had kicked the door shut behind him, followed warily. Amerotke, shocked, was only aware of their soft breath, the shuffling of padded feet and the eyes of these killers gleaming between the black folds across their face.

'What is it?' Amerotke rasped, desperate for time. 'Who sent you?'

'The dead,' a voice behind the mask grated. 'They die, you die. For you, judge, this is the day of fiery judgement.'

'They were blasphemers, robbers.'

'No, judge, they were our friends, our allies.'

Amerotke started forward, swinging the copper cylinder. One assassin lunged, dagger snaking out. Amerotke turned and, using the container like a club, fended off the blow. The assassin darted back, and his companion sprang forward. Amerotke could feel the sweat bursting out, wetting his face; his throat had gone strangely dry, and he found it hard to breathe. The assassins were waiting: one mistake and they would be in, those wicked curved daggers ripping his flesh.

'My lord!' The door to the chamber swung open, and a temple usher entered holding a tray. He took one look at the scene, dropped the tray and ran screaming down the Hall of Two Truths. The assassins, desperate, closed once more, but Amerotke, anger now replacing fear, moved quickly from side to side, recalling all the tricks he had been taught during his military training. The assassins, unnerved, drew back and edged towards the door, where there were the sounds of voices and hurried footsteps. Convinced their attack had failed, they lunged once more, driving Amerotke back, before fleeing through the doorway. Amerotke slumped to the floor even as Asural and the temple guards burst in. The judge convinced the captain he was well, urging him to pursue the attackers even though he realised it was futile. The Temple of Ma'at was a warren of passageways with many doors to its outer courtyards and gardens.

Amerotke sat gasping for breath, aware of the noise outside his chamber. Asural was calling for more guards, scribes and acolytes to help him in his search.

'They've escaped.' The captain came back into the chamber. 'But they left this.' He dropped into Amerotke's hand a scarab; the small stone, polished until it shone, bore the hieroglyph of a man kneeling holding a bow.

'The Sebaus,' Amerotke whispered. 'I've come across them before in my investigations. They take their name from demons. They are professional assassins; they may have been involved in the plundering of the tombs.'

'Are you hurt?' Asural asked.

'Only my pride.' Amerotke grinned up at him. 'And before you speak, Captain, it was my mistake. If I've heard you once, I've heard you a hundred times. I should have guards outside my chamber. Well,' Amerotke got to his feet, 'I'm half convinced you're right.'

He sat on a stool whilst Asural organised ushers to tidy the room, clear the mess from the fallen tray and bring more food and wine. A temple officer came hurrying in to announce that the temple grounds had been searched but there was no trace of the assassins.

'Professional killers,' Amerotke declared. 'They come and go like the desert wind. They will take off their black garb and mingle with other plaintiffs and pilgrims. Now, leave me for a while.'

Asural and the guards left. Amerotke heard the captain issue orders so that the chamber and the passageways to it were guarded. He ate the food, drank some of the wine and lay down on the couch. He didn't want to think why the assassins had come; that would have to wait.

He seemed to have slept for only a few heartbeats when he heard the door open and, struggling up, stared at Shufoy. The dwarf stood like the Prophet of Doom garbed in his striped desert wanderer robe; his little scarred face, framed by a shock of iron-grey hair, was creased in concern.

'Master, what has happened? I heard . . .' For such a small man, Shufoy had a deep, carrying voice. 'I've told you before.' Shufoy pointed his staff at Amerotke. 'The lady Nofret will not be pleased. You have guards, you should use them!'

'The lady Nofret will not be told.' Amerotke drained the last of the wine from his cup. 'More importantly, where have you been?'

The judge was eager to divert his manservant.

Shufoy opened the leather pannier across his shoulder and took out what looked like a lump of charcoal, an oval piece of black rock. He handed this to Amerotke, who exclaimed at its heavy weight.

'You see,' Shufoy gabbled, 'it's a sacred stone which fell to earth. It came from beyond the Far Horizon, a gift from the gods. If I smelt it down and break it up, I can sell small pieces as scarabs to protect pilgrims against all dangers.'

Amerotke stared at the piece of hard black stone. The more he examined it, the more he became convinced it was not so much a rock as a piece of unknown metal. He recalled travellers' stories of how the Hittites in the north had invented a new form of metal which could smite through copper and bronze. Was this it? He'd also heard stories of fiery rocks falling into the desert burning hot to the touch. Many regarded these rocks as sacred, more precious than gold.

'I bought it from a scorpion man,' Shufoy explained. 'I had to haggle for hours, and pour a large jug of wine down him, before he agreed to a sale. Now, master.' Shufoy's voice rose to a wail, clearly annoyed at Amerotke's attempt to distract him.

'Ah, very well.' Amerotke got to his feet, tied his sash round himself, checked on the guards outside and closed the door again. He sat on a footstool while Shufoy perched on the chair. Amerotke stared at the great ugly scar where Shufoy's nose and upper lip had once been.

'I'm sorry.' The judge smiled. 'Shufoy, you are correct. If you had been here, those assassins would never have attacked.'

'Why?' the dwarf asked. 'Why did they come?'

'They were sent,' Amerotke explained.

'But I thought you had caught the tomb robbers?'

'No, Shufoy, I caught some of them, but perhaps not the leaders.' Amerotke held up his hands. 'Across the Nile lies the City of the Dead, the sepulchres of very wealthy noblemen, court officials, generals and priests. Beyond the Necropolis lie the Valleys of the Kings and Queens, the

Houses of Eternity, the Mansions of a Million Years, where the great ones sleep and dream their eternal dreams. Now, Shufoy, these tombs are the glory of Egypt, but they are also treasure houses. They contain caskets, coffers, precious jewels, chairs and beds, pots of exquisite perfume, chests full of every form of treasure, bars of gold and nuggets of silver—'

'I know that,' Shufoy intervened.

'Now the Divine One,' Amerotke continued evenly, 'has tightened her grip on the neck of Egypt. She is the ruler, the Mistress of the Great House, but to achieve that, she has had to fight enemies both here and abroad.'

'She was distracted.'

'She was distracted,' Amerotke agreed, 'and so was Lord Senenmut, as well as others of the Royal Circle. Egypt is like a garden. You tend one patch and the weeds start to grow in another. A great conspiracy was formed; it included merchants, officials, soldiers and some of the custodians of the Necropolis. Now tomb robbing is like the desert, it's always with us, but this was more serious. Many of the imperial tombs are hidden, their entrances concealed and closely guarded; even if you broke into one of them, you'd need a map to find your way through.'

'And they did this?' Shufoy asked.

'Yes, they did. Now, as you know, I investigated their crimes. I found one merchant more greedy than the rest; a man who stupidly tried to sell some of the plundered treasures in Memphis. I arrested him and his brother and took them to the House of Death, where the imperial torturers questioned them closely. They broke and provided more names. Entire families were involved.'

'What was the result?'

Amerotke waved a hand. 'You saw what happened this morning, or rather you heard: the tomb robbers were arrested and sentenced.'

'But not all of them.'

'No.' Amerotke rubbed his face. 'I have said to the Divine One and to Lord Senenmut that two problems remain: the leaders and these assassins. In my searches I found that the leaders had hired the Sebaus not only to protect them but to steal the treasure and dissipate it through various cities of Egypt.'

'So the game is not finished.' Shufoy leaned forward, almost tipping off the chair.

'No, it's not finished.'

Amerotke was about to continue when there was a loud knocking on the door and Lord Senenmut entered. Behind him thronged members of the Imperial Bodyguard, 'Braves of the King', warriors who had excelled in battle, killing an enemy in hand-to-hand fighting and taking his head as a trophy. They all wore the distinctive blue and gold headdress, and each wore a collar with a silver bee in the centre, the highest award for bravery that could be won by an Egyptian soldier.

'My lord,' Amerotke bowed, 'have you come to arrest me?' He noticed how each of the soldiers carried a shield, as well as an oval war club and curved daggers thrust in the sashes around their waist.

'I heard about the attack.' Senenmut told the guard to stay outside the chamber. 'I thought this business was finished.' He held up a leather bag. 'Now we have proof it is not.' He cupped Amerotke's cheek in one hand. 'You are unmarked? The Divine One was concerned.'

'I am well,' Amerotke replied. He pointed to the leather bag. 'But you are not just here about my welfare.'

'The treasure from the looted tombs?' Senenmut asked.

'It is kept below in the strongroom.'

Senenmut asked to see it. Amerotke took him out of the chamber and along the passageway. He noticed how the court was beginning to fill again. Scribes and priests, having satisfied their hunger in the temple cookshops and rested in the shade of the gardens, were now returning to the hall for the second session of the court, which would last until dusk. All these hurriedly stood aside as Pharaoh's First Minister and principal judge, ringed by the Braves of the King, hurried along the gleaming passageways and down the steps to the great cavernous storeroom below. The doors were guarded by sentries wearing the regalia of the goddess Ma'at. Amerotke took the keys from the officer of the guard, broke the seals, unlocked the doors and led Senenmut in.

The storeroom was long and low-ceilinged. They waited for a while as the torches fixed into the wall were lit to reveal heaps of treasure, caskets and coffers which had been seized from the temple robbers. For a while Senenmut, whistling under his breath, moved amongst these, examining the beautiful mirrors and mirror cases decorated with coloured glass and semi-precious stones; ointment cases, gloves, sandals, diadems, ivory bracelets, pectorals of blue faience, collars of gold, statues and scarabs, earrings and bracelets, ritual couches, headrests carved in gold, exquisitely fashioned funeral boats, silver-plated shrines, canopic jars and dozens of shabtis, carved statues plated with precious metals which represented the servants of the dead person. Amerotke explained how each item had been carefully listed and noted, even the chairs of state and the beautiful miniature chariots. Senenmut ran his hand through a box of jewels, letting them cascade back in a glittering hail of colour.

'It was easy enough,' Amerotke explained. 'Once we knew what had been stolen it was only a matter of matching the list. We managed to seize about three quarters of what was taken. Some of it is damaged, but once things are sorted and purified, they can be returned to their rightful owners.'

Senenmut took Amerotke by the arm and led him over to a small polished table under a cresset torch. He undid the sack he was carrying and gently eased out a solid gold pendant depicting a squatting king with a string of pure pearls tied round his neck. The pendant weighed heavy; the pearls were particularly exquisite.

55

'Another piece found?' Amerotke asked.

'This,' Senenmut tapped it with his fingers, 'was not found in any local marketplace but in northern Canaan, a town in the Amki region.'

Amerotke stared in disbelief.

'One of our envoys discovered it. This means the temple robbers were able to take their ill-gotten gains beyond our borders.'

'But there are guards, customs posts,' Amerotke exclaimed. 'Treasure like this would be hard to conceal. It would be highly dangerous to transport such goods.'

'Well it was,' Senenmut replied drily, his voice echoing through the chamber. 'Here is a golden pendant which weighs as heavy as any sword. It once belonged to the Divine One's grandfather and was buried in his tomb, yet it was taken out, carried through Egypt and offered for sale in a Canaanite town.'

Amerotke stared in disbelief at this beautiful object, precious for so many reasons.

'Can you imagine,' Senenmut continued, 'what this means to the Divine One, the treasures of her ancestors, the glory of Egypt, being sold abroad?' He paused. 'It also means that these robbers were arrogant. This treasure was part of a hoard. If the carrier had been caught by a customs official or border guard, or the chariot squadrons which patrol the Horus road, it would have meant certain death. You were correct, Amerotke: only part of this gang has been destroyed.'

'We interrogated them, but there were no further names?' Amerotke shrugged. 'You don't need to answer that. Of course the leaders wouldn't let their identities be revealed. They know all there is to know about the Valley of the Kings, the secret entrances to the royal tombs and the way each sepulchre is laid out. They also have the means to have such treasure safely removed from Egypt. But who? The only survivors are those two women whose sentences were commuted to life imprisonment in a prison oasis.' Amerotke stared round at the treasures; his eye was caught by a particularly exquisite silver statue of a crouching leopard. Its skin was of gold, the spots precious stones, with two large rubies as eyes. 'But why,' he asked, 'stir up a hornets' nest by sending assassins against me? A warning? Punishment?'

'Or,' Senenmut added, 'because they are frightened you might know something which could lead you to the leaders of this sacrilegious sect. You must ask yourself: what do you know? Go carefully through your records. Is there anything you have missed?'

He walked away and then came back. 'Oh, by the way, I bring not only the good wishes and praises of the Divine One. You have been approached by the Lady Nethba?' Amerotke nodded. 'The Divine One wishes you to visit the Temple of Isis.' Senenmut dug underneath his robe and brought out a scroll, which he handed to the judge. 'You are to enquire about the Lady Nethba's father, and there is further business: four hesets of that temple have disappeared.'

'And?' Amerotke snapped sharply. 'There is something else?'

'Yes, the captain of the guard at the Temple of Isis has been brutally murdered. They found his corpse, hands and feet bound; his testicles and heart had been removed, and he'd been left to bleed to death.'

'Mafdet!' Amerotke exclaimed. 'That was the name of the captain of the Isis temple guard, yes?' He paused. 'His name was mentioned in my investigations into the robbery of the tombs, just a passing reference. Mafdet once served in the Necropolis as a guard. He was also a member of Vizier Rahimere's retinue before that great lord's disgrace. I wonder if there is any connection between his death and the robberies?'

'Did he fall under suspicion?'

'No, no.' Amerotke shook his head. 'It was just that I drew up a list of all those who had served in the garrison at the

Necropolis, and I remember Mafdet because of his link with
Rahimere. He was also recommended by General Suten,
who, as you know, died so hideously.' Amerotke ran a finger
around his lips. 'Talking of temples,' he continued slowly, 'is
it possible that the people responsible for these robberies,
who organised and planned them, are high-ranking priests?
Many of them have attended royal funerals. They know the
Valley of the Kings better than I, and because they escort
the coffin caskets to their resting place, they learn about
the inside of the tombs in considerable detail. Wouldn't the
archives of a temple like Isis hold maps and plans?'

'Perhaps, but you've discovered no evidence for such a
theory?' Senenmut replied.

'None whatsoever. No temple fell under suspicion, be it
that of Isis, Amun or any other. And yet,' Amerotke clapped
his hands, 'even as I finished that investigation, even as I
sentenced those criminals to death, I recognised that some
had escaped.'

Senenmut walked away into the darkness.

'I do not think you will find criminals at the Temple of
Isis.' Pharaoh's First Minister kept his back to Amerotke.
'The Divine One regards Lord Impuki and Lady Thena as
close friends.'

'I shall bear that in mind.'

'And now you must decide upon the death of General
Suten.' Senenmut turned and came back. 'The Divine One is
deeply interested in the outcome of that case. Was it murder
or some unfortunate accident?'

'I know what my lord Valu would reply.' Amerotke smiled
thinly. 'He is going to ask how a nest of horned vipers
mysteriously appeared on the roof terrace of one of Egypt's
leading generals, who was famous for his deep loathing of
such vermin.'

'An accident?'

Amerotke spread his hands. 'No, my lord, I suspect it was
murder.'

THETTET: ancient Egyptian, 'to destroy'

CHAPTER 3

You hold the hidden flame,
Who give birth to the truth,
Oh come forth,
Lady of strength, divine daughter of truth . . .

The chapel priest of the Temple of Ma'at intoned the hymn of praise to the Goddess of Truth. He sprayed holy water over the small naos containing the statue of the Goddess and lit the two thuribles before her shrine, sprinkling them both with incense before opening the doors of the tabernacle to expose the statue itself. Amerotke, kneeling on a cushion, bowed his head. He intoned his secret prayer that, despite the dangers and the worries which confronted him, his heart would be true and his tongue utter just judgements. He bowed, pressing his forehead against the cold, hard floor. The priest once more incensed the tabernacle and quietly withdrew. Amerotke got to his feet and took his seat in the Chair of Judgement. The tabernacle was situated on a plinth behind him, but the judge felt the power from that holy place all around him.

'This court of the Hall of Two Truths,' Amerotke intoned, 'is now in session. All those who have business before the Divine One's justice, approach and state your case.'

Amerotke finished the usual ritual and the court settled

down to deal with the business of the afternoon. The day's
heat had now lessened. The shadows in the gardens outside
had grown longer, creeping across the grass, whilst a cool
breeze wafted in the perfumed fragrance of the flowers. The
sacred bar was in place, dividing the place of judgement
from the rest of the court. Amerotke, face oiled, adorned
with all the regalia of the Supreme Judge, sat more easily
in the Chair of Judgement, grasping the flail and the rod. He
tried to lessen the tension caused by others hurrying to their
places by staring to the left through the great window which
opened up on the pastures of Ma'at, where the flocks of the
Goddess, her trained gazelles and dappled deer, grazed on
the lawns. To the right of the window squatted the line of
clerks, Prenhoe amongst them, heads bowed, pens at the
ready over scrubbed sheets of vellum. These scribes would
take down what was said. Amerotke's Chief of Cabinet, his
collector of words, would write up the official report, copying
it for the Divine House and for the office of the Eyes and Ears
of Pharaoh.

Lord Valu, he of the fat face and the bland smile, had
apparently enjoyed a good lunch. He knelt on his cushion
behind the bar, tapping his fingers on his stomach; now
and again he would pick up a small bottle of perfume to
savour its sweetness. In a semicircle behind him squatted
his retainers, the carrier of his sandals, the holder of his
wig and the guardian of his portable toilet, for the lord
Valu's insides were sensitive in the extreme. Nevertheless Valu, despite his indulgent ways, was a mongoose
in human flesh. Keen of mind, with a dagger-like wit, he
was apparently very satisfied with the convictions he had
won that morning and more than pleased with the secret
arrangements he had made with the Chief Judge regarding
two of the prisoners not sentenced to death. He now smiled
conspiratorially at Amerotke. The judge hid his unease. The
tenor of the day was growing more complex, and once this

session was finished, he still had business in the House of Chains below.

Amerotke accepted that the matters before him were very serious. To his right, further along the bar, squatted the three leading members of General Suten's household, his lady wife Lupherna, Chief Scribe Menna and the dead general's valet Heby.

'My lord Valu, we are ready?'

'I call on General Omendap.'

Amerotke moved slightly. He now realised which path Valu was going to pursue. General Omendap was the Divine One's favourite commander. He had played a vital role in Hatusu's seizure of power four years earlier. Suten had been Omendap's lieutenant, so an attack on Suten was an attack on the power of Pharaoh.

General Omendap, in his pleated robe, a pectoral of dazzling blue lapis lazuli glittering on his chest, was called to kneel on the witness cushion to Valu's right. A tall, elegant patrician, sharp-faced, with close-set eyes, he bowed towards Amerotke and grasped the gold-cased Feather of Truth brought across by Prenhoe as he took the solemn oath and declared his identity.

'You're most welcome,' Amerotke declared. 'Yet General Omendap, why are you here?'

'I knew General Suten,' Omendap's voice was low but carrying, 'when he was a colonel in the Swallows, one of the swiftest and bravest chariot squadrons of Egypt. He was honoured by the Querret.' Omendap used the old Egyptian word for the Royal Circle. 'He won collars of valour and the silver bees of bravery—'

'Yes, yes,' Amerotke broke in tactfully. 'But why are you here?'

'Nine years ago,' Omendap took no offence at the interruption, 'Colonel Suten, as he was then, took a force of chariots out into the eastern Red Lands. He was pursuing a band of Libyan marauders who were attacking villagers, isolated oases. So ruthless was he in his pursuit . . .' The court was now hushed as General Omendap launched into a graphic description of an ordeal many people in Thebes regarded as a legend. 'So ruthless was he in his pursuit of the enemy,' General Omendap repeated, 'that Colonel Suten became lost in a violent sandstorm which must have come straight from the Underworld. By the time the storm was finished, he had become separated from the rest of his companions. He made sacrifice to Red Eyes, Lord of the Storm, but his luck had run out. He and his charioteer were captured by a band of Libyans. They took Colonel Suten to a place of snakes in a rocky valley, a narrow tunnel scooped out from beneath the rocks. It was known as a place of abomination because of the hordes of snakes which swarmed there. Colonel Suten and his charioteer were placed in that place of horror and both entrances to the passageway were sealed with rocks.'

Omendap raised his hand at the low moan from the people standing at the back of the court.

'Can you imagine, my lord judge, Colonel Suten and his charioteer squatting in that underground cavern while horned vipers, poisonous and deadly, curled and snaked all about them? The heat was intense, their mouths and nostrils were coated with sand, their eyes stinging. The sun turned the cavern into an inferno, baking the two men, provoking them to move, yet Colonel Suten sat still. He did not panic, he did not surrender to hysteria, but for hours persuaded his charioteer to stay as motionless as himself.'

General Omendap paused for effect.

'Any other man, my lord, would have died from the heat, his ravaging thirst or the sheer terror of what was happening around him. Yet we have the evidence of Suten's own charioteer, a soldier who has since gone across the Far Horizon, that the colonel showed no fear and persuaded his companion to remain still.' General Omendap paused again to sip at a beaker of water brought by an attendant.

'Now Colonel Suten had been captured early in the day. The Libyans thought he would die in the horror they had created. They decided to light a fire and celebrate their success, sharing out the plunder taken from Colonel Suten's chariot. The smoke of their fires was seen by the rest of the squadron, who moved quickly to attack the marauders. They launched an assault at dusk. The Libyans had drunk deeply and were incapable of organising any defence. Our chariots swooped in like hawks. Every Libyan was put to death, except a young boy who showed the squadron where Colonel Suten and his companion had been imprisoned. The place of horror was opened, Colonel Suten and his charioteer were found safe. Even then the brave colonel did not panic or give way to hysteria. He ordered his rescuers to stay outside, quietly telling them to bring fire brands. Eventually a path was cleared and Colonel Suten and his companion escaped unscathed.'

'My lord,' Valu purred, 'I thank General Omendap for his evidence, which is vital to this case. Colonel Suten's escape from that abode of abomination was an act of bravery but it scarred his soul. I can produce witnesses by the score who will testify that General Suten had a deep, abiding detestation of snakes. He survived the torture of the Libyan marauders but it cloaked his heart in darkness. Even members of his own household will testify that General Suten was most insistent that his house be searched morning, noon and night for traces of any snake. He imported specially trained mongooses to eradicate such reptiles, whilst his practice of using the roof terrace of his house was not just to catch the cooling breath of Amun; he also saw it as a place of safety. On the night he died, as witnesses will testify, General Suten, as was his custom, ordered the roof terrace to be scrupulously searched. This included baskets, the sheets upon his bed, beneath chairs and tables. No trace of any horned viper could be found. Yet within an hour of his household leaving him, General Suten was heard screaming in terror. When his servants returned to the roof terrace they found a swarm of horned vipers. I ask, my lord, how could so many snakes appear on a roof terrace unless put there deliberately?'

Amerotke nodded in agreement. Now the three principal members of General Suten's household took the oath. Lady Lupherna spoke first. She was a small, comely woman with a delicate, pretty face. Amerotke had to ask her to speak louder so the rest of the court could hear. She was followed by Chief Scribe Menna, a strong, harsh-faced man who spoke bluntly and to the point. Finally came slender, thin-faced Heby, who kept plucking nervously at his robe as he described how he had guarded the steps leading up to the roof terrace.

Amerotke moved on swiftly. Other witnesses, servants and retainers were called. Valu kept his main thrust of attack very clear: General Suten had hated snakes. On the night he had been murdered – Valu deliberately used that word – Suten had dined with his wife, chief scribe and valet on the roof terrace. They had eaten dishes of fish and drunk beer and wine before General Suten declared he would continue writing his memoirs, a favourite pastime, which he hoped to present to the Divine One. Before they had retired, Menna, Lupherna and Heby, along with other servants, helped the general search the roof terrace for signs of any snake. Of course, none was found. The household left and General Suten returned to his memoirs, with Heby guarding the stairs. Suten's screams had been heard, the household was roused, but there was nothing to be done. They had contacted a member of the local Medjay, Standard-Bearer Nadif, who had hurried in to help. Nadif too gave evidence, in a clear, strong voice, about his surprise at how General Suten had died.

'There is,' Valu finished, spreading his hands, 'only one conclusion. Those horned vipers were placed there deliberately.'

'How?' Amerotke queried

Valu smirked. 'A question I keep asking myself. Could they have been thrown from another roof? That's impossible, there is no other building. The mansion stood in its own grounds. Could they have been hoisted up from a window below? But the rooms below were occupied by others; such a task would have attracted attention. There is only one way those horned vipers could have been brought to the roof terrace: by the steps. The only person on those steps that night, a man who by his own confession never left his post, was Heby.'

Amerotke gazed at Heby, who put his fingers to his face and moaned, staring around at his companions for help.

'Why should I do that?' he wailed, ignoring the shouts of the court ushers to keep silent. 'I loved my master. I always guarded the stairs, I never saw or heard anything amiss, not until my master's screams rang out.'

Amerotke raised a hand for silence. The valet was clearly terrified. If he was convicted, he would die a hideous death out in the Red Lands, bound to a thorn bush and burnt to death.

'The court must answer the question,' Valu pressed his point, 'why should a general with an obvious and understandable hatred for snakes be found dead on his roof terrace with horned vipers curling all about him, bitten at least fifteen times, a roof terrace which, according to everyone, was scrupulously searched for even the smallest snake? Can horned vipers fly?' Valu paused at the ripple of laughter his words provoked. 'Can at least two score of them crawl up the walls of a house without being noticed? Perhaps someone in the garden was able to hurl them up?' Valu clapped his hands softly. 'Such explanations are foolish. There is only one answer: Heby placed them there.'

'But why?' Amerotke asked. He turned to the valet. 'Heby, how long had you served General Suten?'

'For many years.'

'And you were happy in his service?'

'Oh yes, my lord.'

'And he was happy with you?'

'I believe so. He rewarded me lavishly with new robes.' Heby held up his hand. 'A ring. I have my own chamber, more than enough to eat and drink.'

'And his wife?'

Valu's question cut like a lash through the court. Lady Lupherna put her face in her hands and started to sob quietly.

'What is this?' Amerotke straightened in his chair. 'Lord Valu, what path are you taking now?'

'Lady Lupherna,' Valu grasped the bar of the court and peered down at the general's wife, who knelt on a cushion between Heby and Menna, 'you have nothing to fear.' Valu's voice was sickly smooth. 'Lady Lupherna, tell the court.'

Lupherna raised a tear-streaked face, coughing and spluttering as she tried to clear her throat.

'Tell my lord judge precisely what happened,' Valu urged.

The court waited in delicious silence at the prospect of some savoury sex scandal which would be discussed in houses, shops and beer tents throughout the city. Lady Lupherna, small and ripe as any plum, with her smooth skin and pretty mouth and gentle doe-like eyes! Amerotke, like the rest, guessed what was going to happen next. Lupherna did not disappoint the court. She confessed in halting phrases how, over the last few months, Heby had pestered her with his attentions, buying her presents, gazing all moon-eyed at her, accosting her when she was alone, even coming into her bedchamber. She gave her evidence reluctantly; she confessed she liked Heby, and always had, until he began his pestering. Throughout her evidence Chief Scribe Menna knelt, head down. Valu next turned on him, and Menna had to confess that two weeks earlier Lady Lupherna had eventually confessed all to her husband. At length, the general had summoned Heby to his presence and lashed him with his tongue, threatening that any further harassment would lead to him being flogged and thrown out of the house to fend for himself.

Valu, a born practitioner of the art of questioning, gently teased out the truth. Both Menna and Lupherna were reluctant to betray a member of their household, but the more they chattered, the more obviously Heby's guilt unfolded. Valu prompted them, a question here, a question there, backwards and forwards, until eventually he turned on Heby, reminding him he was on oath, and asked him two important questions. Had he pestered the Lady Lupherna? And had he been severely reprimanded by General Suten? At first Heby refused to answer. Amerotke intervened, warning the valet that if he didn't answer the prosecutor's questions he would be taken to the House of Chains below. Heby, sobbing uncontrollably, whispered yes to both questions. The sigh from the spectators was audible.

'You see, my lord judge,' Valu raised a hand, 'we have the motive and we have the means.' He would have continued, but Amerotke gestured for silence.

'My lord prosecutor, we do have a further problem.' Valu's head snapped up quickly, and the spectators at the back fell silent. 'Picture in your mind,' Amerotke raised his hands, 'the good general on the roof terrace. He has eaten and drunk well; a hero of Egypt, he sits writing his memoirs. His wife is busy in her chamber, Chief Scribe Menna goes about his duties, the hall of audience is empty, only Heby guards the stairs. Now, if I follow your line of argument, Lord Valu, Heby has decided to murder his master, out of either revenge or lust for his lady wife, or possibly both. He climbs the stairs with a leather bag in which these horned vipers swarm and curl. He goes on to the roof and scatters these serpents about. Wouldn't General Suten object, wouldn't he cry out and raise the alarm?'

'Ah!' Valu clapped his hands together and bowed towards the judge. 'My lord, I was going to mention that!'

'What?'

Amerotke was cross at having walked into one of Valu's traps.

'The poppy seed! General Suten's wine had been mixed with an infusion of poppy seed. The general became sleepy and lay down on his bed. Heby had hidden away his leather sack containing the horned vipers. At the appropriate time he creeps up the stairs, sees his master asleep and goes back down to fetch the sack. He takes this up, stealing through the darkness, and empties the contents on and around the general.' Valu spread his hands as his voice rose. 'Can you imagine, my lord, this great hero of Egypt awakening to find he is suffering his worst nightmare. Yet this nightmare is no phantasm but the horrid work of a son of Seth. The general cries out and the vipers strike. The general falls to the ground, arms and legs flailing; such movements would only excite the snakes even more. He is bitten time and time again. He screams and perishes. Such an unworthy death for such a worthy man!'

Amerotke nodded in agreement.

'Then, my lord Valu, I have one further question, or rather two. First, was General Suten accustomed to mixing poppy seed with his wine?'

'He was.' Lady Lupherna spoke out strongly. 'My lord judge, I must tell you this, something we have only learnt since his death: my husband was suffering from pains in his stomach. He had visited the Temple of Isis and been examined. Such pains always came after he had eaten, especially at night. The Chief Physician, High Priest Impuki, prescribed a few grains of poppy seed to be taken late in the evening.'

'Good.' Amerotke glanced at Lord Valu, who didn't disagree. 'My second question,' Amerotke continued, 'is even more important. If Heby murdered his master, surely he would have known he would be caught? After all, he has openly confessed that whilst he was on duty no one climbed those steps, that he never left his post, while you, Lord Valu, have clearly demonstrated that those snakes must have been brought on to the roof. I find it difficult to accept that a man in his right senses would murder his master in such a public way when the only conclusion to be reached was that he was responsible.'

Valu stared stonily back.

'Look.' Amerotke gestured at Heby. 'He protests his innocence. Why should he kill his master so openly and thus entrap himself?'

'Perhaps he didn't realise he would be caught.' Valu couldn't keep the spite out of his voice.

'Not so.' Amerotke shook his head. 'My lord prosecutor, if Heby was going to kill General Suten, he would plan, he would have to go out into the Red Lands to collect the vipers, hide them away in his master's house and seize his opportunity. If I follow your argument, Lord Valu, Heby is not irrational or impetuous but a single-minded cold-blooded killer, so I return to my original question. If he was going to kill his master, why didn't he take more care to look after himself? Moreover,' Amerotke pointed to Lady Lupherna, 'we have the question of the poppy seed. It could be argued that Heby placed an opiate in his master's drink, but we do have the evidence of his wife, which can be corroborated by Lord Impuki at the Temple of Isis, that General Suten needed such poppy juice to ease the cramps in his belly as well as relax his heart.'

Amerotke paused and stared out of the window. The sky was turning a fiery red, the sun sinking fast, the shadows lengthening; the breeze had shifted, bringing in the smells from the river. I should be going home, Amerotke thought wistfully, to play with my children and sit on my own roof terrace.

'My lord, will there be a judgement?'

Amerotke watched a wood pigeon, its thick, heavy wings fluttering slowly, glide over the lawn.

'My lord?' Valu repeated.

'The case will be deferred,' Amerotke replied. 'Heby is to be placed under house arrest at General Suten's mansion. If he tries to leave he will be taken to the House of Chains. He will stay there whilst I investigate further. The case will be brought back to me within two days.' He raised his hand at the clamour which had broken out at the back of the court. Shufoy and Asural immediately left, and Amerotke realised a court usher must have brought an urgent message. 'The business of this court is done,' he declared swiftly, then he rose and left the Chair of Judgement.

'You'd best come down to the House of Chains.' Valu had followed Amerotke back into his chamber. 'You heard the clamour in the court, which is why your retainers left. Those two women you sentenced to life in a prison oasis, one has murdered the other, strangled her with chains.'

'What?' Amerotke put the flail and rod down on the cedar-wood table.

'I know.' Valu rubbed his bald head. 'One trouble after another, my lord judge. Oh, by the way, I still think Heby is a murderer.'

Amerotke didn't reply, but went to the door and called for Shufoy and Asural. He told them to guard his chamber and followed Valu out along the corridors to the rear of the temple, down flights of stairs and into a gloomy narrow passageway. This was lit here and there by a dancing torch which revealed heavy doors on either side, securely bolted, with small grilles high up. The stone floor had been washed with crushed herbs but the place still smelt rank and fetid. Leading off the passageway were small chambers where the guards gathered.

The appearance of Amerotke and Valu immediately brought everyone to attention. The Keeper of the Chains came hurrying up, glistening with sweat which dampened the black leather jerkin he wore. He grasped a torch from the wall sconce and led them further down a set of steps into what he called the Am-duat, the Underworld. It was hot and stinking like some animal cage. Halfway down an ill-lit tunnel, the Keeper of the Chains paused and unlocked a door, ushering Valu and Amerotke into the blackness. Torches were hastily lit to illuminate what was nothing more than a stone box which reeked like a latrine pit. It contained earthenware pots, bowls and two cot beds. On one of these sprawled the corpse of a woman, her dirty face almost masked by thick black hair; another woman in a soiled scanty linen robe slouched sullenly on the floor. She kept her head down. Amerotke glimpsed gleaming eyes in the tangled mess of her hair.

Valu found the stench offensive; he would have leaned against the wall but hastily withdrew his hand in disgust at the slime there. 'I cannot talk here,' he protested. 'Bring the prisoner to the place of questioning.' He swept out of the cell.

Amerotke crossed to the bed, pulled back the hair of the corpse and touched the gruesome marks around the throat. He turned the body over, flinching at the stench. The dead woman's face was an ugly mask contorted by her death throes. Amerotke raised his hand and touched the chains fastened to the wall which had been used to strangle her.

'You did this?'

The woman sitting in the corner nodded. 'I had to.' Her voice was soft and girlish. She pushed back her hair; bruises marked her cheeks and lips, evidence of how the gaolers had used her for their own pleasure. 'I had to,' she repeated. 'She said if she was freed she would go back to the Sebaus, silly bitch!' She spat the words out. 'They would have killed me and her.'

Amerotke snapped his fingers at the Keeper of the Chains. 'Bring her up.'

A short while later Amerotke and Valu, seated behind a table in the place of questioning, stared across at the prisoner. She had tied her hair back and been given a filthy wrap to cover her nakedness. She squatted on a stool and gazed stony-eyed at them. Amerotke found it hard to imagine that once she'd been a beautiful prostitute in a famous house of pleasure in western Thebes.

'What is your name?'

'You know my name, judge. It is Sithia.' The woman gazed round the room. The guards had been told to leave. Only the bloody table in the corner, as well as the chains and implements of torture hanging from hooks on the wall, gave any indication of what happened here.

Amerotke was distracted by the dire warnings some scribe of the stake had painted on the plastered walls: *This is a place where the Flame of Truth burns all lies*, followed by *True terror is not the judgement of man but the work of the Devourers of the Underworld*. Finally, above the door, *In the Place of Annihilation, no criminal survives*. He did not like this chamber or what happened here. His task was to sift the evidence, find the truth, give judgement, and, wherever possible, act as compassionately as circumstances would allow. This was truly a place of terror where the questioners and torturers interrogated Pharaoh's enemies and those brought here for judgement.

'Why did you kill your friend?' Valu asked.

'She was not my friend. She was my enemy. Anyone who offers to betray me cannot be my friend.'

'We could send you to the wood.' Valu used the word for execution.

'If she had lived, the Sebaus would have done the job for you.'

'Sithia,' Amerotke leaned across the table, 'let's start from the beginning. The tombs of Pharaohs and their Queens, the sacred Houses of a Million Years, were cruelly plundered in the Valley of Kings. The Eternal Mansions of nobles were violated, the mummies in their caskets were used as torches to help the plunderers in their work. The treasure they stole cannot be assessed. The Divine One asked me to investigate. I uncovered a web of conspiracy and deceit, one name leading to another. I discovered a coven, a gang, plundering the glories of Egypt. I captured one, a merchant, selling such plunder in the marketplace of Memphis. He was brought here to the House of Chains.' Amerotke gestured round. 'In time he confessed and one name led to another, including yours, Sithia, you and your former friend. What was her name?'

'Tifye.'

'Ah yes, Tifye. Now both of you should have been condemned to death with the rest, but you had words with Lord Valu. You promised, after the trial, to tell the truth about the conspiracy, in return for which your sentence would be commuted and, if the information was truly valuable, you might even be set free. We made no such offer to any of the other conspirators because we thought they would not tell us the truth or had nothing to offer. You two, however, worked in a house of pleasure. You knew more than the rest. You hinted at this, and the Divine One believed your offer was sincere. Lord Valu here and I planned to come down here and listen to what you'd tell us, then make a decision.'

'Yet you killed your companion,' Valu drawled. 'You committed murder.'

'Because I'm frightened.' Sithia sat as if fascinated by the cockroach crawling across the table. She lifted her manacled hands to wave away a fly and wetted her lips. Amerotke rose and gave her a beaker of water. She thanked him with her eyes and drank greedily.

'My lord Valu, you call yourself the Eyes and Ears of Pharaoh, and you,' Sithia pointed at Amerotke, 'a judge in the Hall of Two Truths, but you haven't uncovered the conspiracy. You've plucked the flower but not the roots. You know nothing! Nothing about the terror! The Sebaus are everywhere; they could even be here in this dark corner. How do you know, my lord Amerotke,' she pointed at Valu, 'that he is not one of them? How do I know that you yourself may not be a member of their coven?' She ignored Valu's sigh of exasperation. 'I had to kill my companion. She wanted to confess to mislead you. She would have named innocent people, won her freedom and returned to our masters. She may already have done her damage communicating with one of the guards, gaolers or court ushers. I had no choice.' Sithia drew a deep breath. 'I told you nothing before but now I will. I have met Sebaus, I have even seen one or two of their faces. I am speaking now because the rest are dead, their Kas cannot send messages to their master.'

Amerotke moved uneasily on his stool. He tried to hide his shiver of real fear. He had interrogated men and women, produced a list of names, laid evidence against them and judged them guilty, yet even as he had done so, he had sensed, like an archer who'd loosed his arrow, that he'd missed his mark.

'Tell me, Sithia,' he urged. 'Tell me the truth, what you know. You will be freed, taken to another place where you can live again.'

The woman sat staring at the floor as if listening to the faint sounds from the passageway beyond. She asked for another beaker of water. Amerotke gave her one. He thought she was talking to herself but then noticed how she spread her hands, palm upwards, and realised she was quietly praying.

'The Sebaus,' she began, 'are not just a gang of assassins and thieves. True, some are nothing more than peasants, but others are educated men, Egyptians, Kushites, Libyans, even foreigners from the great Green. They are summoned individually and very few know their comrades. They are the ones who actually rob the tombs. They approach the guards and officials in the Necropolis or the Valley of the Kings. They will offer bribes and, if that doesn't work, threaten blackmail and violence. One official was brought to my house of pleasure. I provided him with everything he wanted, I gave him an ounou of silver to spend and he was in their power. A few men couldn't be bribed; they were swiftly despatched. The Sebaus raid the tombs and bring the treasure to houses like mine. We would be given strict instructions to hand it to this merchant or that. The people who came,' she waved her hand, 'Canaanites, Hittites, sand-dwellers, Libyans, Egyptians, they would buy the treasure and take it away.' She lifted her head. 'Some of them seemed very powerful, rich men, others just messengers. They always came in disguise.'

Amerotke nodded. He had discovered the same: treasures being mysteriously taken into the city then out on to barges, either north to the Delta or south into Kush.

'The Sebaus,' he said, 'may be violent and ruthless, but many of the tombs are hidden away, their entrances concealed; some even contain traps. Where do they get such knowledge?'

'The Sebaus only carry out orders,' Sithia replied. 'They are given the time and the place and told where to take the treasure. The same person who organises them will send a message to this merchant or that, how a statute, a cornelian necklace or a jewelled gorget can be bought, and the merchant will visit my house or some other.'

'Who gives the orders?' Valu demanded.

'No one ever knew,' Sithia replied. 'One of the Sebaus was much taken with me and, in his cups, told me his leader's name, or at least his title: the Khetra.'

'Khetra.' Amerotke echoed the title given to the Watchman of the Third Division of the Underworld. He pushed back his stool and came round and crouched in front of the woman. He ignored the foul smell and gently touched the bruise on her cheek.

'So, the Sebaus would raid a tomb and bring the treasure to a place like yours? A merchant would buy it, pay the price and take it away?'

Sithia nodded.

Amerotke went back to sit behind the table. 'But that leaves two problems. The first is who gave the information about the tombs and what each contained. Secondly, some of these treasures have been taken beyond Egypt's borders. Now, Sithia, you know that is very dangerous. It is easy to transport the gold statue of a former Pharaoh to Memphis, or to Avaris, but across Sinai? Even if you hide it away in a jar on a pack pony or in a bundle of cloth you are running a terrible risk. You have to pass customs posts, border guards, not to mention desert patrols.'

Sithia smiled bleakly. 'Now you know why I'm terrified, Lord Amerotke. Some of the merchants who visited me told me that they would take their goods from the soil of Egypt. I asked them how, and they just laughed and said they had passes.'

Amerotke ignored Valu's sharp intake of breath. Sithia had put her finger on the heart of the problem. Only high-ranking officials, men like himself, chief scribes in the various houses of the palace or high priests in the temples, possessed imperial seals which allowed travellers to pass unhindered across Egypt's borders. Such seals were not personalised but were simply copies of the imperial cartouche.

'Have you reached the same conclusion as I have?' Sithia asked softly. 'This Khetra must be a member of the Divine House. Perhaps even a member of the Royal Circle. So who is he, Lord Amerotke? Or she? I didn't commit murder,' she continued breathlessly. 'I killed in self-defence. The Sebaus are totally ruthless. If someone like myself stole a pearl or a scarab from the treasure horde, sentence of death would always be passed. I've heard of men and women being scourged, bound and tossed into a crocodile pool. Others are taken out to the Red Lands and buried alive. A merchant who didn't pay the full price as promised lost two of his children and, when he did pay, was only given their corpses in return.' Sithia moved the hair from her face. 'One of the guards who pleasured me told me what happened to you, Amerotke, about the attack in this very temple at Ma'at.'

'Do you think that was revenge?'

Sithia smiled, wincing at the cut on the corner of her mouth. 'Oh yes, it's revenge. They will kill you, Lord Amerotke, for the same reason as they would kill me. You might not realise it but you know something you shouldn't, and for that you have to die.'

Valu made a dismissive sound with his fingers.

'Do you think your title will save you, Lord Prosecutor?' Sithia, clearly enjoying herself, drank greedily from the cup. Amerotke noticed she kept touching her stomach and leaning slightly to the left.

'Have you ever heard of the Shardana?' she asked.

'It's the name for a mercenary,' Valu replied.

'No, *the* Shardana,' she repeated. 'He was an officer in the mercenary corps. He was court-martialled for stealing from the regimental chest and discharged from the army. He became a high-ranking member of the Sebaus. I was one of the few who knew his identity. The Shardana wasn't an Egyptian, but came from the lands north of the Hittites. He had fair hair, one eye—'

'I remember him,' Amerotke interrupted. 'He appeared before me in the Hall of Two Truths; he killed a man, but claimed it was self-defence.'

'He was an assassin,' Sithia replied, 'who would enforce the Khetra's wishes. A bully boy and a braggart. He often visited my house of pleasure and insisted on taking two girls together. He was coarse and rough but paid well. I never allowed him to be with me. One night he became involved in an argument with another customer. Knives were drawn and the Shardana cut the man's throat. He was drunk so he couldn't escape. There were plenty of witnesses. The Medjay arrived and arrested him.'

'Yes, he appeared before me in the second week of the

Season of the Sowing.' Amerotke mused. 'He should have been sent to the wood but claimed self-defence and said he could produce witnesses. He hired an advocate, one of the most expensive in Thebes, a priest lawyer from the Temple of Thoth.'

Valu, too, now recalled the case and sat nodding to himself.

'I sentenced him to life imprisonment out in the Western Red Lands, as far as possible from the Nile.'

'There were bribes offered,' Valu added, 'anonymously, for the man to be released, but his victim was the son of a powerful nobleman.'

'Now this Shardana,' Sithia continued, 'was sent to an oasis a hundred miles west of Thebes. Why not go to the House of War, Lord Amerotke, and ask what happened at the Oasis of Bitter Water?'

Amerotke tried to rack his memory. The woman's words recalled certain events, proclamations in the marketplace . . .

'The Oasis of Bitter Water was attacked,' Valu declared. 'Its small garrison was wiped out by Libyans who killed not only the soldiers but also what they guarded. Not one prisoner escaped. It happened about five months ago. The Divine One sent out a chariot squadron. The Libyans had broken their treaty, they'd promised never to attack such prison oases, and why should they, there is no profit in them.'

'Shall I tell you why they attacked?' Sithia was now holding her stomach as if in discomfort. 'I—'

'Are you well?' Amerotke asked.

'Stomach gripes,' she gasped. 'Perhaps the water was too cold. But let me finish. The Oasis of Bitter Water was attacked because the Sebaus paid the Libyans to do so. I don't know how and I don't know when, but it shows the length of their arm as well as their power. They wanted the Shardana killed just in case he talked, so they hired the Libyans, one of those wandering tribes, to launch an attack.

They wanted to make sure the Shardana never changed his mind and tried to negotiate for a pardon.'

Amerotke whistled under his breath. Prison oases were poor, rather desolate places, their small detachment of soldiers usually mercenary sand-dwellers, ruthless fighters. The Libyans would usually leave such places alone as there was little to gain and a great deal to lose.

'The Sebaus,' Sithia was clutching her stomach in pain, 'they show no mercy . . .'

Amerotke, alarmed, got to his feet. Sithia was pale-faced, sweat coursing through the dirt on her face.

'These are not cramps,' he declared. 'Lord Valu, quickly, get a physician.'

But even before the prosecutor had reached the door, Sithia fell to the floor. She opened her mouth to scream but could only gag; she retched, coughing and spluttering. Amerotke tried to hold her but she broke free, legs kicking, lost in her world of pain. Valu was in the passageway shouting for the Keeper of the Chains. Amerotke crossed to the water jug, picked it up and sniffed at the rim; the water was brackish but he smelt something bittersweet. Sithia was now in convulsions, head banging the floor as her body jerked, legs and arms flailing. Guards came into the room but the woman was past any help. The sound from her throat was hideous, eyes popping, mouth gagging as she forced her breath. She gave one final convulsion and lay still. Amerotke felt for a blood pulse in the neck but could find none. He turned the body over, pushing back the hair. Sithia's face was now relaxed, though death betrayed little of the beauty she had enjoyed in life. Amerotke gazed up at the Keeper of the Chains, the gaolers thronging about him.

'Who fetched the water? Asural!' he shouted. The Captain of the Temple Guard, summoned down by the clamour, pushed his way through. Amerotke got to his feet and gestured at the water jug. 'Have that destroyed, it's poisoned.' He glanced across at Valu, but the royal prosecutor, clutching his own stomach, fled the cell, shouting for the nearest latrine.

Amerotke returned to his chamber in the Hall of Two Truths. The hall itself was empty except for the occasional guard. He found Shufoy sleeping, gently shook him awake and told him what had happened.

'Poisoned? But how?' the dwarf exclaimed.

'I'm asking myself the same question.'

Lord Valu came through the door looking a little more relaxed and, without being asked, sat down in Amerotke's chair. He tried to act courageously but he was visibly shocked and soon left the chamber again, only returning when Asural came back to report.

'Nobody knows anything,' the captain declared. 'The guards remember servants coming and going. The assassin must have known you would take her up to the place of questioning, that she would be thirsty, eager for a drink.'

'I suppose it was only a matter of time,' Amerotke declared. 'They must have known that either she, or Lord Valu or I would take a drink. Perhaps they were hoping for all three. You are sure no one saw anything suspicious?'

'My lord,' Asural replied, 'you have been down to the House of Chains; it is full of dark passageways, people coming and going. It would be easy to draw off a jug of water, poison it, and hope for the best.'

Amerotke thanked and dismissed him, and sat for a while in silence.

'My lord,' Valu straightened up in his chair, 'that dead woman spoke the truth. We have plucked the flower but not the root. This is serious and I am very, very frightened.'

'And so am I,' Amerotke whispered. 'And so am I.'

REKHU: ancient Egyptian, 'fire'

CHAPTER 4

Amerotke was glad he'd drunk the goblet of wine the heset had given him when he and Shufoy arrived at the Temple of Isis. They had hurried from the Hall of Two Truths, through the busy streets, skirting the basalt-paved Avenue of the Sphinxes, and been admitted to the temple by a side gate. Challenged by the guards, they had been met by an acolyte priest who had taken them across the moon-washed gardens to a painted pavilion, where they were served sweet pancakes soaked in fruit juice and strong Canaan wine. The acolyte had examined the cartouche Amerotke carried, and apologised for the lord Impuki being extremely busy, saying that until the High Priest was available he would look after the visitors. The man listened intently as Amerotke explained why he had come to the Temple of Isis, then clearly nervous, he hastened away and returned saying that he would take Amerotke to the wabet, the Place of Purification, where corpses were embalmed to complete the soul's journey into the Far West.

The underground cavern was indeed a strong contrast to the exotic temple gardens, a gloomy, low-beamed chamber lit by pitch torches and bitter-smelling oil lamps. Amerotke had to pinch himself to be sure that he had not fallen into a nightmare. He stood just within the doorway and stared around. Such places always surprised him, even though he was used to visiting the Houses of the Dead and scrutinising the hapless victims of some killer. Cauldrons bubbled over. Small fires burned in their open brick hearths. Corpses in varying stages of being embalmed lay like slabs of meat on tables, slightly tipped so the body fluids, as well as the juice of the ointments, could run down to the wide earthenware pots placed judiciously beneath. Priests wearing the masks of jackals, hawks, rams and the smiling face of the goddess Isis moved like sleepwalkers or stood next to the tables chanting the Office of the Dead.

> *Go out, go out*
> *To the Far West.*
> *Enter the secret sanctuary,*
> *Enjoy the splendour*
> *Of the Lords of Eternity.*
> *Follow him into shrines in the Far Horizon.*
> *May you be with the Lord of Years.*
> *May your Ka be ravished by the beauty of the eternal*
> *fields.*

On the whitewashed walls similar prayers were painted in red.

> *O heart of my mother,*
> *O heart of my mother,*
> *O heart of my mother transform me!*
> *Do not rise and testify against me*
> *Do not stand against me at the Great Tribunal*
> *Do not be my enemy in the presence of the Guardian of*
> *the Scales.*

Amerotke stopped to admire the exquisite paintings of the goddess Ma'at. In one she had a golden skin, in another the royal blue of the gods. She stood holding her scales next to Osiris, the green-skinned falcon-headed god who decided the eternal fate of souls.

The acolyte led Amerotke across the cavern. They had to pick their way carefully, as each corpse was surrounded by a range of caskets, coffers, pots and the tall canopic jars which would receive the sloppy entrails of the dead. The smell was rank and cloying, mixing with the salty odour of the natron in which the corpses would be bathed and dried out once the intestines had been removed. Trails of perfume, cassia, frankincense and myrrh teased Amerotke's nostrils as the priests, still chanting their prayers, wound the corpses in thick linen bandages. Shufoy picked up a heart scarab from the floor and paused to watch an acolyte priest push a wire up the nose of a corpse to break the bone and draw out the brain. Amerotke turned and grasped the little man by the shoulder.

'Shufoy,' he leaned down, 'this is not a place for the curious.'

They crossed the cavern, the priests around them oblivious to their presence. Their guide escorted them into an adjoining chamber, where other corpses, yet untreated, lay beneath white shrouds covered with the Words of the Gods, the sacred hieroglyphs from the Book of Thoth; these would protect the dead until they received the ministrations of the priests. It was a stark chamber where the Scribe of the Dead, sitting on his low stool, carefully described each corpse as it arrived. Amerotke noticed with some amusement that above the stool a scribe had painted a quotation on the wall extolling his profession. He nudged Shufoy. 'You should take careful note of that!'

Shufoy, peering through the ill-lit room, spelt out the words. '*Be a friend of the scroll and the pen, this is more pleasing than wine. Writing is better than all professions, it pleases more than bread and beer, it satisfies more than clothing and ointment, it is even richer than a tomb in the West.* I don't know,' he whispered back. 'I still believe a shrewd merchant can make a fortune.'

'My lord judge.' The acolyte paused at one table and

pulled back the linen cloth. The corpse underneath looked frightful, the face still contorted in the final convulsions of death, with popping eyes and snarling mouth. It was the corpse of a soldier, muscular and scarred. The acolyte moved the blood-stained linen poultice which covered the groin. Shufoy gagged and looked away; Amerotke stared in horror: the man's genitals had been removed, both penis and scrotum.

'May the gods of Egypt guide him,' Amerotke prayed. 'By all the terrors of the night, who did this?'

Shufoy turned back, hand over his mouth. The priest too had difficulty controlling his stomach. Amerotke pinched his nostrils. It was a truly horrid death. The removal of a man's genitals was the final indignity; it would hamper his journey to the Eternal West, for if his body was incomplete, so was his soul.

The priest removed the second poultice, on the left side of the chest. Amerotke already knew to expect the great gaping hole where the heart had once been. This dead soldier's fate was sealed. According to the Rites of Osiris, when the body was embalmed, the heart was always protected by a sacred scarab. If the dead person had no heart, what could be weighed in the Scales of Truth? Murdered in life, Mafdet had also been murdered in death, and unless the compassion of the gods intervened, his soul would be doomed to wander the gloomy caverns of Am-Duat, the Underworld, for all eternity.

'What happened?' Amerotke asked.

'Lord Impuki will tell you more,' the acolyte gabbled, 'but this morning the captain of the guard did not report for duty, so a messenger was sent to his house. The door was off its latch, the lamps had burnt down low. The stench was so offensive the messenger realised something was wrong. Guards were summoned. Mafdet was found stripped naked, a gag in his mouth, hands and feet lashed together. His bed and the ground beneath were soaked in blood. Lord Impuki immediately organised a search of Mafdet's chamber and found the remains of a drink with a sleeping potion. Someone apparently drugged our captain of the guard, bound him whilst he was asleep and committed these atrocities upon him.'

'But why?'

The acolyte stared back owl-eyed. 'I cannot answer that,' he replied.

He hastily re-covered the corpse and took them to another table, folding back the linen sheet. The corpse underneath was that of an old man, well past his sixtieth year, a scrawny body with spindly arms and legs. The face was composed in peace; two sacred scarabs covered the eyes.

'This is Sese, Lady Nethba's father. He died some days ago and his body was first kept cold before being brought here.'

Amerotke quickly scrutinised the corpse. Apart from the blemishes of age and the passing of time, he could see no mark of violence. He told the priest to cover the corpse.

'How did Sese die?'

The acolyte shrugged and, going over to a table, picked up a scroll. He unrolled it and peered down the entries. 'According to the scribe, he suffered severe pains in his stomach, a great deal of blood passed through his stools, in the last few days he was given the undiluted juice of the poppy.' He put down the scroll. 'And virtually slept to death.'

'My lord Amerotke?'

The judge turned to greet the young man dressed in the fringed robe of a high-ranking priest.

'My name is Paser, priest of the Royal Chapel in the Temple of Isis. The Lord Impuki will now receive you.'

Amerotke clasped the young priest's hand. Paser was of medium height, his head completely shaven. He had a soft, effeminate face, gentle eyes, a snub nose and a laughing mouth. He wore a pendant around his throat depicting Isis suckling the infant Horus, and faience bracelets displaying the same theme around each wrist. His robe was spotlessly white and gave off a fragrant smell every time he moved. He was not barefoot but shod in sandals, and as he turned, Amerotke noticed that the heel of one was considerably thicker than the other.

'Before you ask, Amerotke,' Paser had seen his glance, 'I was born with one leg shorter than the other. My mother thought I was to be lame for the rest of my life. She dedicated me to the House of Life to strengthen my limbs.' He grinned. 'It is a wonder what prayers and a sturdy heel can achieve!'

He led them back through the wabet, up the steps, across the gardens and into a deserted temple courtyard, where a fountain surrounded by glowing braziers still splashed water up to the night sky. The High Priest's mansion stood amongst gardens screened by a cypress grove, a beautiful place with its porticoed entrance. The walls within were painted a resplendent gold, depicting scenes extolling the exploits of Isis as the goddess fought to protect Osiris, raise her son Horus and challenge the malicious fury of the red-haired Seth. The small hall of audience was a chamber of opulent splendour, its ceiling supported by palm columns, the leaves at the top painted gold, the roots dark red, the columns themselves a deep refreshing green. The floor was of marble, with a small pool of purity just within the entrance on which blue and white lotuses were floating. The blue lotus had opened to exude its own singular perfume.

Impuki and his wife Thena were seated on a dais behind veils at the far end of the hall under a small window. The tables before them were covered with pots and platters of delicious-smelling food. Impuki rose to meet Amerotke, coming down the steps of the dais to clasp his hands courteously. Then he solemnly greeted Shufoy before escorting his visitors up into the eating area and introducing them to his wife. Amerotke and Shufoy were seated on feather cushions before the small tables prepared for them. Servants stood in the shadows, but Impuki insisted on serving them himself, filling the jewelled goblets with white wine and sharing out the rice and spiced chicken on the silver platters placed in front of them.

Whilst he did this Amerotke looked round appreciatively. The walls of the eating area had been painted a rich gold. On one side was an eye-catching picture of Isis being reconciled with her son Horus, on the other Isis making her triumphant appeal against Seth before the Tribunal of the Gods. The robes of the goddess were ornamented with jewels, but close up Amerotke realised these were cunningly carved niches to hold glowing oil lamps in alabaster jars which served not only as a wall decoration but also as a source of light. The cushions he sat on were soft and comfortable, dark blue with golden tassels, the napkins snow white, fringed with gold, the knives, platters, goblets and jugs all fashioned out of precious metals.

Lord Impuki was a tall man with a scholar's face, a thick, sharp nose, deep-set eyes and a strong chin, but the mouth was pleasant, his voice soft yet firm. The Lady Thena must have been a beauty in her youth; of middle age, she bore herself like a queen. She had a rather haughty face, with high cheekbones, but her eyes danced with mischief. She'd immediately teased Shufoy about the small good-luck ring he wore on his finger. Both, like Paser, were dressed in gauffered linen robes with blue fringes and sashes depicting the red and gold colours of Isis around their waists. Lady Thena was rather small, and was already comparing her height to Shufoy, while tactfully waiting for her husband to stop serving, whisper the prayer and commence the meal.

'I'm sorry you had to wait.' Impuki broke a piece of bread, crumbling it with his fingers. He popped a morsel in his mouth and chewed thoughtfully. 'The temple day is long and we have a great deal of business to complete. I know

91

what you are thinking: physician, look after yourself, we are dining far too late. However, we always do so in the cool of the evening, followed by a walk in the temple gardens or a swim in the pool.'

'All three of you?' Shufoy asked.

'Surrounded by guards,' Thena laughed. 'Our temple is near the river, it is not unknown for a crocodile to join us when the shadows fall, whilst we have a number of snakes.' She paused. Amerotke knew Lady Thena must have learnt about General Suten's death. 'I'm sorry.' She looked away in embarrassment and returned to her food.

'Lord Amerotke,' Paser put his goblet down, 'we heard the news from the court that the tomb raiders have been condemned and punished. Such a blasphemy.' He made a face. 'Royal tombs, those of nobles! We even heard they discovered and ransacked the sepulchre of Lord Rahimere, who was disgraced and buried secretly. Such a pity! Rahimere's widow died here recently. She—'

'Tell us what has happened!' Lady Thena interrupted rather swiftly.

Amerotke gave a short description of what had occurred, half listening to the beautiful song of a nightingale from the gardens beyond.

'It's not wild.' Impuki smiled. 'We keep the songster in a cage, hanging from a branch outside. Its call is so haunting, but . . . to business!'

'First,' Amerotke pushed his platter away; he wasn't hungry, his stomach felt agitated, yet he had to be courteous, 'the architect Sese, father of the Lady Nethba.'

Impuki sighed. 'Lord Amerotke, Sese was a man well past his sixtieth summer. He complained of deep pains in his stomach, sometimes he would vomit blood. He was an architect and worked in the quarries; sometimes these places can cause infections in the lungs, though this was not the case with Sese. The source of his sickness was his stomach. I examined him most carefully, here.' Impuki used his hand to demonstrate. 'Low on the left side I felt a large lump, some sort of abscess or tumour. I examined his anus and detected a similar lump just within the rectum. I considered all the signs. Sese was dying; basically his internal organs were rotting away. This was causing obstruction and bleeding. There was nothing I could do but use poppy juice to ease his final days.'

'Yet the Lady Nethba claimed he was in good health?'

'Go into the House of Twilight,' Thena replied. 'In our hospital you will find men and women who look healthier than anyone around this table, but their days are counted short. Some deaths are silent and swift. My husband is right. Sese died of a malignancy within, there was nothing we could do.'

'He made a bequest to the temple?'

Impuki threw his hands up in desperation. 'My lord Amerotke, you are in one of the richest temples in Thebes. Walk round our gardens, visit our storehouses and granaries, the House of Silver, the House of Life; we do not need such contributions. Sese was grateful for the kindness and solace he received.'

Amerotke nodded understandingly.

'There's much more important business.' Paser rapped his nails on the table. 'We can call on any physician in Thebes to confirm that Sese's death was of natural causes and that he received the best attention from our physicians. Lord Amerotke, I am chamberlain of this temple, responsible for its day-to-day business. You are not only here because an old man died?'

'No, not just that. The captain of your temple guard had his testicles and heart removed and was left to bleed to death. Captain Mafdet was a respected veteran, a high-ranking official in what you have described as the richest temple in Thebes. Who killed him and why? Secondly,' Amerotke placed his cup on the table, 'four of your temple girls have disappeared. Hesets, virgins dedicated to the

Mother Goddess; these are the daughters of powerful merchants who have petitioned the Divine House about their fate. But let us begin with Captain Mafdet.'

'He may well have been respected by the House of War,' Paser replied angrily, 'but Mafdet was also a thief and a charlatan.'

'A thief?'

'On a number of occasions we found items missing from the House of Potions, our dispensaries where medicines, either created here or imported from outside, are carefully stored. Some of these potions are very valuable; the juice of the poppy is one. On a number of occasions the Scribes of the Tally found jars disturbed, medicines stolen.'

'And you blame Captain Mafdet?'

'The thefts began shortly after his appointment a year ago.'

'Did you like him?'

'He was lazy and insolent,' Impuki explained. 'He liked to strut before the temple women, and sometimes he drank more beer than was good for him. He liked to boast that he'd once been a prominent member of Lord Rahimere's retinue, until he recalled how that nobleman had fallen in disgrace. He hid behind the recommendation he'd received from General Omendap. He was, in fact, a lazy braggart. On the night he was murdered I had ordered him to take torches and search the temple grounds.'

'For the hesets?' Shufoy asked. 'At the dead of night?'

Impuki wiped his mouth on a napkin. 'Over the last few months four temple girls have disappeared. The first vanished late in the afternoon; that was the last time anyone in the temple saw her. A few weeks later two more went missing, as if they had been spirited away. The final one disappeared in the middle of last month. Now, temple girls,' Impuki gave a half-smile, 'well, they differ, don't they, from temple to temple? Some are dancing girls and suffer all the tribulations such a profession brings. The hesets of

Isis are, however, vowed to virginity. They are daughters of the Great Mother, she who lives in eternal light. They come from good families and live a life of great comfort.' He raised a hand. 'Never once in the history of this temple has a sacred heset ever run away. Oh,' he shrugged, 'there have been scandals, but that is part of life: a beautiful young woman may catch the eye of a visiting soldier, priest or courtier.'

'But they never run away?'

'No, my lord Amerotke, they don't! What has happened, and our records will prove this, is that temple girls have been raped, violated.'

Lady Thena was now nodding in agreement.

'In the reign of the Divine One's father, shortly after he had returned from his war in Canaan, two army officers violated a temple maiden and were impaled alive on the cliffs above Thebes. But why should a girl run away? In this temple they are safe, pampered, looked after; it is the only life they know. Outside, well it would be like placing a baby gazelle amongst a pack of ravenous hyaenas. So you see, my lord Amerotke, I believe these girls are still here. May the Great Mother have mercy on us. They may have been killed, their bodies buried. The Temple of Isis is like a small city, with its extensive gardens and rich orchards; some places are rarely visited.'

'Did you suspect Mafdet?'

'Mafdet was a soldier,' Impuki agreed. 'He was not married but he liked the ladies. I know he visited the houses of pleasure. He liked nothing better than to strut like a cock in front of the temple girls.'

'Were they friendly with him?'

'He thought they were, but you are talking about young, immature women. Lady Thena is responsible for the temple virgins. On a number of occasions,' Lady Thena nodded in agreement, 'she had to have words with Mafdet about his attitude and manner.'

'If you didn't like him,' Shufoy asked, 'then who appointed him to the post?'

'Little man,' Impuki smiled, 'you know the way of the world. As I've said, Mafdet was recommended by the House of War, by Generals Omendap and Suten. In these matters we have little choice but to keep the Divine One happy.'

'Mafdet was strong,' Amerotke mused. 'He was used to violence. He liked his beer and the ladies. He also knew the temple grounds and precincts. Are you saying, Impuki, that he lured these girls to some assignation, raped and killed them, and buried their corpses in the temple gardens?'

'It's possible. The disappearances started after his arrival.'

'So we come to the motive for his killing.' Amerotke gestured at his three hosts. 'You are hardly grieving.'

'Lord Amerotke,' Paser laughed, 'to the faithful we may look devout, even holy, as we raise our hands amidst gusts of incense and pray to the Goddess. However, among my colleagues there are those I don't like and there are those who don't like me, yet it doesn't mean we are going to commit murder.'

'What happened the night Mafdet died?'

'I met him,' Impuki explained. 'I had harsh words about his arrogance. He left and returned to his house, where he drank some beer—'

'I understand,' Amerotke interrupted, 'poppy juice was mixed with that?'

'Undoubtedly,' Paser agreed. 'Mafdet's killer, once he was drugged, simply lashed his hands and feet and carried out that dreadful deed. On that night, Amerotke – and you may ask the temple guards and servants – Lord Impuki, Lady Thena and myself were here. We had worked late that day and had a great deal to prepare for the Feast of Jubilees. We retired in the early hours and never left this building. As I've said, you are free to ask the servants.'

'And nothing suspicious was reported?'

'If there was,' Impuki replied, 'we would have told you.'

'These girls . . .' Amerotke picked up a piece of meat and chewed it carefully. The wine was very good, filling his mouth with sweetness. Although the hour was late, he felt alert; he was glad to be here. This beautiful chamber with its oil lamps flickering, the fragrant wine and savoury food: such elegant opulence drove away those images of black-garbed figures swirling at him, or Sithia's dying convulsions.

'Four girls have disappeared.' He glanced at Lady Thena. 'I can talk to their friends?'

'Of course.'

'And none of them have reported anything untoward?'

'Lord Amerotke, it was as if the girls had never existed. They were temple girls, being trained in the service of the Divine Mother. They loved gossip, they liked to sing and dance, perhaps flirt with priests or guards. They looked forward to the jubilees and festivals, visits from their relatives, then one day they were gone. Four girls disappearing over a space of five months.'

'Have the temple precincts been searched?' Shufoy asked.

'As much as we can, but there are places where corpses could be secretly buried and lie for years undetected.'

Amerotke cradled his cup and stared above their heads out of the window. The songbird had now fallen silent, and the only sound was the night wind moving amongst the trees. The smells which drifted in reminded him of his own garden: the mingling of fruit and flowers, the smell of freshly cut grass.

'You talked about what happened in the Hall of Two Truths today, and you mentioned General Suten. According to the evidence, Suten was mingling poppy seed with his wine.'

'General Suten,' Lord Impuki replied, 'was a good man, a war hero, a cunning, valiant commander. He was a man who could not escape from his fears, particularly the nightmares which had seized him out in the Red Lands.

He often came and talked to me and I would give him advice. You see, Lord Judge, I can heal ailments of the body but not the mind. Sometimes General Suten lived in a world of shadows. He may have been very brave when captured by the Libyans, but the horror never left him. You do know that the charioteer who was captured with him later committed suicide, drowned himself in the Nile?'

'And you prescribed juice or powder of the poppy for the general?'

'I examined General Suten very carefully, I searched his body for any ailment. I asked him about his stools and his urine. A special physician in this temple, a guardian of the anus, examined him internally. We could find nothing wrong. Little man,' he turned to Shufoy, 'when you are happy, does your belly tingle?'

'Aye,' Shufoy growled, 'and when I am in fear I belch like a trumpeter!'

Impuki laughed. 'Somehow the heart affects the belly; that was the case with General Suten.'

'Did he talk about his household?' Amerotke asked.

'He was deeply in love with the Lady Lupherna, very pleased that he had good retainers like Heby and Menna. I gave him a pouch of powder so that General Suten could enjoy his food and sleep at night. He kept this as a secret from his household. I was horrified to hear the news. General Suten would often come here to look in our kha, the library.' Impuki added, 'Paser here is our Sieau, Chief Librarian.'

'Why was that?' Amerotke asked. 'I mean, why your library?'

'General Suten was very proud of his memoirs,' Paser explained. 'The Swallow squadron was part of the Isis regiment. The swallow is sacred to the Great Mother. We keep a temple history here, as do other temples; he often came to consult our books.'

'Was he murdered?' Lady Thena asked. 'I heard rumours from those who attended court that those snakes were deliberately brought up, that General Suten was drugged. I wondered,' she glanced quickly at her husband, 'I wondered what really happened?'

'What my wife means,' Impuki hastened to explain, 'is that on the few occasions General Suten came here, he talked about ridding himself of his nightmares. He wondered if he had a demon within him which should be exorcised.'

Shufoy moved restlessly. He loved such talk and often wondered if he should become a uab sekhmit, an exorcist who drove out demons.

'You believe in demons?' Amerotke asked the High Priest.

'I believe the soul, like the body, can collect ailments. One question General Suten did ask was if he underwent his nightmare again, if he purified himself, made offerings to the gods and entered a place of snakes . . .' Impuki paused. 'I have dealt with people who are terrified of open spaces or of being locked in a room. They cannot explain what happens: they feel panic, their insides turn to water, they sweat like an athlete who has run far and fast. Sometimes I give them a powder to sedate their hearts and take them into the place they fear.'

Amerotke lowered his cup.

'Are you saying that General Suten could have brought those snakes on to the roof terrace himself?'

'His death is reported over all of Thebes. General Suten was well known; the gossip about what happened in your court today will be on everyone's lips tonight. How the general was alone on his roof terrace, how the steps were guarded by his faithful retainer, and yet he died, bitten by the very creatures he so loathed. I do wonder if General Suten did try to confront his nightmare, like any true soldier would his enemy?'

Amerotke stared back in disbelief. At first he dismissed

the idea as preposterous. Yet if Impuki was correct, it would resolve the mystery.

'But it doesn't explain,' Shufoy spoke up, 'how the snakes got there in the first place: at least two dozen horned vipers! If General Suten had brought them up, someone would have seen them when the room was searched.' He drank from his goblet. 'He would certainly have been seen if he had tried to bring them up after the meal. Anway, if General Suten was responsible, why did he organise the search in the first place?'

'According to his wife, he never told anyone about the powders,' Impuki mused. 'Perhaps, a man of routine, a typical soldier, General Suten did not want to rouse suspicion. Yet if he did bring them up,' he added, 'where did he get so many vicious snakes?'

'He was a leading general,' Amerotke replied. 'He could call on the services of many old soldiers, swear them to silence . . .'

Shufoy could see his master was already wondering. Amerotke was about to continue his questioning when the clash of cymbals, at first low and muted but then more strident and harsh, shattered the silence. On the breeze came the sound of shouting, of doors being opened and shut, the patter of running feet. Impuki, startled, put his cup down and went to the window. Amerotke caught it – the smell of burning. The door at the far end of the hall was flung open and a servant hurried in, gathering his robe about him.

'My lord,' he gasped, 'there's a fire over near the barracks, it is out of control.'

Paser sprang to his feet, knocking over a table. They all hastened out into the gardens, their sweet fragrance marred by the stench of acrid smoke. Other people had also been roused as the clash of the cymbals was answered by the long wailing of conch horns. They hurried across a lawn, past garden beds and pavilions, through a pomegranate grove, its scarlet red flowers glowing in the eerie light. Birds fluttered in the branches above them. As they crossed the lawn, Amerotke glimpsed the shadows of tamed gazelles and ibex galloping away in fright. They went through a walled garden to where a range of buildings stood. One of these, set slightly apart, was a blazing inferno. Flames crackled through the windows and were already shooting through the flat roof, which collapsed with a roar as Amerotke and the rest reached the scene. Guards hurried up with buckets, and officers tried to organise a line so as to bring water from the various wells and fountains, yet their task was impossible. The fire had complete control. Impuki gave the order to let the flames burn themselves out.

'May the Great Mother protect us,' Lady Thena whispered. 'But that's Mafdet's house!'

Amerotke walked closer to the conflagration. He had attended many fires, some of them accidental, others the work of assassins, and he sensed that this was no accident. A fire which started so quickly and burned so fiercely had to be deliberate.

'The assassin did that, didn't he?' Shufoy, who had fallen behind, came up all breathless and slipped his hand into Amerotke's, who squeezed it and looked affectionately down.

'I can smell the oil from here.' Paser stood behind them. 'My lord Amerotke, that's arson; whoever killed Mafdet wanted to finish what he started.'

Or hide something, Amerotke reflected. He quietly cursed himself for not demanding that he search Mafdet's house from top to bottom.

'You will stay?' Paser asked. 'The hour is now late, it must be well after midnight.'

'I will stay,' Amerotke agreed.

They stood for a while watching the fire burn down. Officers declared they were mystified at how the blaze had started, whilst the guards reported no strangers in the temple precincts. Amerotke, his eyes and mouth stung by the smoke, turned away. Impuki and the Lady Thena bade them goodnight, and Paser showed them to the guest house, an attractive, pleasant building standing in the far gardens of the temple. At the moment the guest house was vacant, and Paser said they should make it their home. It had eating quarters and a room below, whilst the chambers above were all prepared. Paser took them up the staircase and made sure they had everything they wanted. He said he would send servants with water, jugs of beer and wine, as well as fresh robes whilst the washerwomen of the temple cleaned theirs.

Once Paser had left, Amerotke sat on a stool and gazed around. The walls were washed in a light green with a red frieze top and bottom, and decorated with knots of Isis and gleaming blue and gold wadjets. The beds were comfortable cots, protected by linen drapes against the cold night air and the myriad of flies which flitted through the shutters to dance above the oil lamps. Shufoy had an adjoining chamber, and was full of admiration at the intricately carved chests, stools and chairs.

'I still wish I was home.' Amerotke stretched his head back to ease the tension in his neck. 'But it's too dangerous; I mean, to cross the city at night.'

'Are you frightened, master?' Shufoy teased.

Amerotke grasped him by the arm and pulled him close. 'No, Shufoy, I'm not frightened, I'm truly terrified, and so should you be. Those assassins today, they were professional killers, well disguised, and they reached the heart of our temple. Sithia was a prisoner, closely guarded, yet they settled with her.' Amerotke drew a deep breath. 'The Lady Norfret must not be disturbed, she would only worry. I've had a word with Asural. My house will be guarded and watched, every inch of its walls, every gate; she'll be safe enough.'

The judge, followed by Shufoy, went downstairs to the

washroom, where they stripped and poured cold water over their heads, using perfumed oiled rags to clean themselves. Once they had finished, they returned to their chambers, where servants had laid out linen robes from the temple storerooms. A sleepy-eyed girl came to collect their laundry; Amerotke had to guide her out of the chamber, her eyes were so heavy. Shufoy went down and brought back two beakers of beer. Amerotke sniffed at it carefully and pronounced it was good, and they sat and talked for a while, half listening to the sounds of the temple fade. Amerotke recalled the flames, Mafdet's house burning like a funeral pyre. Had it been destroyed as an act of vengeance, or was there something which had to be removed? Why had the captain been so cruelly killed?

There was a knock at the door and Shufoy came back carrying a leather pouch tied around the neck.

'A temple servant said this was for you, a gift from the lord Impuki.'

Amerotke opened the pouch and peered inside. He gasped and shook the contents out on to the bed. Small, hard wax figurines, two larger than the rest, crudely fashioned to represent a man and a woman, the other three smaller as if representing children.

'Or a dwarf,' Shufoy muttered.

Amerotke, his throat dry, his stomach curdling, stared in disbelief. He picked up the figurine depicting an adult male. It was brownish red and spiked with small thorns where the head and heart should be.

'Blood and faeces,' he muttered. 'A curse.' He snatched up the leather bag – a scarab fell out, black and shiny but clearly displaying a white-lined figure kneeling clasping a bow. The piece of parchment with it was yellowing and frayed at the edges. Amerotke, losing his temper, knocked it away, but Shufoy picked it up and read the curse inscribed in blood.

'*At dawning, at midday, at evening, at night, the Devourer*

103

always lurks in the doorway. The river monster with huge jaws will be your shadow and behind him all the horrors of the Underworld hound your footsteps. The Lady of the Red Linen casts her bloody shadow over you.'

Before Shufoy could stop him, Amerotke had sprung to his feet and left, hurrying downstairs. He opened the door and went out into the night. As the cold night breeze sobered his mind, he knew instantly his mistake. The assassins slipped out of the blackness, one from his left, the other running at a crouch from his right. Amerotke stepped back and bumped into a vine pole resting against the wall. He grasped this and tried to go back through the door, but the pole became jammed and the first attacker was already on him. Amerotke lashed out with his fist, hitting the black-garbed figure on the face and sending him reeling back to fall over some flower bowls. Grasping the pole like a spear, he turned in time to block the killing blow of the second assassin, but this time he was not so fortunate. He only hit the man's right arm, and the assassin sprang back but came in again, a dagger in one hand, a small axe in the other. Amerotke became engaged in a deadly dance, aware only of his opponent, of his own fear, desperate to look the other way to see what had happened to the second assassin.

Suddenly he felt himself pushed from behind as Shufoy, like a shot from a sling, hurled himself through the door and threw himself at the second assassin, who was still nursing the injuries from his stumble. Amerotke could do nothing to help. His opponent lunged in, leading with his knife whilst swinging with the axe. Amerotke drove him off. The night air was rent with screaming. Amerotke watched the black-clad figure move to the left and right, the eyes gleaming madly at him. He drove the pole towards the man's chest, but his assailant simply leapt back and came in again. Amerotke meant to move to the left, but he missed his footing and stumbled, going down on one knee. He glimpsed other figures and felt a pang of despair. He tried vainly to search for his own opponent, but the man had moved to his far left and was now edging towards him, knife grasped between both hands. Amerotke struggled to his feet. The assassin was about to spring when the judge glimpsed another figure behind his opponent and a club swung down, smashing into the assassin's skull and sending him staggering forward to collapse unconscious on the ground.

Amerotke crawled away and leaned against the wall. The screaming had stopped. Shufoy came stumbling towards him, his linen robe covered in blood, a knife in his hand. Amerotke closed his eyes and shook his head. He felt his arm grasped. It was Paser. The priest gently urged him to stand and led him into the guest house, making him sit in the small entrance hall while he went back outside. Shufoy staggered in and crouched like a dog at his master's feet. Amerotke couldn't stop shivering. He put his hand to his mouth, fearful lest he retch. There were voices outside, a low groan, orders being shouted, and Paser re-entered the house and stood over Amerotke.

'My lord, you are unwell? You want some wine?'

Amerotke tried to speak but couldn't. Paser was talking as if he was far off.

'I went for a walk in the cypress grove. I heard the scream-ing and roused the guards.' He gently touched Amerotke's shoulder. 'Shufoy is unharmed but drenched in blood. You have no wound?' Amerotke shook his head. 'One of the assassins is dead,' Paser continued, 'but the other is only unconscious.'

Amerotke put his face in his hands.

'It was a trap!' Shufoy declared. 'My master ran into the night thinking he could catch the person who had brought the leather pouch. One of the oldest tricks in the slums. They were waiting for him, and if he hadn't gone out they would have come in here anyway. They had us both marked out for death.'

RERT: ancient Egyptian, 'medicine'

CHAPTER 5

Amerotke recovered quickly. He washed himself in a bowl of water over which Paser had sprinkled crushed pondweed and purslane. Impuki arrived, the jaguar skin of a senior priest across his shoulders. The High Priest was all concern. He apologised profusely for the attack and insisted the guards had reported nothing amiss. He checked both the judge and Shufoy for any bruises or cuts but declared that shock was the only thing they had suffered, then he anointed them both with holy oil and drew on the door of the guest house the words *Ankh* and *Sa*, 'Peace' and 'Happiness'. Amerotke could hear sounds in the darkness as the dead assassin was dragged away; the one Paser had knocked unconscious was roughly tended to. Lord Impuki withdrew, saying that he wished to have words with the guards. A servant brought fruit juices and delicious walnut cake cut up and mixed with crushed apple. Amerotke wondered idly if some sort of soothing potion had been added to the mixture.

Shufoy was not at all disturbed by the fact that he had killed a man, and was eager to boast about his warrior skills. The dwarf was also full of indignation at Amerotke's foolishness.

'It's the oldest trick,' he repeated, 'to leave someone a message and wait for them to come out. You could have been killed. I would have been very angry with you.'

109

Amerotke laughed and told him to keep quiet, but wondered aloud why there hadn't been more assassins.

'Too dangerous,' Shufoy retorted. 'Two men slipping through the darkness, waiting for their opportunity, are difficult to detect.'

'Why not loose an arrow?' Amerotke asked.

'In the dark?' Shufoy scoffed. 'These are assassins. They work in pairs. They would have to report back that you were truly dead and not merely wounded.'

Paser came into the eating hall; behind him, temple guards dragged the wounded assassin. The blow to his head had been roughly bandaged, the top part of his robe ripped down and his hands bound behind him. He was forced to kneel at Amerotke's feet. The assailant was a man of middling height, a former soldier by the healed scars on his upper torso. He had a sharp face with a snub nose and close-set, glittering eyes; his lips were so swollen they parted to show blackened teeth, and his body odour was acrid, reeking of the cheap oil in which he had coated himself. He showed no fear despite his injury and capture, but began to hum a hymn to the Lady of Silence.

'You will answer my questions,' Amerotke began. The assassin hawked and spat at him. Amerotke slapped him sharply across the face. 'Are you Sebaus?'

'I am Set-qesum.' Bone breaker.

'Why are you here?'

'I bring Setemu.' Edicts for the slaughter.

'Who sent you?'

'The Khaitieu.' The slaughterer.

'Where does the slaughterer live?'

'Kerh.' The darkness.

Amerotke sighed. The prisoner was gabbling in the flat nasal dialect of eastern Thebes. He persisted in using terms from the Book of the Dead. Amerotke suspected he was a soldier but an educated one, perhaps even a fallen priest.

He slapped the man hard across the face once more. 'We shall begin again. Who are you?'

'I am the Breaker of Bones,' the man sneered. 'The Swallower of Shades.'

'We found this.' Paser, standing behind the prisoner, handed across a polished black scarab depicting a kneeling man holding a bow. 'There was that and some pieces of silver.'

'Who are you?' Amerotke repeated.

'Sem-em-senf.' Drinker of blood.

'Take him away,' Amerotke ordered. 'Under heavy guard. He is to be placed in the House of Chains,' he looked at Paser, 'beneath the Temple of Ma'at. Tell Captain Asural he is to be bound with chains and a guard is to be placed outside the door. Only Asural is to feed him or give him anything to drink.'

Paser dragged the prisoner to his feet and pushed him out into the darkness. Amerotke sat and listened to the sounds fade. In a short while the priest returned and asked Amerotke if he wanted any palm brandy or smoked liqueur to make him sleep. Amerotke refused. Paser said he would leave guards around the house.

'You are sure you don't need anything to drink?'

'No, no.' Amerotke smiled. 'Nor do I want any of your powders from the Island of Daydreams.' He stretched out his hand and Paser clasped it. 'I'm grateful for your help. I owe you a life.'

'It was fortunate,' Paser replied. 'I couldn't sleep; perhaps it is I who needs the palm brandy!' He gestured at the stairs. 'Sleep well and safe; you will be better protected than in the Divine One's palace.' He left, closing the door behind him.

Shufoy wanted to talk, but Amerotke was too tired and went up the stairs to his own chamber. He took off his robe and, garbed in only his loincloth, squatted for a while, eyes closed, hands extended, praying to the Lady of Truth for himself, his family and his household.

*   *   *

Amerotke slept long and late. In the early hours he was disturbed by the lowing of cattle and the calls from the various sacred flocks as beasts and birds were taken up into the shrines and chapels for the morning sacrifices. Amerotke lay half asleep. He could smell the smoke from the holocaust fires, the reek of blood and the stench of burning meat. He drifted off to sleep again reassured by the calls of the guards outside. It was mid-morning by the time he woke fully. He washed and dressed quickly in the robes returned from the temple laundry rooms. It was a beautiful day, a cool breeze still bending the flowers and branches of the trees, so he and Shufoy decided to break their fast outside under the deep shade of the sycamore tree with baby gazelles grazing nearby. Servants brought them beer and platters of roast quail, as well as bread sweetened with honey.

'How do you think the assassins got in?' Shufoy began.

Amerotke cocked his head, listening to the distant songs of the choirs who, under the supervision of a lector priest, were rehearsing hymns to the Great Mother, 'The Defender of Osiris, the Defeater of Seth'. He listened carefully to the music of the lines, how Isis was 'The Mistress of Magic, the clever-tongued one whose speech never fails, more powerful than ten thousand soldiers, more clever than a million scribes.'

'I asked a question!' Shufoy crossly waved a hand in front of his master's face.

'By all that's holy, Shufoy, I don't know!' Amerotke snapped back. 'It's easy to scale a wall, they must have known we were here.'

Further argument was ended by the arrival of Lord Impuki, Lady Thena and Paser, resplendent in their fringed robes bound by the sacred coloured sash of Isis. Servants brought them cushions to sit on the grass. Lady Thena asked how they had slept, and once again Impuki apologised for the attack.

'I prayed for you this morning,' he declared. 'After I'd left the food in the Holy of Holies in front of the tabernacle of the Great Mother.' His voice took on a more cynical tone. 'Once that was finished, I gave my guards the rough edge of my tongue. Of course, they apologised and used Mafdet's death as an excuse. The walls are patrolled, but there are blind spots.'

'How would the assassins know that?' Shufoy asked. 'Someone must have told them.'

Impuki glared at the dwarf and shook his head. 'I cannot answer that.'

'And the fire?' Amerotke asked

'Probably started by the same intruders,' Impuki replied. 'It was no accident. At least two skins of oil must have been used. Everything was burnt to black ash. I have sent a message to the Divine House.' His voice faltered. 'What else can I do?'

Amerotke studied Impuki's clever lined face, the sharp eyes and sardonic mouth. The judge concealed his own suspicions. Shufoy was right: temple walls were guarded, high and difficult to scale. Even if it was easy to climb a wall, any intruder ran the risk of being caught by a patrol or being seen from a guard post. The two attackers had had to bring in oil skins and somehow obtain a torch or lamp, unless they had brought a pot of fire with them as well. Impuki was staring up at a buzzard floating in the breeze, as if determined to say no more. Beside him Lady Thena looked the picture of serenity and elegance, a blue faience brooch clasping her robe, with matching earrings and throat collar. Powerful people, Amerotke concluded. He thought of the assassins, the tomb raiders and the mysteries which confronted him. The high priests of the major temples of Thebes also held the imperial seal or cartouche so that they could mark documents or goods to pass undisturbed by border guards or customs posts. Was the person behind those hideous robberies someone like

Impuki, a high-ranking official, one of those who rejoiced in the title of 'Friend of Pharaoh', 'Keeper of the King's Words', a member of the Royal Circle?

Impuki glanced quickly at Amerotke.

'You seem troubled, my lord.'

'I am,' Amerotke agreed. 'And deeply suspicious. I would like to walk this temple, visit your House of Twilight.' He rubbed his fingers together. 'Study its walls and gates.'

'Don't leave the temple without a guard,' Paser intervened. He sat plucking the grass as if agitated. Despite his smooth, effeminate face and ways, Paser seemed unable to sit still.

Are you always restless, Amerotke thought, or has something disturbed you?

'I'm very busy.' Paser's dark eyes smiled as if he could read Amerotke's thoughts. 'So much to do and so little time to do it in. Granaries to check, patients to be seen, pilgrims to be met, accounts to be drawn up.'

Amerotke nodded. He tried to recall how long Impuki had been high priest. Of course he had heard his name and seen him from afar. He was sure his appointment was due to the Divine One's father, Tuthmosis. Wasn't Impuki more famous for his medical knowledge than for any worship of the Goddess?

'Have you always been at the Temple of Isis?' Amerotke asked.

'Since I was a youth.' Impuki patted Lady Thena's hand. 'It's where I met my wife. We exchanged vows in front of the statue of the Mother, oh,' he squinted up at the sky, 'about fifteen years ago.'

'You have children?'

'Had.' Lady Thena's face was now hard, her voice cracked. 'We had children, my lord, until the pestilence took them. All the prayers, all the incense and all the offerings could not save them. They were beautiful.' Tears brimmed in her eyes. 'The boy was seven years, the girl four; the fever came so quickly, followed by a sharp racking cough. I sat by them every hour, my husband used all his skill and knowledge. You might as well have tried to stop the rain falling or the sun shining. They've gone, the little ones.' Her voice broke, her anguish so sharp Amerotke bitterly regretted asking the question. 'They lie in our tomb across the river in our own House of Eternity.' She grasped her stomach. 'I cannot, will not, have more children; even the Great Mother could not save them.'

Amerotke looked at her more sharply. There was something about her words and tone of voice. He had never heard a priestess refer to the deity she served in such a bitter fashion. He glanced quickly at Impuki, but he had his head down, whilst Paser was looking away as if fascinated by a red shrike digging at the grass with its sharp beak. Did these people truly believe in the Goddess? There were times when Amerotke himself stood with the other officials of the court in the antechamber to the Holy of Holies at the Temple of Amun-Ra, a mass of dark columns with only faint light seeping through. The incense would billow about and the dark emptiness would echo with the chanting of the priests. The all-seeing, ever-silent Amun-Ra! Yet Amerotke often wondered if the gods were nothing more than pieces of wood and clay, the product of the human heart desperate for answers.

He shivered and broke from his reverie. Shufoy was watching him curiously. The judge felt like pinching himself. For a moment it had seemed as if they were no longer out on this dew-washed lawn enjoying the fragrance of flowers and the taste of good food.

'I'm sorry,' Lady Thena apologised. 'Just sometimes, on a day like this, the memories come back.'

'Paser is our son.' Impuki tried to lighten the conversation. 'We have adopted him. He has proved his skill and his expertise. I have offered him to Pharaoh and she has shown her face to him and smiled her favour.'

'I follow in the shadow of the great master.' Paser leaned over and grasped Impuki's shoulder, then laughed nervously and got to his feet. 'My lord Amerotke.' Impuki and Lady Thena also got up. 'Do you wish a guide to take you around the temple?'

'No, no,' the judge replied. 'If I can be allowed to wander as I wish?'

Impuki stretched out a hand. 'On one condition, that you will not leave the precincts or enter the great courtyards by yourself.'

Amerotke grasped his hand and promised that he would not. He sat and watched all three walk away, Paser in the middle, holding the hands of his adopted mother and father.

'I don't think they liked your questions.' Shufoy had taken from his wallet the piece of black rock he had shown Amerotke the day before. 'In fact, Master, I don't think they like you!'

Amerotke chewed his lip and watched the three go through a porticoed entrance into the temple buildings.

'I just wonder,' he answered, 'as I always do when I meet priests, do they really believe what they preach? The lady Thena is understandably bitter.'

'Could they be killers?'

'We are all killers, Shufoy, priests, judges, healers; we kill each other in our thoughts. It's just that some of us act on those thoughts.' He got to his feet, brushing away the crumbs. 'And that's why we are here. Four temple girls have disappeared. Lord Impuki is probably correct, their corpses may be buried here. Mafdet, the captain of the guard, was murdered, whilst the lady Nethba believes her father was gently helped into the Eternal West across the Far Horizon.'

'You don't believe that, do you?' Shufoy got up, holding his parasol like a staff of office; he slipped the black rock back into his pocket.

'No, I don't,' Amerotke agreed. 'He died of natural causes. I just wonder why a lady of such intelligence should even contemplate the idea that her father was murdered in a place like this. But come, Shufoy, the last time I walked these temple grounds,' he grinned down at the dwarf, 'I wasn't even as tall as you!'

They strolled across the grass away from the trees. Amerotke found the curtain wall which the assassins must have crossed and studied it carefully, noticing how sometimes it was screened by trees and bushes, cypress, palms and even smaller orchards. He followed it as far as he could until he reached the wall separating the private gardens of the temple from the courtyard beyond.

'They must have crossed this,' he explained.

'Why not the one on the far side?' Shufoy asked.

'Too far away,' Amerotke explained. 'I haven't studied the plan of the temple, but this wall gives access to both Mafdet's dwelling place and the guest house. There are groves and orchards where one could hide at night.'

He pointed at the temple guards, who lounged in the shade or strolled about.

'They carry torches, easily seen, yet a traitor must have given those assassins some information. I just wonder who?'

They left the gardens and entered a large paved courtyard with two-storey buildings on three sides, the limestone gleaming white. A fountain stood in the middle of the courtyard, carved in the shape of a huge fish standing on its tail, throwing up fountains of water through its mouth. In the pool below lotus blossoms floated; the white had opened their petals to the sun but the blue, hiding just beneath the surface, would only flower at night. The courtyard smelt fragrantly of flowers. Amerotke also caught the sharp smell of herbs, peppermint, persea, mandrake and fleabane. He stopped a servant and asked him about the buildings. The man glimpsed Amerotke's ring of office and hastened to oblige. The long building on the far side was the House of Twilight, he said. 'The other two,' he added, 'are the storerooms and treatment chambers. Would you like me to show you?'

Amerotke shook his head. He crossed the yard, Shufoy striding behind him, banging the parasol on the pavement. If the dwarf had his way he would have acted as herald, but as Amerotke quietly pointed out, this was a place of healing, and silence was an excellent physician.

Inside, the House of Twilight was an elegant yet busy place. The floor was of polished wood, the walls limewashed and decorated with motifs, prayers and scenes celebrating Isis. A small antechamber led into the main office of the physician-priest-in-charge, who rose to greet Amerotke. He explained that the small chambers on the ground floor were for the more seriously ill patients, whilst in the long room above rested the acts of mercy.

'The what?' Amerotke asked.

'The acts of mercy.' The face of the priest broke into a smile. 'Have you forgotten, my lord Amerotke? Any man or woman suffering from any ailment – as long as it isn't an infectious fever – who reaches the great statue of Isis in the Courtyard of Flowers and asks for our help cannot be refused.'

Amerotke nodded in understanding. He had forgotten the custom, yet it was a popular one, much used by the poor of Thebes desperate for healing.

The old priest took them along the ground-floor passage-way. They passed narrow chambers, each containing a bed shrouded in linen drapes with a small table and stool beside it. Every room was the same, the walls and floor scrupu-lously scrubbed with a herbal wash so strong it covered any smell, above each bed a large open window to allow in light and fresh air. The young acoloytes of the temple were busy here, tending to the various ailments, though their guide quietly explained how those in the House of Twilight had very little prospect of recovery. Next he took them upstairs to the Long Chamber, a high-ceilinged room with windows above a row of cot beds on either side. Each bed was divided from its neighbours by a small table, on top of which was the same statue, Isis suckling the infant Horus. The floor was so well polished it gleamed and caught their reflection. The walls were whitewashed, and the only decoration under the black-beamed roof was quotations from hymns to Isis. A scribe squatted before a table at either end of the room. Despite the cleanliness and light, the smell of oil and herbs, Amerotke realised he was in a chamber of death. The people in the beds were hidden from him by thick linen drapes to protect them from dust and flies. Every so often a young page boy, dressed only in a loincloth, would process slowly up and down the room carrying a pink-tinged ostrich fan soaked in perfume to sweeten the air. There were no visitors here. Amerotke glimpsed one or two faces lying in the beds, old men and women with straggly hair, their skin covered in the black spots of old age.

As he walked slowly through the room, Amerotke became convinced that Lady Nethba's father could not possibly have been murdered in a place like this. He had reached the end of the room and was about to turn away when he stopped in surprise as his name was called. He glanced quickly around. He had just passed a bed where the linen curtains were pulled back. The old man within had lifted his head, pushing away the quilted headrest. He had a pointed face, a toothless mouth, sunken cheeks, yet there was something vaguely familiar about those smiling eyes.

'Great Judge, don't you remember me?'

Amerotke walked to the bed and sat down. The effort of raising himself had been too much for the old man. He turned slightly to grasp Amerotke's hand, his fingers almost skeletal, the skin dry and hot.

'Amerotke?'

The judge nodded.

'I am Imer.'

119

Amerotke closed his eyes.

'Don't you remember, the woodcutter? At your grand-father's house, to the north of Thebes? I used to slice the wood; I made you a toy sword and brought you a wooden chariot.'

Amerotke caught his breath. He couldn't believe it! He recalled Imer; even then he had been an old man.

'Past my eightieth year now.' Imer licked dry lips.

'How did you recognise me?' the judge asked.

'Just your walk, your face.' Imer smiled. 'I saw you come down the room, you swing your hands slightly in front of you; and your eyes, I always said you had gentle eyes. I've heard the stories. How you entered the House of Life and became a great judge. I used to tell people I knew you but they never believed me.'

'Your illness?' Amerotke asked.

'Old age,' Imer cackled. 'Nothing but old age.'

'Is there anything I can do?' Amerotke looked over his shoulder at the physician-priest, who shook his head imperceptibly.

'There is one thing.'

Amerotke looked down at the old man. 'I'm not bringing you a woman, Imer; you were always one for the girls!'

Imer laughed, which ended in a fit of coughing.

'I would like a deep-bowled cup of wine,' the old man whispered. 'Served by a temple girl. I mean a really deep bowl, and a piece of rich semolina cake, then I will go into the Far West a happy man.'

'I'll see what I can do.' Amerotke kissed the old man on the top of his head, rose to his feet and walked away. At the doorway he turned.

'Before you ask, Lord Amerotke,' the old physician declared, 'Imer is to die; three, four more sunsets, then he will be gone. But you have my promise that before nightfall he will have his bowl of wine and semolina cake,' he grinned, 'served by a temple girl.'

'In which case,' Amerotke grasped the physician's hand, 'you are a man of compassion as well as healing – I commend you.'

He was about to walk away but turned back

'What happens to Imer? I mean, where will he be buried? The funeral rites?'

'The Temple of Isis has its own mausoleum across the Nile. We call it the Divine House of Mercy. Imer will not be laid to rest like a Pharaoh, but he will be sent honourably into the arms of the Divine Father Osiris.'

Amerotke thanked him and left the House of Twilight. He asked Shufoy to go and sift amongst the ruins of the fire at Mafdet's house and watched the little man stride away. He himself would take a tour of the great temple complex, though he would keep away from the mortuary, the House of the Dead. He first purified himself, splashing water from a mottled stone container over his hands and face, before visiting the small shrines, the outhouses, the storerooms and granaries of the temple. He skirted the great farm which housed the sacred flocks, visited the House of Silver, where the temple accounts were drawn up and the treasure stored, then on to the House of War, a sprawling, barrack-like building for the troops and armour of the temple. He was truly impressed with the splendour and the wealth. He realised that a man like Impuki possessed all the means to organise robberies from the royal tombs; he had places to store his plunder as well as the authority to dispatch it up the Nile and across Egypt's borders. He did not suspect Impuki; the High Priest simply represented a whole range of important officials who had the resources and the authority to successfully carry out such blasphemous robberies.

Amerotke sat for a while under a palm tree, sipping at a cup of fruit juice a servant had brought; the man was carrying a bowl of the delicious-smelling drink around the temple grounds with a string of cups about his neck. As

Amerotke sat, he wondered who this Khetra could be, the Watchman who knew the hidden ways into royal tombs and could even command assassins to invade the secret precincts of a temple. He finished his drink and continued his tour. He stayed away from the soaring copper-plated doors of Lebanese cedar which led out to the public concourse. There the pilgrims flocked to pay their devotions and hire a chapel priest to recite prayers for the dead, or a Priest of the Ear to listen to their sins. The hum of noise from beyond the walls was ever present, like that of a great beehive. This was an auspicious day, sacred to the household god Bes, so petitioners were eager to make votive offerings or just come and gawp, to touch the sacred wall paintings or brush against the holy decrees of Pharaoh inscribed in countless stelae throughout the temple. Priests of every kind and status would be swarming about, heads, faces and eyebrows shaved, skin gleaming with oil, garbed in plain linen tunics or the most exquisite gauffered robes.

Amerotke returned to the gardens, where, from behind a row of stunted flowering bushes, he heard the singing of girlish voices, the clash of tambourines and the rattle of sistra. The garden was bordered by the House of Life, the temple school, and the House of Light, where the temple musicians trained. In the centre of the garden, around a pool of purity, a shimmering rectangle of blue water with flowers floating on top, were the temple hesets. They had finished their music and were gathering around the Lady Thena. The High Priestess sat on a throne-like chair brought out by servants who also held parasols and great ostrich plume fans above her. Amerotke's arrival was greeted by shrieks and noisy giggling. Lady Thena commanded silence as Amerotke introduced himself. The girls were about to be instructed on how to adorn themselves, and the edge of the tiled pool was littered with bronze mirrors, jars and pots containing cosmetics, face creams, paints for the lips and the eyes. These were cleared away and Amerotke was invited to sit next to Lady Thena.

The group of girls before him were aged between fourteen and seventeen, all garbed in pleated robes or tight-fitting sheath dresses, their beautiful soft skins coated in gold dust. Some boasted tattoos of Isis on their shoulders and arms; all were decorated with flashing jewellery, their lovely faces almost hidden by thick oiled wigs kept in place by floral fillets. The judge was aware of flashing eyes and gusts of heavy perfume, elegant hands and painted nails. Rather self-consciously he explained why he was here, and as he talked about the disappearance of their colleagues the giggling and smiles disappeared. Lady Thena encouraged the girls to speak but, in fact, they could tell him very little. They knew nothing and could not understand what had happened. The same replies were uttered time and again, slightly above a whisper. Amerotke sensed none of them were lying; there was no attempt to deceive, they were eager to chatter, reluctant to see him go, but the macabre disappearance of the four girls was a complete mystery to them.

Amerotke thanked Lady Thena and the heset chorus and left. He walked under a portico and checked the water clock in a great vase emblazoned with the sacred baboons of Thoth. The water level had dropped towards the thirteenth line; it was time that he left. As he returned to the guest house, he crossed a rather dirty courtyard in which the fountain no longer bubbled. The outside walls were decorated with scenes from the divine life of Isis. The paintings were crudely drawn, but they concentrated on one theme: 'The Battle of the Seeds between Seth, Isis, Osiris and Horus'. In one of the scenes Isis held the severed testicles of Osiris after her husband's body had been dismembered by his red-haired brother Seth. The same motif of emasculation and castration, of the god's seed being spilled, occurred in other paintings.

'Mafdet!' Amerotke exclaimed. The captain of the guard had been cursed by having his heart removed and his testicles severed, a cruel way to die and be damned for ever, yet was the murder an act of revenge or the ritual killing of a soldier who had, perhaps, violated the sacred code of Isis? 'Or am I being fanciful?' Amerotke whispered. Castration was a common way of dishonouring an enemy. During his military training he had come across similar grisly scenes out in the Red Lands.

Deep in thought, Amerotke continued on until he reached the guest house gardens, where Shufoy was waiting for him under the shadow of the great sycamore. The little man ran towards him and thrust a black scarab into his master's hand. It was burnt and cracked, but Amerotke could still make out the faint outline of the kneeling bowman.

'I found it amongst the ash,' Shufoy trumpeted. his scarred face all smudged. 'Because I'm short, I'm nearer to the ground. I have a nose,' he mocked himself, 'for scarabs.'

Amerotke turned the stone over in his hand. It was cracked and burnt from the fire. Had it been accidentally or deliberately dropped by the Sebaus? Had it belonged to Mafdet? Had that veteran been a member of the Sebaus, and his grisly death and the burning of his house an act of revenge by that ruthless gang? Amerotke returned the scarab to Shufoy, who slipped it into his pouch.

'Was Mafdet a member of the Sebaus?' Shufoy asked.

'Perhaps—' Amerotke broke off as Paser came out of a porticoed entrance.

'My lord judge, your escort has arrived. The Divine One has ordered, because of the recent attack on you, that you are not to enter the city without a guard.'

Amerotke and Shufoy quickly proceeded to the small chamber built into the gatehouse of the soaring wall which separated the gardens from the main temple precincts. General Omendap was waiting for them in full battle dress, a leather breastplate covered in shiny mail above a red-fringed white kilt and knee-high marching boots. In the doorway beyond clustered veterans, Braves of the King from the Sacred Band, Egypt's crack regiment, which guarded the Divine House. Omendap grasped Amerotke's hand. He was eager to leave, explaining that the Divine One herself had ordered him here to protect Amerotke.

They waited until Impuki and Lady Thena arrived, then Amerotke made his farewells and left, the Sacred Band, armed with long shields and sharp-edged spears, gathering about him in a protective ring. They crossed the temple courtyard, which was packed with petitioners and pilgrims gathered round the soaring statues or waiting to fill their water jars from the holy fountains. They all stood aside, gaping at the approach of the Sacred Band's standard-bearer carrying the half-moon banner displaying the insignia of Amun-Ra, a scarlet ram's head against a golden background. The escort passed through the soaring pylons, down the steep steps and into the heat, dust and smells of the city. The streets and squares thronged with busy crowds. Amerotke glimpsed passing scenes: a barber on his stool underneath a tree shouting for custom, a fruit seller arguing with a cook next to his portable grill. He felt as if he was out in a carriage, protected against everything, rather light-headed now he was in the centre of such noise after the calm of the temple. Shufoy, however, was full of it, skipping ahead like a boy released from school.

'Did you know General Suten well?' Amerotke decided to draw Omendap into conversation.

'I spoke for him in court, of course I did.'

Amerotke drew a fan from beneath his robe and gently wafted cooling air over himself.

'I'll be blunt,' he declared. 'His death is a mystery.' He paused. 'Is it possible Suten brought those snakes on to the roof terrace to confront his own fears, as a soldier who is frightened of water will immerse himself to overcome his terrors?'

'It's possible!' Omendap scratched his cheek with the tip of his gold-tipped swagger stick. 'Suten was very brave, always in the lead in the chariot charge, the first to bring down an enemy. In battle he was ferocious as a panther. He often expressed his disgust at the nightmares he suffered.'

'And his wife?'

'He dearly loved, and was loved by, the Lady Lupherna.'

'And Heby?'

'You can find the same in any general's household, an honest, loyal valet.'

'And the scribe Menna?'

'A good quartermaster, a soldier himself, totally devoted to his master. A man of little intelligence, mind you. Suten was always recommending Menna for promotion.' Omendap snorted. 'Menna always failed his exams. A good, stolid man with little imagination.'

Amerotke peered through the line of soldiers. He glimpsed a black-garbed figure, but dismissed this as a figment of his imagination.

'Is the prisoner safe? You know we captured one?'

'Oh, I know all about him. Asural will look after him. Don't forget, Amerotke, Captain Asural once served with me. I had a hand in his appointment to the temple. Suten was no different; a born leader, he looked after his men even after they retired. He organised an old fraternity of veterans; Nadif, the Medjay officer who was the first to be summoned when Suten was killed, was a member of this group. There are such gatherings all over Thebes. They meet to feast, to recall the glory days, they pay their dues and club together to construct tombs in the Necropolis.' Omendap raised a hand. 'I'll recall their name in a minute. Ah yes, they call themselves the Heti.'

'That's the word for smoke.'

'That's how these old soldiers see themselves: the fire

has gone out but the smoke remains, here today and gone tomorrow. Well, my lord judge, you must be pleased to be returning home.'

'Not yet.' Amerotke grasped Omendap's arm. 'First I want to visit Suten's house. No, don't object, it's time I saw the place where he died.'

Omendap couldn't refuse. They turned west through the dusty, palm-fringed money-changers' quarter and out through the Gate of Ivory. They followed the avenue along the Nile, through the shabby, sun-baked villages of peasants and artisans and on to the thoroughfare which swept between the river and the city walls to the Mansions of the Mighty. When they reached Suten's palatial residence they quickly gained entrance through the well-guarded gates into a lush garden which reminded Amerotke of his own, with its green coolness, fountains, pools, herb gardens and shrubs. More soldiers stood inside, sheltering in the arbours, pavilions and groves. Amerotke recalled his own order: Heby was under house arrest; these soldiers would make sure he did not leave.

Menna came striding down the garden path to greet them. He was dressed in a knee-length robe with a coloured cape about his shoulders, his thick black hair cropped just above his ears. Up close Amerotke could study the sturdy peasant face, hard eyes, determined mouth and jutting chin. Behind him Heby danced from foot to foot, eyes and face anxious, which probably accounted for the food stains on his robe. Menna bowed, welcoming Amerotke to the house, and explained that Lady Lupherna had retired to her own chambers and been given a sleeping draught by her physician. Amerotke returned the greeting, refused the offer of refreshment and demanded to be taken to the roof terrace. Menna led him through the hall of audience; despite the coloured pillars and frescoes, elegant furniture and tassled cushions, it all seemed rather gloomy. Beyond it lay a small passageway leading to a kitchen and, through a doorway on the left, the staircase to the roof terrace. Amerotke paused at the bottom step.

'Who was here the night Suten died?'

'I was in my writing office. Lady Lupherna kept coming in and out from the hall of audience on this task and the other. Heby guarded the stairs.'

Amerotke nodded and climbed the steps. At the top he flinched at the heat. The roof terrace was deserted except for a few remaining pieces of furniture. It was a huge square, the edge of the roof bounded by a small protective wall and on top of this, as was customary, a sturdy acacia-wood fence about three feet high, sure protection against anyone falling over. Leaving the rest at the top of the steps, Amerotke slowly walked round the terrace. He could see there was no gap in the trellis fence, no adjoining building; the roof looked down only on to lush gardens. He grasped the fence and looked over. There were windows below, but each one was covered by a grill; neither could anyone have hoisted a sack of horned vipers up on to the roof. He walked very slowly around the perimeter again and tried to visualise it on the night Suten had died. There would have been furniture: tables, chairs and stools; he could tell from marks on the floor where the bed had been. There would have been posts at each corner of this, over which linen drapes could be hung as protection against the dust and flies.

'Tell me,' Amerotke called, standing where he was sure the bed had been. 'General Suten was here, sitting on his bed?'

'Lying on the floor next to it,' Menna called back. 'The snakes were curling all about him, there was very little we could do.'

Amerotke walked back.

'The night was cool?'

'Yes, my lord. There was a brazier, chafing dishes if General Suten wanted to warm his fingers.' Menna's hard face broke into a smile. 'But the general always prided himself on being tough. A man who had withstood the freezing cold nights of the desert, and its heat.'

'There was food and wine?'

'Oh yes,' the scribe answered. 'We had all eaten here beforehand; dishes of fruit were left. Why, my lord?'

'For sake of argument,' Amerotke pointed to the steps, 'if Heby had brought the snakes and released them here at the top of the steps, where would they have gone?'

'Why?' Menna scratched his head.

'They wouldn't have gone straight to the general,' Amerotke declared. 'They weren't Libyan marauders but snakes, taken from their pit and released in a strange place. The night was cold, perhaps it was some time since they had eaten.'

'They would have gone towards the heat and food.' Shufoy spoke up. 'That's what they always do in a house. Snakes coil near the hearth or over a dish of food. They only attack when they are disturbed.'

Amerotke patted the little man on the shoulder.

'Which means,' the judge continued, 'the snakes must have been taken directly over to General Suten. Now, if he was awake he would protest, object, raise the alarm. So he must have been asleep. If,' he added with a sigh, 'that's what happened.'

'Or?' Menna asked.

'Or,' Amerotke conceded, 'the general knew all about the snakes because he brought them up here himself. When the roof terrace was deserted, he decided to confront his own terrors and release them. It may sound foolish to us, but a man suffering from a nightmare may do the most extraordinary things.'

Menna shook his head. 'But that's impossible!'

'Why?'

'General Suten came up here for dinner, he finished, the lamps were lit and we went downstairs.'

'But not before most of the food was cleared and the roof terrace, as usual, searched for snakes?'

'Yes,' Menna nodded. 'But you see, my lord Amerotke, as far as I can recollect, General Suten never left the roof terrace, he never went downstairs to bring up a strange-looking sack. Moreover, when we searched the roof terrace, we found nothing. So either Heby brought up that sack on General Suten's orders, which I know he didn't, or he brought it up of his own accord.'

'Or,' Shufoy was determined not to be silenced, 'somehow the general had hidden the sack away on the roof terrace.'

'Impossible!' Menna snapped.

Amerotke shaded his eyes against the sun. It was now mid-afternoon; the heat was intense, not even a whisper of a breeze. He stared across this place of death. Once again he decided to walk the perimeter, holding on to the trellis fence. He was approaching the place where the bed had stood, not far from the perimeter wall, when his hand brushed a piece of stout cord which had been wound round one of the trellis posts. He stared at it curiously. The cord was the toughest twine, the knot tied tightly, but the rest had been cut away. He leaned over the fence and peered down at the cluster of bushes and shrubs below, then returned to examine the cord. It was still fresh, slightly slippery, its oil not yet dried out by the weather.

'What is this?' he called across to Menna.

'What have you found?' Menna came across.

Amerotke tapped the upright post, then stood back, spreading his hands. 'The general's bed stood here, protected by its linen drapes. Is it possible that General Suten did decide to face his fears? Only the gods know how, and I will have to reflect further on this, but did the general obtain a sack of horned vipers in order to confront the terrors which plagued his soul once and for all? It is possible that, earlier on the day he died, General Suten brought a sack here, lowered it over the edge of the roof and tied the cord to this wooden post. No one could see it from the garden below, where there are only shrubs and bushes, no lawns or pools of purity; a deserted part of the grounds. The general did not alert anyone to what he was planning. A soldier, he followed the usual routine of having the place searched, but once the roof terrace was cleared, he drew the sack up, cut the cord around its neck and released the snakes.'

'But we found no sack,' Menna insisted.

'Not yet.' Amerotke walked back across the roof terrace and shouted down the stairs. 'General Omendap! I would be grateful if you could organise your men to search the bushes and shrubs on the far side of the roof terrace. They are looking for a leather sack.'

'A sack? Are you sure?' Omendap queried.

'Yes,' came the reply. 'I think I know how General Suten died!'

HESBET: ancient Egyptian, 'a reckoning'

CHAPTER 6

Darkness had fallen. The flies danced around the lamps. A breeze rattled the shutters over the windows and set the candle flames dancing. The garden outside had fallen silent, although now and again the croaking of the frogs welled up in harsh chorus. Amerotke picked up the flower Norfret had placed on his writing desk and sniffed appreciatively at its lovely perfume. On any other occasion he would have composed a poem; the opening lines of one came like some invited guest into his mind, and he spoke it aloud:

'Hasten now my heart and do not falter on its way.'

He had to keep up appearances, although Norfret was not fooled. They had already quietly decided that tomorrow morning she and their two sons would accept the Divine One's offer to shelter in the palace precincts.

Amerotke leaned back, pulling his white robe more closely around him. He had returned to find his house well guarded, yet Norfret had taken him down along the garden paths to the whitewashed shrine in the cypress grove, a small temple containing a statue of the goddess Ma'at. Amerotke hadn't entered; instead he had gazed in mounting fear at the sinister figure scrawled crudely in charcoal on the shrine wall, a man kneeling holding a bow. The drawing had a macabre power all of its own, as if it were ready to stand, leave the wall and wreak devastation in the heart of Amerotke's paradise.

Despite Norfret's pleas, Amerotke had given way to a fit of rage. Taking water from a nearby pool, he'd tried to wash the drawing off, but ended crouched against the wall, sweat dripping off him. Shufoy had come and quietly taken over, ordering servants to scrub the blasphemy away, whilst Amerotke had returned to the house to thank General Omendap and make his farewells. Norfret couldn't tell him when the drawing had first appeared, though Amerotke suspected it had been done before members of the Sacred Band had taken up guard around the walls of his house.

His two sons had been delighted to see him, totally unaware of the danger which threatened them. They'd jumped up and down, begging their father to play a game of senet. He had given in to their entreaties, allowing both the boys to win against their father.

'It wasn't difficult,' he confessed to Norfret as Shufoy led the children off to play a game of wild goose in the garden. 'It wasn't difficult at all. I was barely aware of playing the game!'

Amerotke had retired to his bedchamber, slept a while and celebrated the evening meal with his family on the roof terrace. Shufoy had once again kept the boys distracted before leading them away for bed.

The Chief Judge of the Hall of True Truths sighed, gazed around, and glanced at the sack lying next to his feet. One of Omendap's men had found it beneath a bush; its dark brown colour had kept it hidden among the all-concealing shoots of the shrubbery. Amerotke picked it up, along with the piece of twine found inside, the same type of cord that had been tied round the trellis post on the roof of Suten's house. He could see where the knife had sliced through it. He pulled open the sack and sniffed its fetid odour. The coarse texture of the inside still bore minute pieces of scaled skin which must have fallen off as the horned vipers coiled there. On the outside were traces of white dust, the occasional thorn and tenacious leaf, ample proof that the sack must have hung for a while against the outside wall of the house before being brought up, the snakes loosed and the sack thrown over the fence into the garden below.

Amerotke had gone down to the garden, and a soldier had shown him the exact place where he had found the sack. Looking back up at the roof of the house, Amerotke could imagine General Suten bringing the sack up earlier in the day, hanging it over the side of the roof parapet and lashing it by the cord to the wooden post. All the servants had maintained that very few people entered that part of the garden. The sack would have hung low whilst the cord would have been concealed by the drapes around the general's bed canopy. Suten, determined to confront his fears, had let the sack hang there until the evening meal was finished. Afterwards, taking a deep draught of wine laced with poppy juice to steady his nerve, he had pulled the sack up, released the snakes and thrown the empty sack into the garden below.

General Omendap had been surprised, yet accepted the logic of Amerotke's conclusion.

'I've done the same myself,' he confessed. 'Deliberately created danger so I know how to confront it.'

Menna, however, had been speechless, shaking his head in disbelief. Heby had cried in relief, whilst Lady Lupherna, disturbed by the noise, had come hastening down, heavy-eyed, to see what was happening. The sack had been carefully examined time and again until Amerotke had pronounced himself satisfied. General Suten's household had been overjoyed, clapping their hands, servants thronging about, although Chief Scribe Menna and Lady Lupherna were still shocked and unbelieving. However, Amerotke had demanded that Heby must remain under house guard and appear before his court the day after next so the royal prosecutor could hear the evidence and the case be formally dismissed.

At first Amerotke had been very pleased with himself, but as he left the house, he felt a little uneasy at what he had discovered. Was it Menna's disbelief? Had he overlooked something? Or was it just his own tiredness? Perhaps it had been that old porter who, as Amerotke approached the main gate, grasped the judge's hand and said how sad he was that General Suten had died. How quiet and withdrawn his master had been for weeks before the event.

'I was a soldier,' the old porter chewed on his toothless gums, 'a member of the Menfyt.' He referred to the shock troops who stiffened the Egyptian battle line. 'I served General Suten's father, and would have been a beggar, but the general saw me in the street and told me I could be porter here until my dying day. Now, wasn't he a good and true gentleman? And yet,' the wizened old veteran shook his head, 'sometimes so sad, so sad.'

Amerotke had nodded understandingly, gently prised loose the old man's talon-like fingers, bade him farewell and continued on to his own mansion.

Now he brushed a bead of sweat away from his forehead and smelt the tips of his fingers, savouring the delicious perfume Norfret had anointed him with just before the evening meal. She was now busying herself deciding what things should be taken, whilst he lurked here in what he jokingly referred to as his hephet, his cavern of writing. He must have sat for an hour at least, watching the wicks in their bowls of oil float in the breeze as he tried to make sense of what had happened, recalling everything he had seen and heard. He picked up the sack still draped across his knees, folded it carefully and put it under his chair, then grasped the sharpened quill, brought a lamp closer and began to write carefully on the papyrus stretched out before him, held smooth and firm by the little weights placed on each corner.

The tomb robbers – he had learnt a bitter lesson. Two days ago, despite a few reservations, he thought he had resolved this case, but he had simply turned over the nest and the hornets were now busy around him. *Who are they?* Amerotke carefully drew the question mark. The gang of thieves, that horde of ruffians who called themselves the Sebaus, were controlled by the Khetra, the Watchman, a powerful, mysterious figure who knew all about the hidden tombs in the Valley of the Kings and Queens, their secret entrances, their false passageways and, above all, the treasures they contained. He could imagine the Sebaus slipping through the valley, forcing their way in and removing the treasures. Many had tried this before, but only the most knowledgeable realised where to go and what they could plunder. Amerotke had studied all such tomb robberies, going back decades, and whenever they happened, some high-ranking official was always involved. The Sebaus, however, were different. They would not only remove treasures, but had the power to move them along the Nile and across Egypt's borders. Such power could only come from the Khetra, a man who must be surrounded by the paraphernalia of high office. Who could it be? Someone like Impuki, a high priest, well known to the myriads who flocked to his temple for solace and relief? The Temple of Isis possessed an extensive library and archives which housed all sorts of secrets, whilst a man like Impuki also held the cartouche, the imperial seal of Egypt. He could organise a string of pack animals to cross Sinai, their burdens sealed against any inspection. Moreover, Mafdet had been Impuki's man. Amerotke could only accept the High Priest's word that he and the captain of the guard had disliked each other. Neverthless Mafdet had been barbarously slaughtered at the heart of the temple and his house burnt to the ground. Was that an act of vengeance, retribution, punishment?

The robberies? Amerotke recalled Hatusu and Senenmut. He could understand their anger. But was there something else? He had detected fury, but also fear. Why? Public humiliation? Being brought into disrepute at a foreign court? Yet Hatusu seemed so personally involved, as if these robbers were blood enemies. Was this true? Or was he imagining it? Moreover, Senenmut had been extremely interested in the stolen goods recovered. They had also directed him to investigate the disappearance of the hesets at the Temple of Isis, yet instructed him not to offend the lord Impuki. Why? The High Priest could be suspected of so much.

Amerotke paused in his writing. He was glad Lord Impuki could not see into his mind. He had no proof against the High Priest except a firm conviction that the Khetra, whoever he or she might be, was a powerful figure at the courts of Egypt. Of course, there was also the Lady Thena. Heset girls had gone missing from the temple, and Lady Thena was responsible for them. Amerotke remembered the High Priestess' remarks about losing her own children, the cynicism in her voice. Did she truly believe in the Mother Goddess, or was she a Kemut, a holder of lies? Someone who disbelieved in the gods and their involvement in the affairs of men? Could she have killed Mafdet? Burnt his house to silence a garrulous captain of the guard who had seen or heard something he should not have?

Amerotke dipped the quill back in the ink. True, they had all been together when Mafdet was killed; they were talking to Amerotke himself when the dead soldier's house was burnt; whilst Paser had rescued him from the assassins. Nevertheless, if the Sebaus were guilty of Mafdet's death, as well as arson and the attack on him, how could they have entered the temple so unobtrusively to wreak such devastation? In addition, what was true of Impuki could be said of many powerful figures in the Divine One's court, men such as General Omendap or even Lord Valu. They too were holders of the imperial seal, men of great power who could wield considerable influence amongst the inhabitants of the city. Except ... Amerotke stared at the wadjet painted on the far wall.

'Except,' he murmured, 'everything comes back to the Temple of Isis.'

General Suten had visited there. Impuki had sent him the poppy juice. The disappearance of the hesets, the murder of Mafdet, the arson and the attack on Amerotke. The judge closed his eyes. The only satisfaction he'd obtained was the business of Lady Nethba. He truly believed the architect Sese had died of natural causes. But why had his daughter raised the complaint in the first place?

Amerotke moved to another problem: the Sebaus. Why were they still pursing him? He looked down at the pile of papers on the floor. He had been through it time and again, the confessions and the evidence against the grave-robbers. He could find nothing significant to make him a danger to these marauders. Which meant, he concluded, it was something he had overlooked. Why had they decided to attack him and not the lord Valu? Yes, that was it! Amerotke had collected the evidence. Valu had simply ordered the arrests and presented the case.

Amerotke felt his eyes grow heavy, and, sitting back, he fell into a light sleep, only to be rudely awakened by Shufoy banging on the door. He started to his feet as Shufoy, breathless, came in, waving his hands.

'What hour is it?'

'Still not yet midnight.' Shufoy leaned against the table. 'That doesn't matter! Captain Asural has sent a message from the House of Chains. The assassin we caught at the Temple of Isis has been found stabbed in his cell.'

'What!' Amerotke yelled, as he strode to the door, taking down his heavy striped robe from a peg on the wall.

'You are not going now, master?'

Amerotke heard the sound of Lady Norfret hastening down the passageway. He swung the robe around him and went out. Before his wife could speak, he grasped her hands, pulling her close. 'I have to go!' He kissed her gently on the forehead. 'I have to see what has happened.

You are well guarded here. I'll take some of the Sacred Band with me.'

He moved quickly before Norfret could protest, ordering Shufoy to bring his sandals. He looped a sword belt over his shoulder, took a dagger from the small armoury, slipped it through the sash on his waist and picked up a heavy club-stick.

'There.' He smiled at his wife. 'Who would dare approach the God of War!'

He collected six soldiers from the camp out in the garden and, with Shufoy ridiculously armed to the teeth scampering beside him, left his mansion, hurrying along the dark thoroughfare towards the postern door near the Gate of Ivory. He tried not to be aware of the sounds of the night, the slap slap of the river, the harsh cries from the papyrus groves or the dull roar of the hippopotami. He strove to ignore the stench of the rich mud, the blackness across the river broken by a few pricks of light from the Necropolis. The soldiers hurried along beside him. Amerotke vividly recalled his own military training, night marches through the desert where the standard-bearer had roared that they should concentrate on the next step and not be thinking of what surrounded them.

They reached the city and were admitted through the postern gate. They hurried down deserted streets, across squares lit by cresset torches and huge bonfires as the city watch burnt the refuse collected during the day. The legion of beggars slunk away at the sound of their approach and the clatter of their weapons. No one accosted them. They reached the Temple of Ma'at breathless and sweat-soaked. Asural, waiting in a side courtyard, his guard all around him, led them into the temple, along a passageway and down the ill-lit stairs into the House of Chains. Guards milled about in the corridors. A cell door hung open to reveal the prisoner lying sprawled against the mildewed wall. In the light of the flickering torch he looked ghastly, clothed only in a loincloth, ankles and wrists heavily manacled. He had slumped to one side, eyes half open, mouth gaping. The cell itself was filthy, containing pots in which to wash, and for prisoners to relieve themselves, a battered stool and a mattress of straw in the corner. Amerotke pinched his nostrils and crouched down. The knife thrust into the man's chest was embedded deep; a curious dagger, its blade long and very thin, its handle not much different, more a narrow shaft of bronze without any wood or leather grip. Amerotke pulled it free. A gasp of air escaped from the dead man's lungs and a small trickle of blood followed the dagger out.

'My lord?' Asural handed him a dirty piece of cloth. The judge unrolled it and stared in disgust at the severed finger encrusted in blood. He glanced quickly at the prisoner's hands; there was no wound.

'It was found next to the corpse,' Asural explained.

'Where did the dagger come from?' Amerotke got to his feet. 'Asural, you were in charge.'

The captain bowed his head, shuffled his feet and muttered something.

Amerotke pushed him gently on the shoulder. 'What was that? Speak up.'

'He was chained and manacled,' Asural explained. 'He could move round his cell but no one ever visited him. I hold the keys; only I served him bread and water. There was a guard outside.' He pointed at the half-open door.

Amerotke went across and examined the narrow slat, high in the wood, which the guard could pull away to check on the prisoner.

'Nobody came near this cell,' Asural insisted. 'There's no window. He had no visitors. The guard outside reported nothing wrong.'

'Bring him in,' Amerotke ordered.

After a great deal of shouting, Asural returned to the cell. The guard who followed him in was young and fresh-faced, dressed in a leather breastplate, kilt and high-tied sandals.

Around his waist was a narrow belt with a wooden sheath for a dagger. He seemed as nervous as Asural and could only tell Amerotke that he'd stood on guard from the ninth hour. Now and again he had checked on the prisoner.

'He kept to himself,' the guard declared. 'He wandered around the cell; I could hear the chains clink. Sometimes he drank from the water bowl, but mostly he just lay on his bed humming a song as if he hadn't a care in the world. About an hour ago everything went silent. I thought he was asleep. I pulled back the slat and peered in. I was carrying a torch. The bed was empty. It was the way he was slumped against the wall which made me curious. I called the captain of the guard.' The man shrugged. 'The rest you know.'

Amerotke stared down at the severed finger, thin and elegant, its smoothness marred by the blood-caked stump.

'What, by all that is light, is happening?' he whispered. 'Here we have a man caged in a box with no weapons.'

'He was stripped and searched,' Asural agreed. 'And so was his cell.'

'No one is allowed in,' Amerotke continued. 'Except you, Asural.' Again the captain of the guard agreed.

'So how did he get the knife, and what on earth is a severed finger doing lying next to his corpse?'

Amerotke crossed to the slat in the door through which the guard could peer. The gap was really a grille, far too narrow for anything to be slipped through. He shut the door, leaned against it and looked down at the prisoner's chains. They would allow him movement to the privy jar and the bowl of water, but only so far. They'd stop him at least a yard from the door. Amerotke ignored the reeking stench and stared at the dirty whitewashed walls, the cobwebbed ceiling and hard paved floor.

'There's no way in,' he murmured. He turned to the guard. 'And you, who are you?'

'Sir, I've worked here since the Season of the Peret, the year before last. My record is without stain, ask the captain.'

'It is,' the Captain growled. 'He's one of my best men, that's why I gave him the post.'

The guard seemed nervous but sincere. Amerotke thrust the piece of rag back into Asural's hands and summarily left the cell, returning to the courtyard. The night breeze had grown strong, the torchlight garish against the blackness, the sounds of the city muted. Amerotke rubbed his arms and stared up at the stars, cold darts of light against the night sky. He was on the verge of panic at the unnamed terrors which threatened. Like a soldier in the battle line who knows the enemy is advancing fast and in force but can do little to prevent it. Who were these Sebaus who could enter a closely guarded temple and, somehow, slip through stone and wood to silence an imprisoned comrade? That severed finger, what did it mean?

Amerotke walked across to one of the braziers to warm his hands. The root cause of this threat was the tomb robberies. They had begun about a year ago, a trickle at first, but more and more as the looters became more audacious. Surely the Sebaus must have existed before that? How were they organised so quickly?

Shufoy ran up to question him. Amerotke snapped back, then apologised.

'Come.' He picked up the club-stick from where he had left it. 'We must go home, there's nothing more we can do here.'

Surrounded by their guard, they left the temple and returned safely home. Amerotke checked all was secure and went up to his bedchamber. Norfret was asleep, or pretending to be. Amerotke slipped off his robe, eased himself into the bed and lay staring into the darkness.

The next morning he woke early, pretending nothing was wrong. He helped Norfret and the boys pack a few belongings and toys and took them down to the Great Mooring Place, the principal quayside of the city. It was still very early, so the warehouses on the wharf had not yet opened, and the workers sat grouped around fires, sharing their food and chattering. The fishing folk had brought their night catch in and were now busy gutting it, soaking it in vats of brine before it was loaded into baskets and taken into the city markets. A group of marines was already there, waiting to receive Norfret. A short while later an imperial barge, the *Pride of Anubis*, nosed in along the quayside with its high gold-coloured brow carved in the shape of a snarling jackal's head. In the stern stood the pilot and captain; its great purple and silver sail had been furled, the rowers raising their oars so it seemed as if there was a host of spearmen on board. Lady Norfret moved to the steps, then came back and pressed her fingers against Amerotke's lips. 'Please don't lie,' she murmured and kissed him gently. 'This is very, very dangerous. You must take care. Come to me soon.'

Amerotke embraced his wife and kissed the boys goodbye and watched them go aboard, as they were escorted to the elaborately carved, exquisitely painted cabin in the centre. He gave a sigh of relief: the barge had a full complement of marines, with an escort of smaller barges full of Syrian bowmen. The ram's head standard of Amun-Ra was lifted. Orders rang out, the barge pushed off, oars were lowered gently, steering the craft through the sandbanks covered in the green leaves of the melons which grew there and out into midstream. Amerotke watched them go. For a while he studied the crowd thronging the quayside. He wondered how many of them, people from so many kingdoms, were studying him. The officer of the escort coughed tactfully behind him. Amerotke raised his hand and, spinning on his heel, was about to leave the quayside when he abruptly stopped. He had been so immersed in his own fears and anxieties over the departure of his family that he hadn't realised: Shufoy was missing.

*   *   *

Shufoy, garbed in a striped robe, its hood pulled up, one hand resting on the hilt of the dagger pushed into his belt, the other grasping his parasol as if it was a war club, had crept from the house whilst Amerotke had been busy with his family. No one had seen him steal through the gardens and scale the wall, nimble as a monkey, before scampering down the trackway. Shufoy ran, fleeing like a little shadow before the sun. He dodged carts, donkeys, the crowds going for the day's trading, in through the Lion Gate and on to the main thoroughfare of Thebes. He hastened along the spacious avenue lined with date, palm and sycamore trees. Every thirty paces there rose a huge carving of a crouched lion, so lifelike with their bodies of gleaming sandstone, black stone for their ruffled manes and precious red rocks for their eyes.

The avenue was busy as peasants and merchants wheeling barrows, guiding oxen, carts or a line of pack animals, went up to do business in the various markets scattered around each quarter of the city: lithe, dark-skinned men from Punt, the Land of Incense, with their bundles of fragrant sandalwood and other perfumed grains and powders; Nubians bringing gold, silver, ivory and malachite as well as exotic animals such as baby giraffes, brilliantly plumaged birds and cages of trained monkeys. A platoon of Kushite mercenaries on their early-morning watch went by, the soaring painted ostrich plumes in their headdresses nodding in the breeze. They looked magnificent in their leopardskin kilts, their hard bare feet slapping the ground as they marched in rhythm behind their panther standard. Shufoy stared enviously at their oval shields and wicked-looking spears. One day, he promised himself, he would buy one of those to place on the wall of his own chamber, perhaps embroider some story about how he'd obtained it in battle.

Shufoy stared up at the branches of a sycamore tree. He wanted to do well, to please his master and impress him with his wisdom. Last night the judge had snapped at him, a rare occurrence, and watching Norfret and the boys prepare to leave, Shufoy had realised that his master confronted terrible danger. He had lain awake half the night wondering what he could do before reaching his decision. It might be dangerous, but at least it might help.

The dwarf continued on his way, only standing aside as a unit of imperial chariotry, gleaming carriages of electrum and gold, horses sleek and fat, rattled by. He moved from one stone lion to another. Every so often he would stop in the shade and peer round to see if he was being followed. He could detect no danger, and halfway down the imperial avenue he abruptly darted down a side lane which turned and twisted into the poorer section of the city. Shufoy crossed rutted tracks, shabby squares, past the mud-caked houses of the peasants and artisans with their outside fires. Swarms of beggar children with red-rimmed eyes, sore mouths and stick-like arms hurried up to beg for alms. Vermin dogs, yellow-skinned mongrels with snub mastiff faces, lunged at the end of ropes; they were deliberately kept hungry so that they would be forced to eat the human refuse strewn about. Petty marketeers touted for his trade. Shufoy cursed them, trying not to gag at the smells from the midden heaps, the refuse tips, the oil-caked ovens of the poor where they burnt their meat and baked their dry bread. Everywhere hung the pervasive smell of the special vinegar, drawn from home-brewed beer, which the peasants used to sprinkle their houses to ward off flies and rodents.

Shufoy forced his way through flocks of sheep, geese, goats and asses, using his parasol to knock aside the pedlars with their trays offering a range of goods, cheap jewellery and salted meat. Eventually the needle-thin alleyways gave way to broad paths and he reached the House of Deliciousness, one of the most exotic brothel houses in Thebes. The Restu, the Watchers, let him through a gate into the courtyard. He introduced himself and was immediately ushered into the presence of the Queen of Pleasure, the heavy-wigged, obese, perfume-drenched owner of Thebes' most notorious establishment. The Queen of Pleasure was sitting on a dais in her pink-painted eating hall surrounded by cushions, feasting from a tray of seafood delicacies. She raised her face and fluttered beringed fingers.

'Shufoy,' she cooed, wiping the juices from her double chins. She lifted a jewel-encrusted wine cup and toasted him. 'Would you like to work with me? Dwarfs are always popular. Some of my customers would like you to stand and watch.'

Shufoy smiled briefly and squatted on the cushions. 'Do you still smuggle goods?' he asked.

The Queen of Pleasure paused in her gobbling and fingered the Nekhbet around her neck, as if the jewel-encrusted vulture could protect her against this dangerous little man.

'You are here on official business?'

'From the mighty judge the lord Amerotke, who might like to question you about smuggling, receiving stolen goods, kidnap, bribery, blackmail,' Shufoy kept his voice to a monotone, 'blasphemy, sacrilege, ridiculing the Divine One . . .'

'What do you want?'

'Have there been any slayers?'

'Slayers?'

'Men who like to kill young women before they take their pleasure.'

'The last one was impaled two seasons ago on the order of your master.' The Queen of Pleasure wiped her fingers on her robe. She didn't like the look in Shufoy's eyes and wanted to be rid of this little pestilence. 'There are no slayers, no killers. Oh, the occasional priest or official who likes to slap and hurt, but there again,' her fat lips parted to reveal gold-plated teeth, 'some of my girls enjoy that.'

'Is there a hunger for fresh flesh?'

'Fresh? People always want fresh.'

'Virgins,' Shufoy explained. 'Voluptuous young girls, nice and ripe for some wealthy client who, perhaps,' Shufoy narrowed his eyes, 'is not too keen on the mature woman?'

'Oh, we get those from the slums.'

'What about hesets? Temple girls of Isis?'

The Queen of Pleasure picked up a fan and tried to cool herself.

'I know what you are saying, Shufoy, I've heard the rumours. Everyone visits the Temple of Isis. But I have nothing to do with that business, it's too dangerous. Anyway,' she shrugged one plump shoulder, 'they could have been killed, their bodies secretly buried.'

'And if they weren't?' Shufoy persisted. 'Come on, dearest,' he cooed mockingly. 'If they weren't killed, what could have happened to them? Kidnapped?'

'For what?'

'For a special customer,' Shufoy explained.

The Queen of Pleasure shook her head. 'Wouldn't you like to stay, Shufoy? I have a girl from Punt who can perform the most incredible—'

'A special customer,' Shufoy repeated.

'It's been heard of but it's very, very dangerous. I mean,' the Queen of Pleasure swallowed hard, 'they could have been kidnapped, sold to a flesh-seller and transported up the Nile to Memphis or the Delta. But if the kidnappers were caught or those who bought them arrested, they would scream their lives out on the end of a stake.'

'The Sebaus?'

The Queen of Pleasure shook, a mound of quivering jewelled flesh. Eyes staring, she raised a finger to her lips. 'I know nothing.'

'You're a fat liar. I'll tell my master about your little customs. Do your girls still steal from their clients? Perhaps,' Shufoy gestured around, 'the Medjay could visit here. Who knows,' he leaned forward, 'they might even find items stolen from the tombs.'

The Queen of Pleasure picked up her goblet, quietly vowing she would never welcome this little man again. She slurped the sweet white wine and pressed the goblet against her hot cheek.

'The Heret,' she snarled. 'The scorpion man who lives in the Mysterious Abode.' She fluttered her fingers. 'Now get out before I call one of my lovely boys.'

Shufoy left the House of Deliciousness and threaded his way through the narrow streets. At the end of a lane he was accosted by a troop of Wild Ones who served the goddess Hathor, Mistress of Drunkenness. At the sight of the dwarf they shouted in glee and tried to seize him as part of their procession, but he side-stepped, ran along the Street of the Bead Makers, past the stalls of the purveyors of skinned mice and into the Square of Mystery, the Mysterious Abode. Here, a teller of tales standing on a stump of a tree was regaling a small audience about the journey to the kingdom of Osiris, visible in the sky, so he said, in the north-east part of the heavens.

'A perilous journey,' the teller bawled, 'across fiery plains infested by serpents, savage animals and rivers of boiling water. Great monkeys lurk there armed with nets to trap your soul . . .'

Shufoy caught the teller's eye and made a sign with his fingers. The teller of tales hastily brought his story to an end, asked for alms and, once his audience had dispersed, jumped down from the tree stump. He led Shufoy into the courtyard of a house where workers were busy mummifying the corpses of cats. The stench was so offensive Shufoy grabbed the perfumed rag from his purse and covered the lower part of his face.

'I thought you couldn't smell,' the teller taunted. 'You've got no nose!'

'You've got no brain, but you still think!' Shufoy bellowed back. The teller laughed and led him into the beer shop, a small comfortable chamber with reed matting on the floor.

It smelt richly of meat juice and spices. A man sitting with his back to the far wall paused in his scrutiny of a pile of precious stones.

'Who is it?'

'Shufoy, servant and herald of the great lord Amerotke.'

'Ah yes, Shufoy, I've been expecting you. I trust you haven't brought the Sebaus with you? I mean, they would follow you like hyaenas would a trail of blood.'

'No one has followed me.'

'Well, come.' The Scorpion lifted a hand. 'Come and tell your old friend what you want.'

Shufoy settled himself on some cushions and stared across at the Scorpion. He was of middle age with a lean face, harsh cheekbones and staring, mocking eyes. A luxurious beard and moustache, coated in balm, hid the lower half of his face, whilst his forehead and cheeks were emblazoned with tattoos of a scorpion. Similar insignia marked the back of his hands, and the costly robe he wore was decorated with silver snakes and other venomous reptiles. Shufoy gazed around.

'Business must be prospering.'

The Scorpion scooped the precious stones into a sack. 'A little here, a little there; a man works from dawn until dusk to earn a crust. What do you want, Shufoy?'

'The Sebaus?'

'I don't like them.' The Scorpion moved restlessly, his gaze shifted. Shufoy realised that, in the shadows on the far side of the room, this robber king's bodyguard was watching him intently.

'I thought you wouldn't,' Shufoy agreed. 'You see them as business rivals?'

'They are what they are, a bloody nuisance. They have attracted the attention of the Medjay, not to mention the imperial palace, the Eyes and Ears of Pharaoh and now that great meddler in mischief Lord Amerotke.' He leaned across. 'The last thing I want, Shufoy, is eastern Thebes being ransacked by imperial troops.'

'Who are the Sebaus?'

'I don't know. I'm telling you the truth, so don't threaten me with your master.'

'But you must have suspicions?'

'Yes, I do, and they are yours for a price.'

Shufoy opened his wallet, took out the piece of hard black rock and handed it over to the Scorpion; he seized it greedily, turning it over in his hands, banging it hard on the acacia-wood table before him.

'Stone from the heavens,' he murmured. 'I've heard of this, even owned a few splinters, but nothing as big as this. I'll talk to the merchants, those who've done business with the Hittites in the north. They talk of a new metal which can shatter bronze and copper. I would like to take this and smelt it, if I can, and see what happens. Is this payment?'

'It's a gift.' Shufoy smiled. The black rock disappeared into the leather bag.

'You've been to the Queen of Pleasure?'

'You've heard about the hesets who disappeared from the Temple of Isis?'

'Probably murdered,' the Scorpion scoffed. He turned to a side table, filled two goblets of wine and thrust one into Shufoy's hand.

'Don't worry, it's not drugged.' He sighed and exchanged his for Shufoy's. 'The temple girls haven't been murdered,' he whispered. 'They've probably been kidnapped. Why is a mystery. If they were brought to me to sell to a pleasure house, I would curse and run like the wind.'

'And the Sebaus?'

'The problem is, Shufoy, no one knows who they are. Contrary to popular rumour, they are not another gang from the slums. They've emerged recently. They have assumed a name and receive orders from whoever controls them. More than that I cannot say, except for one thing. I would wager my best amethyst to a ruby that something, or someone, links them all together.'

'What do you mean?'

'They . . . all have something in common. You see, Shufoy, there are gangs in Thebes, guilds of assassins, usually they know each other, but the Sebaus are different. From what I've learnt, it's possible for a man to be a member but not even realise his brother also belongs to the same group. There will be ones more trusted than the others. They will be given a few names, told to gather at this place or that, carry out this task or that. I only wish they hadn't chosen to plunder royal tombs. I heard a Sebaus was captured, taken to the House of Chains?'

Shufoy described what had happened. The Scorpion nodded wisely, like some Priest of the Ear listening to the confession of a penitent.

'It was the finger,' Shufoy declared, 'which puzzled my master.'

The Scorpion stared at Shufoy and began to laugh. 'Haven't you realised, little man, the Sebaus wasn't murdered, he committed suicide! Someone went down to the House of Chains.' He smiled at Shufoy's exclamation of surprise. 'Think, little man, you are a prisoner. You are going to be handed over to the torturers to be questioned. Suddenly a severed finger appears in your cell, along with a dagger. I wonder whose finger they took: the Sebaus' wife, one of his daughters, perhaps a son?'

'But how?'

Shufoy closed his eyes. He thought of that heavy wooden door and the narrow slats; the prisoner in his chains.

'Of course,' he breathed. He recalled the door to the prison cell. No one had thought of looking for a gap between the bottom of the door and the floor. 'The guard,' he whispered. 'The guard on duty outside, he must have been bribed or threatened.'

The Scorpion grinned from ear to ear. 'That's right, little Shufoy, welcome to the world of the Sebaus!'

154

KEFA: ancient Egyptian, 'to uncover'

CHAPTER 7

The guard from the Temple of Ma'at whom Amerotke had questioned regarding the mysterious death of the Sebaus felt secretly relieved to be taking the assassin's corpse down to the Place of Slaughter near the Wall of Death which overlooked a desolate stretch of the Nile. The corpse had lain in the cell until Captain Asural decided to have it thrown into the crocodile pool before it began to stink. The cadaver, now bound in sheepskin, so as to inflict further indignity, was dragged on a hurdle drawn by two oxen through the Gate of Anubis and down through the city. An executioner walked either side, macabre in their black leather tunics, jackal masks covering their faces; a third one led the oxen, now and again prodding them on with a jab from a goad. A few of the curious watched it pass; most city dwellers believed such processions to be accursed and unclean. They hastily drew aside and the executioners were soon out of the city, going down into the dusty palm grove, following its winding path.

The inhabitants of Thebes regarded this entire area as a place of abomination to be avoided at any cost. At the far end of the grove, rising above the trees, was a crumbling limestone wall which stood on top of a bluff overlooking the lush papyrus groves and the crocodile pool, a place where the river monsters gathered to feast on what was thrown there. No one knew who had built the wall. The ancients said it was the great Pharaoh Ahmose, many years ago, when he had launched his attack on the Hyksos, those invaders of Egypt, during the Season of the Hyaena. The wall soared six yards high, with steps cut into the land side. The condemned were often hung there until the ropes rotted and the remains fell for the crocodiles to finish. Sometimes the mercy of death was withdrawn and criminals were hung alive. It was not unknown for a crocodile to reach up and snatch a body from its gibbet.

The guard noticed how silent the grove had become. No birds clustered there, probably because the pool which had once bubbled in the centre had either dried up or been deliberately dammed. It was like some eerie mausoleum, a place haunted by ghosts, which was why the executioners wore masks, and why the guard had also been given one, to conceal his face lest the demons recognise him. He hadn't worn his, however, but had hung it on the end of the hurdle so that he could sweat more easily and breathe the early-morning air.

The guard was truly frightened. He had enjoyed working in the Temple of Ma'at until that visit by his cousin a few days previously. Cousin was always welcome, a veteran of the Osiris regiment who had won the collar of valour and fought under the standard of General Omendap. He'd plucked the guard by the sleeve of his tunic and invited him down to one of the riverside beer shops, where he had plied him with beaker after beaker, making sure his platter was piled high with delicious spiced quail. Cousin had reminded him how he had recommended him to General Omendap for the post at the Temple of Ma'at, and how he would always look after his career in the service of the temple. The guard, half drunk, had nodded in agreement. The evening had worn on. Cousin had raised the problem of the tomb robbers. He had been loud in his condemnation but claimed there were two women who, unlike the rest, had received a commuted sentence. Only then was the pouch slipped across the table.

'Everyone drinks water.' He smiled. 'Just make sure that's mingled in it.'

The guard had opened the pouch and sniffed the acrid smell. He was about to object, but Cousin had filled his beaker again, edging closer to explain how the women were liars and daughters of liars. They would try and implicate innocent men, good comrades, former veterans, and that wasn't fair, was it? The guard had taken the pouch and the quarter of ounou of silver, any doubts overcome by his cousin's promises of more and the heady prospect of further promotion. Cousin had winked and tapped the side of his nose.

'You're doing what's right,' he urged, 'and you will make very good friends.'

Now the guard sighed so noisily that even one of the executioners stared at him. Well, he had done it. That silly bitch who had murdered her companion had almost upset matters, but when she was taken up for questioning, the guard had realised water would be needed and had made sure the powder was mixed into the jug before it was taken in. Afterwards he had almost been sick with fright. He hadn't realised Chief Justice Amerotke, not to mention Lord Valu, had also been in the cell. What if they had drunk from the water? The guard had been too terrified even to tell his betrothed.

He had thought it was the end of the matter until that assassin had been brought in and he was chosen to share guard with Captain Asural. Once again his cousin had appeared, just before noon, offering bribes, but this time he was more menacing, pointing out that he had already killed once, so why not again? There would be more silver given and guaranteed promotion before the end of the year. Cousin had even made a veiled threat against the guard's betrothed; that had settled matters. He couldn't refuse. In the early evening he had met his cousin and taken the severed finger and that needle-thin dagger. He knew what was being planned; just a look at that bloody stump convinced him. He had studied the cell door and found the gap between the floor and the wood wide enough for both the dagger and the severed finger. He had waited until the corridor was empty and used the tip of his spear to push both towards the prisoner. The assassin had remained quiet. He had, eventually, cried a little, a low, heart-rending moan, before plucking up the dagger and taking his life. Afterwards the guard had taken a vow to Ma'at. He told his cousin that was enough. Once the corpse was disposed of at the Place of Slaughter, he'd never allow Cousin to pluck him by the sleeve again.

The guard looked up. They were close to that forbidding wall, its crumbling steps covered with lichen and moss. The oxen stopped. One of the executioners unhooked the goat skin full of animal blood which he would first sprinkle over the wall to attract the beasts. The guard dropped his spear and shield. He was about to crouch down and rest when the figures came slipping through the grove behind him. A rustle in the undergrowth betrayed their approach. One of the executioners spun round in alarm; after all, this place was haunted. The guard looked over his shoulder, fear freezing his body sweat. Five men, all garbed in black, each carrying a heavy Syrian bow, arrows already notched. The guard died first, then the attackers turned on the executioners. One took off his mask and tried to flee through the grove. The assailants killed him, and the other two. Then they took the skin of blood, raced up the steps and sprinkled it wildly, splattering the rocky ground which stretched down to the river and that lush papyrus grove where the water bubbled and cruel snouts hovered just above the surface. Finally they tossed in the bodies of their victims, whilst that of the assassin was cut from its shameful canvas covering and carried away.

* * *

160

By the time Shufoy reached the House of Chains beneath the Temple of Ma'at, the news of the massacre at the Place of Slaughter was common knowledge. Shufoy found Captain Asural praying for the victims in one of the small temple shrines.

'Very little,' the captain declared, coming out and wiping the ritual dust from his forehead, 'very little was found of them: a skull and a few bones.'

'What are you talking about?' Shufoy asked.

'Isn't that why you are here?' Asural demanded, 'the Place of Slaughter?'

Shufoy shook his head in bewilderment, so Asural briefly explained what had happened. Shufoy groaned and described what he had discovered. Asural sat down at the bottom of a pillar and put his face in his hands.

'You're saying the guard, the one who was murdered this morning, was responsible for the death of the assassin? But he was one of my most trusted men.'

'And he also killed the woman Sithia.' Shufoy muttered.

Asural found this difficult to accept, so Shufoy insisted they both return to the cell where the assassin had been held. Shufoy, crouching down, peered through the gap at the bottom of the door.

'We wouldn't have noticed it at night,' the dwarf exclaimed. 'Now I do. It's obvious. Look, the central paving stone even dips a little.'

Asural fetched the dagger and a peg of wood about the same thickness as the finger. Shufoy showed him how they could both be pushed under and, using his long Libyan dagger, moved them even further so that they fell within the reach of the prisoner.

'The assassin was being warned.' Asural grasped Shufoy, getting to his feet. 'That finger was removed from a wife, a sister, a child, a lover. The assassin was not meant to be taken as a prisoner or to be questioned. He was invited to take his own life, and yet,' he scratched his head, 'they came back for his corpse, as if that was part of the arrangement, to receive an honourable burial.'

'And the guard?' Shufoy asked.

'A former soldier. He served in one of the city garrisons and did good work out in the Red Lands. Like me, he was recommended to this post by General Omendap. What's happening here, Shufoy?'

'I don't know.' The dwarf walked to a side door of the temple and stared at the elaborate carvings on a pillar. 'I truly don't know, but I'm sure my master will.'

Amerotke's anger at Shufoy's abrupt departure from the mansion soon disappeared as the little man knelt on a cushion in his writing office and told him all he had learnt. The judge was still angry and disappointed at the assassin's death, yet he openly wondered if the Sebaus had not made a mistake.

'They killed their comrade,' he declared slowly, 'then stole his corpse for burial. They also used that guard.'

'Couldn't he have been one of them?'

'I doubt it.' Amerotke shook his head. 'My impression is that the guard was either bribed or threatened, but later killed because he couldn't be trusted. We must concentrate on that.' He patted Shufoy on the head and handed him a goblet of wine. 'And it was good of you to barter your rock.' Amerotke smiled. 'I shall not forget that. Now, let's go back to the Queen of Pleasure. She's steeped in villainy and knows what could happen. I agree with her, and the Heret, that those four hesets were not murdered. If they had been, their corpses would have been found. The same is true if they had fled: one of them would have been discovered. So, let's argue that they were kidnapped. The first question is why, and the answer is simple: a virgin, soft-skinned, well fed and pampered, would command a high price in the flesh market. But a heset is consecrated to the Goddess. If anyone was found selling or buying such a girl, both they and their family would face excruciating and humiliating punishment. The girls would have to be transported to some other city, yet I doubt if they would remain silent. One word and their captor, as well as any who supported them, could face death by impalement or burning alive in a bush.'

'Nevertheless, you believe they were kidnapped?'

'Yes, Shufoy, I do, but why and what has happened to them remains a mystery.'

'And their kidnapper, possibly Mafdet?'

'Possibly,' Amerotke agreed. 'He was Captain of the Temple Guard, a man who liked to flirt with the ladies – but how would he get them out of the temple? Why would they go so quietly? Who would receive them?'

'Mafdet may have been a member of the Sebaus,' Shufoy argued. 'Again we have no proof. It's possible they killed him, burnt his house and left that scarab as a signature of their work. But there again we must ask the question, why? More importantly, what would the Sebaus need with temple girls? They are not pimps. Unlike the Queen of Pleasure, they do not run a brothel. They are more interested in the treasures of the dead.' Amerotke tapped his foot on the ground. 'And even if it was Mafdet, he apparently did what was asked, so why should the Sebaus kill him?'

'Perhaps his murderer was someone else in the temple?'

'Again,' Amerotke smiled, 'the question is, who? According to all the evidence, and I have no reason to disbelieve it, Impuki, Lady Thena and Paser were busy in a meeting the night Mafdet died. Anyone can take a sleeping draught, put it in a jug of beer and wait for the drinker to become vulnerable. We also know that the High Priest, his wife and adopted son were talking to us the night Mafdet's house was burnt down.'

Amerotke sipped from his wine.

'Now we come to what you learnt from the scorpion man.

I understand his resentment: the Sebaus have attracted the attention of the Divine One and the power of the law, yet they are unlike the other gangs in eastern Thebes. I have revised my opinion of them. They are not a tribe or clan, but men picked by the Khetra, this so-called Watchman. So what binds them together? A society which will force one of its members to commit suicide and yet remove his corpse for honourable burial?'

'We could search for the corpse,' Shufoy declared. 'Even send a messenger to the Temple of Isis and other places of healing, enquiring about anyone who has come for a wound to be bound.'

'The corpse will be most difficult to trace,' Amerotke murmured. 'Whilst the person with the missing finger could be tended by a local physician. I'm sure it belonged to a woman, and even if she did go to the Temple of Isis, what information would she give about herself? No, what interests me is what binds the Sebaus together. What is the invisible thread? I think they made a mistake over that guard. Yes.' Amerotke tapped the table top. 'After court tomorrow, I want you, Shufoy, to discover as much as possible about that guard, his family, his friends, his relations. Do the same for Mafdet. Finally,' Amerotke gestured at the rolls of vellum on his desk, 'I want you to go through the lists of all those implicated in the robbery of the royal tombs. They all came from different professions, merchants, scribes, officials; some lived in Thebes, others came from Memphis, but there again, is there some thread which binds them all together? There's something in this information which the Sebaus do not wish me to discover; that's why they've marked me down for death.'

Shufoy agreed. Amerotke was about to continue when there was a knock on the door, and his steward entered to say that Chief Scribe Menna and the lady Lupherna were here to see him. Amerotke pulled a face, but asked the steward to bring them in. His guests were rather flustered as they took their seats, apologising loudly for disturbing the judge.

'I came,' Menna mopped the sweat from his strong square face, 'to show you something, my lord.' He glanced quickly at Lady Lupherna, who nodded. 'I found it difficult to accept the evidence about the sack. However, I was going through the master's papers when I came across his memoirs.' Menna opened the leather writing satchel on his lap and took out sheets of papyri closely bound together. 'They are dedicated to the Divine One. Lady Lupherna believes they should be presented to the palace. Anyway, I wondered how far General Suten had reached.'

Menna leafed through the book then handed it over, stubby fingers pointing to a passage. The writing was in the hieratic fashion, done in dark red ink, though now and again General Suten had used hieroglyphs for certain names and terms.

'*I have studied,*' Amerotke read aloud the passage Menna had indicated, '*the Book of Crossing Eternity.*' The judge looked up, puzzled.

'It's a treatise,' Menna explained, 'about what happens when a soul travels into the Far West.'

'*I have reflected,*' Amerotke continued, '*on the Eater of Eternity.*' He pulled a face at this rather ancient name for the god Osiris. '*And when the sun sets,*' he read, '*confronted by the Watchers of the Night, I go back to that hellish cavern and the vipers curling all about me. The clammy terror of my fears is round my heart yet these nightmares do not leave me when I wake. I cannot walk through a field but look for a snake. I cannot relax in the shade of a tree, the fear haunts me. I have talked to the exorcists and healers, little help there. I gave offerings to the Great Mother, the blue-skinned Isis, and I have found some comfort. High Priest Impuki has comforted me. He has told me to reflect on the soldier's way but be careful. I have a demon hunting my soul. I must confront this shadowy swordsman. I must entice him out of the land of shadows. I, Lord Suten, must show, prove there is more to life than the fear of death.'* This section of writing had finished abruptly. General Suten had drawn five hieroglyphs and, beside these, time and again, the word *hefau*, snake. Amerotke glanced up.

'At first,' Menna explained, 'the lady Lupherna and myself found it difficult to accept that General Suten may have brought about his own death.'

'Did your husband talk about this to you?'

'On a number of occasions,' Lady Lupherna replied. 'It was a problem he was forever discussing. Last season we went for a walk along the riverside. I was telling him how sometimes I was frightened to cross the Nile, particularly in one of those light skiffs or punts. When I was a little girl I used to scream. My husband put his arm around me,' Lady Lupherna began to cry, 'and told me to confront my fears, as one day he must do his. I never realised,' her voice faltered, 'what he truly meant.'

Amerotke closed the memoir and placed it on the table. 'May I keep it?' he asked. Lady Lupherna nodded.

'I've also spoken to Heby,' Menna declared. 'Tomorrow, my lord, he appears in court in front of you. With your permission I would like to act as his advocate.'

Amerotke agreed to his request, and the two were about to leave when the judge's hand brushed the seal on the table. He picked this up and called them back.

'Your husband, Lady Lupherna, was a high-ranking general. He was a holder of the imperial cartouche, the great seal of Egypt.'

'But he was retired,' Menna reminded them. 'When he gave up his staff of office, the seal was broken and returned to the Divine House.'

'Was your husband on friendly terms with Lord Impuki, the High Priest of Isis?'

'He liked him,' Lady Lupherna agreed. 'He would often go to the temple for advice. Now I understand why. Those cramps in his stomach had to be examined. He also studied in the library, gathering information for his memoirs. I suppose he and the High Priest were more acquaintances than friends.'

Amerotke thanked them and escorted them back to the garden and his waiting steward. He had hardly returned to his writing office, where Shufoy was stealing a peep at the memoirs, when the steward ran back saying that Lady Nethba was at the gate and needed to see the judge on a matter of urgency.

'Bring her in,' Amerotke sighed. 'It seems as if the whole of Thebes wishes to see me!'

Moments later, Lady Nethba, wearing a gauffered robe, with a little maid trotting behind her, swept into the chamber. Without being invited she sat in the great chair before Amerotke's desk, gesturing at the maid to crouch at her feet. She held up her hands, the nails painted a deep purple.

'I know,' she gazed at the bemused judge, 'how busy you are, my lord, but I just had to come and see you. I've heard all about what is happening in Thebes.' She leaned closer. 'It's on everyone's lips, I mean the attack on you, the deaths at the temple. As I used to say to my late husband, although he always claimed to be deaf, matters are going from bad to worse. Now, I know you are very busy—'

'Yes, yes,' Amerotke intervened.

'My father—'

'Lady Nethba, I have been to the Temple of Isis. I have talked to the High Priest Impuki and to the Scribe of the Dead. Your father, may he be happy in the fields of Osiris, had a severe malignancy in his stomach which killed him. He was given the best possible treatment, but he died, and his body is now being honourably treated in the House of the Dead. As for his offering to the temple, that is customary—'

'I know,' said Lady Nethba, eyelids fluttering. 'But his

death was so swift.' Her face crumpled into a look of sadness. 'I just wanted to make my farewells properly. Are you sure, my lord judge?'

'My lady, I would take an oath upon it.'

Lady Nethba patted her maid on the head and got to her feet.

'In which case,' she extended her hand for Amerotke to kiss, 'I thank you for your troubles. Perhaps I was too upset.'

'Lady Nethba?'

She turned, her hand already on the latch on the door.

'Why were you so suspicious about the Temple of Isis?'

'I had an old washerwoman once,' she pulled a face, 'one of those ladies who always seem old. Her name was Kliya, she was a freewoman. Two seasons ago she fell ill and left her cottage, which stands just beyond the walls of my house. She said she was going to the Temple of Isis. The months passed, I heard nothing, so I went up to the Temple of Isis. I made enquiries of the Scribe of the Dead but he had no record of her. I thought it was strange, because I was sure she had said she was going there. I mean,' Lady Nethba opened the door, 'where else would she go?'

Djed, the cousin of the guard killed near the crocodile pool at the Place of Slaughter, felt pleased and content. He sat in his coloured pavilion at the far end of the small garden which surrounded his square two-storey house in the north-east of Thebes. A salubrious area, as his wife called it, the avenue outside and the lanes leading to it were spacious, paved with basalt stone and lined with thick-bushed persea trees. A comfortable house, Djed thought, in a comfortable area. He pushed aside the platter of duck and chickpeas and grasped his beaker of Buto wine. He loved the evening, to sit here at the end of the day and peer through the half-open door, let the breeze ruffle his light robe and, when darkness fell, stare out at the stars. The saluki hound who patrolled his garden barked and snarled. The dog would be busy tonight, Djed reflected, driving off the genet and the mongoose which came to poach his ponds or climb the trees hunting for eggs or small birds. Nevertheless, the dog's snarl pricked Djed's feeling of serenity. There was something wrong but he couldn't place it, a danger which couldn't be marked. Ah well.

He sniffed at the wine. When he had served in the army, his officers had always said Djed could never think for himself but was excellent at carrying out orders. He shook himself, narrowing his eyes; tomorrow he would work in the garden amongst his beloved beehives. As a soldier he had served in the regiment of Anubis but now considered himself an authority on bees. In fact the bees reminded him of army life, the military organisation of the hive, the unquestioning obedience shown to the queen bee. Djed could tell at a glance the difference between each species by the minor variations in the length of the wing or the colouring of the belly. He knew how to clear the hives with smoke, as well as imitate the call of the queen bee so that he could sift out the honey in order to vary its richness. He considered himself a true ftui, a beekeeper, and one day he hoped to enroll in the Guild of Beekeepers. He had been out to the House of Life at the great Temple of Isis, and had learnt how Pharaohs had once been called the 'One of the Bees'. He revelled in the story of how the god Ra had wept and the tears from his eyes had turned into bees.

Djed picked up a small pot of honey and sniffed its delicious aroma. The very sight of this fragrant substance soothed his mind. After he had retired from the regiment, he'd used the little wealth he had gathered to grow vegetables and run a small stall in one of the markets. But the garden had been blighted and Djed and his family had faced a bleak future. At last, he had gone to the Heti – the Guild of Veterans – to seek help for his family. Late at night, soon after, he had been seized by black-garbed

169

figures who'd taken him across Thebes to a lonely place. He'd been questioned closely by this strange group who'd told him his fortune would soon change. At first his new status had shocked him, but a deben of copper here and a deben of silver there had transformed his life. He had grown wealthy. The Khetra had instructed him to tell people that he had benefited from the legacy of a rich relative in the Delta. Djed had told his wife to keep quiet, not to ask questions or pry, but simply tell their neighbours how the gods had smiled on them.

One task had led to another: messages to be delivered late at night or just before dawn. Mysterious visitors would come, faces masked; they would whisper instructions and flit away like shadows. Djed had met the Khetra in the disused Temple of Khnum, a ghostly place where the Khetra had sat in the shadows as Djed knelt before him, head bowed. He couldn't distinguish the voice. He couldn't even tell if the Khetra was male or female. All he remembered was that cloying smell of jasmine. There had been others present but, like Djed, their faces had been masked, their heads hooded, and that was the way it was. If any of them were captured they could not betray their comrades simply because they didn't know who any of them were. Like the rest, Djed would receive orders, be told to gather here or there, always to be on time, and at the appointed hour, others would join him. Sometimes he was in charge; on other occasions a different leader would issue the orders. At first they had been involved in the robbery of mansions, wealthy houses on the other side of Thebes, but eventually they had turned to the tombs, and the stream of wealth had swollen to a torrent. At first Djed had been terrified as he and the rest poured like bees – yes, Djed smiled to himself – like bees from a hive, silent and formidable, following their leaders up through the rock and shale, the night air freezing their sweat. They'd entered the Valley of Kings, that ghostly place, and climbed up its sides searching for secret entrances.

On the first occasion Djed had been so terrified he thought he would faint with the biting-cold wind, the hideous roar of the night prowlers and the heart-stopping fear of being caught by the guards. Nevertheless they had been successful. The guards had looked the other way and Djed couldn't believe his eyes as their guide had led them to what looked like an impassable rock face before disappearing into the cunningly contrived entrance. Once inside that ancient Pharaoh's tomb, Djed's fears had grown. There were traps to be avoided, hidden pits with stakes, false doors which led nowhere, trip ropes which would bring down a fall of rocks and, finally, a chamber swarming with asps and snakes. A place of concealed terrors, its darkness broken only by the pinprick light of torches which brought the pictures on the wall to flickering life. Five of his companions had been killed that night, but the Khetra had brought their corpses out; they'd all been promised that, alive or dead, they would be well looked after.

Djed had soon forgotten his terrors when he reached the treasure tombs and the ransacking began. Chairs and tables inlaid with gold; ivory and silver precious caskets full of jewels; jars brimming with exquisite trinkets. They had filled their sacks and left the way they had come. The Khetra had organised everything: the bribing of guards and officials, the transporting of goods from this house of pleasure to that, leaving the booty where the merchants and buyers could collect it and move it on. Djed had played his part. Sometimes he had been tempted to keep an earring or a jewelled bracelet, but he knew how dangerous that was. On his second robbery two of the Sebaus had done just that, filling their pockets with small debens of silver. Both men had been captured by the Khetra and stripped, their bodies lashed before being staked out in the desert for the night prowlers to feast on.

The robberies had become commonplace. Djed felt he knew some of those he worked with, old comrades from the regiment, but he could never discuss this secret life in the beer shops or wine booths. Nevertheless he was certain that some of those who drank with him were the same shadowy figures who clambered up the sides of the Valley of the Kings to pillage the Houses of Eternity. A few had betrayed their new-found prosperity – perhaps that was where the mistake had been made – and Amerotke, that interfering judge from the Hall of Two Truths, had brought their depredations to an abrupt halt, picking at a loose thread and beginning to pull away at the entire fabric. The great conspiracy had been revealed. Merchants, officials and soldiers had been arrested at the dead of night, or just before dawn, their households swept up and taken to the imperial barracks or the House of Chains beneath the Temple of Ma'at. Courtesans and prostitutes, temple musicians, money-changers from the marketplace: there wasn't a profession in Thebes who had not dabbled in the buying and selling of stolen goods. Yet none of the Sebaus had been arrested. Of course, Djed smiled, how could they describe someone they didn't know? How could you arrest someone always cowled in black?

Djed had watched and listened as the fear swept through Thebes. Of course the robberies had stopped. He had been summoned back to the ruined Temple of Khnum, and the Khetra had come and issued orders he could not refuse. He had achieved some success; the attack on Amerotke had been fruitless, yet he had arranged the killing of that bitch Sithia and visited his cousin the temple guard. That had worked out well, though it was a pity about his cousin. He should have taken the silver and joined the Sebaus. However, he had told Djed he would do no more, so Djed had received fresh orders, to strike, and strike hard. He recalled the events of that morning: how he had led the attack on the executioners at the Place of Slaughter, the death of his cousin, and the rescue of their anonymous dead comrade. They had taken the corpse to the Temple of Khnum, but before he had left, he'd pulled back the sheet and seen a face he recognised: a veteran he had glimpsed in the beer shops, near the barber's tree in the silversmiths' square.

Djed drank from his beaker. The garden had fallen strangely silent; even the faint strains of music from the house had faded away. Hadn't his wife said she wished to practise the harp? He half rose to his feet. He was sure he heard his saluki hound whimper. He put the beaker down, his hand going to the knife on the table as the door was flung open and Amerotke, Chief Judge of the Hall of Two Truths, came up the steps and into the pavilion.

Djed's mouth went dry with fear, so shocked, so surprised he stayed at a half-crouch. Surely he was dreaming? The judge was staring down at him, one hand slightly extended, the other tapping his leather breastplate.

'What?' Djed slumped back in the chair as the judge picked up the dagger from the table and threw it from hand to hand, studying Djed's face closely as if he wished to memorise every detail.

'You have the eyes of a killer.' The judge's voice was soft. 'And the mouth of a man with no mercy.' He sat down on a bench and pointed the dagger at Djed. 'Have we met before? Surely we have. Did you come into my chamber in the Temple of Ma'at? Were you there when Sithia was poisoned?'

Djed felt as if he was in a nightmare. He tried to pick up the beaker but it slid from his fingers and crashed to the floor.

Amerotke half smiled, and pushed open the door further so that Djed could see the Syrian bowman standing outside. 'He has an arrow to his bow,' Amerotke confided, 'and there are others around this pavilion. They are under strict orders to take you alive. No, don't be nervous.' He smiled again. 'Your wife, child and servants are safe. They are under guard in the house. It's a pity about your dog, but I know the type, a killer, just like its owner. Please,' he held up a hand, 'don't lie to me. Don't start protesting, or quoting the law about trespass. I know all about you. How you are a former soldier who seems to have grown rather wealthy. I know about your friends and relations including your dear, dead cousin who was a member of my temple guard.' Amerotke sniffed. 'Earlier this evening I visited his betrothed; poor girl, she hasn't stopped crying. She told me all about your visit. It was shortly before I was attacked and Sithia was poisoned in prison. After your second visit, a certain prisoner was found dead in the House of Chains. You bribed your cousin, didn't you? You told him what to do, but he wasn't a killer like you. He became nervous and agitated.'

Amerotke dropped the dagger so that it fell to the floor, making Djed jump.

'Your cousin muttered about how he resented your visits and never wanted to see you again. It was only a matter of time,' he played with the sash around his waist, 'before he would talk to someone. You know it was a mistake, don't you?' He narrowed his eyes. 'Or perhaps you haven't reached that conclusion yet?'

Amerotke leaned forward, lecturing Djed as a teacher would some dim-witted scholar.

'It was obvious your cousin was bribed; he was the only guard outside the cell – apart from the Captain Asural, and I would trust him with my life. Now your cousin is dead. It was only a matter of time before I began to ask questions. Who had he been speaking to? Who had visited him?'

Djed sat impassive, so tense he could feel the cramp in the back of his legs. He quietly cursed his own stupidity. He had made a mistake, the Khetra had made a mistake, but what could he do? He fought for breath. Of course, no Sebaus ever showed his face, and if he did, it was a rare occasion. The Khetra must have been desperate. Or was he? Had the Khetra marked him for death but not moved fast enough? Was that the real mistake?

'I'm sure,' the judge picked up the knife, balancing it in his hand, 'I'm sure, Djed, that if I hadn't visited you tonight, others would have done. You showed your face, your true identity to your cousin. All would have been well if he'd co-operated fully. You told the Khetra, who ordered his death!' Amerotke smiled. 'As he has ordered yours. The Sebaus would have come. They would have killed you, your wife, your child, your servants, as well as your dog. Who knows,' he gestured to the knife, 'perhaps the assassins already know we are here. So, which way are you going to jump?'

Amerotke paused as Shufoy came up the steps into the pavilion. He listened to his whispers, then spoke again.

'We've discovered nothing, Djed,' he sighed, 'apart from small items from the days when you fought for the Divine One rather than against her. So, tell me, where do you hide your wealth? And the scarabs you carry? You must have a little hiding hole. Where do you think, Shufoy?'

Djed stared at the hideously disfigured dwarf, who stared unblinkingly back.

'I think we should kill him, master. He tried to kill you. Perhaps we should torture him, take him out to the Red Lands, bury him for a while beneath the hot sand, see how he likes to be cooked.'

Djed tried to swallow but he couldn't. Shufoy was tapping a sandalled foot on the wooden floor. He stared down at his feet and gave a crooked smile.

'Master, why does he come here?' Shufoy pointed at the wooden boards. 'I think what we seek lies just beneath us.'

175

KHENRIT: ancient Egyptian, 'prison'

CHAPTER 8

The Leopard Chamber at the heart of the imperial palace was a room of breathtaking beauty. Its walls, floor and ceiling were of a glowing ivory marble, adorned with leopards of various colours, red with black spots, gold with green spots, deep yellow with black spots, which crouched, slept, sprang, or prowled in a variety of poses; magnificent beasts painted by the best artists in Egypt. Amerotke always believed that if he half shut his eyes these great cats would surely come to life. The chamber had a great window at the far end overlooking the flowerbeds of the palace. The fragrance of the shrubs wafted through the chamber, mixing with that of the perfumes in the small pots placed in countless niches within the wall. The chamber had little furniture, but all the pieces were of highly polished acacia and sycamore, the edges, legs and arms inlaid with the purest ivory and silver. On either side of the door wild flowers, planted in pots of cobalt blue, sprouted from their beds of rich Canaan soil.

The doors to the great chamber were locked and barred so that Hatusu, Pharaoh of Egypt, King and Queen of the Two Lands, could swim in the rectangular Pool of Purity. Its water was the clearest blue, and on its surface floated the finest white lotus blossoms. The Queen turned fast as any dolphin, swimming just beneath the water, the languorous strokes belying her speed and skill. Amerotke took a deep breath and tried not to sigh in exasperation. At the far end of the pool, squatting on a cushion, Senenmut, Hatusu's lover and First Minister, watched his Queen's every movement. Again the Queen turned, kicking away from the wall at the edge of the pool, streaking fast through the water, her black hair floating out behind her. She reached the far end, grasped the gold-rimmed edge and pulled herself up. Wiping away the water with one hand, she pressed against the side of the pool and stared up at her Chief Judge.

'You look tired, my lord.' Hatusu's eyes did not share the smile on her lips. 'You have brought me news? I will be able to impale all those robbers on the cliffs above the Valley of the Kings?'

'I have brought you nothing but information, Divine One.'

Hatusu grasped the gold flail lying on the edge of the pool and made a cutting movement at Amerotke's ankles. The judge didn't flinch.

'My lady, if you do that again . . .'

Hatusu stared at him angrily, then, laughing softly, hoisted herself out of the pool and slipped her feet into gold-thonged sandals. As she walked round to where Senenmut was waiting with linen cloths to dry her, Amerotke turned his back and paced over to the window. He could tell by the stars, the coldness of the night, that it must be well past midnight. The Divine One was correct, he was tired. He had visited his wife and sons in their quarters but had been interrupted by Senenmut, who had said that the Divine One would see him immediately.

'You know it's discourteous to turn your back on the Divine One?'

Amerotke sighed and turned. Hatusu, clothed in diaphanous linen robes, was sitting cross-legged on a stool sharing a dish of sugared dates with Senenmut, who knelt at her feet busy filling three goblets. Hatusu beckoned with her fingers and threw a cushion on the floor beside her. Amerotke sat down, and a goblet was thrust into his hands.

'Are you not pleased to see me?' Hatusu, her hair still wet, leaned closer, shaking herself so that some of the water splattered Amerotke.

'My heart is glad and my soul sings,' Amerotke intoned the usual protocol of court, 'at the sight of your face.' He kept his voice flat and monotonous. 'Your radiance, Divine One, strengthens my limbs whilst the power of your smile—'

'Thank you,' Hatusu interrupted harshly. 'I understand what you are saying, Amerotke. You are tired, frustrated, frightened and you want to sleep. So tell me again, what happened?'

Amerotke described the murders at the Temple of Ma'at. How the guard who had killed the imprisoned Sebaus must have been bribed or threatened, a conclusion which was strengthened when that guard was murdered as well.

'So you've captured this Djed?' Hatusu declared. 'And is he dead?'

'No, he and his entire family have been taken to my house. Captain Asural is under strict orders. The woman and child are to be confined but protected. The prisoner is to be locked in my cellars and closely guarded, two in the cell with him and two outside. Asural is never to leave the house.'

Hatusu put down her wine cup.

'And he is definitely one of the Sebaus?'

'Oh yes,' Amerotke agreed. 'We dug beneath his garden pavilion and discovered a leather sack. It contained everything an assassin would need: the black garb, a dagger, and a pouch of scarabs displaying a kneeling man holding a bow.'

'And?' Senenmut asked.

'Two items provoked my curiosity.' Amerotke toasted the First Minister with his goblet. 'One was a pass allowing Djed into the Temple of Isis, a clay tablet bearing the seal of Paser.'

'He's one of the principal priests, Lord Impuki's assistant.'

'Djed claimed his father had been sent to the House of Twilight and that he had often visited him there; that was why he had been given the pass.'

'Do you believe him?'

'His father bore the same name as him, so he can be easily traced. Apparently he was a soldier and a mason, and therefore worked for the Divine House—'

'Of course,' Hatusu interrupted. 'And any member of an imperial regiment can present himself to the Temple of Isis and ask for healing free of cost.'

'Why did Djed keep the pass hidden?' Senenmut asked.

'Apparently his father died three seasons ago. What I suspect is that Djed used the pass to visit certain friends there, perhaps Mafdet.'

'What else did you find?'

'A map of the Temple of Isis. You can buy them in the temple squares, it shows you the main chapels and sanctuaries, but this one has been embellished. Again Djed refused to answer my questions, saying he used the map when he visited his father. He claims to know nothing about Lord Impuki or Paser and has never met Captain Mafdet.'

'Djed was a soldier?'

'Yes, he served with General Omendap, as did his cousin, and if we check the records, so did Captain Mafdet.'

'But the general is the Commander-in-Chief of Egypt's forces.'

'Djed said that the general always looked after old comrades. I asked if he also knew General Suten. He shook his head. He had once approached General Suten for help but Chief Scribe Menna had driven him away.'

'And the Khetra?' Senenmut asked.

'Oh yes, our Watchman by the gates.' Amerotke smiled. 'When I mentioned the name Djed looked terrified. He shook his head and refused to say any more. Shufoy threatened to torture his wife but the prisoner mumbled that he didn't care; if he didn't speak she would be tortured, and if he did she would certainly be killed.'

'And your conclusions?' Hatusu asked. Amerotke could tell by the way she moved her head that the Pharaoh Queen was not pleased at what was happening.

'Divine One, I don't know. Certain matters are becoming clearer. According to all the evidence, General Suten may have introduced that bag of horned vipers on to the roof terrace himself, a foolish attempt to confront his own fears. In his memoirs he virtually admits that he was considering such an act. Tomorrow morning the court reconvenes. Chief Scribe Menna will act as Heby's advocate and the case will be dismissed.'

'I don't think so.' Hatusu's voice was sharp. 'Only yesterday afternoon Lord Valu visited me. He brought me a new white lotus which he claimed would blossom during the night, though I've yet to see that. Now you know Lord Valu, a man who keeps his secrets as close as his shadow; all he would say was that he had interesting questions to ask. I was busy.' Hatusu shook her head. 'Perhaps I should have questioned him more closely.'

Amerotke hid his own disquiet. Lord Valu was the sharpest of prosecutors. Had he discovered new evidence, or was Amerotke simply betraying his own unspoken reservations about General Suten's death? He felt something was amiss yet couldn't explain it, he'd become so distracted about the events at the Temple of Ma'at.

'And Lord Impuki and the Temple of Isis?' Senenmut asked. 'There is no trace of those four hesets? Or why Captain Mafdet should be so barbarously murdered and his house burnt down?'

Amerotke, ignoring Hatusu's hiss of disapproval, shook his head. 'All I have discovered at the Temple of Isis,' he conceded, 'is that Lady Nethba's father died of natural causes and was treated most honourably. There is some connection between Mafdet and the Sebaus but I don't know what. The same is true of his death. He may have been killed for a private grievance, or the Sebaus, thinking he was about to betray them, took the law into their own hands.'

'And the tomb robbers?' Hatusu insisted.

'Pearls on a string, my lady. I admit I made a mistake.' Amerotke held Hatusu's gaze. 'We pulled up the plant but not the root. Those whom we prosecuted were simply the people who bought and sold, but the actual thefts were carried out by the Sebaus. I was wrong about these, they are not a gang from the slums. They are controlled by this individual who calls himself the Khetra. Djed told me little, but what I have learnt, what I guess at, is that most of these Sebaus are former soldiers. They leave the imperial ranks and fall on hard times. They are resourceful, vigorous men, used to danger as well as carrying out orders. I suspect they don't know each other but are told to gather at a certain place, at a certain hour and given instructions. They are well looked after and rewarded. They receive a lavish price for their work and are managed with a ruthless ferocity.'

'Where do they gather?'

Amerotke shook his head. 'I don't know, I don't think we ever will. This Khetra issues the orders. We must capture him, or her. Once the Khetra is dead, the robberies will cease.' He put his cup down. 'The principles on which the Sebaus work are simple and clear. Once you have been involved in a robbery, or the murder of some official, be it a temple guard or a judge, you are part of the group, there is no escape. And why should you want to leave? After years of hardship you are suddenly offered a life of riches and ease.'

'But who could have approached these soldiers?' Hatusu asked. 'A general like Omendap or Suten?'

'Possibly,' Amerotke conceded. 'Or a high priest like Lord

Impuki. Many former soldiers visit the Temple of Isis; Captain Mafdet had served in the imperial regiments. But why stop there?' Amerotke picked up his cup. 'Lord Valu is the Chief Prosecutor of Thebes; like me or Lord Senenmut, he can demand to see the army muster roles, discover where former soldiers live.'

'And there's the royal tombs,' Hatusu reminded them.

'Yes,' Amerotke sighed. 'The royal tombs. Most of their entrances are hidden. Very few people know their approaches or what traps or treasures lie inside. Such records can be found in the House of Books, either here—'

'Or in the Temple of Isis.' Senenmut finished his sentence. 'Priests attend royal funerals, they are often engaged in the preparation of tombs and funeral gifts. They accompany the corpse to its last resting place. I'm sure there are priests and librarians in many of our temples who know the secrets of the Houses of a Million Years.'

'And the seals?' Hatusu asked, biting her lip to control her anger. 'The imperial seal used to send these treasures beyond our borders under the very noses of our customs guards and patrols?'

Amerotke shrugged. 'I hold such a seal, as do Lord Impuki, General Omendap, Lord Valu, Lord Senenmut—'

Hatusu, unable to control her anger, sprang to her feet, snapping her fingers for Senenmut to follow. She turned at the door, whispered to him, then came striding back, her face flushed with fury. She leant down and grasped Amerotke by the front of his robe.

'I am Pharaoh Queen,' she whispered, her breath hot on his face. 'My first task is to defend the tombs of those who went before me. To make the People of the Nine Bows shift like dust under my sandal. How can I do that, judge, if the goods of my father's and grandfather's tombs are being sold by pedlars in a marketplace in Canaan or given to a Hittite prince as a gift?' She pressed her nails against Amerotke's chest. The judge removed her hand and squeezed it tightly.

'Divine One, is there anything else?' Amerotke paused. 'These tomb robbers, you regard them as blood enemies . . .'

Amerotke caught it, just a glance between Hatusu and Senenmut, worried and anxious.

'Divine One?' he repeated.

Hatusu freed her hand.

'Find the Khetra,' she hissed, 'and I will personally watch him burn.'

Amerotke arrived back at his own house. As soon as entered the main gate he knew something dreadful had happened. Asural was waiting for him in the garden, while other guards, holding cresset torches, grouped on the steps before the porticoed entrance. From somewhere inside the house came the low, heart-rending wail of a woman. Asural didn't speak but, shaking his head and gesturing for Amerotke to follow, led him around the house and down the steps into the small cavern which served as a wine cellar. The architect had used this natural cavern to create small four chambers. Djed had been placed in the nearest. Asural opened the door and, going inside with his torch, indicated Djed's corpse. One glance was enough. The prisoner had been manacled at both wrist and ankle and a chain had been run through these and fixed to a ring on the wall. Somehow Djed had created some slack in the master chain, wrapped this round his throat and, by pulling against it, strangled himself to death. He now slouched, still held by the chains, his face contorted in the agony of his death throes.

'Where are the guards?' Amerotke asked. 'I asked you to put two guards with him.'

'We were hardly given a chance,' Asural confessed. 'The prisoner was quiet enough when we manacled him. He claimed to be hungry and thirsty, he wanted to relieve himself. I withdrew the guards preparing for the night watch. The door was left open, but it happened so fast.'

Amerotke, crouching down, moved the dead man's head.

Djed hadn't choked; the slackness of his neck showed it was broken, a powerful witness to the intense fury the prisoner must have felt. He tapped the man gently on the face and tried to close the staring eyes, then moved the corpse away and got to his feet.

'When I was bringing him here,' Asural confessed, 'he said he was already in the Valley of Shadows, that his life was over. He was more worried about his wife and child, what would happen to them. He kept blaming his own stupidity . . .'

Amerotke stared at the dead prisoner. He realised the truth of Pharaoh's words. To capture a Sebaus meant nothing, it would lead him nowhere. He had to catch the Khetra to put an end to all this terror.

'And so, my lord judge, I have sat and listened patiently to all that has been said, but . . .' Valu sniffed and moved on his specially quilted cushion. The Eyes and Ears of Pharaoh was in a most mischievous mood; now he paused for effect, one finely manicured hand slightly raised so all could admire the beautifully painted nails as well as the dazzling rings on his fingers. Valu was staring at the sheets of papyrus on the small polished table before him, head slightly down, as if he'd lost his place. Amerotke knew better. Valu was like a cobra studying its prey before striking fast. He'd sat moon-faced and pursed-lipped as Chief Scribe Menna, looking rather ridiculous in his heavy square-cut wig, had presented Heby's defence. The Chief Scribe, Amerotke reflected, was a man of very little judgement and even less wit, ponderous and heavy. He had sat between Heby and the Lady Lupherna like some rather bewildered mastiff before Amerotke had invited him to act as advocate. The man was now sweat-soaked, the black kohl round his eyes run like ribbons down his cheeks, whilst his heavy wig kept slipping much to the amusement of onlookers. Matters were not helped by Menna's rather strident voice; even Prenhoe, sitting with the scribes, had lowered his head, shoulders shaking.

Nevertheless Menna, with his harsh voice and theatrical gestures, had presented a very clever, arguable defence. He described how the sack had been found, how it reeked of snake scale, how it had been tied to the terrace roof post, hidden behind the drapes of General Suten's bed. He had presented the facts forcefully, quoting from General Suten's memoirs, telling the court how the old soldier had probably decided to confront his own terrors. After this, Lord Impuki and Paser had been called and gave evidence in sharp, pithy sentences. They described how General Suten had visited them at the Temple of Isis, how he had taken the powders to ease his fears as well as the cramps in his stomach.

'Had he discussed his nightmares?' Menna asked.

'Oh yes,' Impuki replied. 'It is well known that one way to curb unknown fears is to confront them. Any soldier bloodied in battle will confirm that.'

Impuki and Paser now sat in the place reserved for witnesses. Amerotke glanced quickly at them. He vowed to have words with them later when this matter was over. But now it was Valu's turn. He still knelt on his cushion, hand slightly raised, then he moved quickly, pushing back the sleeves of his robe, bracelets jangling, rings flashing. He was smiling secretly, a clear sign that a trap was going to be sprung. At the back of the court Shufoy was jumping up and down like a frog, pointing at someone, but the crowds thronging there made it impossible to distinguish anyone in particular.

'My lord prosecutor,' Amerotke sighed, 'we wait with bated breath.'

'My lord.' Valu's face was stricken with sorrow, but his eyes were positively dancing. 'What a story,' he began. 'What a heart-wrenching tale!' The smile faded. 'What a basket of lies!'

'Never!' Heby would have jumped to his feet, but Menna, face all concerned, seized him by the arm.

'Look.' Valu half turned towards Heby, gesturing with his fingers. 'We have these snakes crawling all about, in the sack, out of the sack. But where did they come from? Did General Suten go out and collect them himself? A man with a mortal fear of snakes? Did he drive his chariot out across the desert and whistle for them to come?' Valu waited for the laughter to subside. 'Or did he go down to a market stall? Two dozen snakes, please, why not throw in a few scorpions as well!' Valu's mimicry of a market trader's nasal twang provoked further laughter.

'I appreciate your jokes.'

'No, my lord judge, not jokes but very honest questions. When did General Suten collect these snakes? Where did he keep them?'

The silence of the court was oppressive. Valu was no longer smiling, but tapping one immaculate nail on the table before him. Amerotke gazed to his left. Two snow-white doves were resting close together on the windowsill. Were they the souls of two dead lovers? The birds fluttered up in alarm as Valu clapped his hands before cupping his ear.

'I can hear no reply. The court receives no answer, so I shall speak the truth.' Valu bawled over his shoulder. 'Bring forward the witness Hefau.'

Amerotke glanced up in surprise. Hefau was the name given to the Great Snake or Worm of the Am-Duat, the Underworld. The man who scampered forward to take the oath on the witness cushion did not look so dreadful, with his scrawny hair and gaunt face burnt black by the sun. He wore a striped sand-dweller's robe and clutched a satchel together with a club, its end carved in the shape of the swollen throat of the Uraeus of Egypt.

'Who are you, Hefau?' Amerotke asked, once the witness had taken the oath.

189

'The scourge of snakes. I kill or collect them. I peel their scaly skin and sell it to merchants.'

'And you are here because . . . ?'

'Of him!' Hefau pointed down to Heby. 'I met him in a wine booth near the statue of Osiris, on the corner of the Street of Caskets in the Necropolis. He asked me to collect at least two dozen horned vipers, puffed and swollen. I asked him why.'

Hefau paused as Heby sprang to his feet, yelling his denials. Only when the court ushers grasped his arms did the valet sink back on to the cushions.

'Continue,' Amerotke ordered.

'He didn't give me his name but he offered a good price. He told me to bring the snakes to a palm grove just past the seventh mooring place on the Nile.'

'Very near General Suten's mansion,' Valu interjected.

'When was this?' Amerotke snapped. He was now angry with himself, as well as the dreadful events which had distracted him from this case. Valu, of course, had seen the weakness. Where had General Suten obtained those snakes? 'Well?' He glared at Hefau.

'The night before General Suten died. I have witnesses,' Hefau gabbled on. 'My brother . . .'

'You never asked Heby why he wanted the snakes?'

'I didn't know his name then and, of course, I do not ask questions. I went out into the Red Lands, trapped the snakes and met him as agreed. Only later, when Lord Valu's heralds were proclaiming General Suten's death in the market squares of Thebes, did I suspect what had happened. I read the proclamations posted near the fountains and—'

'He came to me,' Valu purred.

Amerotke held up the flail and rod for silence. He lowered them as Menna raised his hand to speak.

'My lord,' the Chief Scribe was clearly agitated, torn between fear and anger, 'does this man accuse me and the lady Lupherna as well?'

'No,' Hefau shouted. He pointed down to Heby, kneeling with his head in his hands. 'He made it very clear to me he didn't want anyone else to know.'

'My lord Valu.' Amerotke turned to the prosecutor. 'Is your witness being paid?'

'My lord.' Valu spread his hands. 'He will receive his expenses and, if his story is proved true, the reward for anyone who assists in the capture of an assassin.'

Valu sat back on his heels. The only sound in the court was Heby's moaning. Menna was shaking his head, and Amerotke noticed how he and Lady Lupherna had moved away from the accused. He stared down at Hefau. The snake man seemed calm and poised, and his story had made sense.

'Heby!' Amerotke pointed down at the prisoner. 'Heby, lift your head. Are you going to say that you bought those snakes on behalf of General Suten? I must warn you, if you say yes, Lord Valu will ask you why you never mentioned this before.'

'My lord,' Menna raised both hands in supplication, 'we must have more time to answer such questions.'

'True,' Amerotke declared. 'This is my verdict. Heby, you will return to house arrest, under pain of death if you leave. Lord Valu, your witness,' he smiled, 'as well as any other witnesses, will be kept comfortably but securely at the barracks of the Medjay.'

Amerotke stood up, wincing at the cramp in the back of his legs. He bowed towards Lord Valu and swept from the court. Once inside his private chamber, he took off his robe, the pectoral, the rings and bracelets, and placed them gently on the table. The door opened, and from the gust of perfume he knew it was Valu.

'Very clever, my lord.' Amerotke turned. 'Are you sure your witness is not lying?'

'He didn't mislead me.' Valu, uninvited, sat down on a stool. 'He's a former soldier himself; he served in the auxiliaries. He's skilled with the slingshot. He uses leather sacks. Ah,' Valu lifted a finger, 'and before you ask, I also showed him the piece of cord and how it was tied. He could replicate the knot.'

'Oh, I'm sure you did.' Amerotke rubbed his face. 'You want Heby impaled on a stake, don't you? You want to prove to the Divine One that her old general was murdered and you've unmasked the assassin responsible.'

Valu got to his feet and Amerotke regretted his sharp remarks.

'I'm sorry, my lord,' Amerotke stretched out his hand, which Valu clasped, 'but I thought the case had been solved, yet the question you asked was never answered.' He smiled thinly. 'Where did General Suten collect those snakes?'

'There's something else, isn't there?'

'What do you mean?' Amerotke asked. Valu drew closer. His perfume reminded Amerotke of wild flowers, and the judge recalled stories of how the Eyes and Ears of Pharaoh often liked to dress in a woman's wig and the gorgeous robes of a courtesan.

'I've heard about the attacks,' Valu whispered. 'The business at the Temple of Isis.' He stumbled over the word to avoid lisping it. 'Oh yes, if you watch me, Lord Amerotke, I certainly watch you. You know there's something wrong about General Suten's death. Something you've missed. I think Heby is an assassin. He was the dead general's valet. He took that sack up on to the roof terrace before the evening meal and tied it to the post, hidden behind the bed drapes. Once dinner was over and the terrace cleared, General Suten took his drugged wine and fell asleep. Heby crept up, pulled the sack over and emptied the contents out across his sleeping master. I watched him come into court this morning. Menna is a waddling fool, Lady Lupherna very much the noblewoman and Heby lusts after her. I can tell that.'

Amerotke turned away and stared at a small statuette of Ma'at.

'But why didn't he tell us that to begin with?' he asked. 'Why not say General Suten had told him to buy the snakes and tie them secretly to that rail? It would be difficult to disprove such a story. He must have known that Hefau would recognise him. It would have been so easy,' Amerotke continued, 'to give such a story.'

'That's why I think he is guilty. Heby is consumed with lust for his master's wife. Like all assassins he is arrogant. He thought that eventually it could be proved that General Suten had taken that sack full of snakes up himself. If he could prove that he never went on to the roof, and if he could prove, as Menna did, that General Suten was thinking of confronting his own fears, then it was only a matter of time before the court reached the same conclusion.' Valu jabbed the judge with a finger. 'To answer your question bluntly: no one would dare say they knew beforehand that General Suten had bought a sack of snakes, it would have caused consternation. How could they know such a thing if the general was acting secretly? If they did know, surely they would have intervened and asked him why?'

'I agree,' Amerotke conceded. 'Heby made one mistake, Hefau, and for that he will pay.'

Lord Valu bowed and left. He had hardly gone when there was another knock on the door and Lord Impuki entered. The High Priest was not so friendly as before.

'Your dwarf Shufoy said you wanted to see me?'

'Yes, I do, there are certain questions—'

'I must return to the temple.' The High Priest clutched the folds of his robe, half turning to Paser, who was standing solemn-faced behind him. 'We have urgent business, but if you visit us there . . .'

'Then you must go,' Amerotke agreed. 'But I should have words with you. I need your answers to certain questions.'

The High Priest shrugged and turned away as Shufoy led General Omendap in. Amerotke slammed the door shut and gestured at his guest to sit.

'General Omendap, I appreciate you are busy—'

'What do you want, Amerotke?' The general's round face looked rather haggard, his deep-set eyes red-rimmed, and the usually smooth chin betrayed an untidy stubble. 'I have been out on manoeuvres in the Red Lands; all entrances to the Valley of the Kings and Queens are now guarded. The Divine One is insistent that there should be no more robberies.'

'Do you know who the Sebaus are?'

'I've heard the rumours.'

'Do you also know they are former soldiers?'

'You have proof?' Omendap retorted. 'I see what path you are following. Former soldiers are often looked after by their officers.'

'I have enough proof for that,' Amerotke answered quietly. 'You and your staff look after former comrades, veterans who have served the Divine One well.'

'You know the times and seasons, Amerotke. I am Chief Scribe of the Army. I am pestered day and night for favours. Secure this man a post, a pension for another, a gift for a third.'

'Would former soldiers know about the tombs in the Valley of the Kings? Their secret entrances? The treasures they contain?'

'Perhaps.' Omendap wiped the sweat from his brow and plucked at a loose thread on his gown. 'I have such knowledge, as do some of my officers. Soldiers guard the funeral processions, members of the Sacred Band accompany the corpses of the Great Ones to their last resting places. But such information is also known to priests, judges and even Lord Valu. After all, prisoners are used to dig the tunnels and carve the entrances.'

'After which they are silenced,' Amerotke replied grimly.

'Do you have a list of the soldiers and veterans you've helped?'

Omendap shook his head. 'It would take a year and a day to collect. I'll answer your question boldly. Let me give you an example. Mafdet, the captain of the guard at the Temple of Isis, was a good soldier. He served with me and others, so I secured him the post there. However, I do that in cities up and down the Nile, and sometimes I pass such requests to my brother officers. You are talking about hundreds of petitions.'

Amerotke poured himself a beaker of water. He offered one to Omendap, but the general shook his head.

'What is it you really want, Amerotke?' Omendap gestured to the door. 'You have one visitor after another. Why me?'

Amerotke stared at the wall behind the general's head. 'I slept little last night,' he confessed. 'So my temper is short and my speech blunt. Once again I went through the records about these robberies. I recalled a reference being made by the dead woman Sithia to a man called the Shardana; he was a former soldier, definitely a Sebaus, a tomb robber, though he was indicted and punished for another crime. He killed a man and was sentenced to one of the prison oases. Now, if he was still alive, I would have him brought back, but according to Lord Valu, the prison oasis was attacked by Libyans, its guards and all those held there massacred.'

'Yes, yes, I heard about that.' Omendap rubbed his brow. 'It was strange.'

'Why?' Amerotke snapped.

'Prison oases contain nothing, some weapons, a few supplies. You know how it is, Amerotke, the prisoners can move about but they are kept chained. Their only food and water is in that oasis. If they try to escape the desert will kill them; that is if they are not captured or tortured by Libyans, sand-dwellers or desert wanderers.'

'You are not aware why that prison oasis was attacked?'

'I've told you, no idea whatsoever.'

Amerotke ran a thumb round his lips. 'Do we have any high-ranking Libyans in our prison camps?'

'I don't know.' Omendap closed his eyes. 'Most prisoners of war are used as slaves in the quarries; they barely survive a year. Ah yes.' He held up a hand. 'There is one, we never learnt his name, we simply called him the Libyan. He was a chieftain, we caught him raiding villages along the Nile. Usually he would have been killed immediately.'

'Why wasn't he sent to the quarries?'

'Because he was one of their high-ranking noblemen. He would only have started trouble; it wouldn't be the first time a gang of slaves broke out. We also held him as a hostage. One day they might capture one of our officers, and we would trade him, man for man. He is kept in the Oasis of Bitter Grass, about sixty miles into the eastern Red Lands.'

'I've heard of it.' Amerotke got to his feet. 'General Omendap, I want a favour, your best chariot squadron. Twenty chariots in all, each chariot carrying two men. I want to visit this Libyan.'

'Why?' Omendap got to his feet too.

'I want to ask him a question. Why did his people attack a prison oasis when there was little hope of gain?'

'He might be dead.' Omendap scratched his chin. 'No, no, on second thoughts, he'll be alive. The Keeper there would have told me.' He clasped Amerotke's hands. 'The squadron will be ready within the hour.'

Later that day, just as the heat of the sun began to cool, the Ptah squadron of the Horus regiment left its barracks on the outskirts of eastern Thebes, following the rutted trackway into the desert lands. Omendap had chosen well. The Ptah squadron was the fastest and most experienced; their horses, bloodied in war, were arrogant and fast, with their arched necks, flared nostrils and laid-back ears. The carriages they pulled, with their curved wooden sides and thin rails, were sheathed in gold and electrum. They were built of imported elm, birch and tamarisk, and the six spoked wheels placed at the back gave them that lightness and mobility which was the terror of Egypt's enemies. A glorious sight, the harness of the horses gleaming, the plumes and streamers displaying the black and gold colours of their regiment. Amerotke and Shufoy had been given their own chariot, the horses of which had the blue and gold plumes of the Great House dancing between their ears and tassels of the same colour tied to the leather straps.

At first the squadron moved through a haze of dust, across a pebble-strewn plain. As the sun began to sink and the cool wind soothed the sweat, the chariots began to fan out, moving in a swift line across the desert, eager to take advantage of the freshness before the darkness came rushing in. Each chariot was armed with a javelin pouch as well as quivers for arrows. Shufoy, standing beside Amerotke, gripped the reinforced bow with all his strength. The officers of the squadron were all veterans, men used to desert warfare and the rapid change in the hideous weather conditions which prevailed in the Red Lands. They drank sparsely from their leather water carriers and filled their stomachs from the bags of hard rations slung on hooks just inside the chariots.

To begin with Amerotke found it strange to be away from the noise and clamour of the city, nothing but the blue, red-shot sky above him and the barren plain around. He showed Shufoy how to wear a mask across his face soaked in water and bitter lemon to provide sure protection against the whirling dust and stinging insects. Now and again they would pause at a water hole to rest their horses and seek some shade under a cluster of dusty palms. The soldiers asked no questions; their standard-bearer had been told to escort this important personage and that was what they would do. When Shufoy approached to draw them into conversation they just smiled, shook their heads and turned away.

Their journey continued. They were not in the desert proper but on that rocky, sandy plain which divided the Nile from the whirling sands of the Red Lands. At first it felt as though the wilderness around them was deserted, but as the sun set and the blackness fell like a blanket, it became alive with the roar of the night prowlers. The standard-bearer insisted on travelling as far and as fast as they could, but as the stars came out above them, he called a halt at the entrance to a rocky gully. Amerotke helped the squadron set up a night camp. They arranged the chariots in a protective ring, with the horses in the centre, well away from sudden attack by lion or hyaena. Camp fires were lit, guards posted, and the huntsmen in the squadron managed to bring back some fresh meat. They were full of stories about a pride of lions lurking very close by, roused by the smell of cooking and the sweet odour of horse flesh. The meat was shared out along with the watered wine.

After the meal, Amerotke lay down next to Shufoy, a leather pannier serving as headrest, his war cloak as a blanket. He slept fitfully, aroused now and again by the call of the guards or the heart-shrilling roar of a night creature. Shufoy, however, slept like a babe; Amerotke almost had to kick him awake when the camp was roused and their journey continued.

The heat turned pitiless, the sun becoming a merciless tormentor, the dust whirling like a devil to sting their eyes and cake their lips. As the sun climbed to its midday strength, the squadron reached an oasis, where the standard-bearer agreed with Amerotke that they would wait until the cool of the afternoon. When they resumed their journey, Amerotke felt as if he was a sleepwalker. Shufoy had ceased his chattering and become nothing more than a small dust-covered figure standing beside him clutching the chariot rail. Amerotke tried to recall his own training, concentrating on the horses, gently coaxing them with the reins, keeping a safe distance behind the chariot in front, trying to ignore the heat and the stinging dust. He was aware of the sun beginning to set; he no longer felt as if he was being buffeted and pushed by some unseen club. He took the mask from his face, eager to catch the cool breeze, and rewarded himself and Shufoy with a drink from the pannikin and mouthfuls of dates. The sun began to slip in a fiery glow, once again changing the colour of the desert so that it was no longer a place of blinding harsh light, but rather sinister, with dark rocks and racing shadows.

'I'd never be a charioteer,' Shufoy moaned. 'I'm too small, and the wind . . .' He clutched his face. 'My scar throbs worse than a toothache.'

Amerotke tried to distract him by pointing up to the vultures circling high in the breezes above them.

'It can't be far now, Shufoy. Vultures always gather near an oasis; that's where they find their prey.'

A short while later, just as the darkness was closing in, Amerotke heard a shout and the leading chariot came racing back.

'My lord.' The standard-bearer wiped his face and pointed back the way he had come. 'We are almost there. It means cool water and fresh food.'

The chariot column picked up speed, the horses smelling the water, eager to reach their destination. The oasis came into sight, protected by a high wooden stockade. Amerotke glimpsed its guards under the makeshift shades they had built. The narrow entrance gate was open and a soldier, naked except for a leather kilt, a white cloth over his head, came out to greet them. A short discussion took place, the gate was thrown open again and they entered the Oasis of Bitter Grass.

Amerotke had visited such a stockade before and found this no different. A wooden palisade surrounded the gloomy oasis, with its springs, palm trees and thick vegetation. Both guards and prisoners lived in makeshift bothies. There was a small paddock for horses and places where meat could be cooked and bread baked. The oasis was clean enough, refuse being taken out and dumped in the desert sand. Nevertheless there was no hiding the grim conditions under which both prisoners and guards lived. The soldiers who served there were mercenaries who would do a three-month duty before returning to the garrisons outside Thebes. The prisoners themselves looked a pathetic group in their ragged garb, manacled to each other at both wrist and ankle. It was hard to distinguish one from another except for the clay tablets hung from cords around their necks which gave their name and number.

At first Amerotke rested and refreshed himself at the water hole. Despite the oasis' name, the water was clear and sweet. He made sure Shufoy was comfortable before going over to a tent awning just inside the prison gate where the warder and the prisoner known as the Libyan were waiting for him.

'You've travelled all this way to see me?' The Libyan was tall, with a long face, narrowed eyes and high cheekbones. He had his hair gathered in a clump behind him, his groin covered by a simple leather skirt. Amerotke noticed blue and red tattoos on the man's muscular torso.

'So you are a warrior?' Amerotke spoke the lingua franca of the barracks. 'You have killed men in battle?'

'I am a warrior and a chief,' the Libyan replied in a high, clipped voice. His mouth had a bitter twist, his eyes a sly look. 'I have killed Egyptians in battle. Why are you here, what is your name?'

'My name does not concern you. I have come to ask you a question. Why should your people storm a place like this and kill all the prisoners and their keepers?'

'They would never do that.'

'But they did. Look around you, Libyan. Apart from our

chariots and horses, and perhaps our weapons, what value is there here?'

'Are you a judge? I heard one of the guards say you are a judge. Tell me what is happening in Thebes.'

Amerotke was about to refuse, but the Libyan was keen; he could probably sense that this visit was to his profit. He leaned over, lifting his chained hands as if in prayer.

'Speak with true voice, judge, tell me what's happening in Thebes.'

Amerotke described the tomb robberies, the death of General Suten. At the mention of his name the Libyan half smiled, his eyes glancing away.

'We should have killed him,' he whispered, 'or taken him prisoner. Well, judge, what else has happened?'

Amerotke described the slaying of Captain Mafdet and the disappearance of the four hesets. When he had finished, the Libyan asked for a cup of wine. Amerotke agreed, and the Libyan raised the coarse beaker in toast.

'Tell me, judge,' the prisoner asked, 'if you were a Libyan warrior, what would you need out in the desert?'

'Gold and silver to buy weapons and food.'

'We have enough of that ourselves. What we don't have we can always take.' He laughed at Amerotke's puzzlement. 'If I help you, judge, what will happen to me?'

'If you really help me, those chains will be released. You will be given fresh clothing and taken back across the Nile. You will be provided with food and water, a bow, a dagger and a quiver of arrows. You will be free to rejoin your people.'

The smiled faded from the Libyan's face, and he pointed to the chain around Amerotke's neck bearing the sign of truth.

'Put your hand on that and swear.'

Amerotke did so. The Libyan finished the wine and asked for more, smacking his lips appreciatively.

'The temple girls,' he began, 'the hesets, they are virgins of good family? Soft-skinned and beautiful?'

'If the Libyans want women, they raid the villages.'

'What raids?' the Libyan retorted. 'How successful are we? What casualties do we take? A great deal of fighting for what? Some old woman left behind or a peasant girl too stupid to hide?' In a clatter of chains he tapped the side of his face. 'Think, judge: the Libyan tribes wander the desert, women are a scarcity, marriages are dominated by blood ties.' He grinned with sharp pointed teeth at Amerotke's surprise. 'What a prize, eh, for a chief to attack a place like this, kill everyone, take some paltry plunder but receive in reward four of Egypt's finest women! Girls chosen for their beauty and grace. If you think I'm lying, ask yourself this question. How much would an Egyptian merchant pay for one girl?'

'A veritable fortune, but—'

'But,' the Libyan finished the sentence, 'how can such a prize be hidden? What dire punishment awaits you if captured? Your girls are gone, judge, out in the desert. They were the price of that attack.'

SHENSTET: ancient Egyptian, 'wickedness'

CHAPTER 9

Amerotke sat in the audience hall of Lord Impuki's mansion in the Temple of Isis. He stared out of the open window, once again quietly rejoicing at having returned from the gruelling heat of the Red Lands. The squadron had left the Oasis of Bitter Grass long before dawn. Their journey had been exhausting but unremarkable, and they had reached the Sphinx Gate of northern Thebes just before dawn the following day. Amerotke had spent the rest of the day sleeping and relaxing, once again going through the business of the court. He had already dispatched a pardon for the Libyan, whilst Djed's wife had been allowed to take her husband's corpse back to her own home. There was nothing Amerotke could do for her except express his sorrow and whisper a prayer to the spirits of the Underworld.

Shufoy had gone to the palace and had returned with more guards as well as loving messages from the Lady Norfret and the two boys. They were all well but missing him. Amerotke was pleased: his family were now in sanctuary whilst his mansion had been turned into a veritable fortress, with guards in the house and gardens as well as along the avenue leading to it. He'd tried to calm his own anxieties, taking down the scroll of Ma'at and meditating on its sayings: *Speak with true voice and the gods will respond*; *Let truth flower in the heart and justice will flourish.* However, he found such sayings banal, of little comfort, so he returned to his researches. He had scrupulously examined the documentation and tried to recall everything he had seen and heard. He drew some comfort that the wall of lies which confronted him, with their sinister mystery, was beginning to crumble. Ideas, suspicions, theories and reservations were springing green and fresh in his troubled mind.

Towards the end of the day, just after sunset, Amerotke decided to visit the Temple of Isis and question the three individuals who now squatted before him. Lord Impuki had been welcoming enough, inviting him to join them in a brief meal; the wine from Avaris was red and rich, the spiced quail and goose freshened by crisp lettuce strewn with herbs. Amerotke had to close his eyes; with its cool breezes and heavy fragrance this was a different world from the desert. He opened his eyes, sipped his wine and smiled across at Lord Impuki.

'You wonder why I'm here?'

'Of course,' Lady Thena replied for her husband. 'Your face is tired, burnt by the sun, but your eyes are fresh.' She glanced sideways at her husband whilst stretching out to touch Paser's wrist, a furtive gesture. Amerotke wondered if she was trying to warn her two companions.

'Mafdet was a criminal,' Amerotke began. He felt the linen curtains behind him move in the breeze, and out of the corner of his eye he glimpsed a mural of an antelope evading a hunting dog by jumping a bush. 'Is that what I am?' He pointed at the painting. 'A hunter out for the truth?'

'You have already spoken the truth,' Impuki said. 'Mafdet was a criminal.'

'He was more than that.' Shufoy, who had been eating, now spoke up, his mouth full of meat. The High Priest lowered his cup.

'I've come from the Red Lands,' Amerotke explained, 'where I questioned a Libyan prisoner. The four temple girls who disappeared were probably kidnapped by Mafdet, drugged and handed over to the assassins who call themselves the Sebaus. The girls were taken out to the Red Lands and given as a bribe to a Libyan war chief. In return for this, the Libyans raided a prison oasis and killed a man who the Sebaus thought might betray them.'

All three gazed back in shocked horror. Lady Thena's fingers went to her lips; her eyes had a glazed look. Paser could only stare in astonishment.

'This cannot be true!' Lord Impuki lifted his hands.

'It is true,' Amerotke insisted. 'If I gave the date of the raid by the Libyans on the oasis, you would find it took place during the same period of time the four girls were abducted. One girl would be handed over as surety, the other three as the rest of the reward. It could easily be done. Mafdet was a soldier. He could flatter these girls, meet them in some lonely part of the temple and give them a drugged drink, or force them to take it. This could happen at any time, late in the afternoon or early evening. The girls fell into a deep sleep. The Sebaus came at night over the walls; they had maps of this temple and certainly would have sent messengers in. Once away from the temple,' Amerotke shrugged, 'who could stop them?'

'Those poor girls.'

'It's a common enough practice,' Paser agreed. 'Even in Egypt women are kidnapped for the brothels or houses of pleasure. I know something of the Libyans, the way their clans are organised; if they are short of women, a temple virgin would be considered more precious than gold.'

'But how would Mafdet choose his victims?' Impuki asked.

'I met the temple girls,' Amerotke smiled, 'and I've met young women of similar status. Their heads are full of romantic dreams. Mafdet would be like a lion that has chosen its prey; he would take her away from the rest, then strike.'

'But someone would have to come into this temple. Arrangements would have to be made about where and when,' Paser pointed out.

'Do you know a former soldier called Djed?' Amerotke's question was greeted with blank surprise. 'He used to visit his father here in the House of Twilight.'

'We could check the records,' Impuki murmured, still not recovered from the shock. 'As you know, Lord Amerotke, many veterans come here either for healing or just to die. I never saw Mafdet meet anybody.'

'So now we come to Mafdet's murder,' Amerotke continued. 'There are two possibilities: that he was murdered by the Sebaus because he betrayed them, threatened to, or even tried blackmail. But that wouldn't make sense; to betray his masters would be to betray himself, which would mean hideous execution.'

'And the second possibility?' Lady Thena asked.

'That Mafdet was murdered by someone else, as an act of revenge, a punishment for his hideous crimes. But if that's the case, why did the Sebaus come here to burn his house?'

'What makes you think.' Lady Thena asked, 'that Mafdet drugged those girls before abducting them?'

'Didn't you tell me certain powders had been taken, the juice of the poppy?'

'So it was Mafdet!'

'Yes, Lady Thena.'

'Let us return to Mafdet's murder.' Paser spoke briskly. He paused, cleaning his teeth with his tongue. 'If he was murdered as an act of revenge for abducting those temple girls, his assassin must have discovered his crime and decided to carry out sentence. But if that was someone in the temple, surely they would have discovered the crime long before the fourth girl disappeared? And even if they discovered it afterwards, why not just report Mafdet to the authorities? Why take judgement into their own hands?'

Amerotke gazed at this intelligent young priest's face and nodded in agreement.

'I can see why you have been promoted high in the temple hierarchy, Lord Paser. I hadn't thought of that. When I told you the news about the fate of those four girls you were shocked, as any right-minded person would be. What you are saying is that Mafdet was executed for other reasons, which in turn takes me back to the first possibility, that his death was the work of the Sebaus.'

'A good conclusion,' Lord Impuki observed. 'From what I gather, these Sebaus are ruthless; they used Mafdet and decided to dispose of him. A dead man cannot speak, be it lies or the truth.'

Amerotke was forced to agree. He finished his wine and rose to his feet, bowing towards his hosts.

'There are other matters,' he declared. 'I have my guards outside, but I would like to stay in the temple and speak with you again tomorrow.'

Lord Impuki graciously offered the guest house and Amerotke accepted.

Shufoy, still filling his mouth with spiced meat, got grudgingly to his feet. A servant led them out across the silent perfumed gardens to the guest house. Amerotke's guards followed, their officer explaining that they would stay outside with men at every window and door. Amerotke thanked him and was about to go in when he heard his name called. Paser came hastening through the darkness, a servant hurrying beside him carrying a torch.

'My lord, the business of the court, General Suten? Is that manservant guilty?'

'Why do you ask?'

'Oh, it's just that we know him. He and Chief Scribe Menna often accompanied General Suten to the temple when he came for treatment or visited our library.'

'That is why I want to stay here.' Amerotke smiled. 'Tomorrow morning I wish to visit your House of Books. I want to check the records and see what manuscripts General Suten demanded. You have records for the Valley of the Kings?'

'A few,' Paser agreed.

'Then I would be grateful if you had them ready. Goodnight.' The judge stretched out his hand. Paser grasped it, and Amerotke, smiling to himself, opened the door and went up to his chamber.

'You seem very pleased.' Shufoy squatted on the floor examining a figurine of the household god Bes. He gazed across at his master, who had taken off his sandals and lay on the bed staring up at the cedarwood ceiling. 'I know you are pleased,' Shufoy continued, 'you are trying to hide a smile. You certainly made those people jump.'

'I didn't mean to make them jump,' Amerotke replied. 'Lord Impuki and the others are good people, their hearts are pure and they try to speak with true voice, but they are hiding something.'

'What?' Shufoy asked.

Amerotke sighed and pulled himself up. 'Mafdet was a sinner and a criminal. I would wager my life that he was a member of the Sebaus and abducted those four girls; he stole the powders and drugged them. So why should the Sebaus murder him so barbarously and burn his house? At the same time, as Paser ingeniously explained, if he was murdered as an act of revenge for the abduction for those girls, why would someone do that? They would simply have had to report him to the Divine House, produce the evidence, allow Lord Valu and his interrogators loose on him and Mafdet would have died screaming on a stake.'

'So he *was* killed for another reason?'

'Precisely, my little friend. Mafdet was guilty of another crime which we haven't discovered.'

'So why did the Sebaus return to burn his house?'

'Do you remember Djed? And his secret treasure trove?'

'Ah, of course.' Shufoy got to his feet, dancing with excitement. 'The Sebaus returned to destroy any evidence, anything Mafdet might have hidden away. Tell me, Master, could the Sebaus be controlled by the Temple of Isis?'

'Possibly; many former soldiers come here. Yet Lord Paser foiled their attack, and we actually captured a Sebaus because of him.'

'But Paser might have known he wouldn't talk.' Shufoy gestured with his hands. 'And the Khetra, whoever he is, made sure of that.'

'All things are possible,' Amerotke replied, lying back on the bed. 'The Temple of Isis may be the heart of the Sebaus: they control former soldiers, Mafdet worked here, Mafdet died here, whilst the temple archives might hold the secrets of the Valley of the Kings.'

Shufoy squatted back down again. 'What if, Master, what if Lord Impuki is the Khetra? What if he instructed Mafdet to abduct those girls and then decided to silence him?'

'All things are possible,' Amerotke repeated. 'I follow your logic, Shufoy, but I have a feeling, a deep suspicion, that Mafdet was killed for another reason, though I don't know what. There was undoubtedly bad blood between him and Lord Impuki, though all the High Priest will say is that he just disliked the man. There's got to be something else . . . Now, Shufoy, I am tired.'

Amerotke stared up at the polished panels on the ceiling and tried to remember a prayer, a song for the family that his father had taught him, but he had only reached the second line when he fell deeply asleep.

The following morning he and Shufoy washed, dressed, and broke their fast on the temple lawns. They had hardly finished when Paser came over, greeted them and offered to take them to the House of Books. As he led them away from the guest house and across the temple grounds he explained how he had been excused from the early-morning ceremonies. Amerotke could hear the faint sound of the choirs intoning their morning hymn to the rising sun and the Great Mother. The fresh air was spiced with the tang of blood from the sacrifices and the heavy gusts of incense seeping through the windows of the sanctuaries.

Paser hurried ahead, taking them along a colonnaded walk and across more gardens, fragrant, delicious places with rich vines, their swollen purple grapes hanging from trellises fixed to high posts. They passed the great pool of purity, shaded by palm trees, and through an orchard of fig trees where temple acolytes were using trained baboons to bring the fruit down from the overhanging branches. Occasionally the gardens would give way to small meadows where sacred flocks grazed. They passed other buildings, storehouses, slaughter sheds, not stopping until they reached a stone wall guarded by sentries which led them into the library courtyard.

The lintels and pillars of the great cedar door leading into the House of Books were covered in brilliantly coloured hieroglyphs and paintings depicting scribes and scholars, reading and writing, or in debate with their teachers. Paser unlocked the doors and led them into a small antechamber with a floor of Lebanese wood. Light was provided by spacious windows and specially capped alabaster jars placed in niches. The House of Books, a long narrow room, was on the second floor. The sycamore shutters were thrown open but the windows were barred and protected by a wire mesh to deter thieves. The walls on either side were covered with exquisitely carved racks, pigeon holes and shelves to hold the sacred manuscripts. Down the centre of the room stretched a line of tables, with cushions before them so scholars could squat to read and write. Each table bore a writing tray with pens and jars of blue, red and green ink. The smell of gum, resin, parchment and scrubbed leather seeped everywhere.

A young lector priest came out of a side chamber.

'Divine Father.' He bowed towards Paser.

'The library is empty?'

'Of course, Divine Father.'

Paser gestured towards Amerotke.

'Could you tell the lord judge what manuscripts General Suten studied? Do you have them assembled?'

The lector priest nodded, his smooth round face eager to please. 'My lord judge,' he continued quickly, 'General Suten was a great soldier. He was always eager to read the chronicles and history of Egypt: the great exploits and achievements of its army, as well as the campaign both he and his father fought in.'

'So General Suten's father was also a soldier?'

'Oh yes,' the acolyte priest gabbled, 'and very proud of him.'

'What else did he read?' Amerotke asked. 'Tell me what he asked for when he came here.'

'He would look at military records.' The Keeper of the Books was puzzled, and stared at Paser. 'He would always insist on coming up here alone; his valet and scribe had to stay in the hall below.'

'Do you have any records of the Valley of the Kings?' Amerotke asked. 'If I was a thief, a robber, and I wished to break into the tombs of the great ones . . .'

'My lord, my lord,' the Keeper of the Books became agitated, fingers fluttering like the wings of a bird, 'we have some records, but . . .'

Amerotke pointed to a table. 'Then bring them here, as well as anything General Suten studied.'

The lector priest hurried off. Shufoy wandered over to one of the windows, whilst Paser went to sit in the high-backed chair just within the doorway. Amerotke squatted down. The lector priest, eager to please this grim-faced judge, hurried up with baskets of manuscripts and papyri. At first Amerotke felt excited, sure he was on the verge of discovering something, yet the more he read, the deeper the disappointment grew. The lector priest was correct. Suten's manuscripts were nothing more than temple histories and chronicles, whilst the records of the Valley of the Kings were merely lists of funereal goods and the various liturgies used in the burial of the great ones. He sharply demanded of the Keeper of the Books if there were further documents. The lector priest, highly nervous, shook his head. Amerotke hid his disappointment. If he had found records providing detailed information regarding the Valley of the Kings or the Valley of the Queens, his vague suspicions about Lord Impuki would have hardened. There was nothing.

Amerotke watched a butterfly, which had somehow come through the wire mesh, flutter like a sparkle of light and move back towards the window. He recalled how, when he was a boy, he used to collect hardened twigs to make a broom. Sometimes he wouldn't find enough, and that was similar to the problem now. He'd picked up bits and pieces but nothing substantial. He demanded to see the roll of index which listed every manuscript held by the temple library; this too revealed nothing. He left the chamber and walked down into the hallway. Paser came hurrying after him, more than aware that this judge was losing his temper. Amerotke stood in the shadow of the doorway, staring out across the temple gardens. He assured Paser he would be safe enough with his own guards, that he would wander for a while and then leave. He asked the priest to give his thanks to the Keeper of Books, and walked over to the shade of a cluster of palms which grew round a pool, a place of green darkness, cool and refreshing against the broiling morning sun. He sat down on a rock at the edge of the pool and watched the red and silver carp dart amongst the reeds. A pair of grey doves with black collars came and alighted on the far side and began to peck amongst the stones. Somewhere in the branches above sparrows chattered, whilst the distant lowing of the sacred cattle in the slaughter pens echoed ominously. Amerotke recalled the prayer he had tried to recite just before he had fallen asleep, and now intoned it, loud enough for Shufoy to hear, but not audible to the guards who sat amongst the trees chattering to each other.

If you can hear me in the place where you are,
Tell the Lady of Eternity, the daughter of Truth,
About my petition
I have committed no abomination against you!
I have not opposed your will over any matter.
Speak to me then in truth,
Clear the clouds of my darkness.

'Are you so confused?' Shufoy whispered.

'I really thought that the House of Books would have yielded something. I thought I was making progress,' Amerotke replied. 'But the question remains, who killed Mafdet? Who is the Khetra? Where did that evil Watcher at the Gates obtain his information about the Valley of the Kings? How does he recruit and control the Sebaus?' He sighed. 'I still haven't discovered the truth about General Suten's death. Shufoy, the wall still rises dark and impassable before me.'

'How will you resolve General Suten's death?'

'I don't know. The scales of Ma'at will be used and filled with probabilities, then I shall watch which side will dip. Did Heby murder his master? Or is it more probable that General Suten tried to find a way out of his own terrors?'

One of the guards laughed, the sound echoing across the grove, and the doves, startled, flew away in a flurry of colour. What, Amerotke wondered, do I do next?

Nadif, standard-bearer in the Medjay police, was also thinking about General Suten's death. Armed with his staff of office, a red and black cloth protecting his head and neck against the morning sun, he was striding along the

215

causeway towards General Suten's mansion. He had left the baboon at home, as the animal had fallen sick. He paused to clean some dirt from his sandal and flick the dust from his long white kilt, then tightened the embroidered belt around his waist and went to stand under the shade of a sycamore tree. He stared into the distance. He was following the same route he had taken the night the alarm had been raised. Of course, the great thoroughfare was different now, dusty and hot. The city markets had been open for hours and the processions of peasants and traders had long disappeared. They would stay in the city until the day's business was done and the heat had begun to cool; by then Nadif would have finished his tour of duty. The thoroughfare was empty except for the lonely pedlar striding along, a merchant stringing a pack of animals, and the occasional cart pulled by sluggish oxen. Nadif stood and watched them go. He would never forget the evening General Suten had died, those vicious horned vipers coiling around the corpse. It was no way for a soldier to die! Nadif shaded his eyes against the sun, watching the skiffs along the Nile, the fishermen, armed with their nets or long pointed harpoons, eager to catch a fish or bring down one of the water fowl which nested in the thick reedy banks of the river.

Nadif had followed what had happened to General Suten's household with great interest. He had even attended the court when Lord Valu had introduced Hefau, the snake man, who claimed he had met Heby the night before the general died. Nadif unslung his water bottle and crouched with his back to the tree; he took a long sip and shook his head. On that particular evening he had been in charge of this thoroughfare, patrolling it up and down. He was certain no one had come or gone from General Suten's house, and surely he would remember a character like Hefau, carrying his sack heavy with snakes? If he had come across the river Nadif would have seen his boat, whilst if he had walked along the path, Nadif would have glimpsed him, sooner or later. In fact Nadif was sure the snake man was lying, but why? Hefau was now in the Medjay barracks. Nadif would have loved to question him, but the snake man was under the protection of the court, so the policeman had discussed the matter most closely with his wife. They had argued about it the previous evening whilst they shared a dish of stewed lampreys and a jug of rich dark beer.

'You're just being arrogant,' his wife had taunted. 'You think you see everybody.'

'No, no, listen. I patrol between the fifth mooring place and the eighth mooring place. I know who I saw that night. My eyes are sharp . . .'

On and on the argument had run. Now Nadif got to his feet as he heard the sound of voices. He stepped from beneath the shade and stared back towards the Beautiful Gate. A funeral procession had left the city and was making its way down to one of the mooring places. The procession was led by a group of servants carrying cakes, flowers, jars of water, bottles of liquor and vials of perfume. Nadif forgot his own problem and stood fascinated as the procession passed him by. The servants were also carrying furniture, painted boxes, folding stools, armchairs and even a bed. He reckoned this must be an important funeral, because a second procession of servants brought weapons, masks, helmets and even pieces of armour. Next came the mourners, led by the Master of Ceremonies dressed in a panther skin. On either side of him servants sprinkled the ground with milk and scented water from golden spoons. Finally came the hearse, shaped like a boat, mounted upon a sledge drawn by a team of red and white oxen. On the boat statues of Isis and Nephthys stood next to the closed cabin which concealed the coffin casket.

Nadif liked nothing better than a funeral. He watched it go, taking detailed notice of how many mourners there were, what treasures they carried, and the mournful songs they chanted. The procession passed in a cloud of dust.

217

Nadif was about to continue his patrol when he noticed something glinting in the sparse grass on the far side of the trackway. Had someone in the funeral procession dropped a precious ornament? He hurried over and picked up a silver filigree chain holding a pendant, a golden hawk with its wings extended. He studied this carefully. He had seen it before, surely? He crouched down and racked his memory. Yes, that was right, on the night General Suten had died, his valet Heby had worn it round his neck. But Heby was a prisoner; what was his necklace doing out on the trackway?

Nadif edged forward, pushing aside the coarse grass and bushes. He glimpsed a dagger encrusted with dried blood and plucked this up. The blade was of fine bronze, the handle of ivory. He placed it in his sack and, now alarmed, hurried along the pathway. He forgot about the heat and sun, the cries of the fowlers and fishermen. He must reach General Suten's mansion! He sighed with relief as he glimpsed the guards at the gate, but instead of approaching them, he went down the narrow trackway which ran alongside the curtain wall and hurried along the dusty path, under the shade from the palm trees, the coarse grass sticking out to scratch his legs. He passed a guard resting in the shade; the man was busy with his water bottle and didn't bother to get up but shouted that all was well. Nadif, cursing the laziness of these recruits, hurried on. He rounded the corner and another guard resting in the shade scrambled to his feet. Nadif waved him away. Everything seemed calm, but the policeman prided himself on having a nose for mischief. He hurried on around the next corner. There was no guard!

'Hello!' he shouted. No reply. Nadif paused. The sun was very high now, dazzling the trackway, with the wall of the mansion to his right and a line of date palms to his left. A hot, dusty place where flies buzzed and, in the branches above, a jay chattered. Nadif caught his breath; it was just like this out in the Red Lands, he thought, going up one of those lonely rocky gullies with the sun beating down like a hammer. He drew his dagger and walked on, his right shoulder brushing the wall. 'Hello!' he called again. Again no sound.

He was halfway along the path when the buzzing of flies drew him to the dark red pool on the edge of the coarse grass. Nadif dropped his leather bag and water bottle; staff in one hand, dagger in the other, he moved into the shade of the trees. Squinting against the dazzling rays of sunlight he moved cautiously, but despite his care he almost stumbled over the sprawled corpse. A member of the guard, by the colour of his striped headdress, but he carried no weapons. Nadif turned the body over and stifled a moan at the bloody gash which tore the man's throat from ear to ear. He stared around, rising to a half-crouch. The date palm trees clustered thick, the bushes and gorse pressing in like a fence, a grove which could conceal a small army. Nadif moved back to the trackway and looked for further signs, but they were impossible to detect. He studied the wall and noticed the dried blood stain on the uneven mortar. Someone had climbed down there, grazing an arm or a leg. Whoever it was, and Nadif had his own suspicions, had caught the guard unawares and slit his throat. Nadif hurried around and hammered on the side gate. It swung open, and a sleepy-eyed soldier looked out.

'Where's your captain?' Nadif snarled.

'Don't you talk to me like that.'

Nadif slapped him across the face. 'I'm a standard-bearer in the Medjay; fetch me your officer.'

The guard hurried away and Nadif followed, walking down the garden path. On any other occasion he would have stopped to admire the well-dug flowerbeds, the coloured garden pavilion and the pool of purity. He paused as the guard returned, his officer running behind trying to make himself look presentable.

'What's this?' The officer was young and tried to bluster.

Nadif gestured at the wall. 'One of your men is dead.'

'What!' The officer would have hurried away, but Nadif grasped him by the arm.

'How many guards do you have in the house?'

'Two, one in the entranceway, one in the hall of audience.'

Nadif pushed him along the path around to the front of the house, up the steps and through the porticoed entrance. The door of terebinth wood was off the latch. Nadif shoved it open with a crash. The guard sleeping on a cushioned bench where visitors would wait jumped to his feet.

'What's wrong, sir?'

Nadif waved him away. The hall of audience lay silent; the dining area on the dais at the far end was deserted, its gauze curtains drawn back. Nadif noticed with distaste the empty wine jug resting against the plinth bearing a statue of Montu, the god of war. The guard there was also half awake, stripped to his loincloth and so much the worse for ale he could only mutter that there was nothing wrong.

Nadif ran deeper into the house. He reached the general's quarters, but a heavy-eyed maid said that her mistress, Lady Lupherna, was still asleep. Nadif withdrew.

'Where was Heby held?' he demanded.

They hurried out of the general's quarters, down a narrow corridor with chambers on either side.

'Shouldn't there be a guard here?' Nadif demanded.

'He was only placed under house arrest,' the officer protested. 'To leave he would have to—'

Nadif ignored him and threw open the door. The chamber was empty, but he noticed robes had been taken off the clothes pegs and the lids of coffers and caskets were pulled up.

'He could be in another room,' the officer stuttered.

'He better be,' Nadif retorted.

They searched the other chambers. As they reached the

far one, Nadif heard a groan. The chamber was hot and rather stuffy; the windows had been completely shuttered, the drapes pulled across as if a sandstorm was expected. As he stood in the doorway, letting his eyes become accustomed to the gloom, he made out dark shapes. One seemed to move. The officer had found a lamp and brought it back in. Nadif snatched it from his hand and lifted it. He glimpsed staring eyes and a balding head, a gag across the mouth, and realised it was Chief Scribe Menna. He thrust the lamp back into the officer's hand and hurried across to open the windows. As the light flooded in, the captain was already squatting on a stool, staring in disbelief at poor Menna. He had been securely lashed to a chair, a tight gag around his mouth. Nadif cut this away.

'It was Heby,' Menna gasped. 'He came here just after dawn.'

Nadif sliced the ropes. He noticed how well and securely the knots had been tied. Menna got to his feet. Like an old man on the verge of tears he hobbled across to his bed and sat on the edge rubbing his arms and legs.

'You stupid ox!' Menna shouted at the officer, tears brimming in his eyes. 'Your men were half asleep.'

'We were told to guard the house,' the officer retorted. 'Not every chamber. You know that. He was allowed to wander around.'

'What happened?' Nadif demanded.

'Heby came in here not long ago, just after dawn. He wanted to see me, he was all agitated. He said he was finished. He wouldn't be given a fair trial but would end his life on a stake. I tried to reason with him.'

Menna turned his fat head and pointed to a bruise on his right temple. 'Heby said he would flee, he would try his luck elsewhere. I tried to reason with him but he wouldn't listen. He struck me here and I fell against the floor. I was dazed. Heby pulled me up, a dagger to my throat. He tied my hands and ankles with two leather belts. He acted like a man crazed with the sun, chattering to himself. He left my chamber and came back with a rope.' Menna pointed to the belts lying at the foot of the statue of the household god Bes. 'He took those off, bound me with the rope and raided my treasure casket.' The Chief Scribe put his face in his hands. 'Then he fled. Perhaps he did kill General Suten.' He lifted a tear-streaked face. 'I don't know and I don't care.'

Nadif walked carefully around the room. He could see signs of disturbance and noticed how the small ebony-lined caskets and coffers had been thrown open and emptied.

'What has happened?' Menna asked.

Nadif was about to reply when he heard voices in the corridor, and Lady Lupherna, hair billowing down like a black cloud, clothed in a night shift, an embroidered shawl around her shoulders, hurried into the chamber.

'Heby!' she whispered. 'One of the guards told me! Chief Scribe Menna, are you well?'

Menna waved her away. She sat down in a high-backed chair, stared at the cut ropes, the open caskets, and turned heavy-eyed to Nadif.

'He did do it, didn't he? He murdered my husband, and now he's fled. We were working so hard to prove it was a lie.'

'My lady.' Nadif smiled at her. 'Did you hear anything untoward?'

'Ask my maids.' Her fingers fluttered. 'I couldn't rest. I mixed a sleeping draught in my wine. I slept until I was woken; my maid said you had tried to enter our quarters.'

Nadif apologised and explained what had happened, how he had found Heby's necklace, the blood-stained dagger and the guard with his throat cut. Menna took up the tale and pointed accusingly at the captain of the guard.

'Your men could have been more vigilant. Well?' he shouted. 'Shouldn't you be pursuing Heby? You, sir,' he pointed to Nadif, 'I thank you for your vigilance. I would be grateful if you went down and informed the Lord Valu;

proclamations have to be issued.' He put his fingers to his face. 'Such woes,' he moaned. 'Such troubles.'

The officer of the guard was only too pleased to leave.

'I can't go immediately sir,' Nadif explained. 'I must question your servants and yourselves. Lady Lupherna, did you see anything suspicious?'

'I've told you,' she retorted. 'Ask my maid.'

'Chief Scribe Menna?'

'Ask the servants.' Menna waved his hand. 'They will tell you that yesterday, morning evening and night, I stayed here.' He pointed to the writing table strewn with papyri and blunted styli. 'I was trying to defend Heby, I wanted to question that snake man. I thought he was telling a lie.' Nadif nodded understandingly. 'I slept for a while and rose just before dawn. Heby came in, the rest you know.'

Nadif thanked them and went back into the hall of audience, where he asked the steward to assemble the servants: the maids, the kitchen boys, even the gardeners. They all told the same story: how Lady Lupherna and Chief Scribe Menna had kept to the house. No one had seen Heby go. Nadif thanked them. He walked out and sat on the steps and recalled what he had been thinking earlier and the argument he had had with his wife. He closed his eyes. That young guard, his flesh so cold, lying in the undergrowth! Nadif reflected carefully. He was tired, he would have to go away and think very prudently before drawing up his report.

AMAM: ancient Egyptian, 'the eater of
the dead'

CHAPTER 10

Amerotke decided to leave the Temple of Isis. He and Shufoy returned to the guest house to pack their few belongings. Their guards gathered, quite delighted to be assigned this light duty of trailing the solemn-faced judge across fragrant temple gardens, or lounging in the cool orchards around Amerotke's house. The judge thought they were too relaxed, so he decided to keep them busy and sent them to search for Paser, as well as offer his farewells to Lord Impuki. Paser came hurrying across to the guest house. He still seemed anxious and wary-eyed, clearly relieved that this inquisitive judge was leaving.

'I meant to tell you,' Paser declared hastily, 'that although General Suten came to consult our manuscripts, he was thinking of leaving his family archives to our House of Life. I thought,' he glanced away, 'perhaps, you might find such records more interesting than ours.' He bowed, then strode out of the chamber and down the stairs.

Amerotke collected their belongings and put them in a leather sack. Shufoy was chattering like a monkey, so his master, more to distract him than anything else, told him to go to the House of Twilight.

'What do you want there?' Shufoy gripped his parasol as if it was a staff, standing on one leg as he had seen a holy travelling man do outside the Temple of Min. The fellow had managed to stay like that for three days without moving. Shufoy often wondered whether he could pass himself off as a holy man; after all, he did serve in the Temple of Ma'at.

'That old man Imer,' Amerotke paused, 'the one I met last time I was there, they said he was close to death. I would like to know.'

Shufoy hopped to the door. Amerotke heard him laughing with the guards outside. He picked up his cloak and the sack and went down and made himself comfortable in the shade of an acacia tree. A short while later Shufoy, his scarred face lugubrious, came striding back with all the sombre majesty of a chief mourner.

'Master,' he intoned, 'Imer has died, shortly after you visited him. He has gone into the Far West. He now rests in the cool green fields of Osiris.'

'Ah, well.' Amerotke rose to his feet and walked across the lawns to the precincts near the great temple. He went down the steps, across another courtyard and down into the wabet, which he had visited when he had first come to view the corpses of Mafdet and Sese. He skirted the priests and acolytes, busy over their funeral rites, walking quickly round the death slabs with the corpses sprawled there, and across to the scribe at the far door who kept the tally of the dead.

The scribe lifted his head. 'My lord?'

'Do you have the body of Imer? He died a short while ago in the House of Twilight. I would like to pay my respects and hire a chapel priest to sing some prayers and hymns for him.'

The scribe lifted a hand and methodically went back through his records. Then he looked up and shook his head. 'I'm sorry, my lord, there is no entry. You must be mistaken, perhaps you were given the wrong name?'

Amerotke was about to protest when he recalled the Lady Nethba. He thanked the scribe and went outside to where his guard was waiting. He sat on a bench and tried to resolve the problem. Shufoy, fascinated by the funeral priests, their faces covered by hawk and jackal masks, drifted back towards the wabet. He stood in the doorway oblivious to the pungent odours of perfume and natron, studying the various inscriptions carved into the lintel of the door, particularly the one about snakes, which he read out to entertain the guards.

'*Go back, dusk crawler, go back into the dark.*'

'Shufoy!' The little man groaned and went back to his master. 'Shufoy . . . no, never mind.'

Instead Amerotke beckoned over one of the guards and whispered an order to him; the man pulled a face but nodded and went into the wabet. He returned a short while later shaking his head.

'I'm sorry, my lord.' He spread his hands. 'There was no record of her.'

Shufoy was now fascinated at what was going on. Amerotke waved away the guard.

'I can't believe it!' the Judge whispered. 'The lady Nethba talked of Kliya, an old washerwoman who came to the Temple of Isis to die. Lady Nethba later made enquiries about her only to be told they had no record. Now . . .'

'Is that why Lady Nethba was upset about her own father?' Shufoy asked.

'Precisely,' Amerotke agreed. 'She became all anxious. So what do we have here, eh, Shufoy? Two old people who come to the Temple of Isis, one of whom I met, I saw with my own eyes, yet now they have no record of them. I wonder if they were buried?'

'My lord judge!'

Amerotke glanced up. A white-garbed temple acolyte, dressed in a sheath-like linen robe, stood on the edge of the lawn. Behind him, some distance away, was a woman, apparently in mourning by the dirty, dishevelled robes she wore and the dust covering her head and face.

'My lord?' The acolyte waggled his finger fastidiously

towards the woman. 'This, er, this lady presented herself into the Chapel of the Ear. She has come to see you. She says the chief steward of your house told her you were here. She claims to have information for you.'

Amerotke waved the woman over. The temple acolyte almost jumped aside, as if she was infected with the plague. She was quite young and kept her head down. Amerotke could glimpse the blood-scarred cheeks where she had scratched herself with her nails; her skin was now the colour of dust. At first he suspected some form of attack and his hand went to his dagger while he beckoned a guard over. The woman, however, fell to her knees and began to keen, rocking backwards and forwards.

'What is it?' Amerotke asked, crouching down and tipping her gently under the chin. The woman glanced up. Amerotke narrowed his eyes. 'I've met you before, you are Djed's wife?'

The woman nodded. 'I came to thank you,' she whispered hoarsely. 'I thought, because of what my husband had done, I would be punished, but you are compassionate. You returned his corpse, and no punishment has been inflicted upon me or mine.'

Amerotke tried not to flinch at the smell of her unwashed body.

'I will observe the period of mourning,' she continued, 'that his Ka finds some peace in the Underworld. Perhaps if I pray, fast and make offerings to the priests . . .' Her voice trailed away.

'What is it that you've come to tell me?'

'I came to thank you for your kindness, and to help. I never knew what my husband did, who he met or where he went, or who provided such wealth. Only once did I become curious. A visitor came late at night, his face all masked. I saw him come to the side gate; my husband was busy with his beehives and he'd lit lamps. I was curious, so I stole across. I heard only one phrase, *the Temple of Khnum.*'

'The Temple of Khnum?' Amerotke asked. 'But that lies at the centre of Thebes. What would your husband . . .'

'No, no.' The woman shook her head. 'I don't think they meant *that* temple, but the other one; its ruins lie to the north of Thebes, an old temple.'

'Ah yes, I remember.' Amerotke nodded. 'Abandoned because the Nile broke its banks. It stands on an island or a large sandbank.'

'That's the one,' the woman nodded. She got to her feet and backed away. 'I thought you should know.'

She shuffled back to where the acolyte was waiting. Amerotke grasped his leather bag.

'Where to, Master?' Shufoy asked.

'To the river.'

They left the temple precincts through the soaring pylons, past the huge stelae proclaiming the Great Deeds of the Divine Mother, or boasting about the exploits of previous Pharaohs, and crossed the square of obelisks, soaring pillars of gleaming red sandstone, capped in gold, silver, bronze or electrum, so as to dazzle in the blazing sun. The heat was like the blast from a fiery oven, the sun a tormenting demon above them. Shufoy offered to open the parasol, but Amerotke said he was in too much of a hurry and lifted his linen shawl above his shoulders to cover his head. He was fascinated by the problem which vexed him; perhaps there was no path through this maze of puzzles.

Shufoy was about to act as herald, to shout at the crowds that the lord Amerotke was approaching, only to realise that his master wished to draw as little attention to himself as possible, so he merely grasped Amerotke's hand as the judge strode across the square. The dwarf almost had to run to keep up. Amerotke often fell into these trance-like moods, apparently oblivious to the crowds milling about and the various scenes in the streets and squares. The smell of incense as priests, clapping their hands, shuffled towards some shrine; the mercenaries from a dozen different nations, gathered eagerly round a group of sinuous Syrian dancers who swayed provocatively to raucous music. Only on one occasion did Amerotke stop. A snake charmer was performing his tricks under the spreading shade of a palm tree. He hurled what looked like a stick to the ground but it abruptly moved, head up, throat swollen: a hooded cobra, deadly and menacing.

'How do they do that?' Amerotke asked.

'Very easily,' Shufoy answered, gasping for breath. 'There's a point on the back of the snake's head. If you press it firmly you paralyse it; throw it to the ground and it breaks free from the spell.'

Amerotke shook his head in disbelief.

'I've tried that trick myself,' Shufoy declared.

'And?'

'It only half worked so I gave up all hope of becoming a snake charmer!'

Amerotke continued on his way until they reached the bustling quayside. The place teemed with people from many nations: merchants from the Great Green; blond-haired mercenaries from the islands to the north of the Great Sea; Nubians, black as night; dour-faced traders from the land of incense; Phoenicians, Syrians, Canaanites, even Hittites with their strange parrot-like faces, hair piled high on their heads and trailing down the back like a horse's mane. A dozen tongues babbled and everything was for sale: ivory from the jungles in the south, precious stones from the mines, creatures and birds of every kind. Sharp-eyed pimps touted for trade amongst the sailors, the women they offered trailing behind, resplendent in their gaudy finery, bangles jingling. Some of them were almost naked, others cloaked mysteriously. Barbers and pedlars shouted for trade and boatmen jumped up and down offering 'the safest boat on the Nile.'

Amerotke hired a small barge with a look-out in the prow, a steersman at the stern and six burly oarsmen.

'Where to, Your Excellency?' The captain, naked except for a loincloth, was delighted with Amerotke's deben of silver.

'Upriver to the ruins of Khnum, then across to the Necropolis.'

The smile faded from the captain's face.

'What's the matter, man?' The judge pinched his nostrils. The smell of dried fish was overwhelming; the captain must hire the boat out to those who fished at night along the river.

'Here, Your Excellency.' The captain pushed a sponge soaked in perfume into Amerotke's hand. 'Why do you want to go to Khnum? Nothing there except ruins.' He pulled a face. 'And crocodiles. I mean, it's . . .'

Amerotke's escort walked closer, fingers going to the swords hanging in their leather sheaths.

'If His Supreme Excellency wishes to visit Khnum . . .' The captain bowed and sighed. 'Then Khnum it is.'

The captain waved Amerotke to a seat in the middle of the barge where he could sit under the ragged awning, some protection against the sun. He also served, in carved beakers, surprisingly delicious ale. The order was given to cast off, and the barge left the busy quayside, threading its way deftly through the various punts and skiffs which congregated as thickly as water beetles. The smells of the city gave way to the marshy, fishy aroma of the river, but there was a breeze to cool their sweat. Amerotke closed his eyes, listening to the rhythmic chant of the rowers as they bent over their oars.

'I knew a girl soft and sweet . . .'

Amerotke smiled as he recognised this old chant of the river.

'A sailor's heaven, a paradise she,' came the refrain. The rest of the song continued, Shufoy joining in as the

oarsmen began to list the charms of this mythical temptress of the river.

Amerotke opened his eyes and stared out across the water. The heat haze hung heavy, but he could make out the quayside of the Necropolis to the west and the soaring red-gold mountains over which brooded the peak of the goddess Meretseger. The river was busy, barges of soldiers going up and down to the various garrisons and barracks, a prison boat taking the condemned across to the quarries in the deserts to the west, merchant craft carrying a wide array of goods as well as animals: oxen, donkeys, and on one occasion a herd of baby gazelles and cages of strange-looking dogs. The barge was now midstream, the oarsmen falling silent as they concentrated on their task. To his left Amerotke watched the gleaming cornices and glittering obelisks and temple roofs of the city disappear behind a thick line of palm trees.

'Would His Supreme Excellency like to tell us why he is going to Khnum?' the captain asked.

'His Supreme Excellency would not,' Amerotke smiled. 'But why are you so frightened? Is the place haunted?'

'Demons hover there,' the captain agreed. 'It lies some way from the river bank. A causeway still stretches out, but the papyrus grove is like a jungle and the crocodile pools are always busy.'

The captain pointed to a small sand bank to his left. Amerotke squinted his eyes against the sun, and saw that what he had thought were gnarled stumps of trees were really stakes on which three men had been impaled, their bodies burnt black by the sun.

'River pirates,' the captain declared. 'They also lurk near the Khnum. But with all these brave men around us, we will be safe.' His voice lowered to a whisper. 'I only hope the crocodiles realise as much!'

They journeyed on. The city gave way to groves of palm trees and the fertile black lands. Farmers were busy; the smoke from their villages hung heavy in the air. Eventually the black lands gave way to rocky outcrops. Amerotke was dozing when the prow man shouted. Getting gingerly to his feet, he could glimpse the great sand bank, almost an island in itself, dotted with trees through which he could glimpse the wind-scarred ruins of the Temple of Khnum. The barge turned, nosing its way through the water as Amerotke inspected the island more closely. The river was constantly changing, eating away the land. A narrow causeway had been constructed, but Amerotke could see the dangers. On either side of it grew thick papyrus groves at least half a mile deep, the breeding place of many different birds, but also the killing ground of the crocodiles who lurked there. In fact Amerotke could see some of these beasts basking on the open ground, soaking up the sun until it began to set and they returned to the water, hunting for any unwary man or beast who came down to the riverside.

'I would say the causeway can only be used during the day,' the captain observed. 'It would be a dangerous place at night. Even now it looks haunted.'

Amerotke could only agree; those lush dark-green groves, the battered causeway and the gloomy ruins justified the captain's fears, though the crocodiles would pose little danger to men armed and vigilant, especially if they carried torches or lit fires, the only real threat these river monsters feared. He jumped at a bellowing roar and whirled round; the grove came alive as birds flashed through the air, screeching angrily at the bull hippopotamus lumbering through their sanctuary, hungry for the juicy green stalks. Amerotke ordered the captain to pull away. They rounded the sand bank and found a makeshift quayside where they could moor. The barge scraped in on the sandy shale beneath it.

Amerotke asked for two volunteers, and at the prospect of silver, one of the guards agreed to follow the captain. He took the pot of fire, carefully tended in the stern, and lit pitch torches, and the four men came cautiously ashore. Here and there they heard grunts as crocodiles, angry at being disturbed, slid into the water. They went up a steep incline and into the ruins. The sandstone walls were now cracked and broken, arches had fallen, doorways collapsed, statues and pillars had been worn down by the windborne sand and the heavy rains of the Inundation. They followed a narrow path into what must have been the Hall of Columns, around the various clumps of stone into the old sanctuary. It was no more than a circle of stone, the plaster covering the walls displaying faded paintings describing the exploits of Khnum.

'Master?' Shufoy grasped Amerotke's arm and pointed. The judge went across and stared at the painting on the wall of an archer kneeling, a bow in his hand. They then carefully inspected the sanctuary. Although some effort had been made to hide the traces, they soon discovered that someone must have met here: the remains of a fire, a cracked wine jar and, beyond the wall in the doorway, what must have been a beautiful cup of faience which had been dropped and shattered. Amerotke picked up this exquisite piece of workmanship and turned it in his hand.

'This is where the Khetra comes,' he said. 'Where the Sebaus meet. It's lonely and dangerous; only men with torches and weapons would dare to come here. And more importantly . . .' He walked to a gap in the wall and pointed back to the waiting barge. 'I'm sure this is where some of the treasure is brought to be packed and sealed and sent north. This cup was once part of a hoard.'

He went back and scoured the ruins, discovering further evidence to prove his theory.

'Think of a merchant leaving Thebes, Shufoy. The Khetra has some splendid plunder from the tombs, something which can't be smuggled into the city. This is where the merchant will pick it up, as you would from the quayside at Thebes, then it's north to Memphis, Avaris, Heliopolis, even across the deserts into Canaan. I'm sure this is where he met the Libyan war chief, and where those poor girls were brought.'

Amerotke pulled himself up the wall; it provided a good vantage point. To the left he could glimpse the river and the waiting barge, to his right, across the papyrus grove, the empty, dusty fringe of the Red Lands. A shout came from the barge, and the four men hurried back to the crumbling quayside. The guards were pointing across the river, to where three small barges had appeared to the north of the sand bank. Their prows were high and carved in the shape of some animal, dark sails flapping in the wind.

'River pirates,' the captain whispered. 'They are watching us, weighing their chances.'

Amerotke ordered the soldiers to stand to and draw their weapons; spears and daggers were hastily produced. The captain opened his weapon locker and distributed bows and quivers of arrow to his oarsmen. The river pirates, watching carefully, realised this was no easy prey and turned sluggishly away. The order was given to cast off, and this time, because the wind was behind them, the blue and white sail was unfurled. To the patter of bare feet and the straining of the sail, the rudder man moving the craft to take full advantage of the wind, the barge reached midstream and turned south, back towards Thebes.

At last the city came into sight, its temple cornices and palace roofs shimmering in the sunlight, and the dark green wall of trees gave way to buildings. The river became busier, fishing smacks and boatloads of pilgrims, pleasure punts and dark powerful war barges thronged about, their lookouts blowing at conch horns to raise the alarm and demand passage. In the end they all had to wait, treading water as the funeral flotilla of some powerful nobleman made its way across to the Necropolis. The mourning barges had been dismasted, the outside of the cabins covered in embroidered leather. The passengers stood, their gazes directed towards the funeral barque, constructed in exact imitation of the sacred boat of Osiris which conveyed the god's body to Abydos. It was swift, light and long and decorated at each end with a lotus blossom carved out of gold which bent gracefully as if eager to reach the water. In the centre of the funeral barque stood a small chapel adorned with flowers and various types of greenery. The close relatives of the deceased crouched mournfully beside this, protected by two priestesses dressed in the guise of Isis and Nepthys. In the prow stood the master of ceremonies, resplendent in his leopard kilt and shawl, before him a huge bowl from which flames leapt up which he fed with generous handfuls of incense, perfuming the river wind. Around the funeral barque clustered smaller craft bearing the choirs and musicians. Their mournful lamentations echoed across the water.

Go West, go into the Far West. May you land in peace in western Thebes. In peace may you proceed to Abydos and across the Western Sea to the islands of Osiris and their green, eternal fields.

The funeral cortège swept into the Place of Mourning. Amerotke's war barge followed. He told the captain to wait, and climbed on to the busy quayside, a place where the dead mingled with the living. Other, much poorer funerals were being organised; corpses wrapped in cheap dyed linen were dragged on sledges or wheeled on carts up through the city and into the funeral grounds beyond. Priests of the poor moved amongst the mourners looking for business, as did amulet and scarab sellers. All the scorpion men of Thebes were there, eager to sell petty trinkets and statues to the relatives of the dead.

'As thick as flies on a turd!' Shufoy whispered.

The tramp of feet, the clouds of dust and the swarm of

insects attracted by the great mounds of refuse and host of unwashed bodies were a constant irritation. A demented priest, face blackened and wizened, shrieked at the top of his voice as he danced and cavorted in front of the soaring statue of the green-skinned Osiris, until he was knocked aside by a gang of drunken sailors. These, in turn, began to curse a circle of mercenaries who were watching a dancing girl, naked except for a cloth expertly arranged to withhold her charms whilst enticing spectators.

Amerotke's guards pushed these away. They went up narrow streets which reeked of the dead and the exotic odours of natron, cassia, frankincense and juniper oil. They passed the corpse shops, where embalmers plied their trade, offering a wide range of services from stuffing the corpses of the poor with scented rags to the full paraphernalia of a proper embalmment. Casket sellers offered coffins and chests for sale, whilst their apprentices were eager to distribute copies so that people could take samples home for their kin. They crossed a broad square, through the Portals of the Dead and into a veritable honeycomb of caverns, tunnels and mortuary temples. Guards and officials milled about, armed with staffs ready to drive away the beggars and petty thieves. Amerotke produced his badge of office and demanded to see the Keeper of the Dead. A short while later this official appeared, a portly individual, greased and oiled and escorted by a group of flunkies carrying fans and perfume jars. He was a heavy-eyed, thick-lipped man who, as soon as he realised who Amerotke was, became cringingly servile.

'Yes,' he declared, nostrils flaring, 'I can take you to the Mansion of Mercy, the mausoleum of the Temple of Isis.'

They had to thread their way up dusty, shale-strewn trackways, through a walled gate and across a courtyard, in the centre of which stood the statue of Isis suckling the infant Horus. The heat was intense, the dust stung Amerotke's eyes and he was grateful to pause in the shade to sip clear water from a clay beaker. Once they were ready, they entered the mausoleum, a maze of tunnels and caverns with quotations carved in the rock and pointed with red paint. One in particular caught Shufoy's eye, and he began to recite it loudly, his voice echoing eerily through the hollow space.

'Oh you who cut off heads and sever necks, who put folly into the mouths of the spirits because of your magic—'

Amerotke gently put his hand across the little man's mouth and raised a finger to his lips. Just within the doorway stretched the entrance chamber, with wall paintings depicting the divine souls as brilliantly feathered birds with human faces. The Scribe of the Caskets, the overseer of that place, squatted at the far end behind a small table, torches fixed on the wall above his head whilst oil lamps glowed on a side table. Next to this, chattering on a perch, were a beautiful pair of tamed swallows, who hopped up and down and gave a full-throated song as Amerotke approached.

The Keeper of the Dead advanced and spoke to the scribe, who sat, fingers to his lips, before jumping to his feet and hurrying over to a casket decorated with the *Ankh* and *Sa* signs. He lifted out a roll of papyrus, brought it back to the table, undid the bundle and began to search. At last he nodded triumphantly, tapped the sheet of papyrus with his finger and beckoned Amerotke to follow him down one of the many tunnels stretching off from the chamber. With the scribe hurrying before him holding a flickering torch, Amerotke truly felt he was in the Land of the Dead. The tunnel was needle-thin, the walls on either side stacked high with the dead, locked in caskets or wrapped in linen cloths, all pushed into their manmade chambers. The air was musty, reeking of corruption, the staleness lightened by the sweetness of juniper oil and resin as well as the ever-pervasive harsh odour of natron.

Eventually the guide stopped in front of a ledge. He

picked up a small ladder pushed against the wall and climbed up to peer at the number carved on the side.

'Yes,' he declared, taking back the torch, which he had given to Amerotke. 'This is the woman known as Kliya. She was embalmed in the wabet and put into a casket in the Nefet Per, the House of Beauty, three seasons ago.'

'Take her out,' Amerotke ordered.

A short argument followed, but Amerotke had his way. They had to leave the tunnel so a low-slung sledge on wheels could be brought. The casket was lowered and taken back to the entrance chamber. The officials muttered about impurity and pollution. Amerotke's guards no longer relished their duties, and grumbled amongst themselves. Amerotke snapped at them to keep quiet, and walked back to the doorway to catch the breeze and dab the sweat from his neck.

'Master, what are you doing?' Shufoy asked. 'This is a holy place!'

'Is it?' Amerotke asked. He stared out across the empty courtyard. If the truth be known, he hated such places with their dusty rituals, mumbling priests and the costly, unholy trade in artefacts for the dead. His visit evoked memories of the burial of his own dear brother. Amerotke would never forget that. He wasn't a heretic, he believed that when the soul left the body it did have a life of its own, but the corpse was nothing more than the cracked, empty shell of a nut. He cleared his mind of such thoughts and concentrated on the problem vexing him at the Temple of Isis. The Scribe of the Dead had had no record of this woman, yet her corpse was here in the Isis mausoleum. A vague suspicion pricked at Amerotke as he recalled his conversations with Lord Impuki and Lady Thena.

'Master?'

'Shufoy.' Amerotke beckoned his servant closer. 'Will you help me?'

'What with, Master?'

Amerotke leaned down and whispered. Shufoy gazed back in shock, but nodded in agreement.

'Good.' Amerotke smiled and turned back, clapping his hands. 'I am Chief Judge Amerotke, the Divine One's own mouthpiece in the Hall of Two Truths. What I do is blessed by the gods, for the good fortune of the Divine House and the Kingdom of Two Lands. This is what will happen.' He pointed at the casket resting on the sledge. 'The body inside belongs to a woman with no relatives or family. I intend to open it.'

Amerotke's words were greeted with shock, accusations of blasphemy and condemnation. The judge declared he would take full responsibility, and once he had shouted them down, he made everyone take an oath of silence. No report would be issued to the Temple of Isis until Amerotke had reported his findings to the Divine House.

A short while later, Amerotke, standing on one side of the table with Shufoy on the other, broke the seals of the casket.

'Notice,' he whispered, 'how fine this casket is, fashioned out of cedar wood.' He pointed at the gold decorations along the side, wiping away the dust. At last he lifted the lid. The smell was still fragrant from the floral garlands, posies and bouquets inside. Amerotke's interest deepened. Kliya had been an old woman, one of the poor of Thebes, yet her mummified face had been covered by a beautiful gold-lined mask fashioned out of linen and papyrus. The bandages, despite the dark resin which coated them, were also of the finest type, usually reserved to wrap the statues and sacred objects of the temple. Amerotke didn't disturb the mask but cut at the linen folds. This was harder than he had expected because the resin had hardened the bandages, turning them into a blackened sheet. As he cut, Amerotke came across the amulets and sacred stones placed there. The corpse had also been coloured with yellow ochre, again usually reserved for the wealthy.

'Master, are you sure we should be doing this?'

'I'll answer to the gods.' Amerotke lifted his head and wiped away the sweat with the back of his hand. 'We are not going to strip the whole corpse, just the chest.'

Assisted by Shufoy, Amerotke cut away a square of the resin-stained cloth. The deeper he dug, the softer it became, evidence of the care the embalmers must have taken with this old woman's corpse. At last the chest area was cleared, and the small chamber they had taken over stank with the funeral oils and spices, the dust from the coffer floating in the air. They had reached the corpse itself. At first Shufoy couldn't believe his eyes. Amerotke smiled to himself as he examined the red cuts running down the neck and the way the left arm had been severed totally from the body.

'What caused this?' Shufoy asked. 'I know the embalmer's art, cuts down the chest and in the left side, but this woman, her chest has been gouged. Look, Master, the left arm is almost severed at the shoulder.'

'I've seen enough.' Amerotke picked up the pieces of hardened linen he had cut away and started to place them back as expertly as he could. Once he had finished, he left the chamber and brought back a narrow sheet of linen, in which he re-wrapped the corpse. Then, helped by Shufoy, he replaced it in the casket, closing the lid and demanding the Keeper of the Dead reseal it.

'Are you finished now?' the official asked, his fat face soaked in sweat.

'I am,' Amerotke smiled, 'but I have one further request.'

The man groaned audibly. 'My lord, you have caused enough confusion.'

'No, no.' Amerotke tapped him on the shoulder. 'I want to visit another tomb. General Suten's . . .'

'It is being prepared,' the man conceded. 'But the period of mourning isn't yet over, and his corpse still lies in the House of Beauty in the Temple of Isis.'

Amerotke had expected this, but once he had washed his

hands and face and anointed himself with oil, he demanded to be taken to General Suten's tomb anyway. They went back out into the sunlight, and the guards, relieved to be out in the fresh air, chatted amongst themselves, trying to draw Shufoy into conversation about what had happened. The dwarf remained puzzled. The old woman's corpse had been honourably treated, but what kind of death had she suffered to have her chest so damaged, and her arm almost hewn off?

They left the mausoleum, following the narrow pathway to the other side of the Necropolis, where the more wealthy and powerful had their Houses of a Million Years. General Suten's tomb lay just within the Valley of the Nobles and was guarded by two priests wearing Anubis masks who escorted them through a gate and across a small courtyard. Just within the gateway a proclamation had been carved on the wall:

The Great Ones have forgiven and purified him,
He has confessed his sins and they are no more
Homage to thee, oh Osiris,
He who hears all our breaths,
He has washed away his sins,
He has justified his mouth,
So in the lands of eternity he will speak with true voice.

The priests were curious as to why Amerotke was visiting the tomb. The general's death had provoked a great deal of interest amongst the workmen putting the finishing touches to this final resting place. Amerotke simply shrugged and said he wished to pay his last respects. He stopped outside the entrance chamber to look at the precious caskets and furniture waiting to be taken in. Once inside the tomb he became deeply interested in the frescoes and paintings on the walls. Some of them depicted General Suten's soul being weighed on the Scales of Truth.

He noticed, with amusement, how the general was portrayed in full dress armour as if he was ready to fight the demons who thronged about, the Great Strider, the Swallower of Shades, the Breaker of Bones and the Eater of Blood. Amerotke went deeper into the tomb to examine the exquisitely painted frescoes on the small chapel wall glorifying scenes from General Suten's life: the General being received by Pharoah; being decorated with golden collars of honour; out hunting antelope or fishing on his punt; or armed with a boomerang and accompanied by his dogs, stalking water birds along the banks of the Nile. Amerotke studied these paintings carefully and asked when they had been finished.

'Only a short while ago,' one of the priests replied.

Amerotke nodded and moved to a further set of scenes depicting the lives of General Suten's ancestors. One painting in particular caught his attention, Suten's grandfather armed with scrolls. The judge became lost in thought.

'Master?' Shufoy whispered. 'What is the mystery?'

Amerotke glanced down at him. 'Mist, Shufoy?' he replied, playing on the words. 'I think the mist is beginning to clear!'

'I wonder,' Shufoy grinned up at his master, 'I wonder what the Divine One will make of her Chief Judge opening tombs? Do you know,' he added absent-mindedly, 'I've studied the list of tomb robberies. Do you realise that the tomb of one of your old enemies, Grand Vizier Rahimere, was robbed?'

'Yes, it was,' replied Amerotke, equally distracted.

'Strange,' Shufoy mused. 'If you look at the dates, that robbery truly disturbed the Divine House.'

UTCHATI: ancient Egyptian, 'judgement'

CHAPTER 11

Nadif, standard-bearer in the Medjay, was becoming more confused by the hour. He prided himself on his powers of observation and logic. When he had served in the army he had always been praised for his astuteness. He recalled how his superiors had whispered that he should, perhaps, have trained to be a scribe. He believed that life should reflect Nature and the Nile. The Great River flowed, the seasons changed. If harmony was shattered, if the truth was twisted, if evil was done and wickedness perpetrated then it was simply a matter of clearing up the mess and restoring Ma'at. Nadif always tried to speak with true voice; he would often remind himself, and his wife, that when he appeared before the Divine Osiris he would be able to make a full confession: '*I have not stolen someone's goods, I have not spoken with evil voice. . .*' His wife always nodded and asked him if he would like more pottage or his beer jug filled.

Nadif prided himself on his own peace, but now he was very perplexed. The day was hot and he was unable to go on patrol because he had to sit in council in the stuffy lower room of the sandstone-built Medjay headquarters, just within the Beautiful Gate to the west of Thebes. Nadif recalled the old adage: 'Do not show your temper, or take out your anger on subordinates, this is a sign of weakness.' In truth he felt like screaming his puzzlement as he gazed round his corps of assistants, a mixture of fresh-faced recruits and grizzled veterans. He was deeply disconcerted at what he had found at General Suten's house, and he still had to resolve the business of the snake seller. Now these men who were supposed to be helping him were only making matters worse. If only his baboon was not ill, he'd be more help than these so-called guardians of Pharoah's laws.

'Let me understand this clearly.' Nadif pointed to a one-eyed veteran, a former spearman from the Seth regiment who had lost his eye whilst hunting wild boars out along the marshes. 'You are telling me that a man fitting Heby's description was seen in the Potters' Quarter to the south of the city?'

'That's what I was told,' the fellow retorted. 'As clear as I can see you now!' The veteran grinned, winking his one good eye.

'This is not amusing.'

'Of course not, sir.' The veteran cleared his throat. 'According to my information, he was dressed quite well in cloak and sandal boots. What caught my informant's gaze was the sword he carried; he also seemed to have considerable wealth.'

Nadif could only raise his hand in agreement and sigh noisily. What the veteran said fitted with what he had learnt from Chief Scribe Menna, who'd reported that Heby had stolen clothes, a weapon and jewellery.

'More importantly,' one of the fresh-faced recruits, eager to prove himself, spoke up, 'there are rumours that Heby was seen at the Fifth Mooring Place along the Nile.'

'It would seem,' Nadif's scribe said, 'that he attacked Chief Scribe Menna, tied him up, robbed the house and escaped over the wall, killing that guard. It wouldn't have been hard,' he added. 'From what you have told us, sir, his guards were lazy oxen. Heby reached the Nile, creeping along the undergrowth next to the bank. In his haste he dropped things. Nothing,' the scribe smiled tactfully, 'escapes the sharp-eyed gaze of Nadif. He must have reached the Fifth Mooring Place, crossed the Nile and tried to raise enough wealth by selling what he had stolen.'

Nadif could only agree. With the small food tables before him, he felt as if he was trapped in this chamber. He wanted to rise, kick them all aside and go on patrol, swinging his stick and marching like he used to when the regiment was going to war. He thanked his officers, dismissed them, then leaned back so that the wall could cool his sweating skin. He closed his eyes and recalled that funeral party passing, the knife he had found, the guard sprawled in the undergrowth, his flesh cold as marble, the blood all congealing. Then there were his questions to the fishing folk and ferrymen along the river. Where was Heby going? Why did he flee? Chief Scribe Menna claimed they could mount a powerful defence, but was the valet looking for something else to prove his innocence? Nadif slipped into a reverie, coming sharply awake as his nephew led in a stranger. The standard-bearer glowered. He regarded the boy, with his moon-like face and slack lips, as simple-minded, yet surely he knew when to knock?

'Great uncle.'

'I beg your pardon?'

'Sir,' the nephew apologised. 'I'm truly sorry, sir, but great uncle, I have brought Apep.'

Nadif waved to the table opposite. The emaciated, yellow-skinned man squatted down, chomping his toothless gums, though his frailty did not stop him from grasping a piece of quail and popping it into his mouth.

'Help yourself!' Nadif leaned across and filled an ale jug while he studied his visitor. The man was garbed in a shabby leather gown, he had tattoos along his forearms and a small carved head of Meretseger on a piece of cord around his neck.

'Why do you call yourself Apep?'

'Snake men always do. They take the name of this god or that god. I am attracted by the idea of being protected by the Great Snake.'

'Horned vipers?' Nadif asked. 'What do you know about them?'

Apep whistled through his lips. 'Nasty, crawling things, vicious and venomous, that's the one snake you avoid. You go down to the snake charmers of Thebes and ask them to play their tricks with a horned viper, they will all refuse. You see, sir,' Apep warmed to his theme, 'take the cobra or the python. Its fangs can be drawn, its poison drained, you can make them sleepy by giving them a nest of mice to eat. It's easy to confuse the crowd. A grass snake can look like an adder, but a horned viper is a horned viper!'

'Have you ever sold them?' Nadif asked, wishing that his nephew, sitting opposite him, would keep his mouth closed and stop gaping.

'Sold one?' Apep drained the beer jug and put it out for more. 'If I saw a horned viper I would kill it. They are responsible for more deaths out in the Red Lands than a pack of lions.'

'Out in the Red Lands?' Nadif queried. 'Can't you find them in the valleys across the river?'

'Oh, you might find the occasional one. But mostly they're out in the Red Lands; look for some lonely oasis where there is some water, but not enough. Next to it, perhaps,' Apep moved his hand, 'a nice rocky gully with plenty of shale and loose boulders, some grass, some bushes, enough water and shrubs to attract the creatures in, rodents, perhaps the occasional nesting bird, and if they're really lucky, a deer or a wounded quail. That's where you'll find the horned vipers!'

'Do they nest together?'

'Small groups.'

'So you wouldn't be able to buy horned vipers in Thebes?'

'You might, but you would wonder why their owners had

them in the first place. There again, in Thebes you can buy anything, can't you, officer? I mean, from a piece of ivory,' he lowered his voice, 'to a jewelled pectoral from a royal tomb.'

'I wouldn't say that in the marketplace,' Nadif warned. 'Let's go back to the horned vipers: you are sure about what you say?'

Apep nodded and, realising that the interview was drawing to an end, stuffed more roast quail into his mouth. Nadif gave him a deben of copper and some flat bread with cooked meat on top and told the man to finish his meal outside.

'What is it, great uncle?' asked his nephew when Apep had gone.

'You heard about Heby?' Nadif replied. 'He may have panicked or he might have fled to look for something. But come, nephew, I gave my word to my sister that you will become a fully trained scout in the Medjay. It's time I took your training in hand.'

Nadif quickly dressed, putting on his chain of office and a striped black and gold headdress over his shaven head. He donned a thick quilted kilt and sandal boots and looped a war belt across his shoulder. He took his staff, inspected his nephew, pronounced himself satisfied and left the police station, grabbing a parasol from one of his assistants in the courtyard. He told his nephew to do something useful and hold it for him as they went out on to the busy thoroughfare leading down to the Beautiful Gate. He deliberately walked quickly so that his nephew wouldn't ask questions, and all the time he studied the faces he passed, the fruit sellers, tinkers and pedlars, the scorpion and lizard men who scampered up the alleyways as quickly as the creatures after which they were named. Nadif knew all their petty tricks and deceptions. He paused to shout at Silver-Fingers, a sneak thief who liked to lift the pouches and purses from ladies and merchants; the man promptly disappeared into the dark recesses of a beer shop.

Soon they were near the Beautiful Gate, where carts and pack animals waited in a cloud of dust. Nadif, displaying his clay seal of office, was allowed through the postern gate and out along his favourite thoroughfare, which stretched between the walls of the city and the lush green vegetation along the banks of the Nile. He found the place where he had sheltered earlier that day and stood as he had done when the funeral cortège had passed. Only when he was satisfied did he move across the trackway to search amongst the undergrowth. His nephew tried to help, still holding the parasol, until Nadif bellowed at him to put it down, take off his leather sack and hold it open. Squatting down, Nadif moved through the undergrowth.

'What are you doing, great uncle?'

'I'm getting ready to make love to a temple girl!' Nadif snarled. 'Oh, don't believe me. I will know what it is when I find it. When I was his scout, Colonel Suten always complimented me on my eyesight.'

Nadif moved deeper into the undergrowth. His nephew, remembering what he had heard about horned vipers, moved cautiously.

'Ah, found it!' Nadif picked up a bracelet of blue faience, followed by a ring, a silver brooch and a comb. He put these into the sack and moved deeper, chewing the corner of his lip, eyes narrowed, as he stared at the thick vegetation in front of him.

At last he pronounced himself satisfied and returned to the trackway. Swinging his stick, he walked past the mansions until he reached General Suten's. He didn't approach the main gate but went along the curtain wall as he had done earlier that day. He found the place where the guard had been killed and stepped into the cool, dark greenery. The sun was still hot and the faint breeze brought the smell of the river. Nadif was pleased to crouch in the silence, listening to the birds chattering above him. Once again he studied the ground, the dry encrusted blood, and turning round he gazed across the grove, wondering which way Heby had gone.

'There's something wrong,' he sighed, getting to his feet. 'There's something very wrong about all this. I was going to write a report, but on second thoughts, I think it's best if I report in person . . .'

Amerotke was in his writing chamber with the window shutters thrown open. He sat in a corner on some cushions, eyes half closed as he gently caressed the statuette of Ma'at which he had taken from its niche in the wall. Shufoy sat across the room, his back to the wall, staring at his master. They had returned to discover that a messenger had been waiting for them with news of Heby's flight and the death of the guard. Amerotke had immediately gone down to General Suten's mansion. The soldiers had left, and Chief Scribe Menna and Lady Lupherna were sitting beside the lake of purity enjoying the shade of a sycamore tree and watching a tamed goose strut like a soldier. Menna explained how he was trying to distract his mistress, her eyes red-rimmed from crying, her cheeks stained with streaks of black kohl. He also described what had happened. Amerotke had listened carefully, yet there was nothing he could do, so he'd returned to the silence of his own house to reflect and meditate.

Shufoy looked at his master carefully. Amerotke appeared calm; garbed only in a loincloth, he looked like a priest praying quietly in some shadowy chapel. The dwarf, however, knew the signs. Amerotke was stripping away the deceit, the falseness and the lies. Like some saluki hound, he was eager to get to the truth.

'Master?' Amerotke opened his eyes. 'The Necropolis, that old woman's corpse?'

Amerotke smiled. 'The truth, Shufoy? The dead don't leave, they are all around us and try to speak.'

Shufoy pulled a face at this enigmatic response.

'And General Suten's tomb?'

'I went to look for something but didn't find it, and yet I found something else.'

Amerotke turned to the side table beside him and took down the dead general's memoirs. Using the light from the window behind him, he once again read the passage he had marked. He turned the pages of the folio carefully, and now and again put the book down and returned to his writing desk, where he was listing everything he had learnt.

The day drew on. Amerotke was thinking about going into the garden when his steward knocked on the door and ushered in Standard-Bearer Nadif and his rather awestruck subordinate. Amerotke had met this policeman before. He appreciated Nadif's sense of duty and had a deep respect for his allegiance to the law and his sharpness in the conscientious discharge of his duty. Nadif still bore himself like a soldier; he stood as if he was on the parade ground, his face all stern, eyes staring, holding his staff like a spearman waiting to salute his colonel.

'Nadif, Nadif.' Amerotke patted him on the shoulder. 'This is not the time or the place for ceremony, for you or your companion.'

'This is my nephew, my lord, a new recruit in the Medjay. I'm trying to teach him some skills.'

Amerotke smiled at the note of irritation in Nadif's voice. Shufoy was fascinated by the sack the nephew carried. He caught the clink and wondered what valuables it contained. Amerotke, however, was keen that Nadif lose the stiff formality of the parade ground. More cushions were brought, beer jugs were filled, whilst the judge insisted that both Nadif and his nephew bathe their hands and faces and dry themselves with perfumed cloths before they discussed the reason for their visit. Nadif was very grateful; he quietly prayed his nephew would behave himself.

'My lord,' he began, 'I thought I would write you a report but I changed my mind. Nephew, empty the sack.'

The recruit hastened to obey. Amerotke stared as the trinkets fell out, though he seemed more fascinated by the way the nephew threw the sack to the ground.

'Do that again,' he ordered. 'Fill the sack and empty it out again.'

The nephew hurried to obey. He was still overawed at meeting this powerful judge, with his quiet voice and sharp dark eyes, yet his uncle had told him that if Amerotke ordered him to stand on his head he must do so. The sack was refilled and emptied again, then Amerotke asked Shufoy to do the same thing. He sat for a while holding the bracelet, moving it from hand to hand.

'My lord,' Nadif leaned forward, 'shall I tell you where I found this?'

'Yes, yes, do so.'

Nadif began his report, haltingly at first but gaining confidence as Amerotke nodded or grunted with pleasure. The standard-bearer described his meeting with Apep, what he had found in the undergrowth when the funeral procession passed, how he had discovered the murdered guard as well as what he had just recently observed.

Amerotke heard him out, sitting as if fascinated by a painting on the far wall. Nadif followed his gaze. The fresco showed the goddess Hathor receiving the sacrifice of harvesters.

'My lord, are you pleased?' Nadif asked.

'Shufoy, I want you to take our guests out into the garden. You are on duty?'

'Till sunset, my lord.'

'No, no, I want you to stay here tonight as my guests. I will have certain tasks for you to do. Now, go with Shufoy, he will look after you, you deserve a good meal. I have some light white wine a merchant brought from the vineyards in the Delta; it is cool and refreshing on a hot day. Perhaps you would like to swim in the pool?'

Nadif could see the judge was distracted but hastened

to obey. Shufoy was also eager to interrogate these new arrivals; he was particularly interested in questioning Nadif about whether, in his patrols, he had ever found a piece of that hard black rock.

Amerotke waited until they had left, then returned to his writing desk. At last everything was making sense, the mist was lifting and the truth about these hideous murders and sinister affairs was growing clearer. He must have sat for about an hour, writing hastily, until the cramp in his back and arms forced him to rise and join the others outside. Nadif, his belly full of good wine and spiced duck, would have jumped to his feet, but Amerotke waved him to keep still and squatted down before him.

'What you have done, officer, is excellent.' Nadif blushed with pleasure. 'I shall remember your name and, rest assured, Pharaoh will turn her face to you and smile at you. You will receive the red gloves of favour and the necklace of honour.' Nadif was now beside himself with happiness. 'But listen, this is what we must do, there are preparations to make.'

The rest of the day was taken up with various tasks. Amerotke bathed in the pool and slept for a while until it was early evening. Then he dispatched a guard to take a message to the palace, and instructed Nadif to go to the Temple of Isis.

'You are to tell Lord Impuki and his household,' he declared, 'that they are to present themselves in the Hall of Two Truths by the ninth hour. If they are not there, they will be arrested. Oh, then visit Chief Scribe Menna. Tell him this business is being brought to an end. I want him there as a witness.'

Nadif nodded excitedly.

'Shufoy,' Amerotke gestured to his manservant, 'I want you to take a letter to General Omendap, and once that's done, go to the house of Lord Valu; you will find him preening himself in his garden. Tell him that he too must be at the court by the ninth hour, and he is to bring the snake man Hefau with him. Once you have left Lord Valu's house, seek out Captain Asural; I have a letter for him as well. Oh, by the way,' he turned back to Nadif, 'tell Lord Impuki I want him to bring the temple records of all those who've come into his sanctuary looking for healing or help.' Amerotke waited until both had left, then turned to Nadif's nephew. 'You too, sir,' he smiled, 'have a role to play. I want you to bring that sack down to the court tomorrow and do exactly what I say. For the rest, enjoy yourself here.'

Amerotke returned to his writing office. He felt relieved, at peace. Once the messages were delivered he would face no more danger this night. He was eager to finish a business which would end in hideous deaths. He wrote out his line of attack like a general planning a battle. He had dug the trap, but was it deep enough? Would he snare the very people who had been hunting him?

The court of the Hall of Two Truths had been closed to all spectators. Fully armed guards wearing the masks of Amun ranged along the steps outside and thronged the central courtyard. Their standard-bearer was under strict instructions: no one was to be admitted. Inside the court Amerotke did not sit in the Chair of Judgement; that was now occupied by Hatusu, beloved of Ra, the Glory of Amun, Pharoah Queen, Lord of the Two Lands. She had swept into the court garbed in exquisite robes, a jaguar-skin sash around her slim waist, her gold-dusted feet sheathed in sandals of silver adorned with diamonds, her hands hidden by the Red Gloves of Majesty. She had risen before dawn and the Keeper of the Royal Oils, the Imperial Perfumer, the Holder of Pharoah's Sandals and Robes, the Keeper of her Cabinet and a host of sloe-eyed maids had clustered about to prepare her to show her face to the people. She had bathed in a rose-drenched pool, then allowed her maids to delicately paint her face, draw the dark green lines of kohl beneath her flawless eyes, carmine her full lips and slip the earrings of mother-of-pearl into her soft fleshy lobes. She had adorned her head with a thick braided wig drenched in perfumed oil and was dressed in the finest linen. The vulture pectoral on her chest glittered and sparkled, her wrists were decorated with bracelets of pure gold, rings displaying the most precious stones gleamed on her fingers, and her nails were painted a deep purple. Over her shoulders hung the Nenes, the Coat of Glory, a vivid display of eye-catching colour, so brilliant it seemed as if a million beautiful butterflies had gathered on a sea of lovely flowers. Around her forehead was the imperial circlet, displaying the swollen-throated Uraeus, ruby-red eyes in its lunging head. This was the female cobra of Egypt, representing the power of Pharaoh, ready to burn millions in defence of the Kingdom of the Two Lands.

Hatusu likened herself to a cobra; she was swollen with fury and eager for vengeance. She had studied the lists of treasure stolen from the royal tombs and screamed with fury at the reports from her ambassadors that some of this was now in the palaces of petty princelings in Canaan. Such passion concealed her own deep-rooted fears. She had eagerly read Amerotke's letter of the previous day and laughed with delight when she realised that her saluki hound, as she called Amerotke, had found its quarry. She had decided that she herself would sit in judgement and had swept along the thoroughfares, the Avenues of the Sphinx, Lion and Ram, not in a palanquin but in the imperial chariot of glory, drawn by war-horses with their heads and flanks adorned with imperial plumes and streamers. The carriage she'd stood in was of beaten gold, a glorious chariot on its red-rimmed leather wheels displaying the full panoply of battle with its jewelled javelin case and gold-sheathed arrow quiver.

Hatusu had driven the chariot herself; Senenmut, in the full dress uniform of an imperial general, standing beside her. She drove slowly but majestically, ranks of Syrian archers and Menfyt veterans from the Sacred Band holding back the crowds. Priests swinging thuribles went before her, purifying the air with sacred smoke, whilst imperial pages scattered rose petals beneath the hoofs and wheels of her chariot. No music, however, accompanied her, no songs of praise or chanting temple dancers. Instead, on either side of the chariot strode members of the Royal Circle carrying huge flabella, ostrich-plumed fans dyed a light pink and soaked in perfume so as to keep away the dirt and fleas from the sacred flesh. The true music was the ominous tramp of the units from the Sacred Band who followed the chariot: the Maryannou and the Nakhtu-aa, the Braves of the King and the Strong-Arm Boys. They were her bodyguard, bound by the most sacred oaths to live and die for their Divine Mistress. Every so often the sombre silence would be shattered by the shrill blasts of war trumpets so that those ahead knew the Divine One was coming. Pharaoh was showing her power. Secretly she was determined to inflict hideous vengeance on those who had dared to try and bring her name down to the dust. Despite Lord Senenmut's attempts to pacify her, she had sworn terrifying oaths to reduce the malefactors to dirt under her sandals, carrion for the devourers, sent into the darkness with no blessing, no prayer, no incense or song.

At the Temple of Ma'at Hatusu had walked imperiously up the steps, turning neither to the left nor the right. Now she sat like a statue grasping the flail and rod, her feet resting on a footstool. On a smaller chair to her right sat the sword of her justice, Amerotke, dressed in his robes of office. On her left, squatting on a cushion, was Lord Senenmut, ever ready to whisper advice.

The court had been cleared, the bar lifted; not even the scribes were present, only lines of archers, arrows notched to their bows. Across the hall were those Amerotke had summoned: Lord Valu, looking distinctively nervous before he bowed his head; next to him Hefau, then Chief Scribe Menna, Lady Lupherna and Standard-Bearer Nadif. After a short gap were Lord Impuki, Paser and the Lady Thena. Once summoned, they hastily knelt and bowed, foreheads against the hard floor as they nosed the ground before their dreaded ruler. Hatusu kept them waiting as a royal herald proclaimed her titles, and when he had finished, a royal chapel priest, crouching before the Chair of Judgement, intoned the longest prayer Amerotke had ever heard. The judge sat rigidly still. He was prepared; he just hoped that the traps he had laid were cunning and subtle enough to trick the murderous children of the red-haired Seth. He breathed in deeply, savouring Hatusu's most delicious perfume. At last the priest ended his prayer. Hatusu lifted a finger.

'Rouse yourselves,' the herald declared in a ringing voice, 'and look upon the face of Beauty. The Divine One has not hidden herself but, like her father Ra, now sees all that is before her. Look,' he intoned, 'and wonder! Marvel at the wisdom of the Dazzling One, holy in thought, sacred in speech.' The herald paused. 'You may lift your heads and enjoy her face.'

They did so. Amerotke glimpsed a variety of expressions: relief, fear, awe and glances of calculated cunning. He remained silent during this ceremony; the ponderous words, the ringing phrases were all part of his trap. It wasn't just an empty, sterile show; he wanted to frighten some of these people, induce fear so that a word or a sentence hastily spoken, without reflection, might reveal the truth.

The silence in the hall grew oppressive. Hatusu, Amerotke's fellow conspirator, never moved; trained in the strict protocol of the court, she kept her face impassive. She knew she was there not only to see justice done but to help this most cunning of judges. Lady Lupherna started to cry, head down, shoulders shaking, whilst Lady Thena put her face in her hands.

'You may begin.' Hatusu's voice cut like a whiplash. 'Make known the truth.'

Amerotke glanced down at the floor, shuffling his feet, praying to the Goddess to guide his thoughts and sharpen his tongue.

'In the beginning . . .' He paused. 'Yes, in the beginning everything was harmonious in Thebes, Waset, the City of the Sceptre. The Divine One's rule had been confirmed by the gods and all was peace and truth.' He paused again, wanting to heighten the tension, to stretch the nerves of those hanging on his every word. 'In the Land of the Dead to the west, across the river, lay the Valleys of the Kings, the Queens and the Nobles, the Houses of a Million Years where the Divine One's ancestors slept whilst their Kas proceeded into the Eternal West. The regiments had been brought home from war, the city was full of former soldiers. The Temple of Isis,' he looked sharply at Lord Impuki, 'was famous for its beauty and the health it brought to the citizens of Thebes. The temple was the glory of the Mother Goddess, much favoured by the Divine One; its Houses of Life and Healing were open even to the poorest, the beggars, the infirm, former soldiers who had fought in the wars. The temple was a paradise, but into this paradise crept an evil being: Mafdet! He was appointed Captain of the Temple Guard at the request of General Omendap, Chief Scribe of the Army.'

Amerotke turned to where Omendap, along with other high-ranking military officers, squatted on cushions. The General looked distinctly nervous.

'Mafdet was an evil being, a man with a dark soul and a twisted tongue. Unbeknown to the High Priest, he was also a member of a secret society called the Sebaus. The Sebaus were a canker, a blight which threatened to spoil the beauty and harmony of Thebes. In the ancient myths the word Sebaus means demons, and rightly so. Mafdet was one of them!'

'I did not know that!' General Omendap shouted, unable to control his anger. Hatusu raised one hand for silence and gestured to Amerotke to continue.

'Mafdet was under instruction,' Amerotke continued, 'to kidnap four temple hesets, beautiful maidens of noble families who had been dedicated to serve the Mother Goddess. He enticed them away, young women, their minds easily turned. He invited them to a lonely part of the temple and offered them a drink, secretly drugged with potions from the House of Powders in the temple—'

'We suspected this,' Lord Impuki said quietly. 'I mean,' he added quickly, 'that he had stolen the powders, but we thought he would sell them in the city. Only when you came to the temple, Lord Amerotke, was the real reason revealed.'

Hatusu made to silence him, but Senenmut whispered quickly to her. The Pharaoh's First Minister recognised that Amerotke was drawing his victims into the parry and thrust of debate.

'Are you saying,' Paser cleared his throat, 'are you now formally accusing us of murdering Mafdet because he killed those four women? May I remind you, Lord Amerotke, that on the night he was murdered – I concede when he received his just deserts—'

'No, no,' Amerotke interrupted, 'you did not kill him because he had kidnapped the girls, though you may have suspected that somehow he was involved. No, Mafdet died for another reason, didn't he? Steeped in villainy, he wanted to collect as much information about High Priest Impuki as he could. Mafdet was not only a thief and a brigand; he was also a blackmailer.' He could tell from the High Priest's face that he was on the verge of the truth. 'Where is it?' he asked quietly.

'Where is what?' Impuki stumbled over the words.

'The secret place,' Amerotke replied, 'where you examine the corpses of those patients without family or friends who die in the House of Twilight at the Temple of Isis.'

'I don't know what you are talking about.' Impuki's voice betrayed him, while Lady Thena rubbed her eyes as if to relieve a pain in her head.

'I went to the wabet,' Amerotke declared, 'looking for the body of Kliya, an old washerwoman the lady Nethba knew. There was no record of her there. In the mausoleum of the Temple of Isis, however, I found her casket. Lord Impuki, I opened that casket, I unwrapped the linen bandages, I know what I saw.'

'That's blasphemy!' Paser shouted.

'And so is the dissection of the dead. Tell me, Lord Paser, where is the body of Imer, an old man I knew as a boy? I met him when he was in your House of Twilight. I was later told he had died, but the Scribe of the Dead had no record of him. I know his corpse has not been taken out across the river. Where is that man's body?'

Lord Impuki gazed back bleakly.

'Mafdet discovered some of this,' Amerotke continued. 'Perhaps he found your secret place, or did he meet an old comrade whose corpse later mysteriously disappeared? He began to threaten you, hint at what he knew. One night Lord Impuki, Lady Thena and you, Paser, met in secret council in the hall of audience. You pretended to be closeted there but already the decision had been made. One of you had taken a sleeping potion from the House of Powders and mixed it with a jug of beer in Mafdet's house. Once darkness had fallen and the temple was quiet, one or all of you crept out of the chamber using the window which overlooks that fragrant eating place. You slipped through the darkness and you killed him.' He stopped speaking and closed his eyes.

'I would like to—'

Amerotke opened his eyes.

'What would you like to do, Lord Impuki? Protest? I can have the temple searched. Imperial troops will go from building to building until they find what I want.'

'This is not—'

'Oh, Lord Paser, do not lie. Your guilt is in your faces. You never desecrated those bodies. I declare that publicly, here in the presence of the Divine One. The old lady's corpse that I examined after you had finished using it was prepared most honourably for burial, wrapped in sacred linen and buried in a fitting casket.' Amerotke wiped the lace of sweat from his forehead. 'I wanted you here,' he declared quietly. 'I insisted on it to mislead any spy of the Sebaus in your temple. Nevertheless, you also have a case to answer and you carry the very evidence I need. You brought the record of those who entered your House of Twilight. You have similar lists of those who die. Lists of the burials in the Necropolis. You know they won't match. Do I lie?'

'You speak the truth.' Lady Thena lifted her head and waved her hand to her two colleagues to keep silent. 'What you say is true,' she continued slowly. 'Everything you have said you can prove, except for two things. First, Mafdet was more wicked than you thought. Secondly, my husband did not kill him, I did! I castrated him not because he had kidnapped those temple girls but because he had made one of them pregnant.'

Lady Thena's words came even as a surprise to Amerotke. Senenmut had to shout for silence.

'Oh Divine One,' Lady Thena bowed her head, 'hear my confession then judge for yourself.'

Hatusu nodded imperceptibly.

'I was only a young girl when I was dedicated to the service of the Mother Goddess,' Lady Thena began. 'I loved my youth in the temple; I fell even more deeply in love with the Lord Impuki. We married and had two beautiful children who were taken by the Great Thief of the Under-world. Paser here became our adopted son. We dedicated ourselves to the service and healing of others. Month passed into month, season into season, year into year. Sometimes the sick, the injured, the ill seemed like a wave around us, a litany of woes, hideous illnesses, secret diseases, most of which we could do nothing about.

'Those who died in the House of Twilight were always taken to the Place of Purity in the House of Beauty to be prepared for their journey into the Far West. However, many who came to the Temple of Isis, as you have said, Lord Amerotke, had neither friend nor family. We were fascinated by the workings of the human heart, the frailty of the body and how disease could wreak its hideous effects. One day an old man came, a former soldier. His eyes were filmed over, his gums swollen, he complained of searing pains in his belly. The rest you can guess at. Lord Impuki is the most skilled of physicians. I argued with him, convinced him to use that old man's body to deepen his own knowledge. What harm would it do if the liver was dissected or the heart opened? Perhaps we could use the dead to find a cure for the living. We made progress, we discovered things other physicians never knew and used our knowledge to help other patients. The corpses were always removed secretly from the House of Twilight and taken to our own house, where you will find, Lord Amerotke, what you call the secret place. The Rites of Osiris were always observed. An obsidian knife opened the left side of the corpse, the entrails were removed and the brain drawn forth. The body was washed in natron, dried and perfumed.'

'But not handed over for burial,' Amerotke questioned further, 'you first used them for your own purposes.'

'Those we took secretly,' she replied, 'we first examined: the stomach, the brain, the heart, the joints, the veins and the arteries. Lord Impuki kept secret records, carefully noting what he observed. He discovered growths, tumours, blockages; he experimented on what he had found, and when we had finished we always resumed the holy rite.

The body would be anointed, perfumed and bound in linen bandages. We always provided the most costly casket and arranged for it to be taken across to the Necropolis. We had no scruples, we believed we were doing good.'

'Until Mafdet arrived?'

'Yes,' Lady Thena's voice turned hard, 'until Mafdet arrived!'

SHETA: ancient Egyptian, 'a hidden thing'

CHAPTER 12

'Mafdet discovered our secret like a snake slithering here, slithering there. He was arrogant, especially when his belly was full of beer, and he liked to show off in front of the temple girls.' Lady Thena spat the words out. 'He liked nothing better than to strut like a goose with what he called his well-muscled thighs and flat stomach. He was always boasting about his exploits. One day a temple girl came to see me, highly distraught because she had missed her monthly courses for the second time. She confessed how she had lain with Mafdet.' Lady Thena shook her head. 'My lord, she was really only a girl, with a child's mind in a woman's body.'

'Did you tell your husband?'

'You can tell from his expression,' Lady Thena smiled weakly, 'that this is the first he ever knew of it. I questioned Mafdet, I challenged him, but of course he denied it. He said if the girl was pregnant she might have lain with my husband or Lord Paser, what proof did I have? I hated him for that. My detestation deepened when he referred to other matters. He claimed he knew what happened in the Temple of Isis.'

'Did he?'

'Oh, he tapped his nose and winked. He said that if you were old and lonely perhaps the temple was not the best place to prepare to go into the Far West. I was distraught. Then the temple girl in question disappeared. At first I thought she had fled; that was the logical thing for her to do, seek sanctuary with family or friends. I wondered if Mafdet had anything to do with it, but again he sang the same hymn: what was I talking about? What proof did I have? How dare I accuse him? I decided to watch and wait.'

'Did you suspect he was a criminal?' Hatusu asked. 'Were you aware that he was in the company of malefactors?'

'Divine One, I grew suspicious because I watched him. I knew he met people late at night, but there again, I had no proof that was a crime. I thought the temple girl would be found, but over the next few months three others disappeared. Mafdet became more bullying and abrasive. I recognised I was dealing with someone with a dark heart, wicked and dyed in villainy. He continued to hint and said that one day he would ask for favours. I didn't know what he meant.'

'So you killed him,' Amerotke said.

'Of course I did. On the night it happened I left the hall of audience not through the window, my lord, but through a side door. I told my husband and Lord Paser to continue talking, to act as if I was still there. Night had fallen, darkness cloaked me. I hastened across to Mafdet's house. I had prepared carefully. The pig was already sleeping. He had drunk deep of the beer and the powder I had mixed with it.'

'Yes, I know that,' Amerotke said. 'Or rather,' he smiled, 'I now realise it. Mafdet had stolen similar powders to drug the temple girls.'

'True,' Lady Thena agreed. 'But the potion he drank could have had a source other than the temple. I reasoned that because of the earlier thefts, we could claim our House of Powders had been guarded more closely, so we would not be suspected.'

'It *was* guarded more securely,' Paser declared, 'but I never thought . . .' His voice trailed away.

'Didn't you wonder if there was any connection,' Senenmut demanded, 'between the theft of the sleeping powders and the disappearance of the temple girls?'

'Mafdet was a great sinner.' Lady Thena spoke quickly, unwilling for her two companions to be drawn in. 'I stood by his bed, I recalled that temple girl sobbing her confession to me. Of course, I had my suspicions about the other three. I did wonder if Mafdet had used the powders to violate them. But in the end I was tired of his hints, of his knowing looks, of his arrogant pride. I bound his hands and legs. I gagged his mouth and I cut him, took away his manhood and plucked out his heart. Read the history of our temple, Lord Amerotke. Study the ancient laws of Egypt. Castration is the sentence for someone who violates a temple maiden, eternal death for a blasphemer—'

Paser went to intervene, Thena gestured at him to stay silent. Amerotke gazed admiringly at this priestess. When he had first met her she had appeared so soft, gentle and supportive, a woman who adored her husband. How wrong I was, he thought. You are as strong, ruthless and resolute as this Queen Pharaoh beside me. He suspected Lady Thena was taking full responsibility for what had happened, shielding her beloved husband and adopted son. Amerotke decided not to question them; he had the confession he required.

'Divine One,' Lady Thena bowed her head, 'I beg mercy from the court. Yet what have I done but executed a malefactor? Lord Amerotke, study your laws: do not high priests have the power of life and death over those who serve in their temples? Do we not have the power to send criminals to the wood? I, a High Priestess, executed Mafdet. I castrated him as punishment in this life and removed his heart as punishment in the next. As for the rest, we took the corpses of the lonely and used them to further our knowledge, to fight the demons of disease, the evil spirits of infection.'

'I would agree.' Amerotke spoke up sharply before Hatusu could intervene. 'Lord Paser, I owe you my life.'

Senenmut was also whispering heatedly to Hatusu, who raised her hands grasping the flail and the rod.

'Lord Impuki, you and your family are to remain here. I shall reflect on all that has been spoken, on all that has been done.'

'Divine One,' Impuki bowed, 'I speak with true voice. We now know Mafdet was a member of a criminal gang, the Sebaus, yet we had no knowledge of that before. Nor are we guilty of the destruction of his house.'

'Of course you're not.' Amerotke pointed dramatically at Chief Scribe Menna. The judge had planned this, a swift, vigorous attack. 'There sits the Khetra, the leader of the Sebaus, blasphemer, violater, murderer, thief.'

Menna sprang to his feet, then knelt back down as a soldier pressed an axe against his shoulder. Forgetting all protocol and etiquette, he tore the heavy wig from his head and threw it to the floor. His face was a mask of fury, eyes popping, mouth gaping. Amerotke sensed it was more pretence than fear.

'You're going to say I'm wrong,' the judge declared. 'In fact, you are correct. You are only part of the Khetra. The Khetra is the Guardian or Watchman of the Third Gate of the Underworld, which represents three: Chief Scribe Menna, Lady Lupherna and Heby, three parts of the same evil root.'

Lupherna, her doll-like face set in shock, gazed in horror at Menna.

'You have no proof.' The Chief Scribe had now found his voice. 'Where is the evidence for these outrageous allegations? Heby indeed! Ask Nadif, your policeman, he found me gagged and bound.'

'We'll come to that by and by,' Amerotke replied quietly. 'My case is this. Menna, you are not the fool you pretend to be, but as cunning as a fox. You are a scribe with military training who knows the Heti – the guild of veterans – because so many served your master. You murdered General Suten because you had to, he was growing very suspicious. He had to die in a certain manner and his memoirs gave you the best way forward. For a while Heby would be the cat's-paw. You would, of course, arrange for him to be cleared of any charge, an easy matter given the evidence you'd fabricated, not to mention the confusion caused to this court by my assassination.'

'Nonsense!' Menna shrieked.

'No,' Amerotke replied. 'A devious plan spoiled by mere chance. But let us begin where it started: the death, no, the murder of General Suten. Let us ignore the nonsense about General Suten wishing to confront his terrors, his fear of snakes. Of course he wanted to, he desperately tried. He talked about it to Lord Impuki. He mentioned it in his memoirs. Yet Suten was an intelligent man and one with many friends, supporters and admirers. Why should he confront the nightmare on his own, on the roof terrace of his house? Why not call his faithful Chief Scribe, or his loyal valet, or . . .' Amerotke shrugged, 'his loving wife?'

'But, but . . .' Lord Valu's voice was scarcely above a bleat as the royal prosecutor turned on Hefau beside him.

'Ah, yes, you!' Amerotke pointed at the snake man, who was so frightened he was trembling, hands grasping his crotch. 'You, sir,' Amerotke bellowed, 'must tell the truth. Did you sell Heby those snakes? Yes or no? If you lie, and I can prove it, I will personally ensure that you are buried alive in the Red Lands.'

Hefau moaned in terror, threw his hands up in the air and prostrated himself on the ground. Such a dramatic, comical gesture made even Hatusu smile.

'Mercy!' Hefau wailed. 'I heard about Lord Valu's proclamation and the reward offered. I . . . I thought . . . Mercy, Divine One, I have sinned!'

'Take him away,' Amerotke ordered. 'Let him reflect on his sins in the House of Chains. Lord Valu, you would agree?'

The Eyes and Ears of Pharaoh, a look of horror on his face, nodded in agreement.

Amerotke used the diversion to stare at Menna; the scribe knelt on the cushions, glaring malevolently at the judge. Amerotke hid his growing excitement. You are my enemy, he thought, you tried to kill me; even now if you had a chance . . . You are in fact the Khetra, a fighter, ruthless and cunning, whilst the other two were your helpers. Lady Lupherna was clearly terrified. Amerotke sensed she was the weakest, the most vulnerable.

The judge rose as if to adjust his robe, then sat down again. This was the agreed signal for Asural standing near the door. Once the snake man had been removed and order restored, Hatusu made the sign to continue.

'So,' Amerotke declared, 'we have proved one lie; let's return to the pursuit of the truth. Do you know where I began? I went out to General Suten's tomb, his House of Eternity, which he was lovingly preparing for his eternal rest. I studied its wall paintings. Most of them were finished over the last few months. I saw no mention of snakes. But above all, I was intrigued that there was no reference to his loving wife, to his Chief Scribe or his loyal valet. Such paintings are a memorial, they capture the scenes and images most dear to us all. Why did General Suten make no allusion to the people so close to him in life? When I visited the general's house I was informed how, in the weeks before he died, he had grown quiet and withdrawn. Why? And then I read his memoirs and I recalled something else I had seen in his tomb in the Valley of the Nobles. General Suten came from a family of soldiers, high-ranking officers.' Amerotke paused for effect. 'Members of the Sacred Band.'

Hatusu gasped as she realised where Amerotke was leading them. 'High-ranking officers in the Sacred Band,' Amerotke repeated. 'Trusted architects, masons, captains and colonels, who help prepare the tombs and supervise the transport of treasure, who would know everything there was to know about such holy, yet secret, matters. General Suten makes reference to this in his memoirs, whilst the wall paintings of his tomb reflect the glorious history of his family. So I began to wonder.'

'Other men have such knowledge,' Chief Scribe Menna declared. Amerotke just stared back.

'Sometimes finding the truth,' the judge mused, 'is like a cook in his kitchen. You have to take things and mix them before you achieve what you want. So here we have an illustrious general whose family played an important part in royal burials and those of other notables. They too must have left memoirs and papers which, I'm sure, will be found in General Suten's archives, those same archives he had decided to donate to the Temple of Isis.' Lord Impuki nodded at this. 'General Suten was also a soldier, a commander-in-chief of Egyptian forces; hundreds, thousands of men served under him. In times of peace these men leave the ranks eager for some new post or sinecure, desperate for work so they can feed their families. General Suten's generosity in these matters was well known.'

'I drove many of them away, I sent them to General Omendap,' Menna declared harshly.

'Oh yes,' Amerotke agreed, 'but you knew their names and where they lived. So,' he summarised, 'General Suten held knowledge about the Valley of the Kings and other rich tombs. He also had lists of former soldiers, many of them desperate men. He was also the holder of an imperial cartouche, the great seal of Egypt.'

'We broke that,' Menna protested. 'It was dispatched back to the royal palace.'

'Oh, I'm sure a seal was sent back to some busy chamberlain who realised it was shattered and threw it away without a second glance. But the original? No, Chief Scribe Menna, you kept that. Now all these things come together,' Amerotke continued. 'Busy, busy Chief Scribe Menna, who knew all the family history, had access to all documents, was the holder of the seal. It was only a matter of time, wasn't it, before you owned the means to rob tombs and send the plunder along the Nile or even across Egypt's borders. However, you had to have help. I'm sure that Heby and Lady Lupherna were lovers. The general was old and distracted.' Amerotke paused. 'It's happened before and it'll happen again,' he added quietly.

'So,' he raised his voice, 'you know where the treasure is, but how do you rob it? You can blackmail Heby and Lupherna with what you know, and they will help you. General Suten was a great writer, he loved the city of Thebes and knew all its temples; his manuscripts mention the Temple of Khnum, a derelict building on a lonely island along the Nile. On a wall of those ruins is a picture of an archer holding a bow: that would become your symbol. Your web is spun, and the flies are drawn in. Heby is your messenger, he goes to this or that former soldier in the dead of night, offering him wealth and the prospect of riches. They are under strict instructions to come to the Temple of Khnum or perhaps some other lonely place. A sinister system with its own terrible beauty. Only the Khetra knows who the Sebaus are; they don't know each other, do they? Garbed in black, heads and faces masked, they are offered riches in this life and, if they die, honourable passage into the Far West.'

'You have proof?' Menna was more composed.

'We'll come to that by and by,' Amerotke insisted. 'The Sebaus are not only thieves but messengers. You steal something, but then it has to be sold to a merchant, or trader. Officials have to be bribed, so more and more people are drawn in. Of course, mistakes are made. You do know about the Shardana? A former mercenary, a prominent Sebaus? He is arrested, tried by me for killing a man and sentenced to a prison oasis.'

'I know nothing of this man,' Menna protested.

'Oh, I suspect you know everything. The Shardana had been stupid. One of the rules of your gang is that the members live public lives of probity, worship the gods, obey the law and speak with true voice. The Shardana broke these rules. More importantly, he was a threat. He was imprisoned and sentenced to lifelong captivity. Prison oases are not healthy places; sooner or later the Shardana's mind would have turned to a pardon or amnesty. Perhaps he would seek an audience with Chief Justice Amerotke and reveal all he knew about the dreadful robbery of the tombs. There are so many strands to the Khetra's web, perhaps this had already begun?'

Amerotke shifted his gaze. Lady Lupherna's right hand was trembling as if she was on the verge of losing control. Menna kept glancing at her. Amerotke quietly prayed that what he had plotted would happen.

'The Shardana had to die,' Amerotke continued. 'But how was it to be done? Bribes were offered for his release, but the Shardana's victim was of noble family. Guards could be bought, but prison oases are small, crowded places. As I've said, perhaps the Shardana had already begun to confide in his gaolers or his companions. I mean, they are lonely, desolate spots, where a man's courage can soon be weakened.'

'Did you bring our enemies, People of the Nine Bows, on to the sacred soil of Egypt to murder and burn?' Hatusu's voice, stern and carrying, silenced the whispering around the court. The Pharaoh Queen was giving Menna the opportunity to confess; to lie, not to speak with true voice in answering a direct question from Pharaoh's mouth was the worst form of treason.

'I did not.' Menna's reply was impudent, and Lady Lupherna's agitation only deepened.

'But you did,' Amerotke contradicted him. 'You sent out a messenger into the Red Lands to bribe a Libyan war band. They were to destroy the prison oasis and kill everyone they found, but the price they demanded was surprising. The Libyan tribes are always looking for fresh blood for their menfolk, women outside their own kin to strengthen their clan or tribe. Above all they prize Egyptian maidens, not some coarse-skinned peasant girl, but the graceful ones of Thebes. That was the price they demanded: four young women of good breeding. And where could you find these? The Libyans are no fools, they would tell at a glance if you tried to deliver some city prostitute or even a courtesan from one of the pleasure houses. Mafdet was your answer. He was captain of the guard at the Temple of Isis. A member of the Sebaus, he was bribed, threatened and cajoled to kidnap those young women. Of course, the first victim was the one he'd seduced. Mafdet would be only too pleased to be rid of her. The temple authorities might suspect, but they couldn't prove anything. Moreover, Mafdet had been busy discovering their secrets ready to counter with his own blackmail. The first girl was stolen, drugged and taken beyond the temple walls at night, then hurried north to the Temple of Khnum and delivered to some desert trader, who took her across the Red Lands to the waiting Libyans. This was your token, the assurance that the price would be paid. The prison oasis was attacked and plundered, a bloody massacre in which no one survived. The Libyans had to be paid in full – you might always need them again – so three other temple girls disappeared—'

'This is not true!' Menna interrupted. 'I know nothing of Libyan tribes or desert paths.'

'Of course you do, you're Chief Scribe Menna, General

Suten's aide. His house has maps and charts. More importantly,' Amerotke moved in his chair, 'General Suten saw service against the Libyans, and where he went, you were sure to follow.'

Menna shrugged and glanced away.

'The Shardana was now silenced, but like all thieves, Menna, you became very greedy. You must have known the Divine One would intervene, but there again, you were well protected. None of the officials or merchants I arrested knew you, whilst the Sebaus remained untouched. You planned to fall silent and wait for another day. Only two problems remained, General Suten and myself.'

Amerotke lifted his hands as if to examine the ring of Ma'at on his middle finger. He stared at Nadif and smiled. The policeman knelt fascinated by what he was seeing and hearing; he had lost all surprise and awe, and was listening intently to Amerotke, now and again nodding in agreement.

'Standard-Bearer Nadif.' Amerotke lowered his hand; the signal had been given, Shufoy would be ready.

'Yes, my lord.' The Medjay officer bowed.

'You discovered a great deal about horned vipers. I believe they must be brought in from the Red Lands, not collected from the city dust as that fool Hefau declared?'

'That is correct, my lord.'

'Who collected them for you?' Amerotke turned back to Menna.

'Nobody did.'

'Steeped in lies,' Amerotke shouted. 'One of your Sebaus did! And you know why? Because General Suten was beginning to grow uneasy. He may have had a fear of snakes, but he also became aware of a different type of viper, closer to his bosom. He became anxious, withdrawn, he suffered stomach cramps and went out to the Temple of Isis for powders to ease his discomfort so that he could sleep more peacefully. General Suten was a good man, an honourable man. What did he suspect, Lady Lupherna? That you were playing the whore with his valet? That he was being betrayed by a man he regarded as a friend?'

The woman opened her mouth as if to reply; Amerotke glimpsed it, and also noticed Menna brush her thigh with the back of his hand.

'Or was it you, Menna? Did General Suten notice you absorbed in the family archives; did he wonder about the robberies or reflect why Heby should slink away at night? Only the gods know the answer to that! Of course he would try and console himself. He'd dismiss such thoughts as impure, unworthy, but you were sharp enough to notice the change. The general had to die. He was the one man who could destroy the Khetra, so you and those other hearts of wickedness concocted a cruel plot.'

Amerotke was about to continue when there was a pounding on the court door. He raised his hand and nodded. Asural opened the door and Shufoy came hastening in and immediately prostrated himself.

'Speak!' Hatusu ordered. 'Speak and approach, little man,' she added gently. Shufoy, shuffling on all fours, came forward, acting out the role Amerotke had taught him. He came in front of the Chair of Judgement and, pressing his face down again, waited for Amerotke to speak.

'What is it?' the judge asked.

'My lord,' Shufoy raised his face, 'the body has been found! We have discovered his corpse! It was not as you were told—'

He would have continued but Amerotke raised his hand for silence. He asked his manservant to withdraw and stand next to the captain at the door. Shufoy's entrance had been enough; the look which passed between Menna and Lupherna confirmed their guilt.

'We shall continue.' Amerotke clapped his hands gently. 'General Suten had often talked about confronting his demons, and you decided to use that as a means of murdering him. One of your Sebaus brought in a bag of horned vipers. Once the evening meal was over, the usual search was carried out. In fact that was rather clumsy. Why should General Suten order such a search in view of what you say he had planned? Moreover, as I said earlier, why should he confront his fears alone on his deserted roof terrace? In fact the general was more intent on being by himself, on drinking a goblet of wine and continuing his memoirs. The roof terrace was cleared. Heby had arranged for the general's wine to be heavily drugged.' Amerotke shook his head. 'You lied! You claimed to know nothing of the powders Lord Impuki had given your master.

'So that night, tired, his stomach full of wine, his mind dulled by the potion, General Suten decided to retire to his bed. Lady Lupherna and Menna were in or near the hall of audience; Heby controlled the steps to the roof. The sack was given to him and up he went. It was full of horned vipers especially brought in by a Sebaus, some former soldier who had knowledge of snakes and was skilled in their capture. I doubt if that particular Sebaus lived a day after he handed the sack over. The Khetra would have regarded him as far too dangerous. So,' Amerotke drew in a deep breath, 'the sack was emptied over the general and the pouch of poppy powder tossed nearby. The vipers, angered and excited, struck and struck again, and General Suten woke and found his nightmare was a reality. One of Egypt's great heroes died a death he had always feared. The rest is as you know. Standard-Bearer Nadif, you have brought the sack with you?'

The Medjay officer nodded; his nephew had been too nervous to attend court.

'Please stand up and empty it.'

The policeman obeyed. Getting to his feet, he undid the cord around the neck, emptied what he had found in the undergrowth and threw the sack to the ground.

'Notice what he did.' Amerotke got to his feet and bowed

to the Chair of Judgement. He walked over, picked up the sack and came to kneel before Pharaoh. 'Divine One, when someone empties a sack, and I've watched this happen on a number of occasions, the sack itself is no longer important and is thrown away. On the night he died, we are supposed to believe that General Suten had taken this sack up to the roof terrace and tied it to a rail behind his bed where it could be hidden. Apparently, or so the story goes, once the roof terrace was clear, General Suten took his knife, sawed through the rope and emptied the contents on to the bed beside him.'

'He would have thrown it to the ground,' Senenmut declared. 'Tossed it away.'

'But according to the accepted story,' Amerotke declared, 'for some strange reason General Suten took the sack back to the edge of the roof terrace and threw it down amongst the bushes in his garden. Why should he do that? What was so important about the sack? Why not just leave it on the ground? If we are to believe Menna's story, General Suten would be more concerned about the vipers than the sack.'

'Nonsense!' Menna cried. 'Why should I go to such ridiculous lengths? After all, Heby was accused.'

'No, Heby was investigated because that was the way you wanted it.'

Amerotke retook his seat and sipped from his goblet.

'Murder, I suppose, has its own logic, its own hideous harmony. First came my arrests. True, in my foolishness I never discovered the Sebaus, their true organisation, the awesome power they wielded. Nevertheless, I had begun to overturn stones, and perhaps I appeared more dangerous to you than I really was. That's why you tried to kill me. You knew I had gone to the Temple of Isis; Mafdet would have provided you with detailed plans, so you struck. You burnt Mafdet's house to hide any evidence of his wrongdoing, whilst your assassins attacked me to silence me, first in my own temple, then at Isis. Your heart had conceived my murder lest I discover that the Sebaus were former soldiers controlled by some high-ranking officer or priest,' Amerotke shrugged, 'or a chief scribe. You wanted me dead as you wanted Sithia dead. My arrests were actually the cause of everything that happened afterwards.

'Let me repeat the heart of my argument. I have explained my theory, which I cannot fully prove, that General Suten was also growing suspicious, though about what I cannot say. Did he suspect his lovely wife and his valet Heby? Was he alarmed by the furtive secrecy of his chief scribe? Or had General Suten become deeply concerned over more serious matters? He must have been worried about the thefts in the Valley of the Kings, his archives held vital information about these. He certainly became quiet and withdrawn, his reservations were apparent, his change in behaviour obvious, even to his old servants in the mansion. More importantly, in his own way General Suten was voicing reservations about his family and household. The wall paintings of his tomb make hardly any mention of them. General Suten could become a major obstacle in a time of crisis, so the Khetra – Menna, Lupherna and Heby – plotted his death. You had to, to survive!'

Amerotke paused so the court could hear Lupherna's sobbing.

'General Suten had to die, but how? An accident? He was a wiry, tough old man, often surrounded by other servants; the more suspicious he grew, the more careful he'd be. A fall from the roof? General Suten was a fighter and he might survive. A poison powder? That would provoke outcry. Whilst a hired assassin is a risk which could leave you vulnerable. But snakes, horned vipers? In a curious way this was the best method, especially after what General Suten had both spoken and written about.'

'A risk, surely?' Lord Valu declared, although his voice lacked conviction.

'Of course it was a risk,' Amerotke agreed. 'But not as

great as being unmasked and arrested. So the trap was sprung. General Suten was drugged, the horned vipers released, and suspicion falls on Heby, which is spiced by rumours of the valet flirting with the general's pretty wife.'

Amerotke raised his hands. 'A good lie always contains some truths. The Khetra knew about the poppy seed the general received at the Temple of Isis. We only have their word that he never told them or they never knew about it. Lord Impuki,' he turned to the High Priest. 'Such powders can be bought?'

'Yes.' Impuki nodded. 'As can a pouch bearing the insignia of our temple.'

'The rest,' Amerotke continued, 'was also a mixture of truth and lies. Heby, of course, was well protected by a series of defences which I am sure Menna would have argued in court. Where did he get those horned vipers? Where did he store them? How could he have brought them up to the roof without anyone noticing? What real motive did he have for murder? What about General Suten's intention to face his own fears? Finally, and most importantly, we have the cord tied on the rail behind the drapes where General Suten's bed stood. Eventually someone, under Menna's direction, would have stumbled on that, if not me then Standard-Bearer Nadif, or some other official. You, Menna, and Lupherna were never suspected. After a little doubt, Heby would also be cleared and the Khetra would be safe. But blind chance intervened. The gods love to upset our best-laid plans. The snake man, prompted by Lord Valu's offer of a reward, made the surprising declaration that he sold those vipers to Heby. Now, if Heby had been calmer, that too could have been dismissed. Why should Heby show his face if he was planning murder? But you hadn't planned for such a mishap and that's where you made a terrible mistake. Your next was to assassinate that temple guard and draw attention to the criminal known as Djed.'

'I know nothing of him!' Menna shouted. 'What proof do you have?'

'Heby's my proof, he became hysterical with fear. What could you do, assassinate Hefau? No, too suspicious. It was much easier to murder Heby. What went wrong? Did Heby accuse you of betraying him? Did he blame you, threaten you?'

'He attacked me,' Menna replied coolly. 'Bound and gagged me, rifled my treasures and fled.'

Amerotke stared at this fat, square-faced clerk. He quietly conceded he had made a mistake, overlooked something. Menna was a wily schemer; he appeared too calm, and kept looking intently at the Pharaoh Queen. Hatusu was unnaturally tense and Senenmut was whispering to her. Amerotke felt a prickle of unease. How dangerous, how cunning was Chief Scribe Menna? Yet it was too late now, he had no choice but to proceed.

'Heby did not attack you,' Amerotke declared. 'You killed him, you hid his body somewhere in that house, you bruised yourself and then Lady Lupherna came slipping along to your chamber to gag and bind you. No one thought of looking for Heby in the house. In a mansion that size, a corpse can be hidden away for a short while.'

'Ridiculous!' Menna snorted with anger, looking to Valu as if for protection. 'If I did all this, then who killed the guard? Who left the dagger and trinkets in the undergrowth near the path?'

'Why, you did!'

'I never left General Suten's mansion, nor did Lady Lupherna.'

'No, that's not true. The guards left at the house were rather lax. You made them even more so. You're a soldier, Menna, you know a lazy sentry when you see one. Moreover, those men were concerned with Heby, not you. On that particular morning, long before dawn, garbed and masked, you left the house, scaled the wall, entered the grove behind the house, came up behind that sleeping guard and sliced his throat. You then hastened along the trackway to throw down Heby's dagger and the jewellery you yourself had taken. It was a lonely time, in a deserted place, with very little risk. After all, you had every right to leave the house. You would have escaped attention,' Amerotke gestured at Nadif, 'if it had not been for the sharpness of this officer.'

He paused.

'When Nadif first freed you, you declared that Heby's attack had taken place only a short while earlier. Nadif was intrigued, because the guard who was killed was stone cold, his blood caked, whilst the blood on the dagger was also dry. More curiously, when Nadif studied the grove behind the house he could see that someone had stolen through there, but when he found the trinkets and dagger the undergrowth around was hardly disturbed. No one had passed through there, forced a way. It looked as if they had just left the path, dropped the dagger and jewellery and returned, which, of course, is what really happened. You'd arranged for those trinkets to be found, just as the day before you'd organised information to provide false reports about Heby being seen in the city or along the Nile.

'Nadif was also curious about the guards; they were not only sleepy but very heavy-eyed, and that troubled me. You would have been responsible for the food and drink given to them. Did you mix powders with their wine? I expect you did. During the night you invited Heby to your room, killed him, and hid his body. You left before dawn and returned to continue the deceit. Lady Lupherna came to your chamber to finish the web of lies.'

Amerotke closed his eyes and quickly prayed to Ma'at, then he leaned forward and opened his eyes.

'Lady Lupherna, Heby did not flee! My manservant Shufoy and his fellow searchers have found his corpse near General Suten's mansion.'

'You couldn't have—' Lupherna spoke before Menna

could intervene, a ringing shout which proclaimed their guilt. Menna tried to grasp her arm, but she pushed him off as the guards pulled them apart. 'You couldn't have,' she moaned. 'You couldn't have.' She was staring fixedly at Amerotke. 'It wasn't supposed to be like this.' She abruptly recalled where she was. 'Mercy!' she shrieked.

Amerotke sat fascinated. Lupherna was apparently broken, but Menna remained resolute. The judge started as Senenmut appeared behind him and dropped a small scroll into his lap. Amerotke quickly unrolled it and read the short phrase: *If the order is silence then it is silence.* He glanced up. Hatusu sat unmoved, although her breathing was rather quick and abrupt. Lupherna, her hands to her face, was rocking backwards and forwards.

'My lady, Divine One,' Menna bellowed like a bull, 'I know nothing of this. I swear by the Book of Secrets I—'

'Silence! Gag him!' Hatusu screamed.

Amerotke sat in amazement as Senenmut sprang to his feet, shouting at the guards. Lupherna, crying hysterically, was bound, gagged and dragged from the hall by the Silent Ones, the deaf-mutes who guarded the House of Adoration. Menna was still shouting something about proclaiming the truth whether he was alive or dead, before he too was seized, a cloth stuffed into his mouth and his hands quickly bound. The Chief Scribe struggled like a bull; tables were kicked over, cushions flung across the slippery floor. A guard hit Menna full in the face but the scribe still resisted, and the High Priest of Isis, together with Valu and Nadif, moved quickly out of the way. Senenmut shouted for the hall to be cleared.

Hatusu rose majestically, slapping Amerotke on the shoulder and gesturing to him to lead her across to his own private shrine and chamber. Once inside, she drew the clasp bolts across, tore off her headdress and sandals, the jewelled Nenes from around her shoulders, and slumped down into the high-backed chair. The judge went to kneel before her but she snapped her fingers.

'Sit where you want!' She pointed to the serving table. 'I'm thirsty, some watered wine.'

Amerotke poured this and handed it to her. There was a knock on the door; Amerotke opened it, and Senenmut almost threw himself into the room. He slammed the door shut and leaned against it, gasping for breath.

'So he did find it!' he exclaimed.

'Yes,' Hatusu sighed. 'He must have. They must be kept in silence, total silence.'

'They have been taken below to the House of Chains; each will be guarded by Silent Ones.'

'They will have to die!' Hatusu whispered. 'Whatever happens, they must go to the wood. Did you hear what Menna was shouting? Alive or dead. Alive or dead, the Book of Secrets will be known.'

Amerotke curbed his own angry impatience and sat silently. Senenmut, still leaning against the door, glanced sharply at him as if only now becoming aware of the judge's presence.

'Ah! My lord judge.'

'My lord judge,' Amerotke shouted, 'is angry, his court has become a travesty. On reflection I am beginning to suspect the truth behind two questions which have occurred to me before but which I unwisely dismissed. First, why was the Divine One so angry at these thefts? Oh, I understand the blasphemy and sacrilege,' he added hastily, 'but the robbery of royal tombs has occurred before and undoubtedly will happen again.'

'Secondly?' Hatusu snarled.

'Something Shufoy noticed. How your rage spilled out after the robbery of the tomb of Rahimere, Grand Vizier under your late husband.'

Hatusu was not listening to him but staring at Senenmut

with some unasked question which he answered with a nod of his head.

'As you know,' Hatusu turned back to Amerotke, 'my late, glorious husband was assassinated by a faction in the royal circle who then tried to oust me. Rahimere was the leader of those criminals. He'd hated me since I was a little girl, and kept a close eye on me, much closer than I thought. He drew up a Book of Secrets about me, scandal and gossip.'

'Straws in the wind,' Amerotke scoffed.

'No, no, much more serious.'

'Such as?'

'That my birth was not divine.'

'Only the gods know that,' Amerotke replied. 'What else?'

Hatusu drew a deep breath. 'That whilst my husband was still alive and involved in the House of War, fighting the People of the Nine Bows, Lord Senenmut and I became lovers, and whilst my husband was away on campaign I was secretly delivered of a female child.'

'Lies, of course!'

Hatusu gazed back serenely.

'Lies, Divine One,' Amerotke repeated.

Hatusu's glance fell away; Senenmut stared at the floor.

'In the struggle for power,' Hatusu's voice was just above a whisper, 'Rahimere died. Well, you know the truth, Amerotke.'

'In which case he didn't die, he was invited to take poison.'

'He was a traitor, a murderer and a rebel!' Hatusu snapped.

'Never mind that,' Senenmut intervened. 'His corpse was handed back to his relatives for burial. Those were frenetic days, Amerotke, we were concerned with the living, not with the dead. To come to the point, he was buried secretly in the Valley.'

'You had the power to discover where his tomb was.'

'We didn't care where he was rotting,' Senenmut jibed. 'He was dead, gone into the Far West, and that was the end of the matter, until about three months ago, when we discovered that Rahimere had kept this Book of Secrets, contained in a sealed casket, which was buried with him. Not just in the tomb but in the coffin casket itself.'

'Who told you this? Ah!' Amerotke took the rings from his fingers. 'The only person who could, Rahimere's wife. She wouldn't have known what to do with the Book of Secrets. Out of respect for her husband she wouldn't destroy it, so she had it buried with him. When I was in the Temple of Isis I heard that Rahimere's widow had gone there for treatment and died. She must have told Lord Impuki, and he reported it to the palace.' Amerotke shook his head. 'Mysteries within mysteries,' he whispered. 'That's why the disappearance of the four hesets was treated so sensitively. Any other temple would have been ransacked by troops from the Sacred Band. No wonder Lady Thena felt confident enough to take the law into her own hands and execute Mafdet; you are in their debt.'

'Of course I am!' Hatusu scratched her arm, a nervous gesture she made whenever she was angry. 'Lord Impuki was most gracious. He heard the dying woman's confession as if he was a chapel priest, yet he still told me. He and his household were sworn to secrecy. I owe them a great debt. Rahimere's widow, however, did not tell him where the tomb was. We searched for it but it was too late. We thought,' she grimaced, 'she would be buried with her husband, but she was too cunning for that, and her corpse rests with her own kin.'

'So the tomb robbers discovered it?'

'Of course they did! When Rahimere was Grand Vizier, a lord of Egypt, he knew the Valley of the Kings. He'd already chosen a lonely spot, a place where the crags of the valleys create a shadow, an illusion.'

'Those robbers found it,' Senenmut came away from the

door, 'like all such discoveries, by accident. They must have done.'

'No they didn't.' Amerotke smiled. 'One thing I did discover, but dismissed at the time, was that Mafdet had been captain of Rahimere's guard. When the Vizier fell from power Mafdet retired. General Omendap recommended him for the post at the Temple of Isis. Menna too may have had a hand in his appointment, but secretly, through General Suten. Mafdet also became a member of the Sebaus. He would have known about the secret of Rahimere's tomb and, like the mercenary he was, gave the information to the Khetra, hoping to share in the plunder. Indeed,' Amerotke shrugged, 'Mafdet would have known about the Book of Secrets. A treacherous villain, he would have deserted Rahimere just in time, played the role of the loyal veteran for his superiors and, when approached by the Khetra, divulged what he knew. Like the blackmailer he was, he nursed the whereabouts of Rahimere's tomb and its contents as a miser would some secret treasure.'

'Once Rahimere's tomb was violated,' Senenmut continued, 'it was no longer a secret. Officials who investigated the robbery found items which led them to the entrance. The tomb had been ransacked, its coffin casket opened, and beside it was a leather case. This was brought to the palace. It was the sort of leather case in which you keep a book or manuscript. You can imagine our concern. If the treasures of other tombs were sold abroad—'

'Why not the Book of Secrets?' Hatusu drank greedily from the goblet clenched in her hands. 'Can you imagine, Amerotke, the damage such a book could cause in the possession of my enemies, either here or across the Horus road? I would have been depicted as an adulterer, perhaps even my late husband's murderer.' She stretched out her hand and brushed Amerotke's face. 'I listened to you in court, a brilliant attack. I could tell from Menna's eyes that he hoped to negotiate, but this is a fight to the death.

As you talked I wondered how much General Suten had known. Did Menna even approach him to join the Sebaus? Ah well,' she sighed, 'we will never know. You must find that book, Amerotke, you are my saluki hound, and both the prisoners must die. Do not approach Menna.' Hatusu's smile faded. 'You must not be infected, polluted by what he has read in the Book of Secrets. Offer the woman a merciful death. She must know something. Mercy now and honourable treatment for her corpse.'

'And Menna?'

'Nothing,' Hatusu snapped back, 'but horror after horror.'

The Pharaoh Queen held Amerotke's gaze, and the judge wondered about the Book of Secrets and the truths behind the mysteries it contained.

A short while later Amerotke went down to the House of Chains. The temple guards, apart from Asural, had been withdrawn, their places taken by the Silent Ones who prowled the narrow, ill-lit passageways like wolves, hardened men in their imperial headdress, leather belts and kilts. They even insisted on searching the judge. When Amerotke gestured with his hands that he needed to question the prisoners, their officer smiled serenely, pointed to a cell door and shook his head. Again, through signs, Amerotke asked if he could at least see Chief Scribe Menna. The officer agreed. They approached the door and he pulled back the high wooden flap. Amerotke peered through. Chief Scribe Menna, stripped of everything except his loincloth, a mask over his face, squatted against the far wall, his arms and legs laden with manacles secured to the stone behind him. Looking down, to his right and left, Amerotke glimpsed the guards sitting either side of the door. Even though Menna's face was veiled, Amerotke could sense the malicious strength of this most cunning of men. He moved to the next cell, where Lupherna, her robe all soiled, her wig removed, slumped sullenly, her face dirty and stained with dried kohl. Amerotke made signs for the door to be unlocked, and this time his escort agreed. In the next cell Menna must have heard the noise.

'No use going in there,' his powerful voice bawled. 'The stupid bitch knows nothing! She'll only mislead you. Is that our noble judge? I can smell your body sweat. I prefer jasmine, the most fragrant of perfumes.'

Lupherna stirred as Amerotke came into the foul-smelling cell with its slop buckets and dirty basins. She was beyond tears now, and just stared at him, lips moving soundlessly. Amerotke crouched down before her.

'I speak with true voice,' he declared. 'I cannot mislead you. You are to die.' Lupherna blinked, tongue going out to wet dry, cracked lips. 'What you must decide,' Amerotke continued, 'is how you die and how you prepare your soul for the journey into the Far West. Pharaoh is inclined to mercy, at least for you.'

'What form of death?' Lupherna whispered, as if fearful that Menna might overhear.

'A goblet of wine with the juice of a marsh plant added, a feeling of tiredness, of falling asleep. Your body will go to the wabet and the House of Beauty. The priests will chant their prayers, your heart will be covered with the sacred scarab. Sacrifices and prayers will be offered for you, and before you drink the wine a chapel priest will purge your sins.'

Lupherna stared down at the ground.

'Wickedness is like a flower,' she replied slowly. 'First the root, then the stem and the branches shoot out before you even know. I come of good family. My marriage to General Suten was most honourable, but my eye wandered and my heart followed. I became involved with Heby, and Menna discovered us. He had the proof which could have destroyed us; he offered us another reality. We became part of the Khetra. It's all there, you know,' she continued, as if speaking to herself, 'in the family archives, all the information about the Valley of the Kings and the tombs. General Suten didn't know what Menna was doing! He could go into the House of Books and read what he wanted. He used to ride out to the valley. He would tell us what he had seen and found. We became aware of how busy he truly was. Veterans would come to the mansion begging for favours. Often Menna would drive them away or refer them to some other scribe in the army, but secretly he would note their names, the places where they lived. He covered his tracks so well, nothing could be traced directly back to him, not even the assassins he sent against you.'

'And he met the Sebaus at the Temple of Khnum?'

'There and other places. He would cloak himself in black and douse himself in jasmine perfume. He liked that, did Menna.'

'And General Suten suspected nothing?'

'Yes, he did. He suspected something was very wrong but couldn't believe it. Menna grew rich. Search the house, judge, you'll find treasures hidden in wells, beneath the soil, in the rafters of the roof. Go down to the goldsmiths of Thebes; Menna would use different names to hide his wealth there. He had Heby and me in the palm of his hand. At first we were reluctant, but then Heby too began to enjoy the wealth. My husband was no fool, he was watching us, so he had to die. Menna conceived the plot. He declared suspicion would fall on Heby, but that wouldn't last.' She sighed. 'Then that snake man appeared. Did you really find Heby's corpse?'

Amerotke shook his head. 'It was only a trick; I had to do it.'

'Menna kept Heby's corpse hidden in an empty chamber. When the guards were withdrawn we took it out by night and threw it into a crocodile pool. I knew then we were truly cursed. I could feel Heby's ghost and my husband's hunting me through the dark.' She paused. 'If you've come to ask for names, I haven't any. Menna was insistent on that; only he kept the master roll, here.' She tapped the side of her head. 'But surely you know all this?'

'Did Menna ever refer to the Book of Secrets?'

'Never.'

Amerotke closed his eyes in disappointment.

'I swear by all that's holy,' Lupherna added hastily. 'Only once, at the end of last month, he was full of himself. He declared that he had found a treasure more priceless than the rest. We used to meet him in the garden, late in the evening. Heby asked to see it, Menna shook his head. He said that the treasure was protected by the potter's wheel and only the frogs knew where it was. That's all I know,' she muttered. 'I need some water.'

Amerotke moved across to the jar, but one of the Silent Ones intervened. He grasped the ladle himself, tasted the water and only then handed it to Amerotke. Lupherna drank greedily.

'That's all I can tell you,' she declared. 'Is it enough to buy me mercy?'

Amerotke left the cell and returned to his own chamber in the Hall of Two Truths. The court was now empty of spectators, the cushions, tables and chairs all tidily replaced; no trace remained of the violence which had occurred earlier. Hatusu's guards were everywhere, even outside Amerotke's own chamber, where Shufoy crouched enjoying a jug of beer. Amerotke joined him, taking off his robes. Sitting with his back to the wall, he described what Lupherna had said. Shufoy could not help him. Intrigued, Amerotke returned to the House of Chains, to be greeted by Menna's raucous shouting and Lupherna's tearful insistence that she didn't know what the potter's wheel meant, though she confessed Heby had suspected it was some place in the house.

'Could it be the Temple of Khnum?' Shufoy asked, when his master returned.

'But there's no potter's wheel there,' Amerotke replied

absent-mindedly. 'Nor any sign of frogs, be they alive, statues or a painting. It must be in General Suten's house.'

Later that day Amerotke and his guards ransacked Suten's mansion. Every room was searched, the gardens dug up, undergrowth cleared from orchards, wells probed, the floors of pavilions turned up. The servants clustered in the garden, frightened and withdrawn. Amerotke, as he searched, had to admire Menna's cunning. Of course they found hidden stores, debens of gold, silver and precious stones, but nothing to connect the Chief Scribe with the robberies at the Valley of the Kings. Apparently Menna had converted the proceeds of such robberies into wealth which could be quickly gathered in case of flight,

The Chief Scribe had been particularly astute in his use of General Suten's House of Books. At first the chamber looked to be what it was, the dusty archives and library of a family, with caskets, coffers, baskets and shelves full of old records and manuscripts. A closer study of these, however, revealed a true treasure house of knowledge they stored: letters, memoranda, chronicles, journals and diaries describing the burials of Pharaohs, nobles, queens and other high-ranking officials. Amerotke reckoned the records spanned at least sixty years and the reigns of five Pharaohs. The House of Books also contained, carefully hidden away, the imperial cartouche, the royal seal with its divine signs, which, if used to mark any letter or bundle, would ensure safe passage anywhere in Egypt as well as across its borders.

Darkness fell, and Amerotke continued his searches. He and Shufoy had food and wine brought in for them, yet although they discovered numerous items, there was nothing, apart from the seal and some manuscripts, which convincingly proved Menna's guilt. Dawn found them still at work. Amerotke went up to the roof terrace, a lonely, deserted place, to feel the morning breeze, the cool breath of Amun, and make his morning prayer as the sun rose in a fiery glow. The household was roused as the soldiers continued their search. Royal messengers arrived demanding news, but Amerotke had to send them away empty-handed.

'Nothing!' the judge exclaimed as he and Shufoy rested in the shade of a palm grove. 'Nothing at all about a potter's wheel. The mansion doesn't even own one.'

'It's got frogs!' Shufoy exclaimed. 'Plenty of the noisy little vermin. They sang their hymn all night.' The dwarf sifted through the manuscripts on the grass beside him, then stared across the grove, lost in thought. 'Frogs and potter's wheels,' he whispered. 'Do you know, Master, sometimes there is an advantage in being a scorpion man.' He jumped to his feet and said he must visit the House of Books again.

Amerotke was dozing when Shufoy returned and shook him gently by the arm.

'Master, frogs, what are they?'

'Frogs!'

'And the potter's wheel?'

Amerotke glimpsed the excitement in Shufoy's bright little eyes.

'The Temple of Khnum,' Shufoy whispered.

'It has no potter's wheel, and frogs do not croak so close to a crocodile pool.'

'The potter's wheel,' Shufoy repeated. 'Don't you remember the legends about the god Khnum? He is one of Egypt's oldest gods. According to the story he first fashioned human life on a potter's wheel before he tired of it and handed that power to the womb of a woman. Khnum had a wife, Neit.'

'Who is often represented by a frog,' Amerotke said, scrambling to his feet. He recalled the derelict temple, the circular sanctuary with its grey-paved stone. 'Of course,' he breathed, 'the sanctuary was built in the shape of a potter's wheel; that's what Menna meant, whilst the reference to frogs was a joke.'

*   *   *

The late-afternoon breeze was cooling the river as the imperial war barge, the *Vengeance of Isis*, stood off the small causeway leading to the island where the ruins of the Temple of Khnum sprawled under the light of the setting sun. The war barge had been there some time, its blue and gold sail furled, whilst the royal cabin, with its red and silver canopy, stood empty, its side doors open to catch the breeze. Those soldiers and marines not sitting in whatever shade they could find clustered with Amerotke and Shufoy along the taffrail, in the prow or the stern. They shaded their eyes and stared across at that lonely island fringed with its reed and papyrus groves. Even now, despite the presence of the barge and its escort craft, it was a lonely place, the haunt of the hippopotamus, the crocodile and the brilliantly feathered marsh birds whirring up in clamour at this unexpected intrusion. Barges of marines, armed with flaring pitch torches, patrolled the banks, driving off the river beasts from this place now sanctified by the presence of their Pharaoh.

Amerotke himself had reported his findings to the palace. Hatusu and Senenmut had wasted no time. The golden-prowed war barge was immediately readied and, with an escort of lesser craft, began the short journey along the river. Heralds with conches and horns wailing warned all other boats to pull aside as the great oared barge displaying the imperial Horus banner swept up to the island of Khnum. Once it arrived, only Hatusu, Senenmut and the hawk-masked Silent Ones went ashore. Amerotke could only wait and hope. The royal party had been ashore for at least two hours. He glimpsed the occasional movement, the glint of sunlight on weapons, whilst the sound of digging echoed faintly across the water. A sharp-eyed look-out pointed to a plume of smoke, a dark drifting smudge rising up above the trees against the blue sky. A short while later Amerotke glimpsed the imperial canopy sheltering Hatusu from the sun moving through the palm grove down towards the waterside. A war horn wailed from the island, and immediately the barge readied itself in a patter of running feet and shouted orders from the helmsman and captain. The vessel, scores of oars rising and falling in unison, moved closer to the shore under the guidance of the pilot, the gangplank was lowered and Hatusu, escorted by Senenmut, swept aboard, going directly to the gorgeously caparisoned cabin. Amerotke was ordered to join them, and Hatusu, smiling and joking like a girl at her first banquet, patted the cushions beside her and thrust a goblet of iced fruit juice into his hand. She leaned closer, her perfumed face laced with sweat, eyes bright with life.

'We found it, Amerotke! The Book of Secrets. It lay beneath the paving stones in the centre of the old sanctuary. We found it and we burnt it.' Her smile faded. 'Now go back to the House of Chains. Tomorrow I shall ensure justice is done.'

The line of war chariots stirred restlessly. The horses, plumed and harnessed, moved backwards and forwards in their excitement; their drivers clicked their tongues, urging the magnificent beasts to stay calm. At least fifty chariots were there, the swiftest and fiercest of all Egypt's war squadrons. They had come out before dawn, silently leaving the city and moving to the edge of the Red Lands, a rocky dry wilderness where, in the grey light before dawn, the wind still stirred the dust devils. In the centre of the line was Hatusu, magnificent in the full war armour of Pharaoh. Next to her in the chariot was Senenmut. Amerotke and Shufoy occupied the place of honour in the chariot to her right. The judge rested against the rail and stared across the empty, desolate plain. He was weary, tired of all this. He wanted to take Norfret and his family back to his house, sit in the orchard and listen to the whirr of the crickets and the song of the birds, not be here, in the harsh wilderness, waiting for a man to die.

Before he had left Thebes, Amerotke had visited the House of Chains, as was his duty, to witness Lupherna drink the poisoned wine. She had gulped it quickly, then lay down and, without a murmur of protest, slipped into death. Now it was Menna's turn. He would die in this place, imprisoned in the great thorn bush which sprouted amongst a cluster of rocks some ten yards away. He had already been bound in a sheepskin, his mouth gagged, eyes blazing with fury. In front of the line of chariots the hawk-masked executioner watched as his assistants thrust the prisoner, still struggling, into the centre of the thorn bush to be cut and lacerated by its spiky thorns. Ropes were wound tightly around the bush, which was so drenched in oil Amerotke could smell it from where he stood.

Hatusu grasped the reins and, talking softly, urged the chariot forward. Senenmut leaned down and took the blazing cresset torch from the executioner. The chariot picked up speed, the fiery pitch glowed, dancing in the breeze as the chariot charged towards the thorn bush then wheeled around it, once, twice, before Hatusu slowed down. She shouted something, then, grasping the torch, flung it at the bush. The flames caught hold, bursting into a raging fire. All watched as Chief Scribe Menna burnt, body and soul being consumed by fire.

Once the flames started to die down, Hatusu turned her chariot back towards the rest, reining in before them.

'Lord Valu,' she called, pointing out towards the eastern Red Lands. 'In this scorching place a Libyan tribe holds four hesets, kidnapped from the Temple of Isis.' Despite the crackling of the fire and the whipping breeze, Hatusu's voice carried full and strong. 'In the olden days,' she continued, 'Great Mother Isis would dispatch her assassins to right a wrong. You will lead an embassy and seek out that Libyan tribe. Tell them the Great Mother has loosed her assassins to bring justice to the Kingdom of the Two Lands and the People of the Nine Bows. Tell them, negotiate with them, but you shall bring those four captives home.' She moved her chariot closer, in front of Amerotke. 'As for you, my lord, chosen of Isis, go back to the palace, take your wife home, and rejoice that Ma'at has been restored.'

AUTHOR'S NOTE

This novel contains many strands of life in Egypt as it
approached the zenith of its glory during the Eighteenth
Dynasty. I have referred to the royal Necropolis as the
Valley of the Kings, though that was a name given to it
by later generations. However, what is a definite fact is
that the robbery of royal tombs became ancient Egypt's
second oldest profession. The robberies were often highly
organised and led by nobles and officials who had access
to secret information. Some of these robberies were breathtaking in their daring. For example, during the Twenty-first
Dynasty, the princess Henttawy, daughter of a high priest,
was robbed even before she was buried. A very interesting
source is the Papyrus Salt 124 (formerly known as British
Library Manuscript 10055), which gives a vivid description
of a gang like the Sebaus robbing tombs during the reign
of Sety II. The organising genius behind this was a high-
ranking official called Paneb who received a great deal of
help from a very corrupt vizier. Surviving records known as
the Tomb Robbery Papyri describe similar robberies during
the twenty-ninth year of the reign of Rameses III. The
target of these robberies was no less than the burial place
of Egypt's greatest king, Rameses II, and his magnificent
House of a Million Years in the Valley of the Kings.

Sometimes important documents were buried with Pharaohs.

In the 1920s, when Howard Carter first discovered the tomb of Tutankhamun, he thought he would find highly confidential manuscripts buried with the boy king. In his search for them, Carter unearthed a dual mystery. Tutankhamun's tomb contained two guardian statues, and it looked as if manuscripts had been hidden there but then taken out and the holes in the statue carefully gessoed over. More surprisingly, Carter also discovered evidence that, shortly after Tutankhamun was buried, the tomb was opened again. The first opening was a robbery which was undoubtedly discovered, but the second was the work of a high-ranking official known as Maya. It would seem from my researches that Maya did not only restore certain goods to Tutankhamun's tomb but may have taken specific items out.

The relationship between Hatusu and Senenmut was very close. Graffiti dating from shortly after Hatusu's reign depicted this relationship in very crude and explicit terms. Hatusu may have had a daughter by Senenmut, although this child never succeeded her. For some strange reason Hatusu also had a special devotion to that rather ancient god of Egypt, Khnum. Her memorial temple at Deir-el-bahri possesses a drawing of the god Khnum creating the Pharaoh Queen on his potter's wheel!

The temple life described in this novel reflects the reality of the early years of Hatusu's reign. The great temples of ancient Egypt were like the cathedral abbeys of the Middle Ages; they were not only centres of worship but businesses possessing their own academies and schools.

There is no clear source which proves that the Egyptians dissected corpses, but sometimes the medical knowledge of Egyptian physicians is truly astonishing, particularly the treatment of wounds and some quite sophisticated internal complaints. Specialist physicians took rather strange titles such as 'Guardian of the Ear' or 'Guardian of the Anus'.

The only conclusion I can draw from their expertise and perceptive comments about certain diseases and illnesses is that dissection was carried out but never discussed. One example of their knowledge will suffice: the Egyptians were very careful to clean wounds. They possessed the herbs to accomplish this and were very careful about how wounds were bandaged, deliberately keeping dressings loose to allow the wound to breathe and clear itself of any pus, a practice the British Army ignored to its cost until after the First World War!